Praise for Scott Mackay's
Outpost

"Mackay avoids the grandiosity that is an occupational hazard of science fiction writers who dabble in cosmic themes. . . . Provocative."—*The New York Times Book Review*

"A fast-paced action adventure."—*The Washington Post*

"Absolutely classic . . . stunning ingenuity."—*The Globe and Mail* (Toronto)

"Moving. . . . Much of the novel's strength lies in its characters, heroic yet vulnerable, facing tough decisions and tough situations . . . stirring."—*Publishers Weekly*

"Ingenious and satisfying . . . a complex and winning heroine. . . . Mackay delivers on the surprises when he needs to . . . and he writes with impressive grace and clarity. His vision is original enough, his imagery vivid enough, and his characters engaging enough, that we might expect even better surprises in the future."—*Locus*

"An intriguing puzzle scenario and tense prison action . . . worth trying."—*Kirkus Reviews*

"[A] fast-moving blend of mystery and Sci Fi adventure . . . a well-written and engrossing tale."—*Library Journal*

THE
MEEK

SCOTT MACKAY

A ROC BOOK

ROC
Published by New American Library, a division of
Penguin Putnam Inc., 375 Hudson Street,
New York, New York 10014, U.S.A.
Penguin Books Ltd, 27 Wrights Lane,
London W8 5TZ, England
Penguin Books Australia Ltd,
Ringwood, Victoria, Australia
Penguin Books Canada Ltd, 10 Alcorn Avenue,
Toronto, Ontario, Canada M4V 3B2
Penguin Books (N.Z.) Ltd, 182–190 Wairau Road,
Auckland 10, New Zealand

Penguin Books Ltd, Registered Offices:
Harmondsworth, Middlesex, England

First published by Roc, an imprint of New American Library,
a division of Penguin Putnam Inc.

First Printing, April 2001
10 9 8 7 6 5 4 3 2 1

Copyright © Scott Mackay, 2001

All rights reserved

Cover design: Ray Lundgren

 REGISTERED TRADEMARK—MARCA REGISTRADA

Printed in the United States of America

PUBLISHER'S NOTE
This is a work of fiction. Names, characters, places, and incidents either are the products
of the author's imagination or are used fictitiously, and any resemblance to actual
persons, living or dead, events, or locales is entirely coincidental.

BOOKS ARE AVAILABLE AT QUANTITY DISCOUNTS WHEN USED TO PROMOTE PRODUCTS OR
SERVICES. FOR INFORMATION PLEASE WRITE TO PREMIUM MARKETING DIVISION, PENGUIN
PUTNAM INC., 375 HUDSON STREET, NEW YORK, NEW YORK 10014.

To my son, Colin

PART 1

CERES

CHAPTER 1

As Cody Wisner looked at the orbital photographs of Ceres he detected a discrepancy between the old reference photographs taken thirty years ago and the ones their own surveillance cameras on the Public Works vessel *Gerard Kuiper* had taken just yesterday. He thought he knew all the Public Works structures on the surface of the abandoned asteroid, but what he saw here in these new photographs baffled him.

"GK 1, magnify," he said.

The computer magnified the image a hundred times. A ramp? A vent? A new surface-to-subsurface entrance? Certainly something man-made. Yet there'd been nothing man-made on Ceres in thirty years. The asteroid was nothing but a big ghost town.

"Ben, take a look at this," he said.

Ben LeBlanc propelled himself through free fall to Cody's terminal. He was a slight, odd-looking man, with a small head and broad shoulders. Dark whiskers covered his chin already, though it was early; Cody often caught him shaving twice a day. Ben looked at Cody's magnification of the unidentified object.

"GK 2," said Ben, accessing the shipboard computer with his own voiceprint, "extrapolate at 90 degrees west."

The screen went blank for a second, then filled with an extrapolated image, a surface-level view of the object.

The image showed a cavelike opening, with the ramp-shaped structure tapering to the dusty, cratered surface of Ceres.

"GK 2, extrapolate, frontal elevation," said Ben.

A hypothetical camera panned to a front view of the unidentified object. The thing looked like a gigantic dorsal fin. Cody tapped in some commands.

"Let's get some measurements," he said.

The computer estimated measurements for the thing: two hundred meters tall at its highest elevation, tapering at a slant more than three hundred meters long, forming a broad right-angle triangle contiguous to the surface of Ceres. Both men stared at the thing for a long time. Cody was mystified. Considerable man and machine power must have been used to build it, and such activity, especially on the surface, would have been detected by the swarm of microsatellites orbiting Ceres.

"Any ideas?" he asked.

Ben stared at the object. "I think we're going to have to go down," he said, "before we start our survey."

Cody had to agree. Anything unexpected had to be checked before they began their infrastructure viability survey for the Vesta City Public Works Department. What bothered him was that there was anything unexpected at all, especially after thirty years of scrutiny.

"There's nothing coming from it," said Cody. "No readings of any kind. Maybe it's space debris."

"GK 2, catalog impacts for current coordinates," said Ben.

The computer cataloged all known impacts down to a millimeter. Nothing.

"No," said Ben, "it was built." He arched his brow curiously. "What's underneath there, anyway?" he asked.

"There's nothing underneath there," said Cody. "The Ceresians never built this far east. The closest utility is seventy kilometers away, the solar-power generating plant at

Actinium on the outskirts of Newton." He looked over his shoulder. "Deirdre," he called, "come have a look at this."

Deirdre Malvern, the crew's structural engineer, floated free of her seat and propelled herself to Cody's workstation. She was in her early thirties, an attractive woman with close-cropped hair the color of burnt sienna and unsettling green eyes.

"This isn't on any of the reference satellite photographs," said Cody. "This is new."

Deirdre leaned forward, put her hand on Cody's shoulder.

"Someone's been tampering with the satellites, then," she said. "Those satellites have been in place ever since the Civil Action. Vesta City should have picked up on this."

"That's what I thought," said Cody.

Cody stared at the structure on the surface. The geometrical precision of the structure unnerved him, was daunting in its angles and its size, like a knife blade rising above the surface of the dusty asteroid, as still and imposing as a gigantic tomb, isolated, secretive. Was this the work of human endeavor? Or could the structure be the product of unknown visitors? If so, what would be the impact on his survey schedule and, ultimately, on the more massive and complicated reconstruction effort? He pressed the communication button.

"Jerry," he said, "could you come up here and have a look at this?"

A few moments later Dr. Jerry Rudnick floated up through the companionway. He was a tall man afflicted with a slight hunchback—bone disease from growing up in the microgravity of Juno, where the capacity spin produced only .2 gees.

"Take a look at this," said Cody.

The doctor leaned forward and peered myopically through his glasses at the screen. He looked at it for a long time. Finally he arched his back, scratched his head, and spoke into the computer.

"GK 3," he said, "search yesterday's orbital photographs for like or similar structures."

Two seconds later the computer identified seventeen other similar structures, all of them brand new, scattered over the surface of the asteroid.

Cody sealed his helmet and went into the lander's airlock with Ben. Ben leaned heavily against the railing, unused to the artificially produced gravity on Ceres—a speck of a singularity inserted into the asteroid's core a hundred years ago, a laboratory-created black hole pulling everything coreward at a force of .5 gees.

"You all right?" asked Cody.

"It'll take some getting used to," said Ben. He was from tiny Flora, a planetesimal where gravitational enhancement couldn't exceed an integrity point of .2 gees; any greater and Ben's small home asteroid would shake apart in the resulting tidal fluxes. "I guess point-five gees is about right for you."

Cody was from Vesta, an asteroid half the size of Ceres that used the same gravitational technology. "We have point-four on Vesta. That's about as high as we can go without running into serious problems. So this will be a bit of a go for me as well."

Cody cycled the airlock, and the two engineers descended the ladder to the surface of the asteroid. Cody was glad he lived on a grav-core asteroid, where such a thing as surface walking was possible. A place like little Flora, where Ben came from, you stayed inside all the time, walking on the inside rim while the whole works spun centrifugally to artificially create a meager .2 gees. No wonder Ben was already out of breath.

"I guess you don't see the sun much," said Cody.

"Not until I joined Public Works," said Ben. "To tell you the truth, the sun kind of scares me."

Both engineers looked at the distant white ball. It shone with a hard brittleness. Through his heavily tinted visor,

Cody made out its disk, round and nearly blue in a hot insistent way. He liked surface-walking, the loneliness of it, the desolation of an asteroidscape, the quiet. But surface-walking always reminded him of Christine, and he couldn't help thinking how he would never surface-walk with Christine again.

"Can you manage?" asked Cody. "Or do you want me to give you a hand?"

"No, I'm okay," said Ben. "Just a little dizzy. It really presses down, doesn't it?"

"You'll be okay."

"We really have to get this place up and running again."

It was all a question of gravity in the Belt, thought Cody. Gravity in the Belt was as precious, in its way, as air. He actually enjoyed the tug he felt coming from Ceres. He picked up a stone and threw it, marked its trajectory in the weak light coming from the sun, saw that it came down a lot more quickly than it would have on Vesta, where the gravity was 20 percent weaker. The children of the Belt had to be able to grow up on Ceres again, as they had thirty years ago. Heart disease. Bone disease. Inner-ear deficiencies. All these maladies and more could be avoided later in life if children could again be sent to the schools on Ceres, where the sheer size of the place made a stronger gravity possible, up to a full Earth gravity without any significant damage to the asteroid's geological structure.

"I wonder what one gee feels like," Cody speculated. "Can you imagine?"

"At this point," said Ben, gasping even more, "I'd sooner not."

They proceeded over the blasted surface toward the unidentified object. Cody felt the crunch his boots made on the age-old carbonaceous dirt. He looked around for signs of construction activity, footprints or machine tracks, but except for the usual pitting of micrometeorites, the surface looked undisturbed—virgin asteroid terrain, beautiful in a cold, sterile way.

A holo-image of Deirdre appeared in the upper right corner of his visor.

"How is it?" she asked.

"Sixty percent on Ben," he said. "He's the one you should be asking."

"Vesta City is still giving us the go-ahead," she said. "Pending what you find surface-side."

"Nothing so far."

"We'll be out of contact for the next seven minutes while we're in occultation," she said. "I thought I'd better let you know."

"We'll be fine," he said.

"Then bye for now," she said, but left her holo-image intact, staring at him with those green eyes of hers until occultation cracked her image into a million pieces.

He thought of his hometown—dim, unimaginative, provincial Vesta City, thrust into prominence as the Belt's provisional primary city after the evacuation here on Ceres thirty years ago. What would become of Vesta City once they got Ceres up and running again? Would it be content to take second place to Newton again? Would its stolid citizens be glad to go back to modest, unassuming lives after three decades in the spotlight? And would Council's government officials uproot themselves and return to Isosceles Boulevard? Did officials with Vestan constituencies not realize that in voting to undertake this massive reconstruction project on Ceres they were in fact cutting Vesta's throat economically and culturally? Yet the fact remained: you could boost the gravity on this seven-hundred kilometer-long rock to one gee without the place shaking apart, and give the children a healthy place to grow up in, to develop as they should, so they could be farmed back to their home asteroids with less likelihood of microgravity-related conditions.

"Who was that?" asked Ben.

"She didn't have it on the open channel?"

Ben grunted. "Deirdre again?"

"You got it."

"She's a nice girl, Cody."

"I know she is."

"I heard her singing the other day."

"You did?"

"She's got a nice voice."

"She's a top structural engineer," said Cody.

"Is that the only thing you can say about her?"

The thing, when they got there, cast a stark shadow to the southeast. The ramp rose three hundred meters, three times the length of the field in Kirkwood Stadium in downtown Vesta City, rounding to a dark, cavelike opening that dwarfed the two men. The sun lit the outer rim of the opening as if with a stroke of white fire, while the inner portion was as dark as ink. Cody took a visor reading, first in infrared, then with the spectrometer, and was surprised to find trace amounts of oxygen, nitrogen, and carbon dioxide shimmering over the walls.

"Do you see that?" he asked Ben. "Check your spectrometer."

Ben checked his spectrometer. "Shit," he said.

"Let's have a look," said Cody.

They proceeded into the gigantic entrance, turning on their guidelights to penetrate the dense shadow within.

Plantlike cilia grew in sparse patches on the metallic walls. Plants. In a vacuum. In deep-space cold and dark, with no water. He moved closer. Each cilium was a thumb-length long, flat, leaf-shaped, bilateral in design, with three rounded points on either side, six points in all; a bit like an oak leaf but blue-green in color and growing in colonies. Sources of oxygen, nitrogen, and carbon dioxide showed up strongest around these colonies.

They shrink-wrapped a specimen in quarantine polymer.

Back on the *Gerard Kuiper*, Jerry put the sample in a larger quarantine study box and gassed it so the shrink-wrap polymer dissolved around it.

"Six-and-a-half centimeters long, 2.2 centimeters wide,

and .7 millimeters thick," said Jerry. "GK 3, compare present sample to all known plant, lichen, fungi, bacteria, and virus specimens."

Cody read the screen two seconds later: comparison negative. In other words, they had a specimen of something entirely new here.

"What I'd like to know is how it could survive out there on the surface?" said Cody. "GK 1, is present sample alive?"

The screen read positive.

"GK 1, run a toxicology analysis," he said.

The inside of the quarantine box steamed over with various chemical compounds designed to test for all known toxins. Five seconds later, the steam cleared and Cody had his answer.

Negative. No known toxins detected.

"GK 3," said Jerry, "analyze molecular structure and extrapolate for possible bacterial, toxic, or viral threat to the human metabolism."

The quarantine box filled with a lighter mist.

Negative for possible bacterial, toxic, or viral threat.

Deirdre pushed her way forward. "GK 4, is current sample innocuous to human life?"

The computer told them that the lichen, or fungi, or cilia, or whatever it was, was indeed innocuous to human life. But to be on the safe side Jerry introduced a lab mouse into the quarantine box. The mouse sniffed the sample, bit into it, tore a chunk off, and began eating. Cody glanced at Jerry, then at Ben, finally checking in with Deirdre, who was staring at the mouse with a small smile.

"He likes it," he said.

"The genetic analysis is coming up just now," said Jerry. "Coding 76 percent similar to the Parasol Mushroom of eastern Michigan."

"What about the remaining 24 percent?"

"Unknown."

"But still innocuous."

"Still innocuous," said Jerry.

"Then I say we go in," said Cody.

"Shouldn't we relay to Vesta City?" suggested Deirdre.

"We'll do that," said Cody. "But in the meantime let's get our gear." He called to their pilot, Joe Calaminci. "Joe, fire attitude jets and bring us into synchronous orbit above Newton."

As Joe followed Cody's instructions, everybody floated against the left wall, pushed there by the mild gee-force, and grasped various handholds until the *Gerard Kuiper* positioned itself above Newton, that city of cities, an idea as much as a city, as mythical as New York, Paris, or London—a place to start, the chosen hub of the reconstruction effort, the heart of the asteroid Ceres, and indeed, of the whole Belt.

They all dealt with it in their different ways, the gravity, .5 gees produced by a utility, that sliver of a black hole in the core that had stayed on-line, if in a degraded form, since the evacuation. Cody glanced around as they walked in their pressure suits down Isosceles Boulevard into the underground city of Newton. Deirdre, who was also from Vesta, forced herself to walk upright, even managed a bounce in her step, as though determined to prove herself. Jerry walked with flat-footed effort, his stooped shoulders a lot more stooped than they usually were, his arms hanging with a nearly apelike droop at his sides. Ben got himself into a rhythm, banging each foot down on the macadamized surface of Isosceles Boulevard as if he were stepping on insects, sending small puffs of dust into the vacuum.

Cody glanced around at the other eight members of his survey crew, all good men and women, people he knew he could trust. Russ Burke, Dina Alton, and Peter Wooster stuck together, talking in low voices in the hard-to-follow Perseusian dialect of their home asteroid. Witold Kawlosewicz helped Claire Dubeau because Witold came from Vesta and Claire came from Flora, and the difference was .3 gees. Huy Hai, the waterworks engineer, kept close to the curb by force of habit, inspecting whatever drains they came to, occasionally picking pieces of the strange lichen off lampposts and tossing them into the road. Anne-Marie Waddell, communications engineer, was hunched over like Jerry, but not as badly. Finally, Wolf Steiger, who came from one of the Hundred Towns in the Nefertiti Family, a place so tiny that centrifugal capacity couldn't exceed .05 gees, a big man, muscular, fitter than all of them, but breathing hard, as if he had chronic lung disease.

A holo-image of Joe Calaminci—still up in the *Gerard Kuiper*—appeared in the upper right corner of Cody's visor.

"I just got word from Vesta City," said Joe. "They're giving us the go-ahead in spite of the lichen. They've had a mycologist look at our readouts, and he agrees with us. It's innocuous."

"Do they have any idea how it got here?"

"They're working on it."

"Do they suggest an alien origin?" asked Cody.

"Not when it shares kinship with an earth mushroom, no. Have you found much more of it?"

"It's all over the place. On anything with a carbonaceous base. Plus there's this moss. It glows blue in the dark. We've tested it and it's innocuous as well."

Cody looked around at the little bits of moss hanging like the wispy strands of an old man's beard here and there, patches of it everywhere, lighting up the dark city as if with dim blue stars. He should have alerted Vesta City about the moss too, but he wanted to get on with things; he had been satisfied with their own tests and didn't want to get tied up in further bureaucratic delay.

"Vesta City wants to know if you've found any corpses yet," said Joe. "They particularly want to know about orphan corpses."

"We saw five skeletons laid out next to a garbage disposal unit. The bones were all mixed up. It was hard to tell whether they were orphan or human."

"They're sending a security ship," Joe told him, sounding miffed.

"What for?" asked Cody.

"The *Conrad Wilson*," said Joe. "Kevin Axworthy is commander. I think the crew is forty."

"Why's that name sound familiar?" asked Cody.

"Heard of Artemis Axworthy?"

"Sure."

"Kevin is his youngest son."

"Which means Kevin must be at least in his fifties."

"I would think so," said Joe.

"What are his orders?" asked Cody. "I hope he's not going to take over. This is our project. We know the infrastructure. The last thing we need is a bunch of defense engineers coming in here and trying to revamp the place."

Joe nodded in commiseration. "They're coming for our safety," he said. "At least that's what Vesta City says. They'll be here in two weeks."

"Anything else?" asked Cody.

"They're bringing heavy equipment," said Joe. "They're interested in those outside structures. They want me to confirm with you the depth of the cavelike opening."

"Sixty meters."

"And you ran up against a titanium alloy?"

"Five meters thick. We haven't the equipment to get through it. We're here for a survey, not to investigate unknown structures on the surface with titanium alloy walls five meters thick."

Cody could only speculate about the structures, but their implication made him nervous. He glanced around at his crew, dim figures in the peripheral glow coming from their guidelights. To forge structures of such great size and strength in absolute secrecy impressed him. What he found frustrating as a builder and a Public Works engineer—what made him keep turning the structures over in his mind—was that he couldn't figure out what they were used for. His professional acumen was stumped. He could usually look at any tool, structure, or utility, no matter how foreign in design, and know immediately what it was used for. He kicked a piece of rubble—evidence of the fighting here thirty years ago—and watched it roll heavily across the road. He hadn't the slightest clue what the structures were used for. And he knew that he was going to lose sleep over it.

CHAPTER 2

They set up operations in Laws of Motion Square. Cody dimly remembered a visit to Newton thirty-four years ago, when he'd been five years old, taken here by his father to tour a number of Ceresian boarding schools for the purpose of possible enrollment. He had been amazed by the tall buildings; how the Weather Board had been constantly changing the color of the sky; how all the construction materials had been in funhouse hues, designed to please children. He gazed at the building across the street, a bank building, checkered in meter-sized tiles of white, blue, red, and green, looking like a Piet Mondrian painting. He looked at the maglev station on the corner, a building zapped with diamond-shaped panes of copper-tinted glass, and diamond-shaped tiles of pink, yellow, and purple acrylic, looking like something a harlequin might wear. He looked up at the sky. The sky was now black. Back then the sky had been purple, red, pink, blue, green, and gold. Sometimes with clouds. Sometimes with moons and planets. Sometimes with whales, elephants, and lions.

He glanced around at his crew. Peter Wooster inventoried pressure-suit oxygen tanks. Wolf Steiger mounted an electrical box on one of the bank's multicolored tiles. Huy Hai adjusted the temperature controls on the portable water tank. Cody was glad to see they were getting on with their work despite the unexpected discoveries.

A holo-image of Jerry Rudnick appeared on Cody's visor, optically transmitted for focus directly into his retina by a laser. Jerry's face looked as if it floated two meters in front of Cody.

"We've found one," said Jerry. "He's been mummified."

"Human?"

"No. Orphan. A male."

Cody called up a local map to his visor using his wrist input and pinpointed Jerry's location. "You're on Subtraction Avenue?"

"Two blocks away."

"Are you going to need help bringing him here?" asked Cody.

"No," said Jerry. "I've got Wit with me. And Russ is here too. Has Deirdre checked in? I saw her heading up Spectrum Street."

Cody felt his lips stiffen. He knew Deirdre occasionally ignored safety protocols, but also knew there wasn't much he could do about it. "Let her go," he said. "She's never been here before. She's going to find the structures interesting."

A few minutes later Witold and Russ appeared in Laws of Motion Square bearing a mummified orphan corpse on a stretcher. Jerry walked along beside them, looking as if he might collapse under his extra gee-load any minute. Cody stared at the corpse, fascinated by it, this genetically altered human being, now dead, preserved by the dry airless cold, an orphan who had lived here thirty years ago, in a different time, and who had most likely lost his life during the bitter struggle of the Ceresian Civil Action. A historical snapshot on a stretcher.

"You're really getting along with the lights," said Jerry, looking around.

"Ben was born to wire," said Cody. He motioned toward the supply yard. "Let's put him over here on this cable spool."

Wit and Russ lifted the corpse onto the cable spool.

As with all orphans—Cody had seen only pictures—this

one looked to all intents and purposes human. Genetic engineering had been minimal, only enough to enhance his bones into a more adaptive posture for microgravity. The orphan's arms were longer than human arms, while his legs were shorter. He wore green satin pants and a Schrödinger University T-shirt. He was barefoot, with those odd orphan feet, like monkey feet, only human-looking, with an extra phalange in each toe. The orphan would have been young, no more than eighteen, but, because of the extreme cold and zero humidity, had been freeze-dried, looked wizened, like an old man.

Cody shook his head. "I never agreed with the way they handled that," he said. "They should have negotiated. Look at him. He's just a kid."

Cody stared at the orphan's face, wondering what it was like to grow up without a mother or father, to be incubated in a test tube, to have your code genetically altered by someone else's design. To climb, to swing, to jump. To instinctively pack with your own kind. To repudiate the people who made you. To renounce humanity. To rob. To rape. To kill . . .

"Okay," he said to Jerry. "Perform an autopsy and send the results to Vesta City. I'm sure they'll be interested in what you find." Vesta City, habituated to a posture of vigilance, would always be interested in looking at dead enemies. "Then give him a proper burial."

The airlocks. Sixty-eight of them citywide. Eighteen leading to installations on the surface. Another eighteen used as access points to electrical, water, oxygen, and heating mains. The remaining thirty-two strung along various transportation routes at the city limits. All of them with backup airlocks, and backup airlocks for the backup airlocks. One-hundred-and-ninety-eight separate units in all. All of them closed, when, by rights, they should have been found wide open, the way the evacuation authorities had left them thirty years ago. Who had closed them?

Cody shook his head as he gazed at the surprising finding once more on his visor's GK link, a link that downloaded data into the visual hookups of his visor. After the Ceresians had evacuated the asteroid; after the Ceresian Defense Force had launched multiple bioextermination warheads; after they had opened all the airlocks—after anybody and everybody who had been left behind should have been dead, fried to a cinder from the inside out by microwave radiation—somebody had gone around and closed all the doors. A lot of doors to close in this once-thriving city of five million inhabitants.

He could picture the members of Council back in Vesta City scratching their heads in mystification over the whole thing. The closed airlocks, in conjunction with the citywide bulwarks, now pressurized a tenuous atmosphere of oxygen, nitrogen, and carbon dioxide—the stuff the lichen breathed out—with a barometric reading of eight millibars, as thick as the atmosphere on Mars.

He closed down his data-link. They had one last airlock to check. But they had to get there first. Cody, Ben, and Peter adjusted the gauge of the rover wheels to fit around the Fermi Maglev's central rail so the tires wouldn't rub against the metal. Cody keyed in a command and the chassis rose, creating distance between the rover and the rail so the chassis wouldn't scrape. Now the wheels could ride comfortably in the concrete bed on either side of the rail. He looked around at Ben and Peter and smiled. They were just three guys tinkering with their vehicle.

"I think we're ready," he said.

"Then let's go," said Peter.

They drove in the track-bed over the central rail, Peter at the wheel. They rumbled eastward—the Fermi Maglev line was the most direct route to the final airlock they had to check. The rover headlights pierced the gloom. After about ten kilometers, Peter slowed the vehicle. Ben stood up and peered ahead. The final airlock, decorated with a mosaic of children playing catch with an enlarged atomic model of hydrogen, rose twenty-five meters to the pressure wall overhead. Like all the others, this airlock had been closed. But unlike the others, this one had been damaged. Whoever had closed it had repaired it.

A compound of unknown origin had been puttied over the central seal.

Peter, in charge of materials management, stopped the rover ten meters from the airlock. The three men got out. Peter went to the back of the rover and retrieved a portable materials analyzer. The three approached the airlock.

Cody selected his visor's infrared, looked at the airlock, detected no discernible decline in temperature in and around the airlock, and concluded it was airtight.

"Are you getting the infrared reading?" he asked Ben.

"No leak," said Ben. "We could have popped Newton the minute we got here."

"I'm getting sick of wearing a pressure suit," agreed Cody.

"Look at this compound," said Peter. "It looks like ice."

Peter pressed the retrieval port against the compound and waited for a reading.

"Mainly carbon and nitrogen in polymer-type chains, with a few heavier molecules I can't identify," said Peter. "We're really going to save on sealant. Maybe we'll have enough for Equilibrium."

Equilibrium was Ceres's second-largest city, next on their list.

"Unless all the airlocks have been closed and repaired in Equilibrium as well," said Cody.

"Look at this," said Peter. "The stuff has a melting point of minus 25 Celsius."

"Who would make sealant with a melting point that low?" asked Ben. "What would be the point? Nothing can live at minus 25 Celsius."

Cody thought about it. "Nothing human at least," he said.

He again wondered about the structures on the surface, whether they were, in fact, alien, or whether the orphans—humans of a sort—had been responsible for them. Certainly the possibility of alien design had to be considered. The notion was so momentous he felt ill-equipped to deal with it.

He was a carpenter by trade. The larger ramifications of first contact would have to be dealt with by people who had made a study of such things.

"We're going to have to put some of our own sealant on that before we pop the place," said Peter. "If we pop the place and release the biotherms, that stuff's going to melt."

"Then let's get to it," said Cody.

Cody went to the back of the rover and lifted a thermal laser. He keyed in for a diffuse beam, walked to the airlock, lifted the tool, and pulled the lever. The sealant immediately began to bubble and steam, sublimating directly from solid to a gas heavier than the ambient atmosphere, filling the track-bed of the Fermi Maglev line with dim blue mist.

"You think there's anybody still here?" asked Ben.

"Not in Newton I don't," said Cody. "The place is a giant tomb."

"Joe's going ultrasonic up in the ship?" asked Ben.

"I gave him orders to go to a depth of 60 meters."

"Good."

"I really don't think there's anyone here but us, Ben. Whoever built those structures on the surface . . . well . . . I think they must be gone by now. The *Kuiper* would have detected any life-forms from orbit."

A large chunk of sealant fell away from the airlock like a piece of ice sloughing off a glacier into the sea.

"Unless whatever sabotaged the microsatellites sabotaged our own detection equipment as well," said Ben.

"I just don't see it," said Cody. "This place is dead. Maybe there might have been some survivors, and maybe they were able to huddle together somehow for a few years after the evacuation, and maybe build those structures, for whatever reason, but I think they've all died out since then." Cody shrugged as the last bit of sealant gasified under the diffuse beam of his thermal laser. "I think we're alone."

Back in Laws of Motion Square, where the crew now had the pressurized dorm and office up and running, they received from Joe Calaminci an interesting ultrasonic image of the surface of Ceres. This was essentially an X-ray 60 meters deep. What Cody saw was a disk, measuring 70 meters across, its shape concave according to the computer's extrapolations, dipping a full five meters to the center. Material analysis indicated a composition of bonded silicate—in other words, glass. This huge disk of concave glass was situated in County Hypotenuse, a remote part of the asteroid 250 kilometers away from Newton. Like the other structures, the glass disk hadn't been there at the time of the evacuation.

"Do you realize the kind of kiln they'd need to bond a piece of glass that size?" said Deirdre. "And the heat such a kiln would produce? At least 1,500 degrees Celsius. I don't know how Vesta could have missed it."

"Any speculation as to what the thing is?" he asked her.

She raised her eyebrows. "A photocell?" she said. "To collect solar energy?"

"Why would it be 60 meters underground with no microwave converter in sight if it were a photocell?" asked Ben.

"I think it's a telescope," Jerry Rudnick said quietly, steepling his fingers. "Any time you have a concave disk of glass that large you can be certain it's used for light-gathering purposes. What you've got here is a 70-meter refractor."

"GK 1," said Cody, addressing the computer, "access historical infrastructure blueprints for current coordinates."

The computer showed historical infrastructure blueprints for these given square kilometers of County Hypotenuse in a smaller window off to one side. Nothing. No infrastructure at all. Certainly no telescope. Cratered terrain. No sign of human habitation or economic activity. Cody half thought the old infrastructure blueprint shot might be in error. Ceres was famous for its telescopes, known for its great strides in deep-space optics. A giant telescope in County Hypotenuse would be typical of them. As far as Cody could recall, the Ceresian Astronomical Association had six observatories around the asteroid. But did it have any so big?

"So who built it?" asked Ben. "And why did they put it all the way out in County Hypotenuse?"

Cody shook his head. "I don't know," he said. Again, it was a mystery that he found galling to his professional pride. He was intensely curious about the structure as a builder and an engineer, but as a project manager he knew he couldn't devote any of his resources to finding out what it was. "Let Kevin Axworthy worry about it when he gets here in the *Conrad Wilson*." He thought of his schedule, tried to act like a project manager. "We should have popped the oxygen yesterday. We should have released the bio-therms. We're a day behind. Transmit all this stuff to Vesta City. Let them worry about it."

The next day he was up a ladder stringing lights on Sub-traction Avenue. Ben was helping him. The temporary lights were powered by a generator for the twofold purpose of making their survey easier and lighting the way for the cleanup crews when they arrived six weeks from now.

"Deirdre took me down to the lake," said Ben. "I've never seen ice so hard. And the boats they have down there! Shaped like swans. Hippopotamuses. Blue whales . . . just like a carnival."

"Frozen right into the ice?"

"Yes. We walked out to this island, and they have a gazebo and a bandstand in the park. That's different for me. The civic designers on Flora prefer neon and metal."

"Vesta's not much better," he said. "I notice you're spending some time with Deirdre." He put his screwdriver in his tool belt. "Could I have a bit more cable?"

Ben handed Cody more cable.

"That's okay, isn't it, me spending more time with her?" said Ben.

"Why shouldn't it be?"

"You're not upset, are you?"

"Why should I be upset?"

The light swung eerily as Cody adjusted the cable.

"What I meant was . . . you know . . . you and Deirdre," said Ben.

"What about me and Deirdre?"

"The way she looks at you," said Ben, sounding as if he were explaining something to a child. "She talked about it . . . when we were out on the lake together. She likes you. She likes the way you move. She likes the way you hold a hammer."

"The way I hold a hammer?" said Cody.

"She likes the way you talk. How do I stand a chance with Deirdre if she keeps talking about you that way?"

"I have no interest in Deirdre," said Cody.

"How am I supposed to compete? Look at you. You're tall. You've got that face. And then look at me. A guy with a tiny head who always grows a beard by noon. A guy with an overbite."

"You don't have an overbite, Ben," he said.

"Will you talk to her?"

"About what?"

"Just tell her you don't have any interest in her," said Ben. "That should be enough."

Cody motioned toward the next intersection, wondering how Deirdre could possibly be interested in him when he still hadn't fully gotten over the loss of Christine.

"I'm not going to say anything," he said. "Just go ahead and have fun together if you like. As long as it doesn't affect your work, I don't care. Let's erect the next post. I want to get as far as Vector Boulevard by—"

"Will you tell her?"

"I don't think it will be necessary, Ben," said Cody.

"It'll be necessary," Ben insisted.

But Cody didn't reply. He stopped working and peered up Vector Boulevard. Up to where the darkness swallowed the city, up to the corner of Trigonometry Avenue, where a dust-covered bus sat by the curb and an infant's perambulator lay on its side in the middle of the litter-strewn street.

The impression of sudden fleeting movement, alarming and unexpected, tantalized his eyes.

"Did you see that?" he asked Ben in a quiet voice.

Ben didn't immediately answer. Cody glanced at Ben. Ben's jaw was thrust forward, his bewhiskered chin sticking out. His dark eyes narrowed. "I saw," he finally said.

"What was it?" asked Cody.

Ben's shoulders eased. Cody heard Ben's accelerated respiration transmitted through his com-link.

"I don't know," said Ben, "but it sure was running fast."

Cody stared up Vector Boulevard, perfectly still. The light carried only so far, brightening the facades of dusty and dirty buildings, penetrating as far as a stanchion protruding from the coppery walls of a coffee shop, a flag with a coffee cup and a bagel on it drooping from the stanchion.

"It wasn't . . . one of the crew, was it?" asked Cody.

"No . . ." said Ben. "I don't think so. It was . . . blue."

"Yes, blue, that's what I thought," said Cody, speaking quickly, with a slight jitter in his voice. "Definitely blue."

Sky blue. And not wearing a pressure suit. Where could it have gone? Somewhere up Trigonometry Avenue? And how could it see, whatever it was, through such impenetrable darkness, with only bits and pieces of blue glow-moss to light the way?

"Was it running on all fours?" asked Cody.

Because he was sure it had been running on all fours, at least part of the time, rising on its haunches only to steal a quick look at them, then bolting behind the bus and disappearing.

"I'm not sure," said Ben.

Dressed in only a pair of pants, as far as Cody could see, in a temperature that could freeze the blood in seconds, with no air to breathe. Animallike. And still prowling somewhere out there, a possible danger, maybe alone, maybe with others, its intent unknown, its next move beyond prediction.

CHAPTER 3

Cody held a meeting in the office of the pressurized dorm to discuss the sightings. He told them exactly what he had seen. Their faces were pale, still, quietly alarmed. He glanced out the pressure window at Laws of Motion Square. Something was out there, they didn't know what, and it might possibly pose a threat. A blue thing. A visitor from beyond colonized space? He didn't know. The air inside the office seemed thick with the implications of the discovery. The way his crew waited, worried but patient, forced Cody to acknowledge that they were, after all, counting on him, that they expected him to handle this, just as he handled the more routine situations of their general survey. He controlled his apprehension and prepared himself. His was a position of leadership, a position he was by no means a stranger to. But this was the first time in ten years that he'd exercised such responsibility in the field. An unforeseen and potentially threatening situation out in the field was different from the management glitches and personality clashes he had routinely dealt with when he'd been number-three man at the Public Works Department. But he was out here by choice, and a problem like this was far more exhilarating than eight hours a day in an office. He was back to doing real work. Physical work. He was point man for the Ceresian Reconstruction.

Shaping her words carefully so she could be understood through her Perseusian accent, Dina Alton spoke first.

"If there's one, there could be more," she said.

Cody nodded. "Yes, but so far we've seen only one." He was going to keep strictly to the facts. "And we saw it for less than two seconds. It was dark, and the thing was moving fast."

Wit said, "Huy and I got a good start on the water mains today and I'd like to keep going." Wit's broad face was motionless; he was the kind of man who would bury any concerns in hard work. "Let's not let this slow us down."

Cody glanced at Huy. Huy nodded, but his nod was tentative and he looked anything but certain about going down into the city's water mains now.

"As long as we're careful," said Cody. "As long as we're watchful. We've seen only the one. We have no idea what it is, how it got here, whether there are more, whether they represent a danger or are just . . . just harmless. I don't want to speculate where it came from. I'm sure you all have your own ideas, but until we know more—and who knows, maybe this is the only one we'll ever see—there's no point in playing guessing games."

"Our laser drills have a range of two meters," said Deirdre, half joking, half serious.

Wolf Steiger spoke up. "Maybe we should delay the oxygen pop," he said. "You say that what you saw wasn't wearing any protective clothing, no pressure suit or oxygen tanks."

"No," said Cody.

"So how can we be sure we won't kill it by pressurizing Newton? If we fill this place with air, moisture, and heat, we might harm the thing. Maybe it can't survive in a higher atmospheric pressure or at a warmer temperature."

Cody stared at Wolf. He was surprised by his crew's varying reactions: Deirdre wanted to go out and kill the thing with a laser drill; Wolf wanted to make sure they took every precaution to save it.

Jerry said, "Let's keep with the schedule. Let's not let this affect us one way or the other." The doctor sat forward, rubbed his knees, seemed irritated by the thing out there. "I'm thinking of our children," he said. "Our children haven't been able to grow up on Ceres for 30 years. They've been waiting a long time to come back. First they had to wait for the contamination levels to taper off. Then they had to wait for Council to make up its mind whether we should come back at all. Then they had to wait for the financing to become available, for the planning to be done, and for all the extensive training and preparation of all the crews. I don't want to make them wait one second longer. They've had to grow up in the microgravity of the other asteroids for 30 years. And that's done irreparable harm to at least three generations. Look at any of my pediatric charts on Juno and you'll see a microgravity-related condition in all of them. We need the grav-core." The doctor looked around at the crew, then gestured toward Isosceles Boulevard. "I don't care what's out there. Newton belongs to us. We should go ahead and pressurize."

Cody took stock of his survey crew. "Could we continue working in our pressure suits for just the next few days?" He was beginning to think that Wolf might have a point. "I know we're all sick of our suits, and I know they slow the work down, but the thing we saw . . . I don't know . . ." If the thing out there was indeed a true visitor, and was of a peaceful nature, he certainly didn't want to be the one to inadvertently kill it. "I'm going to see what Vesta City says," he said. "I think we need direction on this."

Wolf shifted in his cot, disappointed. "You know what they're going to say, Cody," he said. "They're going to want us to go ahead with the oxygen pop one way or the other. You know the way they think. Something like this isn't going to stop them."

In the suburb of Actinium, on the outskirts of Newton, there stood perhaps the oldest Oxygen Production Utility in the whole Belt; two hundred years old, decommissioned seventy-five years ago, and preserved up until the time of the evacuation as a museum. Cody looked around the old control room. Through the years, a succession of curators had refurbished the plant so that the OPU, if supplied with the necessary kilowatts, might in a pinch still produce oxygen; this was done more out of historical interest than any real practical need. Cody brushed dust off one of the panels. The original power plant for the OPU consisted of a solar-power generating station located directly above, on the surface. In its heyday, the station had produced enough current to power a good portion of Newton, as well as much of the surrounding area, sending electricity over the cratered surface of Ceres by means of a microwave converter. Wolf sat in a chair, still easily tired by what to him was a strong gravity. Cody wanted to make enough power with the solar-power generating station to get the OPU working again. He turned to Ben.

"What do you think?" he asked.

Planners for this initial phase of the reconstruction had decided to revamp this particular antiquated utility because it did indeed run on solar power; the *Gerard Kuiper* didn't have the cargo space to bring the large fusion cell units needed to power the more modern Oxygen Production Utilities.

Ben was their power specialist in this area. "I think it can be done," he said. "At least to a limited degree. This panel here, when it was running, indicated which cable conduits were on-line. Remember, this plant is two centuries old. That means cable. We can repair a lot of the impact-compromised cable on the surface. Once we get some power, we can at least make Newton livable for the cleanup crews and the contractors, make it so they don't have to keep popping the place with oxygen."

"What's this panel for?" asked Wolf.

"Solar panel calibration," said Ben. "There's going to be a lot of cleaning to do, especially in those calibration beds."

"Look at this," said Cody. "Transom valve indicators."

Ben took a closer look at the panel. "For rerouting the oxygen to emergency shelters. An old safety measure."

Cody pondered this. "Why don't we see if we can reroute oxygen to the emergency shelter across the street from Operations, in Laws of Motion Square? At least for starters. Then we'll be able to spread out a bit, have more of a headquarters."

Ben considered. "It's possible," he said.

"It'll be a good way to test the system before we go full-scale," said Cody.

"Then we should check the cable upstairs," said Ben. "Out on the surface."

Cody looked around. "I really like this old place," he said, patting the control panel affectionately. "If we could clean off some of the panels on the surface, fix some cables, and get this utility up to maybe three or four percent output by Monday, I'd be really happy."

They climbed seven flights of stairs, then two different companionway ladders to get to the surface. Wolf was so tired by the time he got to the top that he had to sit down on the control deck floor.

"You two go ahead," he said. "My knees are killing me. I'll be out in a minute."

Cody and Ben went out onto the surface by themselves, using a power pack to cycle the airlock.

Solar panels, each ninety meters square, stretched as far as the eye could see, a neat checkerboard of solar-gathering silicon arranged in photovoltaic cells. The transmission tower stood half a kilometer away, rising white and dusty from the carbonaceous surface. On top was a large object— the microwave converter—like a radar dish, with a transmitting baton rising from its center like the stamen of a hibiscus.

"Look at these cells," said Cody. "Silicon. We haven't used silicon on Vesta for a hundred years."

They walked across the surface. It wasn't like the surface of Vesta, which was studded with igneous rock and shone like a rough-cut gem in the sunlight. Ceres was dark. Gray. Monochromatic.

"What about the microwave converter?" asked Ben. "Have we come up with a plan to target the current to the various intake grids yet?"

Cody nodded, thinking of the powerful beam of current that the microwave converter would generate once the solar panels were collecting sunlight again, how that beam would cause a lot of damage if it weren't targeted properly toward the designated intake and conversion grids. "Claire has a program for it," he said.

He heard Ben sigh through his com-link. "Claire has a program for everything," said Ben.

"I don't think she has one for your overbite," Cody replied.

"Funny guy," said Ben.

"She says once we get it interfaced, the targeting accuracy should be within one square meter."

"Good," said Ben. "I'd hate to be hit by that thing when it starts transmitting."

In the morning, Peter Wooster, in charge of stores, discovered oxygen tanks were missing. Cody stared at the remaining bright yellow tanks, standing like little soldiers braced one next to the other in a steel rack; only seventy-five left now, enough to last twelve people six days.

"And they were all here yesterday?" he asked Peter.

"Yes."

Cody looked at Deirdre. Deirdre gazed at the tanks through her visor with wide speculative eyes. Cody looked at Jerry, who shrugged, and then at Ben. Finally he stared down Isosceles Boulevard. They had temporary lights running for three blocks, small lights, harsh lights, ones that did little to dispel the gloom, a small finger of incandescence truncating abruptly at Decimal Place.

"Those tanks are heavy," said Cody.

His words sounded small and distant, scraping through

the near-vacuum on brittle radio waves, riding the open channel into everybody's helmets.

"I say we pop the oxygen with or without Vesta City's go-ahead," said Deirdre. "They took our tanks. They're compromising our life support. They can't go around stealing our stuff."

They. But who were *they?* Cody stared up the street to Decimal Place as if he thought he might find an answer somewhere out there in the darkness. Twenty-seven tanks gone. He had to conclude that the theft, because of its magnitude, had been perpetrated by more than one individual.

"There's 12 of us," continued Deirdre. "We're here on our own for the next 10 days. We have no weapons. Vital supplies have been taken from us. We have to guard what's left. We have to conserve it. And in order to do that we have to pop the oxygen."

"But why did they steal just our oxygen?" asked Jerry. "Why didn't they take our biotherm canisters as well? Why didn't they steal some of our shovels, or our cable, or our lubricant? Why steal just our oxygen? Especially when the one Cody saw wasn't wearing a pressure suit or using an oxygen tank? Why would they need oxygen when they live in a place that doesn't have any?"

Cody didn't want to jump to conclusions, but he feared that whoever had stolen their oxygen in fact realized that oxygen was vital to human life and that stealing it would undermine his crew's life-support capability. Before he could offer any thoughts on this, a holo-image of Joe Calaminci appeared in the upper right corner of his visor.

"I just received word from Vesta City on the oxygen pop," said Joe. The image flickered for an instant; Ceres had a small and occasionally disruptive magnetic field. "They want us to go ahead."

"Did everybody hear that?" Cody asked his crew. He thought that Council back in Vesta City must be having conniption fits by now.

Everyone nodded. For several seconds no one said anything. Were some of them thinking, as he was, of Wolf Steiger's oxygen pop concerns, how if they filled the place with heat and air they might kill whatever happened to be out there?

"It's about time," Russ Burke finally said. "I'm getting sick of my own stink. I want to get out of this suit."

Cody stared at Russ. His shoulders felt suddenly heavy. He was relieved that the decision had been taken out of his hands—he was a builder after all, and he wanted to get on with the practical side of things—but he couldn't help feeling at least some concern about the possibly fatal consequences of the Council's go-ahead.

"Then that settles it," he said. "As for the missing tanks . . . we post a guard. We go in shifts of three, four if necessary, round the clock. Anne-Marie, could you draw up a shift schedule, please? I guess we have to get out of these suits sooner or later. We can't work effectively when we're in them, and work is what we're here for."

CHAPTER 4

The oxygen pop, or Portable Atmospheric Release Tank, contained a magnetically pressurized parcel of 80 percent nitrogen, 20 percent oxygen, and a few other trace gases. In other words, air. Cody watched the pop at the foot of Isosceles Boulevard hiss and steam, white jets billowing like the huffing and puffing of a dragon. Each tank released 2.5 million cubic feet of air at a pressure of 1,000 millibars. The Public Works crew had ten such units, spherical tanks twenty meters across, white, with the green Public Works emblem—trees and clouds—painted on two sides. Cody watched water vapor, meant to humidify the air, crystallize as it left the release valve. Ice particles floated upward, refracting in the lights, breaking into the colors of the spectrum.

Deirdre stood beside Cody gazing at the small rainbow the refracted ice crystals made.

"It's pretty, isn't it?" she said.

He tried to concentrate on the oxygen pop. Before utility contractors had a chance to build proper OPUs, the oxygen pops proved invaluable for extended construction or survey projects on new asteroids, allowed crews to tunnel and excavate without the encumbrance of pressure suits, made labor easier, more productive, and cost-effective. But as much as he tried to concentrate on the oxygen pop, Cody found he couldn't. He still couldn't get over it. She liked the way he held a hammer. The thought made him uncomfortable.

He gestured at the oxygen pop. "This is going to make work a lot easier," he said. He felt awkward around her now. "How are the building inspections going?"

She took a moment to answer. He could see she was picking up on what he was feeling about her.

"They're all . . . going to have to be cleaned . . . down here, downtown." She looked away. "And the plumbing's all shot. About half the wiring's gone." She turned to him, looked up at him. "But the basic structures are sound." Could she really read him so easily? "A lot of them were built to the old codes, pressure-resistant. They've stood up well." She looked away again, and he could tell she was trying to ignore the new dynamic between them, trying simply to be a fellow worker. "The decorating . . . the drywall, the paint, and the trim . . . it's all gone. Plus we're going to need a hundred glaziers working a full year to get all the broken windows fixed." She put her hands on her hips, shrugged. "As for Planck's Constant," she said, "where the heaviest fighting was . . . we might as well bring in earthmovers and level the place." In sudden apprehension, she asked, "Ben talked to you, didn't he?"

The oxygen pop continued to hiss like a rocket. He cringed inside his pressure suit. He just wanted this to go away. But it was there, a fact now, and conversational smoke and mirrors would only go so far to disguise it.

"Have you been to any of the residential sectors?" he asked. "Hemholtz or Kepler, or any of those places?"

She played along. "I was out in Kepler earlier today," she said. "A working-class and off-campus neighborhood. Three- and four-story walk-ups."

"You went inside a few of them?" asked Cody.

"A few."

She reached in a large pouch attached to her tool belt, moved things aside, pulled out something wrapped in cloth, and unwrapped the cloth. Inside lay a piece of varnished pine. She took it out and offered it to him. He peered at her through his visor and saw her smiling, but it was a tentative and apologetic smile, as if she wanted him to understand that he could trust her to do her job as well as she always did, no matter what she happened to feel toward him.

"It's a piece of plate rail I found in one of the walk-ups," she explained. "I thought you might like it. I know how much you like working with wood."

He looked at the wood and frowned. *She liked the way he held a hammer.* The pine she held in her hand had to be worth a thousand dollars, nearly a week's wages. And it wasn't just any pine; it was Corsican pine. He loved wood; he wanted to work with this piece of pine, carve it, especially because any kind of pine on Vesta was so rare, but he knew he couldn't take it from Deirdre, knew he might end up sending her the wrong signal if he did.

"I can't take this wood from you, Deirdre," he said. "I appreciate the offer. It's a fine-looking piece of wood, but I can't take it from you."

She hesitated. "Okay," she said. "I just thought you might like it."

He sighed. "Because if I take it from you . . ." He turned away.

"It's okay, Cody," she said. "I understand. But you don't have to worry. I know how to handle it." She gave him another shy look. "You're sure you don't want the piece of wood though? You'll have fun with it. I'm giving it to you, friend to friend."

He admired the strength he heard in her voice. He admired her fortitude in dealing with this unexpected strain, this sudden feeling she had for him; they were all just human, after all. They'd been sharing close quarters, and in close quarters this kind of thing could easily happen. Yet he couldn't stop a certain coldness. He couldn't help thinking of Christine.

"I'm widowed," he said. "Is that something you can understand?"

She paused.

"Of course," she finally said. He heard her breath through the com-link. "But that shouldn't stop you from taking this piece of wood, should it?" She placed the piece of pine gently in his hands, as if it were indeed a peace offering. "Here," she said. "Do something nice with it. Carve something that Christine would have liked."

She gave the wood a pat and walked away.

Cody followed Huy Hai through the main water trunk under Isosceles Boulevard up toward Decimal Place. With the oxygen pop completed, the crew had released the biotherms. All the water in the filtration systems had melted. Huy Hai strode ahead of Cody. Lake Ockham had melted. The temperature in Newton was now a balmy plus seven. The water in the fifteen reservoirs had melted. So had all the water in the mains and sewers. This was making Huy Hai's job a lot easier, helping him pinpoint leaks and fractures in the city's water delivery and drainage infrastructure with much greater accuracy.

The diminutive Chinese man eased his pace, waited for Cody to catch up. Cody held up his guidelight, glad to be out of his pressure suit. The strange lichen covered the sewer walls like oak leaves, clustered in colony after colony. He picked some off and looked at it. It seemed to be growing well in these moist conditions, just as it did in the freezing-cold vacuum. How could it be so adaptable? The biotherms, engineered organisms designed to produce heat much the same way bioluminescent organisms like fireflies produced light, fought for a toehold, clinging like a fine white dust on the walls over the clusters of lichen.

A trickle of water ran down the middle of the trunk. It fell down a giant crack at the juncture of the next crossway, at Subtraction Avenue.

"Here's another one," said Huy. "I'm going to try and plug it. We'll see if we can get the water to drain over this crack so we don't get any subsurface frost pushing up on the general structure and making it worse. It's got to flow to that vertical drain down there," said Huy, waving his guidelight toward the juncture at Decimal Place. "That drain's the second-last run before the used water reaches the recycling plant. If we can get this downtown grid working before the cleanup and construction crews get here, they'll have an extra source of water as backup."

Huy took a large caulking gun from an array of leak-stopping tools, aimed, and fired. A fine gray polymer issued from the end of the tool. As the polymer touched the crack it expanded the way shaving cream expands, sealed the leak in a matter of seconds, then shrank to a perfect fit, the nanogens in the compound guiding the fit so that the polymer ran contiguously with the adjoining sides of the damaged sewer. This allowed the water to drain properly, without any damming, toward the downspout up ahead. The water found its new route and flowed toward the drain.

"Let's check it," said Huy.

They walked to the drain and looked down.

"Help me set up the pulleys," said Huy. "I don't think we should trust those rungs. They're rusted right through."

Over the next ten minutes they set up two pulleys. They hooked in two lines, one for each of them, and descended the drain, rappelling along the sides like rock climbers descending a cliff. The temperature dropped. The rungs had icicles on them. The strange lichen thrived everywhere, now reminding Cody of bunches of leaf lettuce.

At the bottom, they found another corpse lying on a ledge next to the main channel. Not an orphan corpse. Not a human corpse. A corpse like none they had ever seen.

This corpse was blue.

The first thing Cody thought was that maybe the oxygen pop had killed the thing after all, that the new atmospheric pressure and warmer temperatures had indeed proved lethal to the creature. But then he saw that it had the same mummified look that the orphan corpse had had. It looked as if it had been dead for a long time.

"Look at its leg," said Cody. "The way it's bent like that."

Huy Hai looked at the leg, then peered to the top of the drain. "Maybe he fell," he said. He turned his attention back to the corpse. "His leg looks broken."

Cody nodded. "He fell down here, broke his leg, and dragged himself to this ledge to get out of the water."

Huy Hai brought his guidelight closer. "It's human, isn't it?" he said.

The creature certainly looked human, at least in its basic configurations, with arms and legs, a face with two eyes, a nose, a mouth, and hair on top of its head.

"I think so," said Cody.

"But he has much longer arms," said Huy, "and much shorter legs. Like an orphan. And his torso's not exactly bilaterally equal. Look at that bulge on the left side, below the rib cage. What could that be?"

Cody touched the bulge in and around the stomach.

"We'll get Jerry to perform an autopsy and find out for us," he said.

Back in the small infirmary adjoining the portable office, Jerry and Cody examined the corpse carefully. The victim, a male, might have had a human design but certain features looked positively alien. His eyes, for instance. Nearly three times the size of normal eyes: beautiful doelike eyes, neither brown nor blue, but violet. Then there were his ears, large and slender, twice the size of human ears, shaped like a fairy's, delicate-looking, with a translucent porcelain quality, dim blue but showing red veins underneath.

The doctor ran his hand over the creature's bare abdomen.

"Feel that skin," he said. "Even taking into account the corpse's mummification, the skin somehow feels . . . reinforced . . . I don't know . . . with mesh."

Cody felt the creature's skin. His flesh did indeed feel tough, with a gridlike texture that wasn't readily discernible to the eye but could easily be felt.

"What about his stomach?" asked Cody. "The way his abdomen sticks out on the left side like that?"

Jerry shook his head. "If this were an ordinary human corpse, I might suggest a tumor. But really . . . who knows? Look at his hands. Fingerprints, just like you and me. Fingernails. Four fingers and a thumb. He's wearing a ring. I'll admit his fingers are a little longer than our fingers, but all in all his hands look like human hands. Same with his feet. They look just like human feet except for the longer, stronger toes."

"What about his hair?" asked Cody. "Blond?"

"Too white for true blond. I don't think the hair has any pigment one way or the other. Reminds me of albino hair."

Over the next few hours Jerry performed an autopsy on the unusual corpse. As expected from the clinical examination, he discovered an extra layer in the epidermis, a tough gridwork made of a material resembling cartilage. He quickly concluded that the victim had to be a genetically altered species of human.

"Which means he must have originated in the five or six places—the Moon, Mars, etcetera—where genetic legislation is lax enough to allow for this kind of thing," said Jerry.

Even though the creature derived from a human model, there were major differences. As the autopsy continued, they discovered a highly developed sylvan fissure in the frontal lobe, the part of the brain responsible for intuitive functions; a stomach roughly twice the size of a human stomach, with a lining of unidentified cilia; three sets of extra muscles in the calves, and two extra sets in the thighs.

"He could jump, that's for sure," said Jerry.

Cody stared at the creature, wondering about it, in awe of it, nervous about it, but also feeling sorry for it, the way it had died, falling down that drain, breaking its leg, not being able to get out, most probably starving to death.

Jerry was most interested in the victim's stomach. Especially the cilialike growths.

He lifted the stomach onto the small-parts dissection table, made an incision, and sliced a patch of cilia away.

"I'll make a slide of this," he said.

"Look at the size of his lungs," said Cody. "Human lungs aren't that small, are they?"

"No," said Jerry. "His lungs are roughly half the size of human lungs."

"Genitalia are similar, though, aren't they?" said Cody.

"There's no difference," said Jerry. "He has human genitalia."

"But no pubic hair," said Cody.

"No pubic hair," agreed the doctor.

Cody squinted in puzzlement. "Is he a child, then?" he asked.

"No," said Jerry. "If I had to guess, I'd say he's about twenty-five or thirty."

Twenty-five or thirty, thought Cody. A young man. Too young to lose his life. To die all alone. Cody shook his head, feeling as if he had had enough.

"You finish up," he told Jerry. "I'm going outside to get some air."

Cody sat in his small office holding Deirdre's piece of Corsican pine in his hands. His office was crude, no more than a cube fashioned out of riveted metal, a far cry from the opulently furnished space he had left behind at the Public Works Department. He was tired, having spent most of the day conducting safety inspections, walking from building to building marking with yellow crosses the ones that had to be torn down, spray-painting fluorescent orange crosses on bridges that had to be rebuilt, filling out checklist after checklist on more than a hundred different items. Real work. Physical work. Work that mattered. He turned the piece of plate rail over a few times. He thought of Deirdre Malvern. He wasn't going to think of Christine anymore. He wasn't going to brood about her. He wasn't going to pity himself for the way she had died so young. Just like that young man who had fallen down the drain. He was through with brooding. He was going to get on with his life. He was going to move on . . .

He shook his head.

Old clichés weren't going to work.

He rubbed his hand along the grain of the Corsican pine. Was he going to go through the rest of his life as a widower? He thought he might. What Deirdre felt for him scared him more than it pleased him. He took out a piece of sandpaper and sanded the splintered edges of the plate rail. What did he really know about Deirdre? This morning, while walking from building to building with him, she had been professional, appropriate, focused. But . . . but somehow too careful, her voice at times strained, as if she felt she had to walk on eggshells around him. He stopped sanding and looked at the edge of the plate rail. Beautiful. Like the smooth curve of Christine's hip. Sex. Maybe that was his problem. Maybe that's why he was having such a tough time with Deirdre. When he looked at Deirdre he sometimes looked at her in that way, like she had smooth curves that needed to be stroked, caressed.

It bothered him.

He didn't want to think of Deirdre that way. Not if he couldn't feel some sincere affection for her.

He put the piece of wood down. He needed a shower. A cold shower would do him good.

In the shower stall he let the cool water pepper his back. He let his head hang down so his chin touched his breastbone. He held up his hands and looked at his calloused palms, hands that loved to work, to build things, but most of all hands that had once touched Christine. He wondered if those hands would ever touch Deirdre. He was thirty-nine, past the point where he believed in love at first sight; he knew that love was a uphill battle, something that had to be worked on.

He was just thinking how unfair things could sometimes be when he slipped to the floor of the shower stall and hit his hip hard. He was surprised to find himself on the floor. It was as if suddenly his whole sense of balance had given out on him, as if the weight of his feelings about Christine and his ambivalence toward Deirdre had caused a crazy malfunction in his inner ear. He felt his heart beating. He couldn't figure it out. It was as if a great hand were pressing him to the ground. Holding him there. It took him a full minute to finally realize that it had nothing to do with his state of mind. He now recognized this great pressure as an actual outside physical force—gravity, lots of it, too much of it, an avalanche of it.

His whole body hurt.

The water from the shower spout, rather than dropping on him like a gentle rain, shot at him like bullets. He tried to get up, but he couldn't. He lifted his arm and felt as though he were lifting 100 pounds. He heard Anne-Marie calling from the dormitory outside the shower room door, realized that she too had fallen to the floor. He heard a distant rumble from outside, then a big bang. The dormitory shook for a few seconds, then stopped.

He had to get out of this shower. The water hurt so much. He forced himself to his hands and knees and crawled out of the shower, then carefully lowered himself to the tiles. He heard Anne-Marie calling again.

"Just hang on, Anne-Marie," he answered, barely able to get the words out through the crushed feeling in his throat.

Three gees, he wondered? Five gees? He thought of the grav-core deep in the center of the asteroid. That little piece of black hole the Ceresians had so artfully contained in its own self-sustaining control pocket was playing a trick on them. He felt his heart working hard to pump his blood against the crushing gee-force. He wondered if anybody had been up on a ladder. He hoped everyone had been wearing their hard hats.

He thought it was never going to end. But then, after five minutes, he found himself breathing a little easier. He pushed himself up, broke into a sweat, felt as if he had 250 pounds of bricks sitting on his shoulders. The load lightened again. He crawled to the bench, struggled to a standing position, inspected the big bruise that was forming on his hip, then felt the load lighten a third time. Lighten so much that, taking a step toward his dressing gown, he actually left the floor and floated a bit, as if the little piece of black hole had suddenly switched off, leaving this 700-kilometer-long chunk of an asteroid with no more pull than what it derived from its own meager mass, .07 gees, which meant escape velocity was down to around 25 kilometers per hour.

"Anne-Marie, are you okay?" he called.

"What's going on?" she said.

He heard sudden rain outside; Lake Ockham, in gravitational chaos, must have shot up an unexpected spray that reached all the way downtown, five kilometers away.

He settled back to the floor with the slowness of a dust mote. He pulled on his dressing gown, his motions pitching him first one way then the other. He maneuvered himself to the door, floating most of the way. He didn't sink back down this time. He frowned. Even a small rock like Ceres should have pulled him down. But it didn't. It was as if the singularity in the middle of Ceres now repelled rather than attracted. He waved his hand in front of the sensor and the door slid open.

He found Anne-Marie floating in front of the communications console. A bar of soap, a pencil, a clipboard, and several globules of orange juice floated freely in the air.

"What's going on?" he asked.

"I have no idea," she said. "But we've lost contact with Joe."

Anne-Marie tried to raise Joe on the communications console, but no matter what she tried she got no response. Orbital decay, he thought. In such strong gravity the *Gerard Kuiper* would fall.

She looked at him, worried. "Nothing," she said. She typed yet more commands into the communications console. "This is the last we have from him."

Cody turned to the console, his skin tingling coldly at the prospect of imminent bad news.

A holo-image of Joe Calaminci appeared in front of them. Joe looked tired, pale, as if he had spent too much time alone on the *Gerard Kuiper*. His hair needed washing, he needed a shave, and he had the wild look of cabin fever in his eyes.

"Newton, this is the *Kuiper*," said Joe. "Repeat, this is the *Kuiper*." He stared at them, waiting, perplexed that he wasn't getting an immediate response. "Have gone into unexpected orbital decay. Computer estimates escape velocity now at 55 kilometers per second." Joe double-checked a panel of control displays. "Engineering status indicates insufficient thrust." He turned back to them, his face settling, swallowed, and in a much lower voice said, "Impact in 35 seconds. Am downloading shipboard files to base computer."

They watched as Joe issued the necessary commands to the ship's mainframe. Then he turned and looked directly at Cody and Anne-Marie. He didn't say anything. He looked too scared to say anything. His face was white. The rims of his eyes were red. He looked like a man who had just been badly cheated. Then he glanced up at something on the control panel.

And that was that.

The holo-image filled with snow.

CHAPTER 5

Cody, Deirdre, Ben, and Jerry flew in the lander over the surface of Ceres toward the Angle Territories. Gravity had cycled back to .5 gees and had remained stable for the last four hours. According to last-known coordinates, the *Gerard Kuiper* had gone down in the southeast corner of the Territory of the Angle of Refraction, a hundred kilometers beyond any settled area.

"Why doesn't Vesta City get back to us?" asked Deirdre. "They've had six hours."

"I imagine they're doing their best," said Jerry. "This is the grav-core. They're going to have to get their team of particle physicists to examine the data we've sent. And if there's something wrong with it . . . it's going to take them a while to come up with an answer."

"Yes, but I thought this was never supposed to happen," she said. "I'm no physicist, but it's never happened on Vesta. Six downtown buildings collapsed. Peter's got a broken ankle and I've got a fractured rib, and everybody else has muscle sprains."

"At least no one is dead," said Ben.

"The grav-core on Vesta is a bit different," said Cody. "It's limited. It can't go any higher than point-five. During the initial testing phase, as we moved from a rim-grav to a grav-core, after we had virtually turned the city upside down and were ready to go live, it reached point-six . . . and we had a collapse . . . in Residential Sector 5 . . . my old neighborhood." Everyone was quiet. Cody couldn't help thinking that as a highly placed member of the Public Works bureaucracy he should have been able to do something to stop that collapse. "Since then, they've fixed it," he said. "They've made sure it can never go above point-five. They keep it at point-four to be on the safe side, well within the range of Vesta's tidal flux tolerance. The grav-core here . . . well, it's a lot older, the design features aren't as refined, and the containment fields not as stable. And because Ceres is bigger, the grav-core here has to be stronger. Remember, it can go all the way up to one gee. It's like a big, strong horse. It can get away from you if you don't keep a tight rein on it."

"What do you think Council will decide?" asked Deirdre.

Cody thought about it. "They'll probably schedule the particle physicists and their crews sooner," he said. "Don't worry. I'm sure they'll get it working again. They've got ten percent of Vesta's GDP invested in this project. They'd all be voted out of office at the next general election if they abandoned it."

Silence ensued. The shadows below grew longer and longer. Cody and his crew reached the asteroid's terminator, where day ended and night began. The sun dipped out of sight behind them.

"It's just up here," said Ben, gazing at the beacon coordinates on the screen.

Cody gave the port ancillary thrusters a burst. The craft eased marginally to the left. He turned on the floodlights and the landscape below brightened.

"I'm picking up tags," said Ben, meaning the microscopic particles of ionized tungsten embedded in the *Kuiper's* hull, a way to find even the smallest bits of wreckage from an orbital altitude.

Cody lowered the landing craft, skimmed a hundred meters above the surface. The screen filled with tags, little green dots scattered all over the place. He stared at the green dots, didn't want to believe in those green dots, knew all too well what they meant—the end of a man's life, the passing of a friend, and the destruction of the spacecraft that was meant to take them home. For the time being, they were trapped on Ceres. In a separate window on the screen the computer extrapolated the wreckage trail. Cody slowed the craft and brought it even lower, fighting the urge to close his eyes, not wanting to see yet again, as he had seen with Residential Sector 5, just how easily things could be wrecked, not wishing to be reminded of just how fragile everything was.

Soon they saw the wreckage, jagged chunks of metal strewn along the surface, as haphazard, bent, and fragmented as a spilled bag of potato chips, one chunk with the green Public Works logo of trees and clouds. The *Kuiper*'s remote surveillance orbiter, previously carried in the spacecraft's bay, now lay at the foot of a small hill, one side of its spherical hull flattened like a cantaloupe dropped on the floor. A piece of landing carriage, speared into the dirt by the force of the impact, stood straight up out of the surrounding wreckage like a monument.

"Look at that," said Ben. "The forward pod came off in one piece. He still might be in there."

Cody landed the craft. His hands felt stiff from gripping the controls so tightly. He and the crew clamped on their helmets, pressurized their suits, double-checked their communications, and prepared to disembark onto the surface. He couldn't help feeling responsible for all this. He caught Deirdre looking at him, and was glad she was there. They got into the airlock and cycled the air. Then they stepped out onto the pitted surface.

"A standard search grid," he said. "You know the routine. Vesta City's going to need a report. Jerry, let's you and me check the forward pod."

As he approached the pod—a piece of the *Kuiper* that looked like the head of a praying mantis—he saw that its hull had a meter-wide gash in it. There couldn't be any air in there, he decided. And he knew the pilot hadn't had the time to suit up.

They found Joe Calaminci jackknifed over the navigation console, his neck and back broken, his skull fractured, the urine and feces sucked right out of him, his tongue sticking out, bloated, several lacerations along the left side of his head, frozen solid but, by the look of it, mercifully dead on impact, spared the excruciating death of the vacuum. Cody turned to Jerry. Jerry stared at the dead man. Cody felt frozen. Then he forced himself to move. He put his hand on Jerry's arm.

"Let's go get the stretcher," he said. "I'm going to call off the search."

Back in Newton, Cody and Jerry waited while the computer completed the final phase of the blue corpse's genome mapping. Both were subdued. The death of Joe Calaminci hung like a pall over the whole crew. Cody had given crew the option of taking time off to deal with it, but everyone was out working; working was a way to get their minds off the entire incident. Jerry wasn't convinced that the grav-core flux had in fact been an accident.

"I'm not sure that they would be able to control something like the grav-core," said Cody. "Think about it. We have this victim." The body of the blue man lay on the autopsy table, sewn up roughly. "He's walking through a sewer, he falls down one of the vertical drains, he breaks his leg—and he has no way he can call for help? Nothing in the way of a communications technology? No implants?"

"Maybe he was an exception," said the doctor, watching the strands of DNA sort themselves on the screen.

"If they have no communications technology, I don't think they're going to have the know-how to control the grav-core. And this whole idea you have, that they would use the grav-core as a weapon against us—"

"Let's remember," said Jerry, lifting his finger, "it looks like these blue people disabled the microsatellites, or at least tampered with them as far back as 25 years ago, and tampered with them in such a way that Vesta City didn't even realize it.

That's know-how, Cody. They were probably the ones who built all those structures out on the surface, including that huge interstellar telescope or whatever it is out in County Hypotenuse. And it's a good bet they're the ones growing this lichen and glow-moss all over the place, in conditions where such organisms shouldn't in theory stand a chance. That's know-how. Keeping all that in mind, as well as the fact that they've already stolen our oxygen, why couldn't they just as easily manipulate the grav-core against us?"

"As far as I'm concerned," said Cody, "they're innocent until proven guilty."

"Don't kid yourself, Cody," said Jerry. "I'm sure Council's reeling from this. I'm sure all the hard-liners are mobilizing. And as for us, our morale's taken a bad blow."

Cody shook his head. "But why would the blue people manipulate the grav-core for the express purpose of making the *Gerard Kuiper* crash?" Cody stared at the screen as the last chains linked themselves together. "We've done nothing to antagonize them."

"Just being here on Ceres might be enough to antagonize them," said Jerry, gesturing at the screen. "Here comes the final result."

As the mapping of the victim's genome completed itself, Cody couldn't help thinking that as compassionate as Jerry might feel toward the children of the Belt, he had nonetheless drawn an ideological line for himself as far as the blue people were concerned. He had an uncompromising streak that surprised Cody, considering Jerry was a highly educated man and a gifted general practitioner.

Jerry issued comparison commands, and together they watched the graphics form themselves on the screen. The blue person's DNA proved to be 99.43 percent similar to human DNA. Cody shook his head, amazed.

"That close," he said. "Yet look at the differences between us."

"Too many differences for my tastes," said Jerry. "GK 3, run a comparison between the current genome and orphan DNA."

The answer came a second later. "Orphan DNA is 99.78 percent similar to the corpse's DNA. The corpse is more closely matched to orphan DNA than he is to human DNA." The doctor gave Cody a wry look. "Why doesn't that surprise me?"

Cody studied the bridge over the Oppenheimer Canal from Americium Avenue, wondering if it could be saved. Chunks of rubble lay strewn over the road and the pavement was cracked and pitted by shell craters, but the bridge itself looked as if it were in fairly good shape. Abandoned hovercars lay forgotten in the middle of the bridge, casting long shadows in the portable floodlights, their once high-gloss finishes pale and dusty. He pressed a sequence of buttons on a hand-held remote and the floodlights rose higher on their poles. Deirdre stood beside him.

"How's that?" he asked when the floodlights stopped rising.

"A little higher," she said, "so we can get a good look into the canal."

He pressed the buttons again and the floodlights rose yet higher. He walked to the railing and looked down. The canal was dry, the pressure-resistant concrete walls discolored to the twenty-meter mark, where the water used to be. Someone had driven a truck into the canal. It lay on its side, battered and ruined. Skyscrapers rose on either bank. They were dim and indistinct in the glow coming from the floodlights, rising toward the cavernous stony sky, flecked with bits of glow-moss.

"Cody?" said Deirdre.

She was looking up at one of the skyscrapers across the canal, a terraced structure made of a pale jadelike material. He followed her gaze. And he saw them. Three of them. This made his fourth sighting so far. They were getting braver. The drastic increase in air pressure from the oxygen pops—from eight millibars to a thousand millibars—along with the corresponding rise in temperature didn't seem to bother them at all. They stood five floors up on the first terrace.

Blue skin, but skin that now looked gray in the harsh white glare coming from the floodlights. The three watched Cody and Deirdre as if they were curious. They never got closer than a couple of hundred meters.

Cody walked over to his camera, which, mounted on a tripod, was used to digitally and spectrographically record structural damage and also detect any venting gases through compromised bulwarks and airlocks. He swung the camera around and engaged its telephoto lens. As the lens zoomed in, two of the blue people darted away. The third remained. A woman. Bare from the waist up. The same woman he had seen on two previous occasions.

She, too, darted away after a moment.

He shook his head.

As long as they kept their distance, he would just have to accept them as neighbors.

Cody sat on a bench next to the bathing pavilion along the shores of Lake Ockham. He had been coming here by himself ever since the water had melted. Coming here because this seemed to be one of her favorite places—the woman he had seen on the jade skyscraper across the Oppenheimer Canal. He knew she was here today, hiding behind one of the buttresses of the bathing pavilion, peeking out at him whenever she thought he wasn't looking. He didn't look at her, gave no hint that he knew she was there, didn't want to scare her away.

Ben, Wit, and Russ had lights strung along a hundred meters of shoreline now. The effect was pretty, nostalgic, like the lights along the boardwalk of some seaside town hundreds of years ago. He glanced surreptitiously to the right, saw her blue head, her white hair, caught a brief glance of her face, a pretty face; she looked about thirty. Since that time on the jade skyscraper a few days ago, he had seen her by the lake twice. She came when he was alone down here. And she always came by herself.

He stood up, arched his back. She immediately ducked

behind the buttress. He walked to the life-size chessboard—chess pieces fashioned after characters in *Alice's Adventures in Wonderland*—and leaned against the Mad Hatter. Vesta City had nothing this fanciful in the way of Parks and Recreation; Vesta City sometimes took itself too seriously. The Mad Hatter poured tea. The March Hare and the Dormouse stood next to the Mad Hatter with teacups poised.

Cody glanced back toward the bathing pavilion and saw the blue woman staring at him again.

"Do you have a name?" he called.

She instantly ducked back down. He shrugged. He wasn't going to force her.

She stood up slowly. She was naked from the waist up, breasts exposed, perfect little mounds with dark blue aureoles. She wore pants, nothing else, trousers embroidered with beads, tinsel, and thread, made pretty in an idiosyncratic way. He wondered how she could stand the cold. The temperature down here by the lake was considerably cooler than it was back in Laws of Motion Square.

"I'm not going to hurt you," he called. "I want to know your name. I want to talk to you."

She didn't respond. She just stood there, looking at him with wide violet eyes. He studied her. Blue skin the color of a robin's egg, long arms, short legs, big eyes, long slender ears, white hair, and a noticeable protuberance on her left side—the enlarged stomach.

He turned away, walked all the way to the White Rabbit, and stood there with his back to the blue woman. He stayed like that for a long time, wondering if she was acting as an emissary. He hoped she could tell him what had happened to their 27 oxygen tanks, property he wished to recover.

When he turned, he was surprised to see her squatting on top of the Caterpillar, the tallest piece around, four meters high, twice his height. She picked pieces of lichen from the Caterpillar's head and shoved them into her mouth, eating it. Then she stopped chewing and contemplated him, as if she were trying to figure out who or what he was.

She jumped with squirrel-like agility from the Caterpillar to the Mock Turtle's shoulder, hooking her arm around the figure's neck for balance. She picked some lichen off the Mock Turtle's face and offered it to Cody, her arm, despite its extra length, stretching with feminine grace. He wasn't afraid. He wasn't suspicious. He felt oddly peaceful as he looked at the woman. His wife's tragic demise seemed far away, as did the passing of Joe Calaminci, and at least for these few merciful moments he didn't feel the nagging ache of those deaths.

He took a few steps toward her and took the lichen out of her hand. He wasn't about to eat it, but he thought he should accept it. She stared at him for several seconds, as if she were waiting for him to eat the lichen, and when he didn't a frown came to her face. She broke more lichen off the Mock Turtle's face and shoved it into her mouth as if to demonstrate.

"Can you talk?" he asked.

She stopped chewing. English had been the Official Language on Ceres. But she looked as if she didn't understand him.

She jumped off the Mock Turtle and stood in front of Cody. She tossed the last bit of lichen to the ground and looked up at him. He felt it again. The peace. He didn't know why he should feel so peaceful. She was slight, appealing, no more than a hundred pounds. So human, yet with that light blue skin, those violet eyes, that white hair, so alien.

She raised her arms in a gesture of supplication. She put her palms against his bearded cheek, and for an instant he felt uncomfortable, as if she had invaded his personal space. But then he relaxed again, made calm by the waves of tranquility he felt coming from her. He waited. He knew she was strong. To jump from one chess piece to another required a lot of strength. He knew she might be even stronger than he was. She might, with a sudden twist of her arms, break his neck. But he knew she wouldn't do that.

Then she did something that startled him.

She tried to kiss him. He pulled back.

"What are you doing?" he asked.

She let her hands fall to her sides. She tried to say something, but he couldn't understand any of it. She talked like a deaf-mute, an ungainly moaning out of which occasionally surfaced a recognizable English word.

"Are you deaf?" he asked.

She shook her head. She tried to talk again, as if she were attempting to explain to him why she had tried to kiss him, but the effort seemed to cause her some discomfort, and she finally gave up. She spit out a wad of chewed-up lichen, and he realized she had been trying to kiss him with her mouth full. He couldn't begin to understand why she would do this, only that it must have some sort of significance to it, and postulated that a kiss might mean something different to this young woman than it did to him.

"Why did you do that?" he asked.

Before she could answer a drop-down holo-image of Ben LeBlanc appeared below the bill of his hard hat.

The holo-image startled the young woman so much that she bolted away.

"No, wait!" cried Cody.

But she didn't stop, ran through the chess pieces toward the bathing pavilion, catlike in her speed. She jumped to the buttress and in three bounds was on the roof, over the side, and out of sight.

"Cody?" said Ben, squinting at him. "Cody, who are you talking to?"

Cody stared at the bathing pavilion, feeling as if he had lost a big opportunity. "No one," he said.

"I think you better get back here. The computer indicates we have breaches in the seven surface airlocks."

Cody listened. Far off in the distance he indeed could hear the sound of air hissing. But why just the surface airlocks, he wondered, the strongest ones in the whole pressure infrastructure, the ones that led right out onto the surface of the asteroid? Why not the internal airlocks, the ones at the tunnel entrances and exits, of which there were a far greater number? The surface ones should have held.

"What happened?"

"A command was given," said Ben. "Not from us. Anne-Marie's trying to track it back. She thinks it was generated remotely. She's working on triangulating the exact position." Ben shook his head, looking scared. "What's going on, Cody? Are they trying to kill us?"

Ben had a point. Breaching the surface airlocks would achieve that end more effectively than breaching any of the inside ones.

Yet as he hurried back to Laws of Motion Square, he couldn't believe that the blue people wanted to kill them, not when he had seen such gentleness in the woman's eyes, not when she had placed her hands on his cheeks and tried to speak to him in her tortured and inelegant way. He swallowed as the dropping air pressure popped his eardrums. He recognized the seriousness of the situation—they would not be able to fix the breaches before all the atmosphere seeped out, they would have to go back to wearing pressure suits, and they would have to work in shifts if they were going to make their remaining tanked oxygen last until Kevin Axworthy got here with his security force. Survival had to be the primary consideration now. But he wasn't prepared to accept this act as hostile until he had more facts. And the only one he knew he could get more facts from was the strange blue woman, the woman who showed up only when he was alone, like an imaginary friend.

Cody told the rest of the crew about the blue woman when he got back.

"At first it didn't matter if I were alone or with other people," he said. "She would show up. Deirdre was with me that time at the Oppenheimer Canal. But now she comes only when I'm alone. I don't know why she does that."

"And you've seen her twice when you've been alone?" asked Deirdre.

"Yes."

"Why didn't you tell us?" she asked.

"Because we've all seen them," he said. "It's not so out of the ordinary anymore, is it? I've been recording the sightings in the log. If you're interested you can see my entries on the GK."

Jerry shifted in his chair and pushed his glasses up the bridge of his nose. "Why do you suppose this particular woman keeps coming back?" he asked.

Cody gazed at the doctor. "I have no idea," he said. "But I can tell you this. She's harmless." He put his hands on his hips, thought about it. "She's just curious. She came right up to me. She jumped on top of one of the chess pieces down there. The Caterpillar. You should see the way she jumps. I tried to talk to her. I don't know whether she could hear me or not. She spoke to me, but she spoke to me like a deaf woman. She shook her head when I asked her whether she was deaf, but I'm not sure she really understood what I meant."

They all stared at him. Ben finally raised his eyebrows, managing to look mystified and resigned at the same time. "At least she's trying to communicate," he said. "That's a step in the right direction."

"I wouldn't trust them too much yet," said Jerry. "They've still taken our oxygen and haven't given it back."

Cody wondered if he should tell his crew how the woman had tried to kiss him. Such behavior was odd, at least by their own standards. He decided against telling them for now; he couldn't see the point in alarming them more than he had to. He wanted them to stay focused on their jobs. And the number one job right now was getting the surface airlocks closed again.

Cody took Wit and Ben to the Wright Access Ramp on the south side of the city. The Wright Airlock gaped half open, revealing dark and rugged terrain outside and a black sky full of stars. Little dust devils whirled up the ramp as the precious air of their oxygen pops steadily dwindled away.

Wit took out an access tool and removed the panel from the control console.

"Looks like we have a dual patch system here," he said. "We're going to need a number three and a number eight."

They hooked in the necessary patches, long strips of optical cable, translucent and glittering with specks of blue. Cody took the remote override console out of the rover, hooked the patches into that, and keyed in the necessary override. The small screen lit up with machine-language encryption, and the console began to break the encryption. After a few minutes, the screen indicated that the code break was complete. The Wright Airlock slid shut with silent majesty. The dust devils swooned, fell to the ground, and disappeared like phantoms back into their graves.

"That's that," said Cody. He radioed Russ Burke, who was coordinating the airlock effort from Laws of Motion Square. "Russ, we've got the Wright one closed. How are the other crew doing?"

A holo-image of Russ appeared in his visor. "Yours will make three," said Russ. "But I don't think we have to worry about the other airlocks now. I've got some news for you."

"Yes?"

"Someone's issued commands to the remaining airlocks," said Russ. "They've all closed by themselves. And guess what?"

"What?"

"We're right back where we started from. Pressure's dropped to eight millibars and temperature's down to minus 50 celsius. Just like when we got here."

Cody frowned, feeling more frustrated than alarmed. "Any biotherm activity?" he asked.

"None," said Russ. "They're all dead. There's not sufficient moisture or air anymore to keep them alive. I'm afraid we have to go back to living in our suits."

To add to their difficulties, Cody learned once he got back to the dormitory that the *Conrad Wilson,* the security ship captained by Kevin Axworthy, had taken a hit.

"A small asteroid," said Anne-Marie, sitting at the communications console in the command center, "no bigger than a fist, but big enough to puncture one of their hydrogen-fuel tanks. Their maneuvers for rendezvous will have to be less aggressive in order to save on fuel, and that's going to slow them down. They haven't been able to give us a new ETA yet, but they think it's going to be at least twelve days from now."

Cody addressed Peter Wooster. "How's that translate as far as our oxygen supply's concerned?" he asked. "I know it can't be good."

Peter took a deep breath, shook his head. "Current reserves in the pressurized dorm and office units give us four days," he said. "The tanks give us another six. That makes ten altogether. Like Anne-Marie says, the *Conrad Wilson* won't be here for twelve. The math doesn't add up, Cody."

Cody's face settled as he went through the possibilities. "Then we'll have to get the OPU in Actinium up and running as fast as possible. We'll have to make it a priority." He turned to Anne-Marie. "Were you able to triangulate the location of the remote commands yet?"

She nodded. "They came from the Edison Foothills Habitat east of the city," she said.

Jerry spoke up. "I think some of us should go into those hills and see if we can find these blue people," he said, not bothering to hide how fed up he was. "We'll take our laser drills and our axes and we'll ask for our oxygen tanks back. They can't go stealing things from us. It's not right."

"I'm not sure that's practical," said Cody.

"Why not?" said Jerry.

He couldn't help remembering how the woman had leaped away from him, how in three bounds she had been on the roof of the bathing pavilion, over the other side, and out of sight. She was fast, far faster than any of them. He remembered Jerry's autopsy results, how the victim's musculature was more highly developed, stronger, more limber. Could they reasonably expect to be a match against these people if it came down to a physical confrontation? Wouldn't it be better to try and outthink them?

"Cody, you don't seem to understand the equation," said Jerry, pressing his point. "We need to breathe. They have our oxygen. Without oxygen, we die."

"All I'm saying is that our time might be better spent fixing the OPU in Actinium and getting some air into the emergency shelter across the street. At least then we'll have a backup. As for the blue people . . . how are we even going to find them when they know how to hide so well? And even if we do find them, how are we going to catch them? Better to concentrate on something we at least have a chance of succeeding at."

CHAPTER 6

Cody, Ben, Huy Hai, and Wit, back in pressure suits, stood guard out in the square while the others slept in the pressurized dormitory.

Cody sat on a cable spool and stared down Isosceles Boulevard. He was thinking of Joe Calaminci, how Joe had a wife and two children on Pallas, the third-largest asteroid in the Belt, how Joe was never going to go back to them now. He thought how Joe's wife and children now had a sudden empty spot in their lives, and how Joe's usual physical presence would turn into a physical absence. He knew how real a physical absence could be, a big chunk of nothingness eating away at you. He wanted to do something for Joe's wife and his two daughters. But he knew from personal experience that in a situation like this nothing could be done.

He glanced at Witold. As transportation engineer, Wit had spent the last several days inspecting the Fermi Maglev, as well as helping Huy, forgoing sleep to get the job done. He should have been tired, should have been sagging under the extra gravity, but instead he sat on the edge of his crate, erect and alert, staring across the square, hands on his knees, poised like a hunter in a blind. Cody patched through to his fellow Vestan on a private channel.

"Wit?" he said.

Wit didn't respond. He stared a bit more, then raised his hand, cautioning Cody to be still.

The others shifted in their pressure suits, looked at Wit.

"What's going on?" asked Ben on the open channel.

"I think Wit sees one," said Cody.

"A female," said Wit. "Standing in that doorway. Maybe she's the one you've been seeing, Cody. I saw her step in there a few minutes ago. I saw her signal to someone further down. She's not alone."

Cody scrutinized the doorway. On Rhenium Lane. Big bright acrylic apples decorated the tiles on either side of the doorway. A railing along the curb out front was made of big brass numbers, pi to the twentieth decimal, all joined together. He saw no sign of the female, saw nothing but the weak shadows cast by the lights.

"Are you sure?" asked Cody.

"She's carrying five of our oxygen tanks," said Wit. "One under each arm and three strapped to her back."

"Really?" said Cody, pleased that the woman might be trying to help them by returning their oxygen tanks.

"She must be strong," said Wit.

"It's got to be her," said Cody. "She knows we're in trouble. She's bringing the oxygen back to us."

Huy Hai spoke up. "Five tanks aren't enough," he said. "We need it all."

"What do we do?" asked Ben.

"I think we should just sit here for a while," said Cody.

Cody heard Wit grunt, as if he didn't agree with this tactic at all but wasn't going to say anything about it.

"Maybe she's going to wait until we go inside," said Ben.

"Did you see that?" asked Huy.

"I saw," said Wit.

"What?" asked Cody.

"A girl," said Wit.

"A girl?" said Cody.

"Teenager," said Wit. "Maybe a young woman. She ran into the doorway. Where the other one is. She had two tanks of oxygen on her back. You think they've actually come to return the stuff?"

"Why else would they be here?" asked Cody.

Huy broke in. "My visor says it's minus 65 Celsius," he said. "And the atmospheric pressure's dropped to three millibars. To all intents and purposes we're in a vacuum right now. How can they stand it? They should be freezing to death. They should be bursting, with blood seeping out their fingernails, their eyeballs, and their ears."

"They have that extra layer," explained Cody. "That meshwork of cartilage or whatever it is. And the cilia in their stomachs I was telling you about? It's remarkably similar to alveolar tissue. Lung tissue. Jerry and I are starting to think they breathe through their stomachs somehow."

"But *what* do they breathe?" asked Huy. "There's nothing in this atmosphere to breathe."

"They see well in the dark, don't they?" said Wit.

"Their pupils can expand to two or three times human size," said Cody.

"I say turn off these floodlights, go inside, or maybe hide over there, and hope they come closer," said Wit. "Once they get close, turn on the floods. Whack them hard with bright light, see if we can take one or both prisoner. Blind them. Distract them. Get them panicked."

"Why would we want to do that?" asked Cody. "They're trying to help us. Why would we want to try and take them prisoner?"

"So they can tell us where the rest of the oxygen is," said Wit, as if it were obvious.

"But if they're trying to help us," said Cody, "why would we want to do something like that to them?" The whole idea distressed him, even though he knew he should be giving the suggestion serious consideration. "Maybe if we let them go, maybe if we wait and see what they do, they might go back to wherever they came from and return with more oxygen, the remaining twenty tanks. Maybe they now realize it was wrong to steal from us."

"Cody, I hate to disagree with you," said Ben, "but I think Wit might be right. I think we might have an opportunity here. And we have to take it." Ben's voice was thin, nervous, apologetic. "Look at the situation we're in." Ben leaned forward, as if he knew he really had to convince Cody about this. "We won't hurt them. None of us wants to hurt them. We'll just go ahead and try to restrain them. What choice do we have? We just want them to tell us where the other oxygen is."

"Yes, but we might end up making things worse," said Cody. "We don't want to antagonize them. We don't know exactly how many of them there are, but we've seen a good number of them now, 27 different ones recorded in the log. And if we antagonize these two, we might end up having to tangle with the whole lot."

Wit leaned forward. "Did Jerry actually look at the dead one's eyes?" he asked. "Did he cut one of them open and take a good close look?"

"Yes."

"And what did he see?"

Cody sighed. "He said the eyes had certain structures in common with . . . with the eyes of a variety of nocturnal creatures that see well in the dark, creatures who might not like the light."

"Because these people live in the dark all the time, don't they?" said Wit. "I mean, look at this place. There's no light anywhere except for what we've strung up here in the square, and except for that crazy glow-moss everywhere." Wit paused, thinking about it some more. "And aren't you curious about them, Cody? Come on, you must be curious. They might be halfway human, but they're still a new species, aren't they? On the strength of that alone we should try and catch them. We've got a real opportunity here, and we should use it. We should get them over here and whack them with the lights. Especially if the doctor says their eyes are nocturnal."

Cody stared down Rhenium Lane. The two women were

obviously here in a spirit of goodwill. He was convinced of
it. From all he had seen of them, they were gentle. But he
was beginning to think that Wit might be right. And he had
to admit, he *was* curious. It might be in their best interests to
learn more about these blue people, even if it meant a certain risk.

"So," he said to Wit, "we hit them with the lights and
then what do we do? Supposing we distract them, blind
them, even for a few seconds. What's your plan?"

"Huy will go inside and stand next to the window," Wit
said. "The one next to the switchbox that operates the outside floods. We'll get him to turn off the floods. When that's
done, you, Ben, and I will hide behind some of these crates
and hope they'll come over. It might take some time. Who
knows, they might not come at all. They might just go away.
But we have to at least try. If they do come, we'll hit them
with the floods. We've got that nylon cord there." He
grinned modestly. "Just in case we should have any success
at this. It should be strong enough to hold them. Unless the
doctor's strength estimates are completely off."

Cody agreed to the plan, but only because it seemed to be
the lesser of two evils.

They hid themselves in various strategic locations around
the supply yard. An ambush like this went against his nature,
but they couldn't count on the possibility that the women
might bring back the rest of their oxygen. Too many variables, and what they needed were certainties. If Wit's plan
could firm up some certainties, why not?

They waited an hour before Cody finally saw the woman
and the girl emerge from Rhenium Lane. It was the same
woman. His friend from the Alice-in-Wonderland chessboard.

She squinted as she entered Laws of Motion Square. Did
even these dim utility lights hurt her eyes, then? She walked
with a fluid grace, her steps elegant, her movements precise
and sure. She carried the oxygen tanks. The girl walked behind her, her arms free.

When they got to the middle of the square they stopped. They looked at the spools of optical cable, the canisters of compounds, the racks of laser drills, the shovels, axes, and temperature-resistant piping, the electrical supplies, the fusion cells for the dorm's portable generator, the tractor, the crane, the backhoe—looked at all this stuff the way kids at a zoo might look at animals.

They walked down the nearest aisle. Human breath in cold temperatures steamed over, but Cody saw no steam. Their chests remained still. They weren't breathing at all. At least not in any human way.

They walked past the backhoe toward the crates of oxygen. Wit raised his hand to Huy inside, giving the signal.

The floodlights came on.

The woman and the girl jumped and dropped the oxygen tanks. They turned and ran instinctively, blinded by the light, ran right into a wall of stacked fusion cells. Both fell, and the tanks strapped to the woman's back came down hard on top of her. Wit jumped out from his spot behind the water tank. Before he could reach the girl, she got to her feet and leaped to the top of the backhoe.

The woman, still hampered by the tanks, couldn't maneuver as well. Cody ran out from his spot and grabbed her by the arm. She turned toward him but it was obvious she couldn't see him in the blinding light. She swung out at him the way a blind woman would, without knowing where anything was, just in the hope she might hit something.

He wanted to say something to her, to reassure her, but he knew she couldn't hear him through his pressure suit. He hated having to do this to her, but felt it was better if he was the one who restrained her rather than any of the others. At least he would make an effort to be gentle, to try to make her understand that they weren't going to hurt her.

Ben came up and grabbed her other arm. The girl jumped to the ground and tried to help the woman, tried to drag Cody and Ben away from her, but her attempts were short-lived. Witold came up and grabbed her.

Huy brought out the nylon cord.

In a sudden move the girl pulled out a knife and stabbed Wit in the leg. Wit cried out. The insta-seal in his suit began to plug the leak. Wit lost his temper, knocked the girl on the back of the head with the butt of his hammer. She went down, stunned but not unconscious. The woman tried to say something to Cody, but through the near vacuum, with no wind to fill her lungs or to power her words, Cody heard nothing, just saw her lips and tongue move in an agonized way.

With the girl stunned, unable to resist, Huy got the cord wrapped around her wrists.

"Check them for weapons," called Wit.

Cody checked the woman for weapons, found a large knife, nothing else, took it away from her, and helped her to her feet.

She turned and looked at him through the reflective visor of his helmet. The fear left her face when she saw who he was.

"I'm sorry," he said, even though he knew she couldn't hear him.

She nodded. Nodded as if she had heard him as plain as day.

The woman and the girl tolerated the increase in temperature and pressure inside the dorm well, with no untoward side effects, just as they had tolerated the previous oxygen pops to the whole city. To be on the safe side, Jerry ordered a slow cycling of the airlock before they came in to protect them from any possible pressure-related conditions.

When Peter and Ben finally escorted them into the dorm, the two women were fine. The young one actually looked older than fifteen or sixteen, now that Cody saw her close-up, maybe in her mid-twenties. The two of them were a little bewildered, still squinting in the bright light, but . . . but both enchanting, like creatures out of a fairy tale—both pretty, graceful, like a pair of sprites.

"Do we have anything they can wear?" asked Cody. Both women were naked from the waist up.

Dina and Anne-Marie nodded and went to their bunks. They opened footlockers and pulled out thermal undershirts.

The women put them on. They stared down at the garments with great curiosity, felt the fabric, acted as if they were familiar with the notion of shirts but obviously didn't wear them that much. They also seemed fearless now that they realized they were more or less captive. They both stretched their arms; the shirtsleeves were too short for their long limbs, and their wrists extended a few centimeters beyond the bottom of the sleeves. Once they were comfortable, the younger one reached into her pants pocket, pulled out some lichen, stuck a bit in her mouth, then gave some to the older one. The older woman wolfed it down.

Everybody just kept staring at them, getting used to their strange but not unpleasant appearance.

"Jerry," Cody called through the door into the small infirmary, "how's Wit doing?"

"He's going to need a half dozen stitches, but otherwise he's fine."

Cody walked over to the bench and sat down next to the older woman.

"Remember me?" he said. "From the lake?"

She hesitated but finally nodded.

"Can you talk?" he asked.

"She's beautiful," said Wolf.

Cody was feeling what he had felt before. The peace. Like he no longer had to worry about anything at all.

"How do you communicate?" he asked.

She tried talking again, but again sounded like a deaf woman, that moaning and half-formed way they have of speaking. He raised his hand and shook his head, stopping her. He lifted his E-pad from the table and typed the following words: "Can you read?"

She nodded. She took the E-pad from his hand and typed the following: "Kiss me."

His eyes widened and his face reddened.

"What did she write?" asked Deirdre.

Cody stared at the woman. Why a kiss? What special significance did it have? If she wanted a kiss, if kissing was the right thing to do, then so be it. Yet he couldn't kiss her without some gesture of tenderness. Instinctively, he raised his hand, touched her hair with the back of his hand, couldn't even think of kissing her without a romantic reflex. Her hair felt remarkably soft. She smiled at him. He looked at her pretty white teeth.

"What are you doing?" asked Deirdre.

"She wants me to kiss her," said Cody.

"Why?" asked Deirdre.

Cody leaned toward the woman. Stiffly, self-consciously. Like he was in a play and had only just met the actress.

He kissed her. She slipped her tongue into his mouth, something he wasn't prepared for. He nearly backed away, but quickly realized she meant nothing sexual or romantic by it, that there was nothing here but the necessary mechanics of communication.

Her tongue tasted sweet. He remembered. The lichen. From the lake. How she had tried to kiss him with the lichen in her mouth.

He now felt a cool breeze blowing through his mind. *I know who you are, Cody.* His eyes widened. The coolness. Like a vaporous layer of menthol surrounding his mind. A physical sensation that was at once mildly irritating yet pleasurable and peaceful. *My name is Lulu.* Her name. Rising out of her multilevel thought-cloud, focused and clear, like sunlight through an icicle. He pulled away, breathless.

"Lulu?" he said.

Her violet eyes glimmered with relief.

"What happened?" asked Deirdre.

Cody didn't immediately answer. He still felt it, not as strongly now, but he still felt the manifold strands of her various thoughts, the tapestry of the human mind working on its many different levels, the cool wind. He looked around at his crew. Many of them had open mouths, were gaping at him in curiosity. Deirdre's face was red. He swallowed, felt bewildered by what had just happened.

"She spoke to me," he said. He felt as if he had just stepped off a tall building and had survived the fall. "Spoke to me with her mind."

Comments, exclamations, questions, skepticism, amazement, wonder, and he didn't hear any of it. He was looking at Lulu again. Because he wanted to feel it again. That joining. That perfect communication. Looking at Lulu, he could hardly fathom the nature of what had just happened. He moved closer and pressed his lips against hers a second time. He again felt the cool wind, but instead of hearing her voice this time, he saw visions—visions conveyed to him through Lulu's mind: a field of lichen, catamaran-like machines hovering noiselessly above the field, blue people eating lichen. She said: *I need lichen to live.* He understood. He pulled away. He turned to Peter Wooster.

"She needs lichen," he said. "She needs it to live."

Peter went outside and got some.

Needed it to live. Was that entirely true? Needed it, yes, but now he sensed she wouldn't necessarily die; she would just get sick if she didn't have it—these thoughts conveyed to him by Lulu, even though he wasn't kissing her now.

"Did she say anything about any others?" asked Wolf.

"I saw an image. Four of them in a floating machine above a field of lichen."

Peter came through the airlock with a bucket of lichen.

They all watched Lulu and the younger woman eat. The two of them grew less restless while they ate. They finally stopped eating, then looked at each other. And it seemed as if they were having a conversation, using the animated gestures and motions of two women talking excitedly, even though no words came out of their mouths. Finally they settled down. The younger one looked at Ben. Then yawned. Then the two of them waited for a bit, as if they were wondering what was going to happen next. But everyone just kept staring at them, mesmerized by how different yet similar they were to human beings.

Then, to everybody's astonishment, the two females curled up like cats on the hard metal bench and went to sleep, as if it didn't bother them at all that they were prisoners.

CHAPTER 7

Cody climbed a pile of rubble—a tangle of prefabricated acrylic planks, pipes, wiring, broken glass—all half buried under chunks of igneous rock, the glittery stuff that made Vesta shine so much in the sun. The flashing blue lights of emergency vehicles cast eerie shadows over the destruction. The air was thin but getting thicker, now that the insta-seal had ballooned over the rupture, and a pervasive charred smell hung in what was left of Residential Sector 5. He saw a 3-D picture sitting in a broken frame, he and Christine at their ski chalet in the Chillicothe Alpine Habitat in tuques and sweaters with the artificial sun shining brightly on the snow in the hills, both of them looking young, vital, with the rest of their lives ahead of them. Built the chalet himself. Always good with his hands. But now his hands didn't seem to be moving fast enough. No matter how much rubble he cleared, there always seemed to be more.

He pulled a piece of drywall up and saw Christine's hand. Covered with dust. Limp. With a deep cut along the base of her thumb. Saw the ring on her hand, emerald, not a wedding ring but the ring he had given her a year before they got married. Purchased from a jeweler, an actual Earthling he had met on the asteroid Davida while on business there for the Public Works Department. You didn't find emeralds on Vesta. A beautiful stone. But on a hand that was now so pale . . .

He opened his eyes.

He stared long and hard at the ceiling of the pressure dorm. His body was rigid. He turned his head. Saw Lulu sitting in the chair next to his cot, her hands and legs now loosely bound, the stray light from outside illuminating her violet eyes. He took comfort in her nearness. The dream, the same old dream, receded. Lulu gazed at him with concern. *You saw?* he said, only he realized he didn't say it, that the words were already there, plucked from his mind by Lulu's enormous talent.

She nodded. *I saw,* she said.

He turned away. He never talked about it. He felt no relief that she should know. He felt like crying.

He said: *I built the chalet for her.* And realized that he didn't have to provide Lulu with context because it was already there for her, painted like a background on a stage set, easy for her to see. *I used cedar paneling in the bedroom because she loved the smell of cedar. Have you ever seen a cedar tree? Have you ever smelled one?*

No.

He imagined the smell of cedar, with its fresh rooty zing, the sense that when you smelled cedar you were somewhere far away in a forest at peace breathing the cleanest air anywhere, air that had the intoxicating scent of planet Earth.

She said: *Oh.*

And he knew she now understood what cedar smelled like.

He said: *So soft, so easy to work with.*

She pulled these words from his mind like she was struggling to get a deaf man to speak.

She said: *Cody, you have to leave.*

He wondered why there wasn't so much background noise in her mind now. She seemed invigorated by her sleep. She leaned forward, like she was going to kiss him again. He reached up and stroked her hair with his fingers. She glanced at his arm, grinned ambiguously, then shook her head kindly, as if to let him know that the kiss, such as it was, should be construed only as a means of communication. She pressed her lips against his. And again she had lichen in her mouth. As if the lichen, chewed up and soaking in her enzymes, constituted a way-point between them. He allowed some of it to seep into his own mouth. He felt the menthol breeze of her thoughts again.

With the lichen working on him strongly this time, he experienced sensory overload, as if Lulu were trying to say too many things to him and make him understand too many ideas all at once. She filled his head with visions. He saw faces. Blue people. He saw the face of a young woman. Not just any young woman but the woman who had stabbed Wit in the leg. *This is my sister,* said Lulu. *Agatha.*

Lulu made him see the face of a man with a fine blond-white stubble on his blue chin, with eyes more slanted than Lulu's, more streamlined, as if fashioned by a strong wind, his lips smaller, purplish, his cheekbones more defined. He sensed that Lulu was afraid of this man in some way. His hair was shoulder-length, parted in the middle, blond-white but dyed with bright magenta streaks. *This is Buster,* said Lulu.

She then tried to convey a whole series of complicated and important ideas. But they came too fast. To Cody it was like trying to sort out a big tangle of wires. He picked up only a broad outline from her—he was new at this. He didn't have any control over it, didn't know how something like the lichen could allow him to read her in even this minimal and mixed-up way. But from this broad outline he sensed that if such a thing as a hierarchy existed among the blue people—and the way she defined the term was a lot different from the way he did—Buster would be somewhere near the top.

She then reiterated.

You must leave this place. Leave Ceres.

He interrupted her: *How can we leave?*

She reacted with surprise. She said: *The* Gerard Kuiper. That she shouldn't know what had happened to the *Ger-*

ard Kuiper exonerated her. He tried to convey the crash to her. He thought of the wreckage on the surface, of the twisted scraps of metal and Joe's frozen corpse. He immediately saw her expression change.

She said: *Oh.*

He said: *You read my mind with lichen?*

She said: *You're fading. Without more . . . you call it lichen?*

He said: *Yes.*

She said: *We call it marrow.*

Marrow. The pith and inner substance of a thing. The best, essential part of a thing. A name that gave Cody some idea of its importance. He swung his feet out of bed and walked to the bucket of . . . *marrow*, lifted out a leaf, and chewed. Bland, spongy, dry, with a bit of tartness. He glanced around at the sleeping crew members. Wolf was awake, staring at him. Cody waved. Wolf waved back, smiled encouragement, then turned on his side and went to sleep.

He said: *Kiss me again.*

They kissed. She let her hands sit in her lap loosely bound by the yellow cord, approached the kiss with clinical detachment, while he, oddly stirred after five years of celibacy, put his hands on her shoulders and drew her near.

You have two days, she said. *Three at most. Buster won't wait any longer.* She pulled away, her lapis lazuli lips moist, inviting. *He won't let you upset our plans.* She said: *We call ourselves the Meek. But we also remember who we once were. We were orphans once. But we changed.* This surprised him, that they had been orphans once, but now that the answer was revealed he couldn't help remembering how closely orphan DNA had matched Meek DNA when he and Jerry had sorted out the genome of the corpse. Yet how could they have changed themselves? *We know how to fight if we have to. That's why you must leave. We know how to call on our ghost codes when we have to. I don't want to see anyone get hurt. Try to find a way. Buster is determined.*

We've been waiting too long for this. We've worked hard for it. We knew you would come back. But you've come too soon. We've been hiding. But now you're going to find us. And when you find us you'll try to stop us. All we want is a home. Is that too much to ask?

He stared at her, sensing a whole tapestry of thoughts behind these words, but none of them seemed to answer his questions. Yes, they called themselves the Meek, who knew why, but they remembered who they once were, the orphans. And what were ghost codes? The Meek. They didn't sound so meek, and he wondered why they would choose that name for themselves. Just how many were there? Hundreds? Thousands? Millions? He couldn't untangle her thoughts effectively enough to find adequate answers to any of these questions.

He said: *What can we do? We have no way to leave.*

She said: *Who is Conrad Wilson?*

As if she thought the security ship were a person. He didn't have to answer her. Her mention of the name triggered everything he knew about the *Conrad Wilson,* how it would now be here in five days, how they had only three days of oxygen left and were counting on the *Conrad Wilson* to bring them more, how he had no idea what the security force aboard the *Conrad Wilson* intended to do once they got here.

She comprehended all of this immediately.

She said: *Let me go. I will try to bring you more oxygen. When the* Conrad Wilson *gets here, go away and never come back. This is our home. You can't take it away from us.*

He felt momentarily affronted. She seemed to forget that the Ceresians had been driven out by the orphans, that 56,000 Ceresians had lost their lives, and that much of the orphan-inflicted carnage had been gratuitous—the killing of women and children just for the fun of it.

He said: *I'm not someone who can make that decision.*

She said: *Now I'm sorry about all the killing.* She had sensed his thought. *But alterations have been made in chromosome three. Twenty-seven million letters have been rewritten. Everything that ever made the orphans violent, everything that ever made them pack together in gangs, made them want to kill, has been recoded with a simple series of pseudogenes. The Meek are a second iteration, an improved version, with an encoding symbiotic to, and in fact, reliant on marrow. We are of this place. We live here in a natural balance created through a minimum of environmental enhancement and a maximum of genetic recoding. The marrow has increased our bodily tolerances to both heat and cold, and we can survive in extremes of either.*

So the marrow changed them from orphans into Meek? he wondered.

We breathe with the marrow. The marrow increases our ability to survive in a wider range of habitats, in a wider range of temperatures and atmospheres. We of the Meek are sorry about what the orphans did. Believe me when I say we've changed. We're the Meek, yes, and the Meek for a good reason. Her face grew exceedingly grave. *For in meekness we find our strength.*

In the morning Cody and his crew sat around the dorm and discussed what they should do in light of Lulu's warning to leave.

"Six hundred thousand?" said Ben, his mouth hanging open, his overbite pronounced. Lulu had finally given Cody an idea of numbers last night. "How can there be 600,000? We've seen a total of 27, not including the dead one we buried."

"She's not lying," said Cody.

"Then why won't she tell you where they are?" asked Huy.

"Because that would put them at unnecessary risk," said Cody.

"And she wants us to let her go?" said Ben.

Cody glanced at Ben. "She says she might be able to bring us more oxygen," he said. "Maybe not our own. But sometimes when they come here to scavenge they find tanks of it. Mostly in Security Detachment Offices. I've checked the city plan. There are 63 such offices, a lot when you consider that Vesta City has only 21. But then, Vesta City never had to deal with civil unrest like they had here on Ceres thirty years ago. Authorities kept the extra oxygen for backup in case officers had to patrol on the surface or in certain unpressurized sections of infrastructure. Lulu says she might find enough to last us until the *Conrad Wilson* gets here."

"And then we're just supposed to leave the asteroid?" said Jerry. He nodded toward Lulu.. "At her say-so?"

"She advises us to leave. She's made it clear that the Meek will do whatever they can to make us leave." Cody raised his palms. "I'm a Public Works engineer. A carpenter by trade. Not a politician. I don't know what Vesta City's going to say. My main concern is the safety of my crew. And that means oxygen. Lulu says she'll try to get us more. I leave it up to Council to make the bigger decisions. In the meantime I'm going to let Lulu go find us more oxygen. I'm going to keep her sister here. As insurance. To make sure Lulu comes back. Peter, Dina, and Russ can go with Lulu. The tanks will be heavy and she's going to need help. Ben, Deirdre, Wit, Huy, and Wolf—you'll be coming with me to the Actinium Oxygen Production Utility and the solar-power generating plant. We've got to see what we can do about getting that place going again. Just in case."

Cody and his team stood on the surface of Ceres as the sun shot like a thousand lasers from the east over the vista of solar panels.

"Ben and I hypothesize that if we can get this plant to generate some power," said Cody, "we might supply the emergency shelter in Laws of Motion Square with enough oxygen to keep us going until the *Conrad Wilson* gets here. The emergency shelter is a self-contained unit, airtight. It can remain pressurized even if the entire city is in a vacuum.

We think we can get enough power on-line to get some air in there." He paused. "I'm sorry it's come to this. I'm sorry we have to spend all our time on survival. We should be fixing Newton, completing our survey, then moving on to Equilibrium. But things haven't worked out that way. Ben and I are going to check the oxygen mine to see how many of the robots still work. You four can start a survey of the underground cable with your wands." He gestured at all the solar panels. "This is old. It uses underground fiber optics to carry raw sunlight to the microwave transmission tower. See how the ground is pitted? This place has taken thousands of hits since it was decommissioned 75 years ago. Some of the cable is bound to be ruined."

"Why can't we hook up one of our own fuel cells to get the air we need?" asked Deirdre.

"Because our fuel cells can't generate nearly enough power to get those old robots up and running in the oxygen mine. Have you seen the GK's archive record of those robots? Have you looked at the schematics for the mine? It's the one just east of here, the oldest in the Belt. Those robots lift tons of carbonaceous rock at a time into the oxygen separator. We need a giant plant—like this solar-power generating station here—to get them going, not our tiny fuel cells. Ben estimates we have to get it running up to at least four percent capacity to fill the emergency shelter with air." He looked around at the others. "And that means we've got to find some working panels." Cody pointed to the panels. "That's why we're here. We might as well get started. Mark the viable solar panels with yellow crosses. You've got six hundred solar panels out there, each ninety meters square. To get four percent power, we're going to need at least 24 of them up and running. Once we find 24 viable panels, we have to clean them."

"So we . . . we sweep them clear?" asked Deirdre.

"That's why I have all these brooms out here," said Cody, grinning at the innocent tone in her voice.

"At least we'll feel as if we're doing something," said Wit.

"My thought exactly," said Cody.

Many of the robots in the oxygen mine were no more than automated pieces of heavy equipment; backhoes, front-end loaders, dump trucks, cranes, carriage-mounted pneumatic drills, bulldozers, and road-graders. The huge open pit, kilometers across, was like a museum. Most of the equipment was over a hundred years old. Cody remembered accessing pictures of this kind of equipment as a boy, recalled how he had marveled at the size of such machines, how foreign they seemed compared to the current generation of micromachines—robots no bigger than a fist working at incredible speed in swarms of a hundred or more.

A microwave relay antenna rose like a monument before them. The sun shone directly overhead, small but angry. Slag heaps—black and unsightly piles of unneeded carbon—blighted the far rim of the open pit like a small mountain range.

The inspection of the oxygen mine took them most of the afternoon—afternoon, of course, being set by an arbitrary schedule. They checked one of the pneumatic drills first, a piece of equipment twenty times as tall as Cody, white, with a red logo of an oxygen atom along the side, tires as big as a house, made out of a compound that could withstand minus 275 Celsius temperatures. A power grid rose from the drill's control console, ready to capture power from the microwave relay antenna. Cody climbed the ladder to the maintenance platform and was gratified to see that after all these years the little orange light was still flashing, that the machine was in standby mode. He took a data scanner out of his tool belt, established a link to the robot's main program drive, and discovered that only seven percent of the application data had been corrupted, an excellent ratio, considering the drill's prolonged exposure to the sun's ultraviolet radiation. He was able to effect repairs on the corrupt data quickly.

The drill was typical of the many pieces they inspected. The cold and vacuum had actually acted as preservative agents in most cases, and they didn't have to do too many repairs.

"That's fully 70 percent of the equipment still operational," said Cody when they were done. He gestured around the open-pit mine. "It's hard to believe all this rock is potential air."

Ceres, rich in carbon compounds—many of those compounds filled with oxygen and nitrogen—had plenty of the raw materials needed for the production of air. Virtually every stone contained at least some atmospheric component. The mine's job was to unglue the oxygen and nitrogen atoms from the carbon by feeding raw ore into a chemical separating plant.

And luckily everything looked good to go.

CHAPTER 8

Cody sat in his office working on his Corsican pine, tired from the day's work. Slowly but surely, with the small kit of carving tools he had brought along, he was shaping the ungainly piece of plate rail into a cat. Why a cat? he wondered. He looked at the cat's eyes. Big. Leaf-shaped. Like Lulu's eyes. He glanced out the pressure window and saw Wit, Peter, and Russ standing guard over the equipment. Lulu was sleeping in the dorm. Outside his door, Agatha sat on the bench, nervously nibbling a piece of marrow. They didn't keep her tied with yellow cord anymore. He sensed no intent from her to escape. As long as Lulu was here, sleeping, she wasn't going anywhere.

He thought of the day's progress.

By the end of the day, the search crew, having investigated forty-two of the sixty-three Security Detachment Offices, had failed to turn up any extra oxygen tanks. Those on his own OPU detail had had better luck, having found twenty-four working solar panels and marked them with yellow crosses. Finding and identifying the panels had been long hard work, and they still had to sweep them off now. Everyone was tired. Everyone needed a good rest.

Agatha was worried about Lulu, he could sense it. She turned to him and said: *Why is she so tired?*

His eyes widened, surprised by the clarity of the communication; it possessed none of the background noise Lulu's communications did.

He said: *She covered a lot of ground today.*

Agatha turned away as if she hadn't heard him, as if she *couldn't* hear him, as if, after no kiss from Lulu for so long, he had faded out, had become, at least to Agatha, a deaf-mute.

Deirdre appeared in the doorway. She didn't say anything. She glanced at Agatha then turned back to Cody.

"You're talking to her?" she said.

He wasn't sure what to make of her tone. Challenging? Yes. Deirdre was always challenging. But he also detected a note of concern. He held up his cat.

"I'm making something," he said.

She looked at the half-completed cat. Her face softened.

"Everyone's a little concerned about you, Cody," she said.

He was surprised. "About me?" he said. "Why?"

She pressed her lips together. "Because some of us think that whatever Lulu did to you with that kiss . . ." She cast an anxious glance toward Agatha. "That whatever she did to you . . . that it might not have been a good thing . . . that it's made you more sympathetic toward them than you should be."

He frowned. "She didn't do anything to me," he said. "She talked to me. That's all. She didn't change me. She didn't make me feel more sympathetic. She didn't co-opt me in any way. I'm still the same old Cody."

Deirdre sighed. "You really think that's true?"

"Deirdre, we're communicating with them now. Isn't that what we want?"

"I just wonder . . . if we shouldn't be more careful." She took a deep breath, lifted her chin. "I just worry, that's all."

"You don't have to worry," he said. "I'm perfectly fine."

He fell asleep in his chair. He had another dream.

He dreamed that Agatha stabbed him in the leg just as she

had stabbed Wit. Stabbed him in the thigh out on the surface next to the carbon slag heaps of the oxygen mine. So odd to see her standing out on the surface, in a vacuum, in the cold, with no protection whatsoever, no pressure suit, bare from the waist up, wearing only a pair of pants.

Stabbed him, and the blue insta-seal sputtered around the gash in his suit, attempted to block the leak, but his suit was covered with dust from the carbon slag and the insta-seal reacted chemically with the carbon slag, wouldn't bind properly, simply dripped to the ground like blue wax. He tried to catch it, struggled to stuff it back into the gash, but his hands were dirty with the carbon slag, and the insta-seal just got runnier, and he felt needles of cold biting his leg. He looked up at Agatha. She was gone. He was alone. There was no one around to help him.

He woke up . . .

And discovered Agatha pressing her lips against his.

He tensed.

Nearly pushed her away.

At first he didn't know who she was. Startling, to wake up and find someone you don't know kissing you.

But then he felt her innocent reassurance filling his mind.

She said: *I would never do that. I would never leave you out on the surface like that.*

So. She had been watching his dream.

She continued to kiss him, her tongue slipping into his mouth to allow for the free flow of marrow. This kiss. He sensed in Agatha a youthful enthusiasm for it. What was it? She was finding pleasure in this? An illicit thrill? A young woman's thrill? In kissing him? He was too old for her. She pulled away, looked at him, her big violet eyes searching and keen, full of feeling but with nothing at all articulated in her thoughts, just a surprising and uncanny affection toward him.

She said: *You won't let the girl hurt me, will you?*

He was puzzled. *What girl?* he asked.

She said: *The girl with the orange hair. Deirdre.*

"I'm sorry we have to keep you like this," he said. She squinted, as if to her Meek ears words pronounced vocally were a rare phenomenon. "But our situation is . . . is not the best. I'll make sure Deirdre doesn't hurt you."

She said: *Deirdre wants to kill Lulu.*

This took him by surprise.

"No," he said, "she doesn't."

Agatha said: *She does. She's not right. She pretends she's right. But she's not. She always has to know where you are and what you're doing. She's always thinking about you. And now she wants to kill Lulu and hurt me.*

Cody knew what was going on. He had to make her understand that when people thought, they thought on many different levels, and the level she had chosen to probe in Deirdre—Deirdre's feelings toward him—was just one level out of many, perhaps a subconscious expression of Deirdre's jealousy and frustration, but not something that she or her sister should worry about in any substantive way.

"I won't let Deirdre hurt you," he said again. "And I won't let her hurt Lulu."

She said: *You like the curve of my waist.*

Of the several thoughts going through his own mind, this was certainly one of them. But that she should pick this particular thought to examine under her particularly clear, noise-free scrutiny bothered him. Certain thoughts should remain private. He felt as if she were trespassing.

He said: *I like the curve of your waist.* If she wanted candidness, he would give her candidness. *But I'm not sure I like where you go with your mind.*

She said: *I like you. I knew you were different the moment I saw you.*

He said: *You dig too deeply right now. I know you're young, but you should try to learn what's appropriate. Lulu stops herself from digging too deeply. She knows how to be polite. You should learn how to hear only the thoughts people wish you to hear. I like the curve of your waist, but it's inappropriate for me to express that, and it's inappropriate of you to probe for that. Is there no mechanism the Meek use to stop unwanted probing?*

She looked away. *We block,* she said. *But I have a special talent. I can get through most blocks. Buster uses me that way sometimes. To get through blocks he can't.*

He said: *Will you stop? You invade my privacy. As for Deirdre, you invade hers too. She won't hurt you. She won't kill Lulu. You don't have to worry about her. She might have those thoughts, but she might not know that she's having those thoughts, so just leave her alone.*

She said: *You're scolding me.* She was upset now. *Just like Lulu does.*

He decided the best thing he could do was change the subject. He said: *Buster uses you?*

Agatha said: *Buster knows I can tiptoe through a mind like a ghost. It's my scent, you see? It's like pine. Not many have a scent like that. And me of the human line.* He wasn't at all sure what she meant by this, the human line; he just picked up on it, saved it for later. *We all have scents, at least that's the closest thing we can call them, but some have stronger scents than others, and I have a strong scent. I smelled pine a long time ago. There used to be gardens here, and sometimes the sap would run, and I've always remem-bered that smell, and that smell has made me strong. When I use this scent I'm like a ghost. I can see everything, and no one knows I've been for a visit. The only drawback is I don't have a filter. I see everything. And sometimes I don't want to. Sometimes I'd rather not. Sometimes I even see things that the Father has seen.* Unlike Lulu, he didn't have the talent for dredging up context, couldn't see the background like a stage set, had no idea whom Agatha was talking about, only knew that she wasn't talking about her own father. *And the Father has seen a lot of awful things in his life,* she con-cluded, without any further explanation, leaving him with just the brief impression that the Father was a leader of some kind.

* * *

At three o'clock in the morning he went outside with Deirdre, Wolf, and Ben to stand watch over the yard. Everything was still. He looked up at the skyscrapers. At floor twenty, he couldn't see any further; the floors above that disappeared into the darkness. His back felt sore, but sore in an odd tingly way, a sensation he had never had before. He tried to ignore the feeling, but it made him think of the marrow, made him think it might be a side effect of the marrow. He had never had a sore back in his life before. If not the marrow, then perhaps a minor injury from the grav-core flux?

"I don't know who she meant by the Father," he said. "Nor what she meant by the human line. I asked her about it but she closed up. Like she was scared to talk about it."

"I find their names quaint," said Wolf. "Buster. Lulu. Agatha. I wonder why they pick names like that?"

"Who knows what kind of cultural or political structure they have?" said Cody.

"What about this blocking?" asked Deirdre.

Cody rubbed his stomach. His stomach felt odd too. He tried to ignore it, but a part of his mind kept running over the possibilities, especially the possibility of a side effect.

"I don't know," he said. "What good is blocking if someone like Agatha can walk right through your mind? I'm assuming she has a special gift for it, that not many can do it."

"I wish we knew more about these orphans," said Ben. "Their predecessors. This pack instinct. That bothers me. And how they killed for fun. I never knew anything about that."

But Cody was only half-listening . . .

He turned toward Rhenium Lane. His mind felt large and open and receptive. He knew this wasn't right. He felt like an eye, fully dilated, taking in all the light. He remembered how his mother had once grown prize peonies on Vesta, how she would cut them, put them in a vase, and how their smell would fill the house, that pungent and sweet smell of fresh-cut peonies. Was that his scent, then, a signature hooked into one of his own memories, a mind radio frequency of sorts? Because that's what it felt like. The marrow had turned him into a receiver.

Nothing moved on Rhenium. Yet the vacuum seemed to be filled with motion. What was it? He was sensing something. He felt the hairs on the back of his neck rise. The sense of somebody out there. His stomach felt odder still and his back started to hurt even more, and it was as if someone were gently massaging his forehead with cold fingers. What was happening? He peered down Rhenium Lane all the way to where the lights ended at Homo Habilis Avenue. His shoulders tensed. And he knew, without doubt, that the Meek were coming. His stomach felt as if it were filling with foam. Didn't feel right. As if his insides were somehow reshaping themselves. He took a deep breath . . . and realized he hadn't been breathing for the last several seconds . . .

"They're coming," he said.

Everyone turned and looked. Through their various visors he saw their faces, slack, deadened the way his mind felt deadened by that multiple mind wave of approaching Meek, emanations traveling through the vacuum in subvocalized thoughts, images, and feelings, like an invisible dam breaking and flooding Laws of Motion Square with the cerebral equivalent of a fast-rising surge.

The Meek appeared out of the darkness at the end of Rhenium Lane, a troop of them, some brachiating like apes, others walking upright. Leading the pack was Buster, magenta-striped hair hanging oddly limp at his shoulders, no air pressure to toss it, no wind, no atmospheric resistance of any kind except a scant few millibars of carbon dioxide. Each of the Meek carried a shoulder bag. From these bags they now pulled small wads of green putty, what looked like pats of half-risen dough, each with a slight metallic sheen, enough to catch a glimmer from the temporary lights strung along the road. The Meek threw these pats with uncanny accuracy at the lights, the putty seeming to lift by itself, some pats even managing right-angle turns in midair as they homed in on their targets. One by one the lights popped out and it got darker and darker. Some kind of target-intelligent nano-putty?

Cody took out his hammer and his laser drill, acting on instinct; not wishing to attack, simply wishing to protect himself, to keep himself from bodily harm. He backed away, turned his head this way and that way, on guard against whichever Meek came near him. He again focused on Buster, and felt Buster's waves rising above the rest, a signal of certainty, of fearlessness, and especially of determination. Buster hopped with great strength to the top of a backhoe. He threw a pat of putty at the pressurized dorm and the pat hit the window. The window burst open and oxygen hissed out in a white jet. Insta-seal began to sputter from the frame of the pressure window, scattering all over the yard.

Cody glanced wildly around the yard as it was overwhelmed. Meek infiltrated the yard around the barrels and spools. So many of them, all with that dull blue glow to their skin, with white hair, wearing only pants, all ready to pitch wads of destructive nano-putty. Cody swung at one of them with his laser drill, didn't want to attack but he couldn't have them wrecking his dorm, depleting his reserves of oxygen. The man jumped back, scowled at Cody, bared his small white teeth, projecting a wave of such ferocity that Cody felt it as a nearly physical shove. He backed away. Was this what Lulu meant by ghost code? This fierceness? The man darted around him, went right up to the dorm and started cycling the airlock, hacking quickly through the access code.

Wolf went after the man, grabbed him by the shoulder, but the man pulled out a knife and stabbed Wolf repeatedly in the chest. Cody felt his mouth open in numb shock. Wolf didn't even get a chance to use his laser drill. He fell hard, and insta-seal sputtered from the holes in his pressure suit. Cody's hand sank to his side. He didn't want to believe it. He heard sudden radio traffic in his helmet, the crew inside the dorm scrambling into their pressure suits, asking each other if they were all right through their com-links. He shook away his paralysis. He had to help Wolf. He didn't want to lose anyone else. Didn't want to explain to Wolf's wife, the way he was going to have to explain to Joe Calaminci's wife. He dodged around some cable spools, saw Lulu come out through the airlock. He watched her raise her hands, felt the mental equivalent of a frantic command telling the Meek to stop. But her command did no good.

Another man leaped in front him, took out a pat of nanoputty, and threw it at Cody, hitting him in the leg. Cody looked down. The putty melted right through. He looked at the hole, and thought for sure he would be safe, that the insta-seal would patch the leak. But the blue insta-seal wouldn't harden. And he realized that this was just like his dream, that his dream had been a highly accurate premonition of what was happening here. The air continued to hiss out of his suit and the insta-seal turned to gel. How could he have dreams of precognition? Something was happening to him. But what? Was it really the marrow?

The insta-seal now turned to liquid and ran down his leg. He tried to smooth it over. Just like in his dream. But just like in his dream the insta-seal was too runny. He looked up at Lulu, feeling baffled by the whole thing. Agatha appeared behind Lulu, escaping from the dorm, and ran to join her fellow Meek. He heard Agatha's emanations: *Lulu. Now. Come. This is our chance.* But Lulu just stood there looking at Cody, at the way his suit hissed air through the sputtering blue insta-seal. He felt suddenly light-headed as the pressure in his suit dropped. Like climbing ten thousand feet up a mountain in the space of a second. Everything now seemed confused. Agatha leaped over the supply yard barrier into Laws of Motion Square. Someone inside the dorm put a metal plate in front of the damaged window. Someone else closed the airlock.

The pressure inside his suit dwindled to nearly nothing. Yet he remained standing. Everything was suddenly very quiet. He could hear ringing in his ears. He stopped breathing—just stopped . . . automatically and instinctively . . .

didn't feel panicked . . . didn't feel any compelling need for air . . . just felt light-headed. His stomach again felt as if it were filling with foam. He thought of the marrow again. He fell to his knees, woozy, giddy, felt the stinging cold, cold that seemed to paralyze his limbs, like being immersed in ice water, only a hundred times worse. His pressure gloves began to shred. Shouldn't have rubbed at the nano-putty. He saw the backs of his hands, unprotected, wondered how long they could stand minus 50 degree Celsius temperatures without freezing solid.

He glanced around. Could anybody help him? He saw Ben keeping two of the Meek at bay with his laser drill. Buster stood at the airlock. A pinging sound came from the dorm's alarm, transmitted through his helmet com-link, barely audible in the steadily decreasing pressure inside his suit. His tank worked at its highest capacity to keep the pressure up—but it was like trying to inflate a balloon with a hole in it.

It was dark now, with only the lights from inside the pressurized dorm shining out into the yard. He felt dizzy. His vision blurred. Lulu was talking to Buster, looked mad at Buster. Buster glowered, and in sudden anger he threw a wad of nano-putty at Ben, lobbing it with expert aim over the heads of the two Meek men Ben tried to keep at bay. The wad hit Ben right in the chest. He clutched at the stuff, tried to get it off, but his pressure suit popped and the force of the venting air knocked him down.

Cody tried to get up to help Ben, managed to climb to his feet even as the biting cold attacked his limbs, but his insta-seal continued to sputter all over the place like an out-of-control lawn sprinkler, and he fell again, overcome by faintness. Buster gave something to Lulu, what looked like a roll of orange tape, took it from his bag and shoved it at her, then turned and walked away. He bounded out of the supply yard into Laws of Motion Square. All the other Meek retreated with him, all except Lulu. Lulu jumped. An astonishing jump. A full ten meters. She landed right next to

Cody. He thought she would warm him somehow. It wasn't
the air, it was the cold. He couldn't feel his hands. The coldness spread up his arms. He was so cold he thought he was
going to die.

Lulu said: *You're not going to die.*

He felt the peace. He felt the safety.

With startling speed she taped the hole in the leg of his
pressure suit. The nano-putty had no effect on the tape. The
tape remained strong. Lulu wrapped his shredded gloves,
turning his hands into big orange mitts.

She was just about to go over to help Ben when Deirdre
attacked her from behind with a hammer.

Deirdre swung with the pronged end of the hammer.
Hooked Lulu right in the rib cage. Punctured her skin two
inches deep with two toothlike holes.

"No!" said Cody. "Get away! She's trying to help us!"

Deirdre backed away, realizing her mistake.

Lulu fell to the ground, clutching her side. Her blood, red
like his, steamed in the cold but didn't freeze the way it
should have. It seemed to have its own internal biotherms.
Someone turned on the big floodlights from inside. He
peered down Rhenium Lane, thinking some of the Meek
might come back for Lulu. But the street was now empty
and he realized in his faintness that he had lost his sense of
time. The Meek were gone. They had disappeared into the
darkness as quickly and as suddenly as they had come.

Once they were all inside the dorm he felt shaky. And
angry. Angry at Buster. Angry at Deirdre. Wolf Steiger, ironically the one who had advised against the oxygen pop in
case it should harm the Meek, lay dead on a pallet in the infirmary. Ben was unconscious, injured, but expected to recover. Lulu was sitting up with a bandage around her ribs,
nibbling weakly at marrow, every so often casting nervous
glances at Deirdre. Everyone was jittery. Two men dead, the
deaths seeming for the moment to paralyze them all, so that
all they could do was sit. Vesta City had been notified, but

had sent no formal response yet. The *Conrad Wilson* had been notified and was working even faster to effect their repairs. They were all waiting for Peter. Cody heard the airlock cycle, saw Peter appear through the pressure glass, watched him wait as the airlock repressurized, watched the doors of the airlock slide apart. Peter came in. He unclamped his helmet. Cody smelled the faint scent of urine; everyone was in the same situation, bags full, living in suits, always these smells around.

"So how's it look?" asked Cody.

Peter stared at Cody steadily. "The outside meter says we've lost about 24 hours' worth of oxygen," he said. "But the meter has some of that putty on it and it could be wrong. Whatever the case, I think we should still go with that reading. Twenty-four hours, gone, just like that."

Cody turned to Lulu. He had a lot of questions to ask her. Like why his stomach felt distended. Why he had gone for several minutes without breathing while she had wrapped him in orange tape. Why he was having dreams of precognition. Why he had been able to sense the Meek coming down Rhenium Lane even before he had seen them.

He projected these questions but she didn't answer.

He sensed she was torn, that there were greater issues now, issues that went far beyond their little drama of whether they had enough oxygen to keep them alive until the *Conrad Wilson* got here.

"I guess it's back to the Actinium OPU then," he said. "We're halfway there. We've got to get that baby up and running or we're not going to have any air to breathe."

CHAPTER 9

He swept.

Sweeping was the center of his universe.

Sweeping a hundred years of astral debris from the photo-voltaic cells out on the surface. Sweeping dust from solar panels so they could once again collect sunlight.

Every fifteen minutes or so Cody stopped to look around. He saw four other lonely figures sweeping debris off other solar panels, sixteen panels swept clear so far, their lives dependent on this repetitive janitorial activity. He lifted his eyes to the sun, wondered if this would be the last time he would see it. They had another fifteen hours to get the old OPU up and running according to Peter's latest oxygen-supply estimates. Cody wasn't sure they were going to make it. Even if they did make it, how long could they keep it running?

So he looked at the sun. Just in case this might indeed be the last time he would see it.

And then he looked at the Ceresian landscape in all its harsh beauty. He listened to his own breathing. Felt the sweat of his hard work on his brow. Ran his tongue over the back of his teeth. Took a moment to contemplate the fact of his living body, to take in his surroundings, to appreciate his own feelings and his own five senses. And then started sweeping again.

He imagined what he looked like out here on the vast concave surface of the solar panel all by himself. He could picture himself clearly—a small figure in a white pressure suit with the green Public Works emblem on either shoulder. A man who had loved. A man who had worked. A man who was good at building things and who loved wood. A man who had skied. A man who had admired the sparkling igneous surface of Vesta. A man who had married Christine and then had lost Christine . . .

A small figure, all alone on a big solar panel, with the sun 257 million miles that way and Jupiter shining like a diamond-bright star 200 million miles the other way. He felt small in all this vastness. He felt insignificant, like a grain of sand, like his death wouldn't matter at all. He reached the edge of the solar panel. He swept. And the astral debris fell from the panel the way snow fell from the roof of his chalet in the Chillicothe Alpine Habitat back on Vesta. Swept until his muscles hurt. A marathon of sweeping, his broom silent in the vacuum, the only sound his own breath coming and going. He remembered sweeping maple keys from the back deck of his parents' cottage in the Wordsworth Lake Country Habitat on Vesta when he'd been a boy, sweeping more as a recreation, sweeping lazily, listening to the water lap against the shore, occasionally stopping to watch some ducks fly by or to observe some programmed rain drift in. He turned around to check his progress. One by one he had uncovered the individual cells, until he felt as if he stood on top of a giant fly's eye. He gazed at the horizon, saw now that they were up to twenty panels; they had only four more to go before they could go to the control center in the Actinium plant and see if all their hard work had paid off.

He went at his sweeping with renewed effort. He again thought of snow. Christine was gone now, but he remembered the snow. The snow was regulated. Always pretty. Never a blizzard. Blizzards were something he had only read about. Snow was worth living for, he thought, even if Christine was gone. Snow reminded him of Lulu's cool menthol wind. He wanted to see snow again. To lift it in his hands. To watch it melt. To see it retreat into the shadows of the trees and glades when the Weather Board brought spring on. He swept and swept, and finally he swept the whole panel clear. His body ached. Three panels now left to go. And he thought that they might make it after all.

In the control center of the Actinium Oxygen Production Utility Cody watched Claire Dubeau bypass the interface to the Municipal Computer, subverting command access to her own portable GK laptop. She ran a diagnostic. A small window appeared on her screen.

"This is the actual number of solar panels sending voltage to the microwave converter," she said.

"Twenty-two?" he said. "But we've cleaned 24."

He felt cheated after doing all that hard work and coming up short.

She shrugged. "Some of the fiber optics on these two panels have been compromised."

"But the crew checked," he said, trying not to whine about it. He was so tired from sweeping that he felt he could whine about anything. "All that cable is fine."

"Cody," said Claire, "the computer's not going to lie. Obviously you missed something somewhere."

He sighed. There was no point in looking into it or trying to fix it now. They didn't have the time. They would just have to make do with 22.

"Can we check the targeting again?" he said, feeling he had to nitpick about something.

"Sure," she said. "GK 5, display microwave targeting."

A 3-D topographical representation of the station appeared on the screen of her laptop. The graphics camera angle drew back, showed the nearest hundred solar panels, the microwave transmission tower, pulled back even further, a kilometer up, two kilometers up, until the open-pit oxygen mine came into view, and finally the mine's receiving dish.

Claire keyed in a command. A dotted yellow line connected the transmission tower to the receiving dish. A second yellow line appeared, angling from the receiving dish to

a relay tower. Then a third yellow line from the relay tower
to the input grids above the Oxygen Production Utility.

Claire said, "GK 5, confirm targeting."

The targeting coordinates were confirmed and all the yellow lines turned red.

"Targeting confirmed," said the GK through the open channel.

Cody took a deep breath, wondered if there was anything else he could do, if he had forgotten anything. He decided there wasn't. He looked around at the others. Then he patched in to Wit, who was still downtown.

"Wit, we're almost ready with this."

"I'm in the emergency shelter," said Wit over the open channel. "I've checked the vents. They're reinforced with titanium, but it's an awfully long run. We'll just have to hope that none of it's been compromised through the years. I checked the GK for the municipal codes, and this kind of venting had to be installed fairly stringently."

"Is everyone all right in the dorm?" asked Cody.

Wit paused. "They're all right. Ben's still out cold."

Cody again checked Claire's screen. "Stand by," he said. He looked at all the panels. All of it so old. All of it so antique-looking. He turned to Claire. "Okay," he said, "let's give it a try."

Claire issued a start-up command. A bar graph appeared on the screen. The bottom line represented zero kilowatts. The top line represented 1,775,000 kilowatts, maximum capacity. The emergency shelter required a lot, 55,000 kilowatts altogether, first to get the requisite number of robots up and running in the oxygen mine, then to keep the shelter itself properly pressurized, heated, and ventilated. A red bar climbed up the side of the graph, first to 20,000 kilowatts. It stayed at 20,000 for about thirty seconds.

"This is a fail-safe," said Claire. "It double-checks the targeting at 20,000 kilowatts. You don't want to be messing around with the targeting once it goes above that."

"Targeting confirmed," the GK intoned again.

The bar graph continued to climb. With twenty-two solar panels up and running, the math indicated they should get just over 65,000 kilowatts of power. Which wasn't a whole lot to spare.

The bar graph leveled off around 62,000.

"Why isn't it going up anymore?" asked Cody.

Claire shrugged. "We've got a bleed-off somewhere. But what we've got here should be enough."

Cody glanced at the manually operated OPU start-up switch. He felt like he was trying to fly to the moon in a wooden sailing ship. Wit stood by, waiting for him. He reached up, yanked the switch down, and turned to the screens.

Remote cameras showed a small cadre of robots spring to life in the oxygen mine.

Cody and his crew gathered round and watched the robots process ore for a while, fascinated, as children might be, by the way the gigantic machines worked. After fifteen minutes a light on the processing panel flashed green. This meant oxygen was ready to pump. Cody threw another switch.

According to the readouts, the oxygen made its long run to the emergency shelter in Laws of Motion Square without mishap.

Cody contacted Wit. "Wit?" said Cody. "Anything?"

"You should see the dust coming out of the vents," said Wit.

"Are you getting any sort of millibar reading?"

Cody waited while Wit took a reading from his visor.

"Nothing you can breathe yet," said Wit, "but there's a definite rise in pressure."

"Are the carbon dioxide scrubbers on-line?" he asked.

"Just a sec." Cody waited. "On-line," said Wit after a few moments, "but not venting anything yet."

"Any rise in temperature?" asked Cody.

"Going up fast. Minus 25 and rising."

The readouts on Claire's screen showed steady at 62,000

kilowatts. Cody looked at the mine monitors where the automated heavy equipment went about its work, then checked the status of the oxygen separator and saw that it was now producing four hundred cubic feet of oxygen per minute, about what they needed to keep the emergency shelter pressurized.

He nodded. "Okay," he said. "Let's head downtown."

The emergency shelter was similar in design to the *Fernando Junio*, the interplanetary cruise liner Cody and Christine had traveled to Mars in to visit his parents just after they had married, with bulkheads, pressure walls, and small rooms with multiple bunks, self-contained like a ship. Cody sat on one of the hard metal chairs, his body aching more than ever. What the shelter lacked was luxury. He could have used a soft chair. The shelter was purely functional, unrelievedly institutional, and painfully uncomfortable for someone who had just spent the last ten hours sweeping. But at least it had air. At least it had heat.

They camped in the shelter's control center.

"So that's it for the dorm's air?" Cody asked Peter.

"Yes. It's all gone."

"And how much tanked oxygen do we have?"

"Three tanks."

"That's not much of a margin."

"It's no margin at all," said Peter.

Cody sat next to Ben, who lay on a mattress on the floor. Ben was conscious but didn't seem to recognize Cody. Exposure to the vacuum had induced a cerebral aneurysm. At the age of 31, in a society where such things didn't happen to anybody anymore, Ben LeBlanc had suffered a stroke. His right eye was bloodshot. The left side of his face was slack and distorted. Cody took a cloth and wiped his mouth.

He turned to Lulu. He lifted his sweater and showed her the bulge over his stomach.

"What's happening to me?" he asked.

She looked away. Cody glanced around the room at the

others. Wit was leafing through a thirty-year-old calendar printed on polymer-base paper. Claire studied the last orbital photographs the *Gerard Kuiper* had taken before it crash-landed in the Angles. Deirdre was staring out the window at the airless square. Cody turned back to Lulu. He wanted an answer. He wasn't angry or upset; he just wanted to know. Lulu kept her face averted for a few moments, then turned to him. He could tell she was trying to project something. But they hadn't kissed in 24 hours. Nothing came through. She beckoned. He leaned forward and they kissed.

She said: *The 27 million letters that the Father recoded in chromosome 3?*

This was the first he had heard that the Father had had anything to do with the 27 million rewritten letters in chromosome 3. Who or what the Father was he still didn't know. It was as if Lulu was afraid to talk about him.

He said: *Yes?*

She said: *They were designed to engage host DNA. I kiss you, I have the marrow in my mouth, my saliva reacts chemically with it, and I produce a genetic catalyst that binds to your own coding. You start to change.*

He said: *So I'm becoming one of the Meek?*

She said: *Partially. Temporarily. You've developed certain of our characteristics. You'll revert once you're no longer supplied with the genetic catalyst.*

He couldn't help frowning. *Will I turn blue?*

She said: *Given enough coding, yes.*

He said: *Why did Buster attack Ben?*

She looked away. The focus of her thoughts blurred. Where Buster was concerned she could never shape her thoughts into words or ideas that he could comprehend. She looked at Ben, then leaned over and kissed him. This startled Cody. Until now she hadn't kissed anyone else. Deirdre glanced at them, then turned back to the window and gazed out at the square, looking lonely and excluded.

Lulu said: *I will mend him.*

Cody was puzzled. How could she mend Ben? She

sensed his puzzlement. She pulled up her thermal undershirt and ripped her bandages away. Nothing. No scar from the hammer attack. No indication of any injury whatsoever.

She said: *With marrow, chromosome 3 codes for repair. The Father added this function. After the evacuation everyone was damaged in one way or an other. After the bioextermination, radiation was seven times the lethal level. Parts of chromosome 3 were coded specifically to repair radiation damage. We soon found that it repaired a lot more.*

He was at first bewildered by what she was telling him, that the marrow should work as a panacea. Then came relief. She was going to mend Ben.

He said: *Thank you.*

She grinned and said: *We have learned to help. We have learned to care for our brothers and sisters.*

Claire called him over to her screen.

"Look at these photographs," she said. The photographs, four in all, showed the surface of Ceres. "These were taken from the *Gerard Kuiper* 22 kilometers above County Hypotenuse seven minutes before Joe crashed. Look at the coordinates."

Cody looked at the coordinates. "Right above where we found that telescope."

"Right," said Claire. "I'll box in the exact location. You've got a lot of shadow. The sun is setting so it's hard to see what I want to show you. Take a look at the first shot. I'll magnify. This was taken three minutes before the gravitational disturbance started."

Magnification showed no change from reference photographs.

"Nothing," he said.

"Right," said Claire. "Now look at this one. This is ninety seconds before the gravitational disturbance."

Cody leaned toward the screen and had a closer look. "A roof or something is opening," he said.

"That's right," she said. "Now look at this third photograph. This coincides with the start of the gravitational disturbance."

"It's fully open," said Cody.

"And I don't think it's a telescope, Cody," said Claire.

Cody glared at Lulu. Her brow was set in a half frown. She was blocking intensely. Cody couldn't get through. She wouldn't look in his direction.

"What about the fourth photograph?" he asked.

"It's essentially the same as the third photograph. But I've done a spectrographic analysis. I'll switch to full motion." She keyed in some commands, the picture unfroze, and the disk, the telescope, whatever it was, slid quickly to the east as the *Gerard Kuiper* sped by. "Here it is with the spectrograph." She keyed in another command.

Cody saw a whirlpool of color—the colors of the spectrum, only in reverse order—being sucked down into the disk. In other words the gravitational pull from the thing was so intense that, like a black hole, not even light could escape it, and in fact, was being drawn toward the thing's event horizon.

Claire cast a sideways glance at Lulu. But Lulu still wouldn't look at either of them.

Lulu said: *They think I did it.*

Cody sat next to Lulu. Jerry sat at Claire's laptop monitoring the OPU. Everyone else was asleep. Cody felt Lulu's pain but he had no idea how he should respond to it. She wouldn't volunteer any information about the gravity disk—or whatever it was—out on the surface, so naturally everybody thought she was at least partially responsible for Joe's death. Nor would she say anything about the eighteen large structures situated in various sites around the asteroid. She blocked. And he found it frustrating.

He said: *Lulu, I'm tired.*

She looked away. She said: *I'm sorry.*

And then she was quiet, as if she understood he wanted the privacy of his own thoughts. The cool wind of her mind faded and he was left alone to think about the gravity disk, and how it might or might not have been responsible for Joe Calaminci's death.

At three in the morning the vents stopped pumping oxygen into the emergency shelter. The sudden silence woke him. He found Lulu curled up next to him with her head on his chest. The air smelled stale, dusty. He eased Lulu's head gently onto the mattress they had dragged in from one of the bunkrooms. Claire, Wit, and Jerry huddled around Claire's laptop. Cody pushed himself up and joined them. The lights were out and they were using guidelights. Anne-Marie Waddell sat at the radio quietly trying to raise the *Conrad Wilson*.

"What's going on?" asked Cody.

"We've lost power in the Actinium plant," said Jerry. "We've dropped below 20,000 kilowatts. And Anne-Marie's having problems raising the *Conrad Wilson*. It's like something's scattered her ability to receive. We've lost monitor access to the oxygen mine so we have no idea what's going on up there. Wit spotted a transom valve malfunction on the screen while Claire was having a rest, and right after that we had this decrease in power."

"Do we have *anything* coming into the emergency shelter?" asked Cody.

"Nothing," said Jerry. "And the heat's off-line too. The temperature's dropped three degrees in the last half hour."

"What about the scrubbers?" asked Cody.

"They're out too," said Claire. "But so far there's been only a marginal increase in carbon dioxide."

Cody put his hands on his hips and thought. "Anne-Marie, you're not getting anything from the *Conrad Wilson*?"

"Just the occasional positional readout," she said. "But I'm not sure I trust it. The signal's constantly breaking up."

"At a rough guess, how long is it going to take them to get here?"

"About seventeen hours," she said.

Cody turned and stared at Lulu, whose skin looked purple in the dim light of the guidelights. They were trapped in a bubble of air with no new air coming in. He did the math. They would probably make it through the seventeen hours till the *Wilson* got here, with plenty of air to spare. After all, the shelter was as big as a stadium and fully pressurized, and ten people breathing normally would take two weeks to get through it all. What made him nervous was the cold. Without any new source of heat they would freeze to death. There was nothing to burn. Everything in the emergency shelter was, naturally enough, noncombustible. Heat for their pressure suits depended on special intersuit biotherms, but their biotherms were gone. And while the pressure suits were insulated, without the biotherms they couldn't be expected to provide any long-term protection against the killer cold that would inevitably insinuate its way into the shelter.

So . . .

So . . . they would have to ask Lulu . . .

He turned to her, said: *Can you keep us warm?*

She said: *I can keep you warm. The marrow codes for increased temperature tolerance.*

He said: *Then let's do it.*

He had to argue with his crew about this. While some were willing, others, particularly Deirdre, had to overcome the cultural, romantic, sexual, and gender associations that were part and parcel of his plan to save them from freezing to death. In fact he couldn't convince Deirdre at all, and she gave in only after the temperature reached minus 23 Celsius.

At that point their continued existence and survival became a surreal nightmare.

Cody stared at Lulu kissing Dina on the lips, Dina sitting rigidly in the cold while this beautiful blue woman provided the cold-resistant genes of chromosome 3 to her. Then Lulu moved to Peter, then to Wit, then to Jerry, and it was easier for the men than it was for the women; at least the orientation was going the right way. When Lulu finally got to

Deirdre, both women kissed stiffly, arms at their sides, and Cody knew that Deirdre was fighting to overcome her aversion, forcing herself to sip, so to speak, the cold-repelling elixir from Lulu's lips, but also struggling to finally accept Lulu, to understand that maybe this blue woman had found a special place in Cody's life. All so surreal, Lulu kissing Claire, Anne-Marie, Dina, then Deirdre again, an erstwhile male fantasy—all the men watching with red-rimmed fearful eyes—but performed in the most harrowing life-and-death circumstances, with everybody shivering, with their breath crystallizing and all the furniture creaking as it contracted in the unspeakable cold. Lulu wasn't cold at all. She moved from crew member to crew member like she was on a tropical beach in a warm breeze, regurgitating, like a mother bird, the stuff that would keep everybody alive.

This went on for hours. Lulu exhausted herself helping them. She went to Peter, Ben, Jerry, Wit, Huy, and finally back to Cody again, in the dark, with only the beams of their guidelights piercing the gloom. Like it was never going to end. Lulu giving each one of them enough of a genetic rewrite with the superscience of the marrow to survive. And they all endured. One way or another, as the temperature got colder and colder, they all stayed alive . . .

CHAPTER 10

After eight hours of genetic recoding in the freezing cold Cody experienced periods of apnea—his lungs shut down for one or two minutes at a time. He shook himself; it was the only way he could get his lungs to start working again. Even when his lungs stopped he didn't feel the slightest need for air. He stretched his arms out in front of him. They all wore their suits and helmets, but the warmth the suits provided was negligible. He let his arms sink slowly to his lap. His body felt sluggish. He tried to form his hand into a fist, but he couldn't move his fingers, couldn't even feel them. He thought he must be freezing to death. His body temperature was down—he saw the data on his biofeedback indicator, a small display projected onto the lower right corner of his visor—but other than temperature all other life signs were normal.

"It says I have a body temperature of 32 Celsius," he told Jerry. "Isn't that five degrees below normal?"

Lulu was now kissing Claire.

"I'm the same," said Jerry. "I should be shaking. My speech should be slurred. But it's not. We're perfectly fine." Jerry watched Lulu kiss Claire. Cody did the same. So odd to see Claire without her helmet on when temperatures like these would ordinarily freeze her nose in seconds. "This chromosome 3," said Jerry, "these 27 million rewritten letters . . . this is . . . it's miraculously advanced genetic science. For it to happen so quickly like this. Far more advanced than anything we have. The kind of genetic transplants we perform on Juno are primitive compared to this." He gestured toward Lulu. "It doesn't seem possible that the Meek could develop such sophisticated techniques . . . for her coding to bind with our coding . . . to start changing us in minutes, so that we can actually withstand killer cold like this."

"I know what you mean," said Cody.

Jerry nodded, a cumbersome movement of his head inside his helmet. "They seem like such a simple people. Look at her. I don't know how she and her people could have done what they've done when theoretically they should have all been fried from the inside out by the bioextermination thirty years ago."

Cody stared at Lulu as she kissed Claire. He looked at the small flowers embroidered into her pants, the idiosyncratic pieces of reflective thread, the haphazard arrangement of the decoration. She seemed such a natural creature, the antithesis of a technological being. Where did she live? The Edison Foothills Habitat? He certainly couldn't picture her living in a place like Vesta City, with its neat gridwork of streets, its drab office blocks, and its conventional suburbs. Or even in a place like Newton, which, though more fanciful and architecturally interesting than Vesta City, lacked the naturalness he sensed within her.

That's what he wanted. A new naturalness to his life. Maybe that's what attracted him to Lulu. That's why he was here, on Ceres, using his clout as number-three man in Public Works to land this project for himself in the first place. To get out of the boardroom. To get back outside. To regain some of the naturalness in his life that had disappeared when he finally found himself behind a desk. Not only that, he wanted to get away from Vesta, where there were just too many memories now, immerse himself in a megaproject, let his job take over.

He turned his head as if through half-frozen jelly. He ob-

served. Observed Lulu. Observed this room. A confining
space. Lulu didn't belong in a room like this. A desk, a chair,
the control panel, a narrow glass vase with some fake flowers, a metal wardrobe with one of the doors torn off, some
plastic hangers hanging from hooks inside. She belonged
outside. He shifted his guidelight to the far wall. A bulletin
board. Some thirty-year-old maintenance schedules pinned
to the bulletin board. Some postcards from Earth, one showing the Grand Canyon, another showing Niagara Falls, and
still another showing the crumbling ruins of the Coliseum in
Rome, printed on that pixel paper, the stuff that could ani-
mate the postcard, a novelty thirty years ago but today just
so much kitsch. He didn't want to die here. When Kevin Axworthy and his crew finally came would they find him
frozen to death in here? Would his own corpse become part
of the tragic corpse motif of Newton?

He felt like asking Lulu to take him to the Edison
Foothills Habitat. At least out there his death would be more
natural.

He took a deep breath, just to convince himself that he
could, and rolled his shoulders twice. Lulu moved to Dina,
kissed her. He was so cold that he couldn't wait until Lulu
got to him. He felt the cold as a biting ache all over his body.
He had to do something to take his mind off it. He lifted his
half-finished cat. Deirdre watched him. He picked up a
piece of sandpaper, started sanding, his hands awkward in
the big pressure gloves. Lulu gave him a sideways glance as
she continued to kiss Dina. He sanded some more. He liked
to work with his hands. When he worked with his hands he
always felt better about everything, even about freezing to
death in a city that had no heating system.

Three hours later, when the temperature reached minus
60 Celsius, Cody heard a big bang. He rose sluggishly to his
feet, again with the sensation that he was moving through
half-frozen jelly, his bones seeming to creak and moan inside his body. He joined Claire at her laptop. And heard an-

other bang. Then another. And finally another. Not an exploding bang, more of a bursting bang. Atmospheric pressure started to drop and a faint breeze stirred the frigid air in the control room. He leaned closer to the laptop's voice-command input.

"GK 1," he said, surprised by how low and faint his voice sounded. "Exterior cameras."

The screen filled with a night-vision view of Rhenium Lane. Outlined in ghostly green, nine or ten Meek climbed the side of the emergency shelter, packs strapped to their backs. He heard two more bangs. The Meek were using their nano-putty to breach the hull of the shelter. Atmospheric pressure began to drop quickly. The screen switched to a new view, showed four of the Meek applying nano-putty to the main airlock. Cody lurched from the screen, his legs so numb he could hardly feel them, and closed the control room's pressure door, twisting the seal tight with the manual closing wheel. It seemed as if the Meek were really intent on killing them, that they had simply been waiting for them to weaken, to become unable to fight back.

Wit got up. So did Peter. Both were moving as if they had stiff cardboard shoved down the sleeves and leggings of their pressure suits, their faces slack, showing not so much alarm as a dull, cold apathy, as if they were too frozen to care about what the Meek were doing.

"They're outside," said Cody, forcing himself to speak louder. He swung his arm as if in slow motion and pointed at the screen. "You can see them on-camera."

Wit and Peter looked at the screen. The Meek, outlined in the phantom green of the camera's nightscope vision, moved as if through a murky beryl sea up the side of the building, planting pats of nano-putty here and there, climbing with the ease of monkeys. Cody felt distant from it all. He felt like a man who was already dead, a ghost marveling at the antics of mortals who would try to kill him a second time. He knew he wasn't thinking right. Was he experiencing some of the confusion of hypothermia?

He sat down. His legs felt weak. Lulu came and sat next to him. He began to take off his helmet, thinking she was there to kiss him, to warm him, but she shook her head, and he sensed she was too tired, that it had taken a lot out of her to keep everybody alive for this long, that she needed a rest. He heard the squeal of the air outside as it seeped out the nano-putty holes, like the sucking sound water made as it drained out of a bathtub. Huy looked at him, his usual coppery complexion nearly white through the visor of his helmet. Peter looked at him. So did Wit. So did Dina. They wanted him to come up with a plan. But he had no plan.

"Let's everybody sit together," he said. "Let's sit on the floor. We might keep warmer that way."

So they all sat on the floor. Warmth was a relative term when the temperature was minus 60 Celsius. But it was good to sit on the floor close to everybody just the same. It was good to be part of this group. He felt like they were all grade-school kids sitting on the floor in class. Far in the distance he heard Lake Ockham cracking. His mouth, his sinuses, and his throat were dry—desert-dry. Every last molecule of moisture had been frozen out of the air. This was death. None of them panicked. It was too cold to panic. Cody checked his biofeedback monitor again. Heart rate was 28 beats per minute. Zenlike. The Meek destroyed his precious bubble of air, and he found he simply didn't care. All mortal concerns seemed distant and unnecessary.

Cody sat on the floor beside Lulu. She stared at him, her violet eyes glowing in the dim wash of light coming from the guidelights.

She said: *They're not going to come in.*

He said: *They know there's nothing we can do to stop them.*

She said: *They'll wait till you suffocate. They fight against their ghost codes. They will not use out-and-out violence if they can avoid it. They will let the cold ease you away.*

Claire got up and went to the computer. Everyone

looked at her. Cody sensed their vague curiosity. But he also sensed their delicious and dangerous apathy, the apathy of those who were about to freeze to death. Anne-Marie got up and tried to raise the *Wilson* on the radio one more time. He sensed thoughts coming from Anne-Marie, but they were faint, weak, and he could hardly make out what they were, could only sense an unarticulated determination. In fact, he now sensed faint emanations from everyone, their apathy jolted by Claire's move to the computer, by Anne-Marie's move to the communications console. He sampled these emanations one by one. Jerry watched the laptop screen, the creatures climbing the sides of the emergency shelter; from Jerry came medical and professional admiration for the genetic reality and superiority of the Meek. From Wit, a hot spark of anger, a need to go out and show those fuckers they couldn't push him around. From Huy, a nagging worry about water supply, whether the ten liters left, now frozen solid, would last them. From Russ, a visual image, a field of daisies on Perseus, a feeling of peace, of acceptance, as if he realized he couldn't do anything about their present situation. From Dina, an image of her mother making cranberry sauce at home, the sound of words, English words but so flavored by the Perseusian dialect Cody could hardly understand them. From Peter, a professional thought, a hope that the Meek outside wouldn't take any more of their equipment. From Claire, a focused effort to reboot the OPU in Actinium by checking for any damaged software. From Ben—too fuzzy from his stroke to make out much of anything, just a vague image of a country road at night somewhere out in the Great Plains Growing Region of Vesta.

And from Deirdre . . . from Deirdre came a huge and daunting sadness. Such a big sadness it seemed to fill the whole room. He turned to her, startled, so big was her emotion. He found her staring at him, her eyes wide and green and moist with tears, tears that would not freeze in the bitter extraterrestrial cold, not when they ran with the juice of the marrow.

He realized she had finally given up on him.

That she had finally disengaged her emotions from him once and for all.

She was different, he could sense it; a much calmer person, even in her current misery, now that she wasn't ruined by her love for him. A sensible person, a likable one, not someone he had to be uncomfortable around anymore, someone he could call his friend. He gave her a tentative smile. She smiled back.

She said: *I'm sorry.*

He nodded. He understood.

Then his ears popped as he heard the vacuum suck on the control room's pressure door, heard the pressure door knock against its seal as it was pulled outward by that dreaded airless specter of the Belt. They were in a precious bubble of air, and soon the carbon dioxide would thicken. Would the marrow help them breathe? Or would the super-science of the Meek fall short? He thought that Buster had to be out there, and that Buster would know if the marrow would help them or not. Buster also had to know that Lulu was in here with them, no matter how hard she tried to block. Cody got to his feet. How far was Buster willing to go? The air in the control room looked misty—the nitrogen was freezing out. Would Buster simply wait until Lulu exhausted herself? She looked ready to collapse. Would Buster let the vacuum kill them? Cody joined Claire at her laptop. She was running a scan on some of the old disks. He could only hope that the *Conrad Wilson* would get here before their air ran out.

He turned to Anne-Marie. "Any contact?" he asked.

Anne-Marie turned to him slowly, as if moving in a dream. One of the guidelight beams pierced her yellow visor and he saw her face clearly, her dark eyebrows standing out against a preternaturally white face, a face whitened by the extreme cold. She was frowning. "I've got a strong positional signal," she said, her voice low, cracking from lack of moisture. "The *Conrad Wilson*'s somehow hacking through all this strange interference."

"And where are they?" he asked.

She turned back, double-checked the signal, and with a flicker of hope in her voice, said, "They're in orbit."

PART 2

VESTA

CHAPTER 11

Kevin Axworthy, at 57 years of age, was a formidable-looking man with a hawk's beak of a nose, a square chin, a massive forehead, penetrating blue eyes, and thick white hair that swept back in an impressive mane. As Cody watched him walk around Lulu, examining her, evaluating her, looking as if he were trying to come to a conclusion about her, he felt both relieved and alarmed by the man's presence. Cody had his life back. He wasn't going to suffocate or freeze. Sixteen hours had passed since that dire moment in the emergency shelter when they had first learned that the *Conrad Wilson* was in orbit. He was safe in this portable military-style bunker, and the vacuum outside in Laws of Motion Square couldn't touch him. What alarmed him was the change of dynamic. He glanced around the room. Uniforms everywhere. Men with weapons. And outside, a supply yard full of automated weapons waiting to be set up. These men were soldiers in an armed camp, ready to fight, and the unpredictability and potentially disastrous consequences of the situation unnerved Cody.

Lulu sat in a chair, her hands cuffed behind her back. Two guards stood next to her, grim-faced men, human pit bulls, dwarfing the diminutive and fairylike Meek woman. Axworthy stopped circling Lulu, put his fists on his hips, gave her one more probing glance, then looked at Cody.

"You're lucky to be alive, Mr. Wisner," he said.

Cody nodded. "She helped us," he said. "I don't see why you have to handcuff her like that. Why don't you let her sleep? She's exhausted."

A crease appeared in Axworthy's forehead. "We just want to make sure she doesn't run away, Mr. Wisner, that's all," he said. "She might have useful information. I'd certainly like to find out about that putty they use. That's going right to the top of the list as far as I'm concerned. If it can breach your dorm, who's to say it can't breach this bunker?"

"She needs marrow," Cody told Axworthy. "She gets sick if she doesn't eat it." Axworthy looked at him in mystification. Lulu squirmed on the edge of her seat. "They breathe with their stomachs. They need marrow to breathe."

"Marrow?" said Axworthy. "That lichen stuff that's growing out there?"

"Yes."

"The stuff that glows?"

"No, the other stuff."

"She won't die, will she?"

"She won't," said Cody. "Some of them just get sick. She's one of those."

"But others die?"

"That's what I've learned."

"She needs it?" said Dr. Tom Minks.

Cody turned to the slim blond doctor. Even he wore a uniform. "She needs it to breathe," he told Minks. "She'll start having withdrawal symptoms if she doesn't get it."

Axworthy spoke to one of the guards. "Bruder, go get her some lichen. Let's lay in a supply."

"Sir, yes, sir."

Bruder left the infirmary.

Axworthy stared at Lulu again. His massive brow sank close to his eyes. Lulu was looking up at Axworthy nervously. Cody moved next to her and put his hand on her shoulder, comforting her. She tried to say something, struggled to convey a complicated series of thoughts, but all he got from her was that she was afraid. Axworthy looked up from his meditation on Lulu.

"You know who my father is," he said.

"I do."

"I spent a lot of time around orphans when I was growing up." He took a moment, as if he still hadn't come to a decision about whether the experience had been a good one or a bad one. "A lot of people who live in the Belt blame my father for the orphans. He just tried to help them. That's what gets me so mad about the whole thing. The original orphans came from Mars. I don't know whether you knew that or not. My father had nothing to do with them when they were there. People forget that. Leonard Carswell made them in the closing decades of the last century on Mars. Ever heard of Carswell?"

"Some," said Cody.

"They gloss over Carswell in the textbooks," said Axworthy. He smiled sadly about this oversight. "And my father's part was really small. He tried to help the orphans, that's all. When they came from Mars to Ceres. I grew up around orphans because of my father's interest in them. I know orphans. That's why Council picked me for this particular assignment. Lulu here, she might be blue, she might be pretty, she might be smaller, she might call herself one of the Meek, but she's an orphan just the same." He looked at Lulu, his eyes narrowing. "I know," he said. He pressed his hands flat against the table and scrutinized Lulu. "I can see it in her eyes."

Cody felt irritated by this. "So what exactly are your orders?" he asked.

"My orders are currently under review by Vesta City," said Axworthy. "The situation has changed since our last communication."

"What were your original orders?" asked Cody.

Axworthy walked to the end of the table, double-checked his com-link, then said to Cody, "Our initial orders were to secure and ascertain the nature of the eighteen installations

on the surface. Once that was done, we were to secure and
determine the nature of the differing nineteenth installation—the disk, the telescope, the gravity well, whatever you
call it. We're also here to guarantee the safety of your work
crew. Finally, we have orders to secure and maintain a defendable perimeter around Newton. Those orders still
stand."

Bruder came back with a container full of lichen.

"What are you going to do with Lulu?" asked Cody.

Axworthy glanced at Lulu. "That's where the first of our
supplemental orders comes in," he said. "I'm glad you kept
this woman, Mr. Wisner. You did the right thing." He turned
to Dr. Tom Minks. "Dr. Minks, you can take the detainee to
the infirmary and start working on her."

Dr. Tom Minks, looking as if he were suffering terribly
from the .5 gees, sagging under the weight of it, nodded to
one of the guards.

"Working on her?" said Cody. The guard unfastened
Lulu's handcuffs and led her away, Dr. Minks following
heavily behind. Lulu was too weak to give Cody even a
backward glance. "What do you mean, working on her?"

Axworthy raised his hands. For a man his age he had an
exceptionally erect figure. "No need for alarm, Mr. Wisner,"
he said. "We've been ordered to do some tests. Simple, routine, baseline tests to see where we stand with her. I have
nothing against Lulu. I don't want to treat her like a prisoner,
I don't even want to think of her that way, but she's . . . she's
here, we've got her, and we've got to go ahead with these
tests. I have no choice. We're not going to hurt her. It will be
for her safety as much as ours."

Cody spent the following two days assessing the damage
to the emergency shelter in Laws of Motion Square. Nano-
putty holes riddled the structure in 33 different places. He
walked around to the south side of the structure and gazed at
one of the holes. Deirdre Malvern, in her capacity as structural engineer, was with him.

"And he wants us to repair the shelter?" she asked.

"He wants it as backup."

"Can he do that?" she asked. "We're not under his command, are we?"

"Technically, no. But I think it makes good sense to have the emergency shelter as backup. And besides, Anne-Marie's received word from Vesta City." Cody tried to hide his disappointment as much as he could. "Our mission has been temporarily suspended."

"It has?"

He attempted to give the news an uplifting spin. "They're happy with our preliminary work, the costing and so forth, but . . . but all these developments have really taken them by surprise, heads are rolling, and certain segments in Council now think the whole thing has been mismanaged from the start."

"Really?" she said. "What are they saying?"

"That they should have sent a security team in first, not us, and that they were too quick to trust their robot and satellite surveillance. That equipment's sophisticated. There's no reason not to trust it. The Ceresian Defense Force fried Ceres from the inside out with neutron bombs thirty years ago, then opened all the airlocks. They made the reasonable assumption that everybody left inside was dead. They watched Ceres for thirty years and saw nothing. Why send in a security team first, especially under such tight budget restrictions, if there's no one here? But the hard-liners are having a field day. In the meantime, we stop. We've been asked to cooperate with Axworthy. And that means the emergency shelter."

She nodded. She seemed much more comfortable around him. She pointed at the hole in the side of the shelter. "So what about this?" she asked. "The metal's slowly melting away."

"They've brought a chemist. Dr. Alex Czaplinski. He's working on the nano-putty, says it definitely has a biological base and it'll just be a question of developing the proper cytocide to kill it."

"What do we do in the meantime?" she asked.

They were out of their suits again. Axworthy had popped some of his own oxygen and wired fail-safe overrides to all the municipal airlocks. It felt good, to be working with Deirdre. To be concerned about materials and repairs and engineering strategies again.

"You're the structural engineer," he said. "I thought you'd have some suggestions."

She took a few steps toward the wall, her breath frosting over. She rubbed her chin with her hand, thinking.

"We cut around it," she said. "Take it out the way a surgeon takes out a tumor. We replace it with uninfected plasti-bond, go to a depth of five centimeters. That should hold."

"What about the airlocks?" he asked, not because he didn't have his own ideas about the airlocks—he had a specialty in airlocks—he just wanted to see what she might know, see if they had airlocks in common.

"The airlocks are going to be harder," she said. "Pressurized door systems are always complicated, you know that better than anybody. A lot of gears and levers, and as for the airlocks in this building, nothing's sized to the current standard. None of our replacement parts will fit unless we tool them all in the machine shop." She shook her head and put her hands on her hips, contemplating the magnitude of the job. "At least it'll keep us busy until Council decides what it wants to do."

It was good to be up on the scaffolding doing construction and repair work again. Cody sprayed plasti-bond around the edges of his precut hole. Working with his hands was a good way to stop thinking. To stop brooding. He slung the applicator over his shoulder, lifted his lock-sheet, placed it against the plasti-bond, and watched the chemical reaction suck the sheet into place. He gazed down Calculus to Subtraction Street. The street here was cobblestoned with a likeness of Albert Einstein playing the violin. He liked working with his hands to stop brooding, only he couldn't stop thinking of Lulu, how they were recording her brain-wave patterns, how they were testing her for various allergies, taking blood and bone marrow samples.

He looked at his lock-sheet, saw that the seal was now complete, took out his caulking gun, and beaded a line of plasti-bond around the edges. The air smelled like burning leaves. Axworthy was destroying all the marrow with a special defoliant within the city limits—in the interest of establishing a defendable perimeter.

Bruder came up to him.

"We're locking down now," said the security officer. "We're going to release the tracking microgens."

Cody descended the scaffolding carefully. Even after nearly a month on Ceres he still felt the extra weight and wasn't about to risk a broken ankle by a careless climb down.

He followed Bruder into the bunker. Everyone else was there. At least everyone in his own crew. Platoons 1 and 3 of the security team were deployed on the surface investigating the various structures. Second platoon was out in the eastern suburbs ready to deploy the tracking microgens. Outside, two security officers sprayed the bunker with a special chemical that would repel the microgens. Cody had been swallowing tablets of the exact same substance for the last two days, to repel and destroy any microgens that got anywhere near him. The tracking technician didn't want to get any false readings.

Axworthy spoke into the radio. "Santiago, this is Axworthy. Everyone's inside. You can go ahead any time you're ready."

Everyone waited.

By and by, a red fog enveloped Laws of Motion Square. The color was gruesome, reminded Cody of blood.

Axworthy looked at Cody. "Why so quiet, Mr. Wisner?"

Cody didn't answer, just continued to stare at the red fog.

"You know, I wish you'd take a more sensible view toward this," said Axworthy. "I'm sorry about Lulu, but what do you want me to do? They've murdered two of your people and destroyed a two-billion-dollar municipal spacecraft. I have to take action. I have no choice. Those are my orders."

Cody motioned at the red fog. "Will this stuff hurt them?"

"Not at all. This stuff gets into their system, they spread it to others like a common cold, but they don't have any symptoms, and there are no long-term side effects. It just helps us know where they are, and that's important, especially since they hide so well."

"So you track them?"

Axworthy nodded. "For their own protection," he said. "And for ours. Everybody will be a lot safer if we know where they are all the time." He turned and looked at a special screen. Small green dots appeared on a superimposed street map of Newton. "What have we got, Azim?" he asked the tracking specialist.

"Several encampments in the Edison Foothills Habitat, Commander," said Azim, "with 623 individuals infected so far in seven different areas."

"How are they reacting to the deployment?" asked Axworthy.

"They're moving. Heading east away from Santiago and his men."

Axworthy turned to Cody. "They see the red fog and they're running," he explained. "We make it red because we want them to run from it. It quickens the vectors of contagion."

"Sir?" said Azim.

Axworthy turned back to Azim. "What is it, Azim?"

"Look at this."

Azim gazed at the tracking screen in mystification. Axworthy got up and went over. Cody craned.

Axworthy's impressive brow furrowed as he inspected the movement of all the little green dots on the screen.

"That's impossible," he said.

"What is?" asked Cody.

Axworthy pointed to a jagged green line at the eastern edge of the city. "This is solid rock," he said. "We've checked the eastern bulkhead thoroughly. There's no way to get through. We checked every square inch. But they're going right through it like a knife through butter."

Danny Vigo reported back from first platoon. He and his men had managed to penetrate one of the eighteen gigantic finlike structures on the surface. After excavating with heavy equipment they blasted their way in with a particle beam cannon, shaking the alloy apart molecule by molecule. What they found inside surprised even Cody. A holo-image of Danny Vigo appeared above the communications panel in the control room of the pressurized bunker.

"Our final count is 24," said Vigo. "Twelve six-megaton and twelve one-megaton. The structure seems to be a silo, Commander. At least that's what it looks like to me."

Axworthy reached up, pinched the bridge of his nose between his thumb and finger, and closed his eyes. His shoulders sank, he took his hand away, and he looked at Cody with weary resignation.

"Why do you suppose they're stockpiling nuclear weapons, Cody?" he asked, using Cody's first name for the first time.

It was a question he knew the man wasn't expecting him to answer.

Cody sat in the infirmary with Jerry and Dr. Tom Minks. Lulu lay semisedated on an examining table, held down by restraints.

"I guarantee," said Minks, "this is harmless. If there were any other way . . . but now that the situation's changed, now that they have all those silos out there, we have to go ahead with this."

Cody glanced at Jerry. He knew what Jerry was thinking, could sense wisps of it emanating from Jerry's mind, realized that the recoding was still with him, at least to some degree. Jerry thought Cody had been co-opted by Lulu through prolonged exposure to marrow. But Cody knew his opinions about the whole situation hadn't been co-opted in the least.

"Cody," said Jerry, "you have to do this. I don't like it any more than you do. But it's the right thing to do."

Cody focused on Jerry, tried to smile, knew that Jerry wanted to trust him, and that he was trying to deal with his mixed feelings as well as he could. Cody turned his attention to Minks.

"What I object to is that we have to do this to Lulu," he said. "Why should we penalize her when all she's ever done is help us?"

Minks looked at Jerry. Jerry leaned forward, put his elbows on his knees, and nodded with an effort at understanding.

"Cody," he said, "I wouldn't characterize this as penalizing Lulu. We're not penalizing anybody. We just have to find out about this. No one in the whole solar system stockpiles weapons this large anymore. These people do. These people were once orphans. When the Ceresians threatened them with bioextermination way back when, they didn't negotiate. What kind of people don't negotiate when they have a loaded gun pointed at their heads? That's not to say we can't trust Lulu. I have no problem trusting Lulu. But at this point we need information, and she's the only one we can get it from. You seem to have the best link to her. All we want you to do is find out why they're stockpiling these weapons."

"I realize that," said Cody. "And I know we have to go ahead with this. I recognize the threat. I know we have to find out what we can about it." He turned to Dr. Minks. "But are you sure she'll be okay?"

"These drugs I'm giving her are perfectly safe," said Minks. "Just extract whatever you can. She won't be hurt, there's no pain involved, there's no fear or anxiety or nausea. The drugs will sedate her and prompt a free association of ideas. That's all. I imagine you'll be collecting a lot of raw data. You can steer her toward the question of the weapons with your own input, and we'll hope she'll freely associate about them from there, but there's no guarantee. Just go in there. Be as kind as you can. Everyone likes Lulu. It'll be over before you know it."

Cody turned to Jerry, again sensed the doctor's concern about whether he had been co-opted or not. He decided he had to set Jerry straight. "You can trust me, Jerry," he said.

Jerry's eyes narrowed. Cody could feel the old trust coming back. "I know I can," he said.

Cody nodded. "Then let's get it over with."

Cody leaned over and pressed his lips to Lulu's. He kissed her, and he had to wonder if she had indeed co-opted him in some way, made him oversympathetic to her cause and the cause of her people. Her mouth tasted faintly of marrow. He tried to sense what was going on in her mind but the cool menthol wind of her thoughts blew faintly, brought only that customary and welcome feeling of peace.

He lifted his lips away.

"I'm not getting anything," he said.

Minks squeezed a few drops of marrow solution from an eyedropper into her mouth. Then Cody kissed her once again, tenderly, forgetting that this was, for all intents and purposes, an interrogation. With the marrow solution in her mouth her menthol mind-wind blew stronger. The room dimmed and he felt as if he were surrendering. His whole body felt cool, rubbing-alcohol cool. He felt as if he were sitting in a great forest at night. He lifted his lips, looked around . . .

He sat in a tree. In a nest of moss. And the moss glowed blue. Where was he? Somewhere inside Lulu's mind? Beyond all the barriers she had erected? Deep inside her subconscious? He wondered if back at the bunker in Newton he was still kissing her.

He stood up. Trees stretched as far as his eyes could see, reminded him of the rain forest trees of the Pedro Cabral

Amazon Habitat back on Vesta. Every tree was hung with
the blue glow-moss. Was this where Lulu lived? The air was
warm here. He felt wind on his face. He smelled flowers—
juniper, hyacinth, rose, and azalea. Heard music, ringing and
clear, a haunting melody that sounded as if it were played on
crystal chimes. Five moons hung in the sky, each one patterned with its own distinct tattoo of craters, each a different
color, ranging from green to pink. Artificial moons, he realized, maybe even holo-images, but so lifelike, so palpable
and substantive, that they looked as real as the moons of
Jupiter.

As his eyes grew accustomed to the dimness he saw hundreds of Meek in the trees nesting in piles of moss, eating
marrow, children playing with children, adults sitting
around in groups, communicating in their silent Meek way,
at peace with this place, a part of this place. He couldn't
sense one cruel thought in any of them.

He nudged Lulu. *Why stockpile nuclear weapons?*

Her answer came in disturbing fragments. *Because we
can't live here anymore.* Fragments that did nothing to reassure Cody. *Because after we leave, we'll need a new home.*
And then some dream images floated through his mind. Of
this new home. A world with an open sky, a cloudy sky. The
image shifted, blurred, solidified, and he saw a group of
Meek walking single file, some of them brachiating like
apes along the rim of a lava-filled caldera. He felt heat.
Smelled sulfur. He felt the dampness of a tropical atmosphere. Was this Earth? He'd never been to Earth. Got nervous whenever he thought of such a large, open, and
unpredictable matrix of ecosystems, one competing against
the other, a place with so many billions of people and with
a gravity he would find crushing. Earth had volcanoes. Did
the Meek have designs on Earth? Was Earth this new home
Lulu was speaking of?

He felt light, untethered, as if he were floating. The
image of the Meek walking along the rim of the volcano disappeared. He now saw Buster. Standing in front of a large

sheet of cellophane. In an amphitheater. With stone bleachers rising all around him. Hundreds of Meek filled the bleachers. Buster sang at the large sheet of cellophane as if to serenade it, sang in a way Cody had never heard anybody sing, not in the tones and halftones of the well-tempered diatonic scale such as was so commonly heard in the popular music of Vesta, but in quarter-tones and microtones, a melody full of glissandi and implied dissonance, a song that at first sounded out of tune but that, like an unfamiliar spice, soon became palatable. Lines started to appear in the cellophane. And he realized that this wasn't a sheet of cellophane at all but a living organism of some kind, one that could translate and interpret Buster's melody into representative symbols and language.

In the dusky purple ambience of the amphitheater Buster etched bright blue lines depicting what at first looked like several concentric circles but soon broadened and flattened to show the elliptical paths of the solar system's planets around the sun. Parts were magnified. Ceres jumped out in luminous pink, Earth in turquoise. Buster sketched their orbital paths in yellow. As Earth and Ceres approached closest opposition, Buster evoked a complicated mathematical equation that described a decrease in Ceres's speed: Ceres slowing down, figures representing a flagging momentum, a growing inertia, a braking force, all the variables of orbital mechanics showing up on the cellophane. A new trajectory was drawn, representing the orbital decay of Ceres, showing how the new trajectory would eventually intersect with Earth's orbit.

Ominous. As if Earth were indeed the new home Lulu had spoken of.

Lulu objected.

She said: *We are not orphans anymore. We are the Meek. We keep our ghost code under control. The Father taught us the ways of peace. He taught us the meaning of the words, Our Home. He taught us that even though we are a people of many clans we are also a people united. He taught coex-*

istence and cooperation as a means of survival. He taught us the philosophy of eternal peace.

But she said nothing of Earth.

The liturgical resonance of her thoughts puzzled Cody. She spoke of the Father as if he were a deity, not a mortal man.

Who is the Father? he asked. *Does he walk among you?*

She didn't answer. It was as if her mind, besieged by truth drugs, was spinning out of control. An image from inside her mind hit him with the force of a gale wind.

She was young. Twelve years old. And her skin was brown, not blue. Her girlish heart beat with ingrained malice. She knew the meaning of arson because everywhere around her the buildings burned. She chased a boy. Her arms were long but not as long as they were now. Her hair was black. She was, in fact, an orphan, tailored to live on the surface of Mars but now here on Ceres, a refugee, loathed by the Ceresians. A girl in a new place at war with the people who had tried to help her, sticking to her clan, fiercely loyal to Buster. At war, running through the burning streets, chasing a boy of seven with a sharpened pole, finally skewering him through the back like a hunted animal. Children killing children. Kids murdering kids. The boy tumbled to the ash-covered street. The girl Lulu, the brown Lulu, the orphan Lulu, watched the blood pump from the boy's back.

She woke up.

She opened her eyes.

The image disappeared. Cody pulled his lips away. He took a sudden deep breath. His stomach felt full of fuzz. He turned to see Jerry and Dr. Minks both staring at him.

"You haven't been breathing for the last seventeen minutes," said Dr. Minks. "By rights, you should be dead."

CHAPTER 12

Cody sat in a chair and watched Dr. Minks and Jerry gently ease a sleeping Lulu onto a gurney.

"She should wake up in an hour or two," said Minks. "And I can assure you, she'll be perfectly fine. You just sit here for a minute. You just rest."

"I'll be okay," he said.

"You look a little groggy," said Jerry.

Cody managed a weak grin. "I feel a little groggy," he said.

The two doctors wheeled Lulu to the adjoining bunkroom.

Cody's body felt stiff, numb. His eyes felt blasted by the bright infirmary, as if, like the Meek, he couldn't tolerate excessive light anymore. He felt dull and slow-witted. One of Axworthy's young recruits came into the infirmary, and Cody looked at it him as if the recruit were part of a dream, as if the black uniform and the gold epaulets, the side-arm, and the truncheon were all simply fabrications of his own imagination. The recruit looked alarmed, his face slack with the seriousness of whatever it was he had to convey, and Cody dimly realized that something bad must have happened; the poor recruit couldn't have had such a bloodless complexion otherwise.

"Where's Dr. Minks?" asked the recruit.

His voice seemed unnecessarily loud to Cody, and Cody

wondered if the Meek, with their long, slender ears, were more sensitive to sound than ordinary humans. He worked to formulate a response, but he kept on seeing the burning buildings, a young Lulu chasing the boy with a sharpened pole, blood pumping from the boy's back.

"He and Jerry just wheeled Lulu into the bunkroom."

The recruit's eyes flicked toward the bunkroom. The young man seemed to be shaking. He beelined for the bunkroom door but he walked in a jerky weak-kneed way, looking as if he were about to collapse. Cody watched him go but felt only a passing curiosity. He continued to sit in his chair, awake but not awake, squinting against the infirmary lights. He thought of the blue cellophane. Ceres in pink. Earth in turquoise. Thought of the philosophy of eternal peace. Of Lulu's worrisome evasiveness. Dr. Minks came into the infirmary on his way to the command center, walking fast. Here was another emergency, thought Cody. He now seemed to live in a world of emergencies. Dr. Minks went out the opposite door. Cody felt he should be doing something to help, but he was enveloped in a mental fog, couldn't control his thoughts—thoughts of trees hung with blue glow-moss, of five moons, of the sound of music played on crystal chimes. Jerry and the young recruit came into the infirmary on their way to the main part of the bunker. Cody roused himself.

"What happened?" he asked.

Jerry turned to him, looked at him the way a sober person might look at someone who was drunk. The recruit didn't bother waiting, continued out the door.

"Danny Vigo and his crew are dead," said Jerry. Jerry's voice, sounding as if it were coming from a great distance, was nasal and tight. Cody at first couldn't comprehend his meaning. The doctor's eyes were wide. Cody shook his head, tried to clear his mind. "They just dropped dead out on the surface," said Jerry. "Their biofeedback readouts in the control room flatlined. The recruit told us they have footage from Vigo's visor-cam."

Vigo. Cody sat up straight. His spine was as straight as a ruler, but he still felt drowsy. Jerry gave him one last look and hurried out the door to the control room. Cody put his hands on his knees. He tried to get the facts straight. Vigo. Recruits dead. He thought of Joe. Of Wolf. Death seemed to haunt this place. Corpses everywhere. And now another ten on the surface. Young men. Yes. He had it right now. At least he thought he did. But he'd better go out and check.

He got up like an old man and walked carefully into the main part of the bunker. Commander Axworthy was holding an emergency session. Cody listened to the scattered, broken, and sometimes panicked conversation, stood there getting his bearings, at first too dazed to make much sense of it, feeling as if he were still in the thrall of Lulu's kiss. But as he put it all together he realized that Jerry was right, that Danny Vigo and his platoon, halfway back from the silo, had mysteriously, inexplicably, terrifyingly, dropped dead, falling like stones one after another into the ageless Ceresian dust.

Axworthy was too busy to listen right away to what Cody had to say about his communication with Lulu. Cody felt too tired to talk about it anyway. He shuffled over to the mess hall section of the bunker, sat on one of the metal chairs, and watched the activity.

Everyone watched the footage from Vigo's visor-cam: a view of meteorite-impacted terrain, a hill off to the left, some rocks in the immediate foreground, the sun slanting at a sharp angle from the left, making the shadows long. Then Vigo pitched headfirst into the dirt and that was it. All they saw was the concave shallow that Vigo's visor made in the ground.

Bruder came in with two other recruits, his face red, his eyes wide, and told the commander that his brother, first platoon's demolition engineer, was dead.

"He died with the rest of them, sir," he said, as if he somehow believed his brother would have been the only one to survive.

Bruder sat heavily in a chair. He was a large young man with a square head, his blond hair snipped into a crew cut, his shoulders and biceps huge, his blue eyes tiny, now filled with tears—tears that he quickly wiped away. Bruder's pain came to Cody in fragments of choked rage, as a nearly uncontrollable urge to run out to the surface to find his brother, and as a smoldering hatred for whoever might have been responsible. Axworthy put a hand on Bruder's shoulder, and Bruder hung his head.

"I've ordered a remote surveillance robot out to the site, son," said Axworthy. "The pictures will be coming back any minute. If you want to leave the room . . ."

Bruder's face hardened and his eyes dried up, and he looked like a soldier again. "No, sir," he said. "I'll stay and watch, sir. If you don't mind. Sir."

A minute later pictures of the grim scene flickered across the screen.

Ten bodies in gray pressure suits that perfectly matched the color of the asteroid—standard camouflage in the Belt—lay in the frigid dirt, strung out in a column fifty meters long, some on their backs, some on their stomachs. The hovering robot fluttered for a few moments over each corpse, took readings for possible life signs, potential agents of contagion, toxins. Biological causes were negative. Toxicity, however, proved positive in the extreme.

"You see?" said Axworthy. The expression on his face was as immovable as stone. "This is what they do. They never fight face-to-face. They like to spring their little traps." He stared at the dead figures on the screen. His jaw came forward and his massive brow pinched toward the bridge of his nose, and Cody realized that despite his emotional armor, Axworthy was taking this badly. Axworthy gave his head a shake, turned to his chemist. "Czaplinski, what kind of poison can act that fast?"

Cody thought of his own attempt to enter one of the surface structures, how he might have lost his own life had he actually succeeded. He now had doubts about the Meek.

How could he not have doubts when they had snuffed out the lives of ten young men?

"We'll have to roll back Vigo's visor-cam footage if we're going to find out," said Czaplinski.

They wound Vigo's video back an hour, trying to determine the exact time of poisoning, starting it just as Vigo and his crew entered the freshly breached structure. Czaplinski enhanced the footage spectrographically. As Vigo went into the main vault of the silo the spectrometer detected a small burst overhead.

Czaplinski, after a few minutes, matched the spectrographic readings of the burst to a known toxic agent.

"It's ricin," he said, "a highly lethal derivative of the castor nut. I've also detected a chemical demolecularizer, something that allowed the poison to pass through the submolecular spaces of the platoon's pressure suits. Skin contact with even a few grains of ricin causes fatal congestion in the heart, lungs, and circulatory system. I would say it took the demolecularizer an hour to get through. They had the ricin clinging to their suits, and because this particular poison takes such minuscule amounts to be fatal, it wasn't detected by the platoon. The ricin finally got through when they were coming back. Once the skin comes into contact with ricin it takes about thirty seconds. That's why they got no warning." Czaplinski glanced at Bruder then turned back to Axworthy. "That's why they just dropped dead like that."

A silence settled over the group. With the facts clearly established Cody could see they were all thinking about what they should do next, that they were in that moment of stasis where shocked reactions now had to make way for practical responses. He turned to Bruder. Bruder just sat there, looking at the infirmary door. Cody tried to read the young recruit's thoughts and was at least partially successful. Bruder was thinking of Lulu. Bruder was blaming Lulu for what had just happened to his brother

*   *   *

Ben was back. Recovered from his stroke, thanks to Lulu's recoding.

Cody and Ben were out on the surface. The Meek had come out here and wrecked a lot of their work by sabotaging the solar-power generating plant's optic cable. Dr. Minks had conducted both psychological and medical laboratory testing on Cody and Ben, had ruled them fit and given them the green light to go ahead and work. Cody was glad. Work always made him feel better. He and Ben discussed the deaths of the recruits as they repaired the damaged optic cable.

"This is what I don't understand," said Cody. "How someone like Lulu can try and save us, how she can work for hours on you so your aneurysm repairs itself, and then all these young men lose their lives to a Meek booby trap."

Ben, subdued from his experience, went about the work of excavating the damaged optic cable in a quiet remote way.

"The Meek obviously have their reasons for protecting the site," he said.

He bent down and cleared some dirt from around a cable with his fingers. Cody felt something coming from Ben, and, closing his eyes, saw it, a vision of rain.

"Why are you thinking of rain?" asked Cody.

"Is that you?" asked Ben. "That flower smell?"

"That's me," said Cody.

Ben nodded, rubbed a little more dirt away. "I'm thinking of rain . . . because . . . because I had this . . . this weird dream . . . I dreamed that I was on a boat with a lot of Meek. I was the only human there and we were in the middle of an ocean or a lake, and it was raining and we couldn't see that far, and the rain was warm, and the waves were getting bigger." He stopped, sounded out of breath, turned to Cody. "What do you suppose that means?"

Cody shook his head. "I don't know." But if it were a dream of precognition, he certainly didn't like the sound of it.

"I can tell you're concerned about something," said Ben. "Look at us. We're a couple of Meek. We can't keep secrets from each other anymore."

"I would never keep any secrets from you, Ben."

"Then what's bothering you?"

Cody took a deep breath, frowned. "I just don't like the way Bruder looks at Lulu now," said Cody. "He's going to hurt her. I can feel it."

Ben stood up. "He's lost his brother."

"So why blame Lulu?" asked Cody.

"Because he doesn't know any better." Ben lifted his hands, looked at the gray dust all over his pressure gloves, brushed them off. "He's 19. And he hurts." Cody felt a sudden concern from Ben, emanations carried through his mind on a scent that was reminiscent of citrus. "Were you able to think straight immediately after Christine died? I don't think you were."

"No, I wasn't. But I didn't want to kill anyone."

Ben turned toward the transmission tower, grew still. "Do you feel that?"

"What?"

"It's Agatha," said Ben.

"Agatha? Are you sure?"

"I can sense her," said Ben. "She's over there by the microwave transmission tower. And she's thinking of you. She wants you to go see her."

"She does?"

"I had Lulu kissing me for hours. She fixed more than my aneurysm."

Cody stared at the microwave transmission tower. The tower rose up into the black starry sky, matte-white, a simple and elegant piece of engineering. He now whiffed the vague scent of pine, Agatha creeping into his head.

Agatha said: *Don't be afraid. It's just me. Buster wants to see you.*

Cody looked at Ben; the sun glistened like a bright nugget of gold in Ben's yellow-tinted visor.

"Should I go?" asked Cody.

"I think you better."

He turned to the transmission tower again. Agatha stepped out from behind the tower into the harsh glare of the sun, wrapped in orange tape from head to foot, reflective and fluorescent, a slit for her eyes, her hands and feet bare, dim blue. Like a creature from a dream. The skintight orange tape—the same tape Lulu had used to fix his pressure suit—accentuated her curves, made her arms and legs look slender, perfect. He felt an unexpected concern coming from her. For Ben. He wanted to reassure her.

He said: *Ben's okay.*

She liked Ben?

She said: *Are you going to come with me? Buster wants to see you right now.*

He turned to Ben. "This might be our chance to talk to them."

"That's what I thought," said Ben. Cody heard him sigh—he was a more melancholy man since nearly losing his life. "How much oxygen do you have?"

"Seven hours."

Ben looked at the exposed optical cable. "She wants you to go alone. I'll stay here. I might as well work."

Cody stared at Agatha, and he did indeed sense this, that she wanted him to come alone, that this was what Buster expected.

Agatha said: *You love my sister?*

Cody was surprised. The notion had never occurred to him. She was digging into levels of his mind that not even he knew about. He was going to have to think about that. But not right now. He unlatched his location transmitter and handed it to Ben.

"Here," he said.

"Good luck," said Ben.

*   *   *

He followed Agatha east of the solar-power generating plant. Strange to see her bare feet leaving impressions in the gray dust. Strange to see her eyes exposed to the cold vacuum of space, to see her hands free and ungloved.

They continued east past the oxygen mine, past the slag heaps of carbon dust, Cody white and bulky in his suit, Agatha orange and streamlined. They ventured into hilly, cratered terrain. The sun shone directly ahead of them—sunrise on Ceres, an angry white ball. They climbed a ridge. On the other side of the ridge he saw untouched asteroidal terrain. Not a sign of civilization anywhere. The black sky of outer space stretched from horizon to horizon, with its stars and its sun, and the tiny crescents of the Ceresian companion asteroids drifting along like a pack of ghouls released from their graves.

Agatha said: *Get ready to jump.*

He looked ahead, thinking he might see a gully, a crevice, a small crater. But the land remained flat, uninterrupted by any particular landform one way or the other.

He said: *Jump where?*

She said: *Right here.*

She jumped. Onto a flat spot in front of him. And disappeared feet first into the ground.

He stopped. Remained frozen for several seconds. Then examined the flat spot. It looked just like the ground everywhere; bits of rock and little unevennesses cast distinct shadows, and those shadows matched the length and direction of the shadows everywhere, something a standard holo-image would never have been able to do.

She said: *What are you waiting for? I'm way ahead of you.*

He squatted and pressed his hand flat to the ground. It went right through. What high technology was this? A holo-image that changed and blended with its environment according to time of day? He lifted a rock and dropped it on top of the flat spot. The rock stayed on top. Pitted the holo-image ground in a natural and convincing way. He shook his

head. He remembered how Axworthy had been so amazed
when Azim's scanner showed hundreds of Meek burrowing
right through the solid rock of Newton's eastern bulkhead.
Now he knew how.

He jumped . . .

He slid down a long tube. He had no idea what the tube
was made from; it was unlike any material he had ever seen
before, frictionless. He moved at great speed, eventually
slowed by wind blowing up the tube, a progressively
stronger wind. He kept rolling and spinning against the
walls of the tube until, eased by the updraft, he finally sank
into a large cavern.

The cavern was lit by glow-moss and populated by blue
people, seventeen altogether, one of them Buster.

Buster stepped forward and peered at him closely, his violet eyes glowing in the light of the luminescent moss. Cody
tried to sense something from Buster, tried to read his emanations, but he might as well have tried to read the brain-
wave patterns of a rock. Buster blocked. Buster was as tight
and as impenetrable as an airlock.

Buster said: *There's plenty of air to breathe.*

Cody checked the atmospheric reading of his visor. Atmospheric pressure was seven hundred millibars: thin, like
high-mountain air, but still breathable. He cycled the air inside his suit to match the pressure outside, swallowing as his
ears popped, and took off his helmet.

He saw that the cavern was a perfectly polished sphere
with ledges and perches for the various Meek to sit. He saw
seven women, all bare-breasted, ten men, also without
shirts, and Agatha, wrapped in her orange tape. The luminescent moss hung from the various perches and gave the
room an azure radiance, reminded Cody of the James Cook
Coral Reef Habitat on Vesta, of the snorkeling trips he'd
taken there with Christine, the water so blue and clear.

Buster said: *What kind of man are you, Cody?*

Cody felt wind in his mind, only it was a hot wind, an
angry wind, smelled like creosote, tarry and thick. Buster

licked his fingers and pressed them to Cody's lips. The wind blew stronger and the smell of creosote became overpowering.

Buster said: *I want to know you.*

Buster put his hands on Cody's shoulders. Cody backed away, but the wind—Buster's scent—was too strong, and Cody's feet felt glued to the spot, buzzing with pins and needles. Buster drew his face closer, then kissed him. Cody had never kissed a man before. He expected revulsion, yet all he felt was fear. He couldn't move, as if numbed by venom, as powerless as a fly caught in a spider's web. The wavering blue light of the moss began to fade. He felt that same sense of surrender, that giving in, as he had felt with Lulu. The spherical cavern disappeared around him. He felt . . . untethered. Brief images flickered through his mind. Not images of Lulu's life, or Buster's life, but images of his own life . . . Buster finding out what kind of man he was.

He saw his mother swimming in the lake at the William Wordsworth Lake Country Habitat, with the hills green and lush around her, slate fences crisscrossing the countryside, sheep penned in, cottage roofs thatched, country roads no wider than a hop, skip, and jump. His mother smiled. His dad jumped out of the waves behind her, splashed her. A perfect marriage, what he aspired to. His brother, Craig, twelve years old in this particular vision, pedaled a pedal boat around the lake, introducing himself to all the various swimmers, a precocious boy with impeccable manners, shaking hands with the bathers and rowboaters in an adult way.

Then Christine at the same lake—they owned the place now; his dad's appointment to the University of Murray City on Mars meant his parents were unlikely to ever visit Vesta again. And Craig, now on the Moon—Earth's fair old Luna—followed his own academic career, a junior professor of history. Craig would be unlikely to return to Vesta as well. Too busy with university life, the three of them; the Wisners were traditionally academic. But not Cody.

Buster said: *You were the oddball, the boy who disap-*

Scott Mackay

*pointed his parents, the boy who did whatever he wanted,
didn't care about school, never went to college, just wanted
to build things, to use his hands, the boy who wanted to mas-
ter every tool ever devised by the hand of man. The boy, and
finally the man, who always went his own way. Is that why
she loves you? Because you're independent? Is that why
Lulu cares so much?*

Back to his own life, the creosote smell cutting it open
with knifelike precision . . .

Stayed on Vesta because he loved Vesta, the whole idea
of Vesta, the safe little rock, brighter than all the other asteroids, loved the challenge of Vesta, how Vesta worked, how
it supported humans, the engineering and structural miracle
of Vesta. Fascinated by the intricate system of airlocks. Took
a course in airlock mechanics. How to build a better airlock.
And the bulwarks. How to keep a bubble of air intact. How
to keep this living cell that was Vesta, with all its millions of
people, its five major cities, 180 natural habitats, its oxygen
mines, space ports, and military installations, a viable and
self-sustaining microverse in the nothingness of outer space.

Buster said: *You love your home. We have this much in
common.*

Then a course in nano-technology: the use of artificial
bioforms in the construction and life-support industries. Finally, trade school. His parents showered praise on Craig because Craig was tenured at the relatively young age of 35,
praised Craig because he sang tenor in an amateur madrigal
group and had published a whimsical article on the history
of Lunar winemaking. But didn't care when Cody built a
walnut armoire with intricate dovetailing and traditional
Georgian carving.

Buster said: *They were on Mars, eighteen days away at
opposition, but as far as you were concerned, they were
gone. Gone for good.* Buster taunting. Enjoying this. Playing this sour note. *To them, you were nothing but a man with
a hammer and a saw.*

A fascination with the potentiality of biological airlocks,

airlocks that would instantly heal themselves at the slightest rupture. As if there were no greater altar upon which to worship than the airlock. An obsession, securing for Cody the position of Inspector-in-Chief, Airlocks Division, Public Works Department, Vesta City, Vesta. Two years of inspecting airlocks all over Vesta, making a lot of money, but finally growing tired of it, finally wanting to do something definitive against the vacuum, against the specter of instant death that loomed in the minds of all Vestans. Buster probed deeper, followed this, the professional side of his life. Cody Wisner on a crusade for the perfect airlock. Talking to industrialists, chemists, and biologists. Single-handedly becoming the catalyst, the man who developed what in the popular press was called insta-seal, what in research they called pressure-triggered bioconnective, a tough, cold-resistant biomorph that jumped from dormancy to full metabolic function in seconds if air pressure varied more than a hundred millibars.

Buster said: *Working for the public good. We have this in common too.*

But then blaming himself for the collapse in Residential Sector 5, such an unimaginative name for such a beautiful suburb. Everything on Vesta was unimaginatively named, including the capital city. Not like on Ceres, where all the names had an educational slant. Blaming himself because he was a builder, had been on the pressure-wall advisory committee for Residential Sector 5, gave the developers the go-ahead, should have looked deeper into the new grav-core, should have warned them to design a sky that could withstand fluctuations in gravity. Blamed himself because by then he was a force to be reckoned with in Public Works, a man with a voice, third from the top, closer to politics than to building, someone who could have actually done something to prevent the collapse.

Buster taunted: *A man with a voice. Only you didn't speak out. A man working twenty hours a day to effect the conversion of Vesta from rim-grav to grav-core, to take a city that rested upside down on the inside of the asteroid's crust and to place it right side up in excavated caverns, to go from centrifugal gravity to centripetal gravity, a measure that greatly stabilized Vesta's tidal flux tolerances. The greatest engineering project the Belt had ever seen. But not without its casualties. Not without the collapse of Residential Sector 5. A microscopic particle of a singularity is an untamed beast. I know. We have one in the core. One that's gone wild. A black hole can easily tear down the roof. You can't tame it. I've learned the hard way.*

Cody surfaced from the kiss. Surfaced because Buster had at last revealed a part of himself. He felt Buster's guilt. And ironically, the guilt was the same; Buster insisted on taking blame just as Cody insisted on taking blame, the root cause identical, a speck of black hole no bigger than a mustard seed, the one inside Vesta, the one inside Ceres. Cody pushed. Felt Buster's surprise. Cody wasn't supposed to be able to push. Cody was human, not orphan, not Meek; how could he push at the mind of someone as talented as Buster? Cody tried to walk through Buster's mind, and again felt Buster's surprise. That someone human could push in this way interested Buster. *You try to know me?* He felt Buster's curiosity. *We suspected you might have talent.* But Buster had to find out. Walked right in. And opened another of Cody's memories, as easily as he might open a computer file . . .

Ceres, 34 years ago, when he and his father had traveled to Newton from Vesta for Cody's possible enrollment in any of the numerous boarding schools. A chance to grow up straight and strong. A one-gee child.

There he was, just turned five, wearing gray because gray was what children wore on Vesta, stodgy, conservative Vesta. Cody was on Ceres undergoing Guthrie Testing to see if he had any psi talent; Vestan children were known for their psi talent, a peculiar coding in, yes, chromosome 3, that had been emphasized and reemphasized in the relatively isolated Vestan population through the centuries, a genetic resource that usually meant free tuition to the best schools on Ceres for Vestan children who had a particularly strong talent.

The Guthrie Tests. He remembered them now. Remembered sitting in a classroom with some other Vestan children. The teacher at the front—a man with no particular psi talent at all—imagined a mortar and pestle. Cody's job was to retrieve and draw. Cody drew a mortar and pestle. The teacher at the front imagined a treble clef, something Cody had never seen before. Cody drew a treble clef. Another teacher walked up and down the rows winnowing, sending children out of the room depending on their degree of success or failure. The teacher at the front imagined a wineglass. Cody drew a wineglass. The teacher was anxious. Cody didn't know how to draw anxiety, so he just left the paper blank. The teacher had another class to go to, was late for it, had to rush the testing. That's why he was anxious. So he skipped a lot and went to the harder stuff.

A fairly detailed image of Buddha, carved in jade. Cody drew Buddha, had no idea what he was drawing, but drew it anyway. The teacher imagined a model of an ammonia molecule—one nitrogen, three hydrogen—and Cody drew that. The teacher imagined the continent of South America. Cody drew that. The teacher spoke to the other teacher. Cody could again sense the man's anxiety. He had to teach a class today—substituting—on an obscure Canadian humorist by the name of Stephen Leacock, was planning on opening with a quote he kept thinking about even as he begged his colleague to take over the final testing so he could make it on time. Cody thought the quote was part of the testing. He raised his hand.

"Yes, Cody," said the teacher.

" 'I am a great believer in luck, and I find the harder I work the more I have of it.' "

A quote that stuck with him for life.

The two teachers stared at him.

The next day he was offered a scholarship and free board.

The following day the orphans attacked the suburb of Planck's Constant.

The day after that he and his father flew back to Vesta.

Buster said: *This is why we need you as our go-between. Because you can talk to us so well. We suspected this about you right from the start. That's why we kept coming to watch you when you first got here. And this is why we must use you now.*

Cody felt himself pushing again, understanding at last how he could trigger a penetration into Buster's mind. By doing it the same way Agatha did. With the smell of pine.

A smell that, as a carpenter, he knew so well.

CHAPTER 13

Cody pushed, and again felt Buster's surprise. Then his anger. Then his struggle to break away. And finally his resignation. The smell of pine, Agatha's scent, was like a password into Buster's mind. A cloak of invisibility. Something he could use to get past Buster's heavy creosote blocking. He slipped past like mist through trees.

The first thing Cody wanted to know was why Buster had killed all those young men.

Buster said: *Because the silos, as you call them, represent our last chance.*

Cody probed for a further explanation, but even with the smell of Agatha's pine Buster's thoughts about the last chance were so safely blocked, so impenetrably encoded in their own complexity, all Cody saw was the mental equivalent of a thousand-piece jigsaw puzzle dumped freshly out of the box.

Buster offered something about himself as a way to change the subject: *I am the original. I am the oldest. I am the one who can never entirely forget the ways of the clans.*

Impressions, images, segments, and, at least to Cody, bizarre episodes from Buster's life floated through his mind. Buster as a child, no mother, no father, born in what the Martians called a genetic crèche; the first child, a small brown child, with long arms and short legs, Leonard Carswell's answer to the future, to design a people who could live in harmony with the Martian ecosphere, and, in particular, could live in the 3,500-mile-long gorge known as the Valles Marineris, where, in its deepest part 10 kilometers down the atmosphere was thick, the temperatures warmer, and the soil could be turned for the cultivation of windbloom. Yes, the first child, the first orphan, the Adam of his race, but so unspeakably lonely, an island unto himself.

Buster said: *But then he made others. It didn't matter. I resented Carswell. I hated how part of my genetic code always made me feel suspicious. I resented how part of my genetic code always made me feel threatened. I understood why Carswell did it. You have to feel threatened if you're going to live in Valles Marineris. But I couldn't forgive him. You can never know peace if you're always suspicious, if you always feel threatened.*

More episodes. Buster as a young man, taped up the way Agatha was taped up, spading the red oxidized soil in the bottom of the Valley, trying to make windbloom grow, putting the spade aside, spraying the ground with what he called splice crystals, chemically treated water that wouldn't sublimate from ice to gas in the thin cold atmosphere, moisture that remained tenable long enough to give the windbloom at least some meager sustenance. Working all day, then climbing, with his extra-long arms, the steep sides of the Valley, up to where his clan lived in the caverns. Cody *became* Buster. Buster knew everyone was afraid of him. Made sure everyone was afraid of him. Fear bred discipline, and discipline was his best weapon in the ongoing feuds with the other clans.

Buster said: *We fight, Cody. Carswell never meant this, or maybe he did, but somehow the fighting took hold, ruled our lives, made us war with each other. We fought over the sunniest, warmest spots in the Valley. We fought over the biggest ice deposits. We fought over the parachute drops the relief agencies in Murray City constantly sent us. Fought even when we had nothing to fight about. I hate fighting, Cody. The Father helped us stop fighting. The Father made us peaceful. At least as peaceful as he could. But there's always the ghost code, the genetic memory that reminds us of who we once were. Those of us who were born in the crèche, of direct orphan stock, might have blue skins, might profess brotherhood and peace, but we still have our black hearts. We know how to sniff our enemies, how to detect a threat, and Axworthy and his crew are a threat.*

These thoughts and feelings came so fast that Cody felt overwhelmed by them. Other thoughts now, about the great plan, about the thing Buster had spent the last 25 years of his life working on, the last chance; quick-edits of a thousand little scenes, a comet out in the Oort Cloud, a building collapsing in Equilibrium, a vast hangar full of landers, a forest of asparagus-like trees, a diagram of orbital trajectories. A volcano, a cloudy sky, and people walking along a caldera. Distressing images. Puzzling images. Images that were the disjointed integers of an inscrutable equation Cody had no hope of understanding. And underneath it all, the ache of Buster's love for Lulu.

Buster said: *She wants a husband. Not a leader. She wants someone who will make sacrifices for the sake of love. I can't make sacrifices for her because I've sacrificed everything for the sake of my people.*

Cody sensed somewhere inside Buster an emotional vacancy. This seemed to be Buster's greatest personal secret, this deficiency. And nothing angered Buster more than to have somebody discover it. Buster's anger flared, and the pine scent was swept away by the overwhelming scent of creosote. Buster said, in spite of himself: *You came here to present yourself as a hostage in the hope that you could stop your own people from hurting Lulu. I could never do that because I believe in my cause. I am the cause. You are making me lose Lulu because I have no choice but to fight for the cause. And that's where you win.*

The kiss ended, reality patched itself together fragment by fragment, and Cody found himself sitting on the floor of the spherical chamber, the taste of blood in his mouth, a gash on his lip, his head pounding with a violent ache. He took a sudden deep breath.

He struggled to his feet and found Buster looking at him with cagey violet eyes.

Buster said: *You will leave. All of you. We ask you this. You will go back and tell Axworthy. This has been decided. We will not harm you if you all leave now. You can do this. You have the* Conrad Wilson *now. We renounce violence. But we of the crèche and of the Valley remember violence. Our blood still tingles with the ghost codes. I have been chastised by the Father for my attack, even though I wished only to free Agatha and Lulu. The Father has censured me for the death of your crewmen, but I tell him that I can never entirely forget Carswell and the crèche, or those cold hard years in the Valley when the Martians made us live outside. I can't forget, for the old ways still run in my blood. You wish to again inhabit Ceres, but I tell you, Ceres belongs to us. If you fill it with air, we will take the air away. If you drink the water, we will poison the water. Ceres is a labyrinth, full of new tunnels, caverns, and passageways, and each one is booby-trapped. Ceres is a deadly place meant to keep intruders away. History repeats itself. I ask you to evacuate. Suffer the consequences if you refuse.*

Cody gave Axworthy a rundown of what had happened, told him about the spherical room and his conversation with Buster. Axworthy stared at him for a long time after that, his blue eyes sharp and clear under the heavy ridge of his brow. Falcon eyes, predatory in their concentration. Axworthy leaned back in his chair, lifted one knee over the other, and folded his hands on his lap.

"You know what you did was reckless," he said. "You risked your life and possibly the lives of others. For a Public Works employee to remove his location transmitter during surface repairs represents, as you well know, a violation of the Labor Safety Act of 2631, and could result in a year's suspension without pay."

Cody contemplated the commander. "For someone who was born on Ceres you sure talk like a Vestan." He rubbed his split lip, an injury from the violence of Buster's kiss.

"My job here is to protect you," said Axworthy. "How can I do that if you decide to do things like this?"

"They're going to depressurize Newton again," Cody said. "Buster wants us to leave. He expects an answer in ten hours."

Axworthy's face remained motionless. "He feels he's in a position to make demands?"

Cody's eyes narrowed. "You know Buster?" he said.

Axworthy looked at Cody steadily. "I know a lot more than you think," he said.

Cody tried to sense emanations from Axworthy, but he got nothing; Axworthy had never been kissed by Lulu or anyone else, hadn't had any long-term exposure to the marrow, and under those circumstances Cody simply didn't have the skill to probe.

Cody finally nodded. "Buster says the whole asteroid is booby-trapped," he said. "If any of your men stray to any of their critical sites they'll end up like Vigo's men."

Axworthy's face looked as hard as concrete. He picked up a computer disk and tapped it absently against his desk a few times. "And he knows that Ceres rightfully belongs to us?"

Cody took a deep breath. "It wasn't that kind of conversation, Commander."

"Call me Kevin. Let's not let formality get in the way of understanding each other."

"In fact, it really wasn't much of a conversation at all. It all happened . . ." He thought about it, then tapped the side of his head. "It all happened up here. And when it happens up there, it's multistranded."

Axworthy nodded. He put the computer disk down. "How are they going to depressurize Newton?" he asked. "We have all the municipal airlocks wired to our own mainframe, guarded by automated antipersonnel units, and watched day and night by surveillance robots. If you were able to wander freely inside his head—"

"Sabotage."

"I'd like to see him try." Axworthy looked thoughtfully at the door. "Still, we'd better take some precautions. Can you scale back your crew at all? How many do you realistically need to get the emergency shelter up and running again? That's a priority now that the Meek have threatened us with this depressurization."

"It depends on how fast you want it up and running."

"How long do you think I can stall Buster?"

Cody shook his head. "No," he said. "It can't work like that. Not with Buster. He can walk right through your mind. You can't lie to him. You can't try to flimflam him. There's no hiding anything from Buster."

Axworthy lifted his hands. "I need a crew of eighteen. We have an oxygen pod in case they get lucky and succeed in depressurizing Newton. It's old, but it can support twenty-four people for 24 hours if it has to. For emergency use only. We still have lots of tanked oxygen left. We'll put the pod in the emergency shelter, make it harder for the orphans to attack it that way, and I'll post automated antipersonnel units everywhere in the vicinity. When the Meek try to force us to leave Newton, we'll use the emergency shelter as our first fallback. If we have to, we'll go to the oxygen pod, not only for air but for protection. That pod's built tough."

Cody's eyes widened. "You mean you're not going to leave?" he said.

"My orders are to stay," he said. "I'm to secure Newton. Or at least hold it until reinforcements arrive."

"Yes, but what's the latest population count?" asked Cody. "Have you been checking the tracking microgens?"

"Six hundred and twenty thousand," said Axworthy. "Most of them out in Torque. Some out in the Angles. Some around Equilibrium."

"And you think you can defend Newton against that many Meek?"

"We don't think the count's going to go much higher."

"But 620,000, Kevin," said Cody.

"We have a lot of ammunition. And if they want to play with poison, we have a lot of that too. We don't want it to get to that, but if it does, we're ready. Those are my orders." Axworthy grinned but it was a melancholy grin, and Cody could see that Axworthy regretted the whole situation. "I'm afraid the tracking microgen does more than just track. It targets. Figuratively paints a bull's-eye on every Meek's back. That's why I hope things don't get much more escalated than they already are. You're right, we're only forty recruits, eighteen when I scale it back, but we're weapons-rated for a full-fledged siege of Newton with all this automatic and remote-controlled equipment we have. We can hold the city against a hundred thousand if we have to, now that we're all set up."

Cody realized the man was serious, that he was talking war. Axworthy saw the look on Cody's face and shook his head.

"Cody . . ." Axworthy took a deep breath and folded his hands on his desk. "Cody, while you were gone, out to talk to Buster, I knew what Buster was going to do. I knew he was going to give you an ultimatum. That's what I remember about the way the orphans worked. They were always full of ultimatums. So I contacted Vesta City and I told them what was going on, and they quickly cobbled together a counteroffer, something, in fact, that they've been looking at for the past several days. They're mostly hard-liners in Council, you know that, but they're not unreasonable men and women, and they're willing to give the orphans a chance. They don't want to see bloodshed any more than you or I, but if it comes to that . . . especially with the orphans . . ."

"They call themselves the Meek now."

"Yes, but they're essentially still the same. You're not

going to get any of those Council members believing otherwise."

"They're human beings."

"I agree with you," said Axworthy. "And when I lived on
Ceres, when I went to college here, nothing infuriated me
more than when my friends or fellow students, even my pro-
fessors, characterized the orphans as . . . well, as . . . you
know. As thieves. As con artists. As killers."

"Isn't that a bit harsh?" said Cody. "That's not what I get
from Buster at all."

"Buster . . . he's going to leave certain parts out. In fact,
I bet he left out half of it. Maybe I should give you a little
background."

"What about Vesta City's counteroffer?" asked Cody,
anxious to know about it.

"In a minute," said Axworthy. "I think this is important.
I think you should know about this." It sounded more like an
order than a suggestion. "I believe in persuasion, and I think
you need some persuading." He sat back, got his thoughts in
order. "You see, my dad tried to help the orphans, like I was
telling you before, and I was always around them, and I
liked them, at least at the beginning." He nodded at the rec-
ollection. "I knew Buster and a few of the others personally.
My father was a compassionate man. He wanted to help
them." Axworthy peered at Cody as if he somehow had to
decipher him. "Whatever Buster told you . . . about how it
all began . . . but Buster . . . I don't trust him to give you an
unbiased picture. Do you know much about how it all got
started?"

"I know a bit about Carswell."

Axworthy nodded. "In the early days, when I was a child,
my father was in constant contact with Leonard Carswell,
was a good friend of Lenny's. My dad was a pioneering ge-
neticist in his own right. Before he was killed, he was a leading agrigeneticist in the Belt. Everything we eat out here, he
had a hand in. So naturally he was interested in the orphans.
He thought he might be able to help. You could do a lot with

genetics on Mars back in those days. You didn't have the same kind of strict legislation there that you had on Earth. You got to try new things on Mars. Murray City became known for technological and biological innovation. They had no laws against making humans in test tubes as long as it could be shown that such practices might benefit the Martian community as a whole. Lenny went ahead and made all these orphans, tampering with chromosome 3, the chromosome that controls pigment, respiration, skin growth, intuition, and survival instincts. He wrote suspicion right into it. Suspicion goes with survival. So do fighting skills. So does bald-faced lying. In other words, he made them tough." Axworthy shook his head. "But he went too far, Cody, and he made them criminally tough. He made 423 of them, raised them in the crèche till they were in their late teens, then sent them out onto the surface. They bred. In ten years there were 3,000 of them. They're designed to hit puberty around the age of nine. Three thousand quickly became 15,000. Except for the original 423, what you had out on the surface was a society of kids having babies. And they didn't like living out in the cold."

"I wouldn't think they would," said Cody. "I'm surprised they could even survive."

Axworthy leaned back in his chair and gazed at the ceiling, thinking about the whole thing. "They could survive, oh, sure, they could survive," he said, "but there's a big difference between surviving and living. That was the basic flaw in the whole scheme. Lenny was a brilliant scientist but he was really simplistic in a lot of ways. He forgot one important thing. People demand the right to live wherever they choose, even ones specifically engineered to populate a certain ecological niche. The orphans didn't want to live out in the cold. They wanted to come inside where it was warm. Buster negotiated for fifteen years. You don't know how surprised I am to find him still alive on Ceres. He must be well into his eighties, my father's age if my father were still alive."

Cody's eyes widened. "He's that old? He doesn't look much past my age."

"Carswell's design," said Axworthy. "The orphans are long-lived. A survival strategy. I bet Lulu is a lot older than she actually looks too."

Cody took a few moments to digest all this. Then he said, "So they finally gained the right to live inside?"

Axworthy nodded. "Buster knew how to agitate. Or, if you want to take a cynical view, he knew how to con a lot of left-leaning Martians into sympathizing with his cause. But it didn't happen overnight. Like I said, it took him fifteen years of negotiating before the Martians finally let them come inside. Most of them were between fifteen and 25 years old by that time. Except, of course, the original group, who were a lot older. They struggled to assimilate. And for a while it worked." Axworthy laid his hands flat on the desk. "Lenny was against the assimilation right from the start. The whole point of the orphans, he said, was to begin the adaptation of humans to life on the Martian surface, a way to spare Mars all the ecologically destructive terraforming they were going to do. If you read the transcripts of the communications he had with my father you see that he's bitter about the whole thing. He thinks Buster betrayed him. He expected Buster to help him form a kind of Martian utopia on the surface. He really believed in that. It was quite an issue at the time. You're too young but I remember endless coffeehouse discussions about the orphans, how they were called the New Solution, the Genetic Answer, the only alternative to the ecological wrecking ball of terraforming. God, I've never heard so much hot air in my life. Carswell and my father were at the center of it all. They believed it was wrong to destroy the Martian ecosystem for the purpose of turning it into an Earth-like habitat for humans. Why change the planet when it made better sense to change humans, adapt them genetically to the new environment? Expand the habitable zone not through expensive and grandiose terraforming projects but by the rel-

ranks. And get this. For two years the penal authorities from the Tharsis Bulge got permission to take their most troublesome inmates, change them into orphans, and send them out to the Marineris Commune. A lot of them, even the worst, were turned into slaves by the orphans the minute they reached the settlements. Some of them formed their own clans. A recipe for disaster if there ever was one."

CHAPTER 14

At this point Axworthy got up from his desk, went to the coffeemaker, and poured two cups of coffee. Cody now saw even more reasons why Council had chosen Axworthy to head this particular security effort; the man knew the historical and political situation intimately. Axworthy put the coffee cups on the desk and sat down.

"When the government in Murray City found out what was happening, how the orphans out in the Valley were turning the new volunteers and the exiled convicts into slaves, it quickly legislated an end to Lenny's genetic overwrite efforts. In fact, it closed the whole program down and, at Buster's instigation, outlined measures for a slow assimilation of the existing orphans into Martian society. That's when the basic faults in orphan genetic code became obvious. Some of the orphans, once they moved inside, tried to get legitimate jobs, but the few who did never lasted. They just weren't built for the nine-to-five mainstream."

"Why not?"

"They would work their way in good with some company or corporation, gain its trust, and then bilk it. It was just another con for them. They had absolutely no respect for authority. To make matters worse they pirated Lenny's genetic overwrite program. Children began to disappear. Hundreds of them. Investigation proved that the orphans were kidnapping regular Martian children, turning them into orphans with the genetic overwrite program, then forcing them to be slaves. This was too much. There was a general roundup, and the orphans were put into camps. A lot of liberals were voted out of office, and a lot of hard-liners replaced them. These hard-liners wanted to get rid of the orphans once and for all, and they had a great deal of public support. Banish them from Mars completely. It wasn't good enough to send them all back out to the Valles Marineris again. The hard-liners wanted them right off the planet."

"So that's how they wound up on Ceres?" asked Cody.

Axworthy nodded. "Ceres . . . well, you know Ceres . . . always so liberal, a bastion of humanist causes and beliefs. My father explained to the municipal authorities in Newton that he was developing his own genetic rewrite program. He convinced Isosceles Boulevard that he could rehabilitate the orphans. He told them he was in contact with several of the clan leaders, and that the clan leaders had agreed to give it a try. What other choice did they have? Of course there were detractors—there have always been those who oppose immigration, even in the name of political asylum—and there was a lot of clamor about the kids in Newton, how if the kids in Murray City had begun to disappear, what was to stop that from happening in Newton? But Ceres was built on democratic and liberal beliefs, and those beliefs outweighed what public opinion and legislators concluded, rightly or wrongly, was a relatively small risk. I remember Buster coming to our house once—by then they'd all adopted the standard costume of pants only. In walks this man with skin as brown as coffee, long black hair, fiery brown eyes, and a large knife sheathed to his belt. I remember his arms because his arms practically hung down to his knees. I remember how candid he was with my father."

"In what way?"

"Candid about the way he was. About the way he wanted to change, and about the way his people wanted to change. He said he didn't want to fight anymore, that he was tired of fighting, and tired of not being able to stop himself from fighting. He said he had long believed that it was just a matter of his own willpower, that he could acquire a peaceful nature if he only tried hard enough. But now he knew that wasn't true. There was nothing he could do to change, he said, not unless he got outside help. My father believed in them. He trusted Buster. He helped Buster."

Axworthy stopped. Some color came to his face. Cody saw that this was no longer a dispassionate account of orphan history. Axworthy's feelings about his father had now penetrated the matter.

"Buster really wanted to change," said Axworthy. "He hated the way he was. He hated living every single day of his life feeling angry. My father really tried. Everyone on his staff tried. Schrödinger U was able to get some money from the government, and my father was actually making headway, identifying those letters in chromosome 3 that, while allowing the orphans to live in the harsh conditions of Valles Marineris, also made them fight.

"He started with a test group. The test group showed definite signs of improvement. The orphans you ran into on campus you knew you didn't have to worry about. Buster mobilized support among the orphans, and the government supplied transportation to and from campus clinics, offered a small honorarium as incentive. At first the numbers were small, 10 or 12 a day, but those soon swelled to 20 or 30. You can see the improvement in the crime statistics. Many orphans started finding legitimate employment and didn't try to scam their employers. My father won the Dr. Francis Collins Award for Excellence in Genetic Research. Everything was going great. He was really helping them a lot. What pleased him most was that they were just generally a happier people once they'd undergone his genetic rewrite."

"So how did everything turn bad?" asked Cody.

Axworthy took a deep breath, slouched a bit in his chair, and lowered his chin toward his massive chest. He seemed to shrink, as if the emotion of a moment ago over his father, that flicker of grief, had collapsed like a star into a hot and smoldering kernel of anger.

"Someone in the Ministry of Health thought it might be a good idea to add an extra digit to the health code numbers of those orphans who had refused to submit to my father's procedure. The orphans didn't like that. They reacted strongly against it. You'd have thought we'd asked them to wear yellow stars or the scarlet letter A. That's how crazy they got about it. All it was ever intended to do was alert the physician. Lenny's orphans, the ones who didn't have my father's rewrite, showed an allergic predisposition to certain prescriptions. The extra digit was meant to tell the physician, in a simple and easy way, that he had an orphan who hadn't undergone the rewrite, and that therefore he should be careful about what he prescribed to that orphan. The extra digit was never meant to brand unrehabilitated orphans. But the police and the Ceresian Defense Force latched on to it as the perfect tool. That's what triggered the initial protests. Then . . . you get thousands of unrehabilitated orphans in Laws of Motion Square all at the same time, and you're bound to get violence sooner or later. The thing that makes me maddest of all is that Buster joined the protests. You can't imagine how hurt my father was. He felt as if he'd been betrayed."

Axworthy looked away, too angry for the time being to say anything more. Finally he got control of himself.

"That's when I quit college," he said. "That's when I joined the CDF." He shook his head. "The violence escalated. The recoded orphans didn't come for their treatments anymore. They reverted. You don't know how happy I was when the Vestan Defense Force got involved. There's something to be said for right-wingers and hard-liners in time of war. Didn't do much good in the end, but we were still glad to have them."

"Why did the recoded orphans stop coming for their treatments?" asked Cody. "I thought you said they were a happier people when they had your father's rewrite."

Axworthy nodded. "Certain of the uncoded orphans believed my father was the biggest enemy of all. They said his procedure was nothing but a snow job to drug the orphans into submission. They threatened the recoded orphans."

Axworthy stopped, looked away, and lifted his hand to his mouth as his eyes grew glassy. For several moments he just sat there, his hand clenched in a fist, his knuckles pressed to his lips, but finally he eased his hand away, slowly, as if it took great effort, and looked at Cody with eyes that were at once stalwart and shaky.

In a much quieter voice he said, "A gang of them came for him one night." His face hardened. "They killed him." He sat up straighter, and his eyes regained their hawklike intensity. "How's that for gratitude?" He flipped his palms over, trying to explain it to Cody. "He spends six years trying to help them, believing in them, having faith in them, and then they come in the night for him, and they take their knives to him . . . and . . . it's always overkill with the orphans. Mutilation comes naturally to them. I don't mean stabbed fifty or sixty times. I mean stabbed literally hundreds of times. They cut off his face. They cut off his testicles. They severed his hands and feet. They cut out his liver. How's that for gratitude?"

Axworthy opened his drawer and took out a bottle of pills. He swallowed a few with his coffee, then seemed to realize he had spittle on his chin. He took a silk handkerchief out of his uniform pocket and dabbed it away. He glanced at Cody, regained some of his composure.

"You know," said Axworthy, "joining the Defense Force was the best thing I ever did. I really wasn't cut out for a college career. I guess you and I have that in common."

Cody asked, "What about this counterproposal? The one I'm to take to Buster."

Axworthy nodded. "Council says they're willing to help the Meek leave Ceres," he said. "We'll need a workforce, though, and we'll expect thousands of orphans to volunteer, maybe even tens of thousands."

"Why will you need a workforce?"

"To refit some of Vesta's larger machine and ice transports into passenger vessels. We've got seven decommissioned ones orbiting in their own Kirkwood Gap not far from Pallas. That's upstream about eighteen million klicks. It wouldn't take much to rendezvous. These old ships are huge. If we bunk the Meek seven high, on sixty levels, we should be able to ship them all."

"Ship them where?"

"To Charon."

"Charon?"

"Pluto's moon," said Axworthy.

"I know what it is. You can't send them there."

"Why not?"

"Because not even the Meek could survive there."

"We don't mean them to survive on the surface. We'll give them the means to burrow. We'll support them for a year. They can build their own damn society, like we've built ours here in the Belt."

"But Charon is too remote. How do you expect them to conduct any commerce with us?"

"We don't. They'll have a year and that's it. They'll be on their own then. We'll give them fusion, we'll allow them to go comet-fishing, but otherwise Charon will be guarded round the clock by hunter-killer satellites. The way Vesta City phrased it, the orphans will be in quarantine."

"So you're going to force them to live out in the cold again," said Cody.

"They've done it before; they can do it again."

"But like you say, there's a difference between living and surviving."

After his talk with Axworthy, Cody spent some time at the GK—the unit had been moved into the VDF bunker. He found an image file of the Ceresian Civil Action, thousands of stills, plus a subsidiary file of ten- and twenty-second clips. He concentrated on the stills, feeling a profound disquiet about the whole thing now. Axworthy was at the weapons console with Azim checking the readiness and interface coordination of all the automated weaponry his recruits had set up around the city. Cody went through the images one by one. Thirty years ago. It seemed like a long time ago now. One image showed three Ceresian Defense Force soldiers squatting next to an overturned and gutted maglev car, rifles held loosely at their sides, eyes wide, the whites clearly visible, accentuated by their grimy faces, as if the whites of their eyes were the whole point of the photograph, all three looking in the same direction, waiting for something to happen.

He looked up, saw Axworthy staring at him. Axworthy turned back to his screen, his prominent features sharpened into relief by the screen's glow.

Cody went to the next image. An orphan girl, no more than three, standing all by herself in a rubble-strewn street, her big brown eyes streaming with tears as she stared up at a burning building, her lips pulled back from her teeth in a rictus of terror, her tiny body odd-looking to Cody, her short legs protruding from the bottom of her torn pink dress, her long brown arms held out at her sides, fingers splayed, looking as if she were about to push something away. Cody shook his head. It had been war. And now it looked as if it weren't over. Now it looked as if a new chapter was about to begin.

Axworthy left the weapons console and stood behind Cody. As Axworthy gazed at the little girl his face settled into an expression of pity and regret.

"Giving yourself a history lesson?" he said.

"I thought I might," said Cody. "I never really looked into this."

He accessed the next image. A picture taken from the ninth or tenth floor of a skyscraper. It showed a hundred orphans swarming Ptolemy Square in the uptown suburb of Kepler, maiming and killing Ceresian civilians.

"This is what they did," said Axworthy. "They'd come out of nowhere. Out of the sewers. Jump from the ledges of tall buildings. Somehow infiltrate our defensive perimeters, God knows how. They constantly surprised me with their guerrilla tactics. They'd strike right at civilians, murder them in broad daylight. As a terror tactic, it achieved its aim. It forced the evacuation. But it also resulted in their own bioextermination."

Cody focused on one particular woman caught in the mayhem, running toward a shrubbery garden carrying a baby, one shoe off, one shoe on. He wondered if she ever made it. He began to understand some of the bitterness certain Council members must have felt about the whole thing. How could the orphans be so cruel? He remembered Axworthy's words. *It's always overkill with them.* He glanced up, saw Bruder come into the control center and talk to Azim in low urgent tones. What now? he wondered. He looked at the still again. *I don't mean stabbed fifty or sixty times. I mean stabbed literally hundreds of times.* Several civilians lay on the ground. The square's paving stones were smeared with pools of blood. In the middle of it all a bronze statue of Ptolemy stood in a flower bed holding up a crystal sun.

Bruder came over. He gave Cody a stony glance, as if because of Cody's connection to Lulu he now somehow blamed Cody as a coconspirator in the death of his brother; then saluted Axworthy.

"Sir," he said. "Dr. Minks's pressure suit has malfunctioned, sir."

Axworthy looked at the recruit, as if at first he didn't understand. "Malfunctioned how?" he said.

"Sir, his chloropathoxin unit accidentally triggered itself, sir. I don't know how. The unit has three fail-safes, sir."

Axworthy's bushy eyebrows rose a notch. "You mean he's dead?"

"Sir, I'm afraid so, sir."

For a moment, Axworthy seemed lost, didn't know what do. "And was he still out at the site of the massacre?"

Bruder gave Cody another cold glance. "Sir, yes, sir. I've got the tape, if you want to see it, sir."

Axworthy looked bewildered. "I guess I better."

Axworthy and Cody followed Bruder to the medical monitoring section of the bunker. Cody looked at Bruder's broad muscular back, trying to sense his thoughts. Bruder had only one thought: to somehow convince Axworthy that this new fatality, though ostensibly an equipment failure, was unequivocally the work of the Meek.

They gathered round the screen and watched the footage from Dr. Minks's visor-cam. Bruder rolled it forward to the pertinent segment.

The visor-cam footage showed one of the dead security officers. Minks was leaning over the man. The name patch on the man's Vestan Defense Force pressure suit read EVENSEN.

"Sir, that's Jorg, sir," said Bruder. "He was a fine officer. Sir."

Cody sensed a sudden sentimentality from Bruder, registered half a dozen clichéd aphorisms about a soldier's duty, and recognized that Bruder wasn't a particularly original or bright man; he simply took orders and rarely thought for himself.

Cody turned his attention to the footage.

Minks looked at Evensen. Then, through the speaker, Cody heard a soft *ping-ping-ping* sound, an alarm going off in Minks's pressure suit. Cody had to interpret Minks's actions through the viewpoint of his visor-cam, like a quick sketch in hand-held cinematography, the camera swinging up as Minks got to his feet quickly, a jerky and constantly shifting view of the rocky gray terrain as he stumbled forward, a shot of the small unit patched to his belt, a red light flashing on the unit, Minks's hands coming into view as he fumbled wildly with the gadget, two red lights now flashing, a desperate clawing at the gadget, then three red lights flashing. The visor-cam lifted, did a quick sweep of the surrounding terrain, as if Minks were looking for someone to help him, and another recruit came into view; they always traveled in pairs when they went out onto the surface.

"That's Cormier, sir," said Bruder. "He's not back yet."

The visor-cam swung away from Cormier. Far in the distance, Cody saw the poisoned silo. Then the visor-cam swung back down. Minks's hand banged frantically at the unit. Cormier's hands came into the picture. The red lights stopped flashing. The screen filled with a fine blue mist and two seconds later Minks toppled into the dirt. Faceup, according to the visor-cam viewpoint. Cody saw a few stars through the blue mist. An overlay of Minks's dead biofeedback lines appeared on the screen.

"What's chloropathoxin?" asked Cody.

Bruder turned to him, and Cody felt a sophomoric sense of superiority emanating from the man. "Every soldier needs a suicide option, Mr. Wisner," he told Cody. "Especially out on the surface. Better chloropathoxin than the vacuum."

Cody went to the solar-power generating station on the surface by himself. Axworthy wanted to send two security officers with him, but he refused. Why risk three lives instead of one? Alone on the surface, he was again reminded of the walks he and Christine had taken on Vesta. He listened to his own breathing. He looked at his shadow stretching far ahead in the gray dirt. Patches of lichen grew here and there—the Meek's telegraph poles. He squatted and touched the surface of the asteroid. The soil was as fine as powder.

He sensed a sudden vibration and stood up, looking toward the microwave transmission tower, where he saw what appeared to be a giant insect skimming over the surface around it. The insect came toward him. Not an insect, but a vehicle. Open, like a dune buggy, propelled and kept aloft

by an unconventional drive utilizing what looked like a particle pulse technology. Two seats, Agatha in one of them, her
hands around a single control—a tiller—the other seat
empty.

She said: *Get in.*

He got in, found the seat small, had to loosen the harness,
but finally got settled. A few patches of marrow grew on the
floor. The plant would pick up the electrical emanations of
his thoughts and emotions, and amplify them for Agatha.
She swung the tiller in a wide curve. The skimmer turned
around, the frequency of the pulses increasing, and they
headed east.

They left the solar-power generating station and the oxygen mine behind, skimming the surface of the asteroid,
never more than two meters off the ground. Cody estimated
their speed at two hundred to three hundred kilometers per
hour, a speed that would have blown him out of his seat
in an atmosphere. In the vacuum, things seemed just as tranquil and silent as they did standing still.

She said: *He's not going to like it.*

She was right. Buster would hate this, hate it in a way
only an orphan could hate it.

They covered a hundred kilometers in just over twenty
minutes. Agatha swung the skimmer up, then brought it
down, nose-first, straight into the ground. Cody's heart
jumped. They dove right through the ground, into a large
tunnel. A substance the color of a ripe pear coated the walls,
and indeed, the tunnel looked as if it were more a product of
agriculture, grown, not built.

Agatha said: *How's Ben?*

He said: *Recovered.*

She said: *How old is Ben?*

He looked at her, grinned, said: *He's 31.*

After another twenty minutes they exited the tunnel.
Down below Cody saw a rain forest with blue glow-moss
hanging on the trees. In the sky he saw five moons, all different colors. Far in the distance, bathed in the moonlight,

stone buildings rose out of the forest. A river snaked its way through the trees, and 20 meters below a flock of red birds flew in formation.

Agatha said: *This is the Forest of Peace and Understanding. This is where I live. That city over there, that's the City of Resolved Differences.*

The Forest of Peace and Understanding. The City of Resolved Differences. Names that had a reason, names that emphasized the orphan struggle toward rehabilitation, reminders to all who lived here that the feuding was over. He checked the atmospheric and temperature readings on his visor. The atmosphere was breathable, nitrogen and oxygen, with a pressure of 750 millibars. Temperature was 17 degrees Celsius, shirtsleeve weather. He cycled the air in his pressure suit, swallowed against his popping ears, and took off his helmet. Agatha, now moving much more slowly, glanced at him to make sure he was all right.

A fragrant wind hit his face, smelling of cardamom and lime. This was a full-fledged real forest, grown here underground, a habitat similar to the ones they had on Vesta, but a lot bigger. This was no trick of holography. He felt the thoughts of thousands drifting up from the forest. He finally understood it, their ability to communicate through thought, why they had made it part of their redesign, why it was so necessary to them, why without it they never would have built what they had here. Unencumbered by the clumsy medium of words, the clans of the Meek were at last forced to understand each other, to empathize and have compassion for each other. The rewritten 27 million letters in chromosome 3 had turned them all into empaths, and, while the ability for vocal speech had atrophied, especially because they no longer used their lungs to breathe, they could better live in harmony with each other by communicating with their minds.

They *had* something here. He could sense it wafting up from the forest in cool delicate waves, a society, a way of life, a vision unique to the solar system, a place that was important, a culture that other cultures could learn from. They had a home here. A home they had made their own. A home that was now inextricably linked to their identity.

And he knew he couldn't let Axworthy take that away from them or make them abandon it for Charon.

CHAPTER 15

They landed under a particularly large tree in a clearing next to the river. Cody had never seen a tree like this before. Its trunk was straight and round, and rose thirty feet straight up to the first branches, which grew out from the trunk at ninety-degree angles, each branch spaced evenly from the next like the spokes in a cartwheel. These branches curved gently upward like bent fingers. Smaller branchlets grew from the primary ones, thatching the whole works like a roof. The leaves were flat, stiff, about half the size of his hand, pear-shaped, dark green in the middle but brightening to orange near the edges. This thatch of stiff green and orange leaves was so thick that people could walk on it up above.

Cody took off his gloves and pressed his hands to the tree, loving the feel of its smooth bark under his palms, breathing in its scent, a rich resinous smell. He tapped it a few times, wondered how it would cure or if it would cure at all.

Agatha said: *We call these hearthtrees.*

She scrambled up the trunk, looped her left arm around one of the branches, and dangled there like a chimpanzee, staring at him with wide violet eyes. The forest floor was a lush blanket of marrow and fallen hearthtree leaves.

She said: *Are you coming? Buster's waiting for you. You might as well get this over with.*

Encumbered by his pressure suit, burdened by an extra tenth of a gee, he wasn't about to climb this tree, especially when he wasn't physically designed for it the way Agatha was, with her long arms and strong feet.

"I can't climb," he said, speaking out loud now that he had his helmet off. "I'm not used to this gravity, and my suit's too heavy. Tell him to come down here. We'll sit by the river."

He sensed two thoughts from her. First, she felt sorry for him, the way she might feel sorry for someone who was handicapped. Secondly, she wondered if Ben would be better at climbing trees than he was. She disappeared up through the branches.

He walked to the river's edge. The river was wide, flat, nearly a mile across, and smelled faintly of algae. The sound of the moving water soothed him. Much of the riverbank looked as if it had been recently flooded. He couldn't help thinking of the grav-core flux, how Lake Ockham had bucked and pitched with tides, how it had finally spewed forth a soaking rain onto the city of Newton. Had the same thing happened here?

He was impressed by the sheer size of the place, by the engineering miracles it must have taken to build it. Had they developed this technology by themselves or had they learned it from somewhere else? To build such a habitat in just 30 years, to recover from the bioextermination, to construct this whole river system . . . well . . . that meant crucial breakthroughs in ecoforming organisms. They couldn't have built this so quickly without such organisms, he decided. Billions upon billions of eco-organisms, little nanoscapers, had been unleashed here, miles below the surface, turning the carbon-rich rock into a fully stocked river-valley system. All that water. How could they make all that water on this small dry planetesimal? Comet-fishing?

He heard a thump behind him. He turned around and saw Buster standing there. The moonlight dappled Buster's blue body. Buster approached Cody, licked his fingers, and pressed them to Cody's lips. The cool wind blew through Cody's mind, only this time the creosote smell remained faint, just one of several scents, one of a multiplicity of aromas, some spicy, some like fragrant flowers, some musky. It was as if with these scents Buster tried to convey the personalities and feelings of not only himself but of everybody who lived in the Forest of Peace and Understanding and in the City of Resolved Differences.

Buster said: *I bring you here because I want you to see us.* Cody now sensed that Buster had at least partially come to terms with the way Lulu felt about him. *I want you to know this. We have a way of life here. We have homes here. They might not be homes such as you choose to call them, but they suit us. The give us peace. They give us the tranquility we must always be vigilant to strive for. Our natures have been changed, but as I've told you before, we remember the way we were. We call it the ghost code, that which was erased from us by the marrow, but which is still there, hiding in latency, needing only a threat, such as the threat you have brought from Vesta.*

"We mean no threat," said Cody.

Buster seemed disappointed by this. He said: *Let's sit by the river.*

They walked downstream until they came to a garden with fountains and flowers, an open spot of riverbank with no trees, a lawn interspersed with beds of marrow. The moons—blue, pink, green, yellow, and red—cast reflections on the wide river. Some waterfowl, like swans but with looping crown feathers, paddled by.

Cody and Buster sat on an ornate wrought-iron bench. Cody looked around at the impressive river habitat. He thought this might be a good time to ask some questions.

"How did you hide all this from us for so long?" he said.

Buster said: *We knew you would come again.* He gazed serenely at the water as it flowed past. *We didn't want to fight. We have no offensive weapons. We thought it would be better to hide. So we worked to build and implement a tech-*

nology of invisibility. The strong organic component in much of our technology hides it from your sensors.

"But why didn't you hide it from us in the *Gerard Kuiper*?" he asked. "You hid it from the microsatellites. You hid it from 30 years of Defense Force probes. Why were we the first ones to see all this?"

Buster raised his eyebrows, looked away. He said: *Because our security system is geared to infiltrate and decode the heavy encryption of Defense Force sensors. The last thing we expected were sensors with no encryption, such as you utilized aboard your vessel. We strived valiantly to break what we thought were your secure codes. When we at first couldn't find them, we tried all the harder, convinced that they must be more heavily encrypted than usual. By the time we realized you weren't protected by any encryption at all, it was too late.*

"But all those surface probes Vesta sent here over the years," said Cody. "How were you able to hide the silos from the probes? I understand how you can make the microsatellites see anything you want them to see, but the probes have no software. They're simple roving cameras."

Buster said: *You've seen the quality of our holography. A structure sits on the surface, but all a probe sees is uninterrupted terrain. The reason you saw what you did six weeks ago was because the silos, as you call them, were undergoing inspection, and so their camouflaging holography was turned off so it wouldn't interrupt or distort our diagnostic testing. And because the silos are so big, it takes considerable time and technical resources to turn the holography back on. By the time we were ready to hide the silos again, you already knew they were there.*

Cody probed Buster for more information about the silos, what their true purpose was, but Buster blocked strongly. So Cody went on to his next question.

"Why steal our oxygen?" he asked.

Buster said: *To give you a nudge. To make you understand we meant business.* Buster looked away. *I didn't par-*

ticularly agree with that strategy. My own idea was to simply keep poking holes in your life-support infrastructure until you finally gave up and went home. But others demanded a more aggressive approach.

Cody said, "And I don't understand why you closed all the airlocks after the bioextermination. Why didn't you just leave them open?"

Buster nodded. *In zero pressure, such as you have on the surface, we have to wrap ourselves in tape. But give us just a few millibars, and our bodies can survive untaped through a special modification of our lymphatic system, a modification that works in tandem with our extra mesh of skin. With the airlocks closed, the temperature and the pressure rise. That makes it more comfortable for us to work and scavenge in Newton. We are able to rove in Newton untaped.* Buster's eyes narrowed. *And we must rove Newton. Newton is the basis of our technology.*

"It is?" said Cody.

Buster said: *All the Belt's greatest universities are in Newton. All the equipment, labs, and other facilities were left intact after the neutron bombardment, all of it at our disposal.*

At that moment, Cody saw something in the air, five children on pedal planes, wings articulated like the wings of pterosaurs, a large propeller out front, powered by bicycle pedals—a pastime common on the asteroids because of low gravity. Children. Born to this place. Their home. He sensed their distant emanations. They were having fun.

Buster said: *These are our children. Meek children. Not orphans. They are not of the crèche. They don't know the loneliness of the crèche. They have fathers and mothers, sisters and brothers. They have uncles and aunts and cousins. They have grandparents. These children have a place. This place. I never had a mother. I never had a father. I never had a place. I was the first. I was Original Man. I never want these children to go through what I went through. I don't want these children to be orphans.*

Like a flock of ungainly birds, the children headed down-river. Cody thought of the children back on Vesta. Prone to bone and vascular conditions, needing Ceres to prevent them. Ceres, the dream. An asteroid big enough to remain geologically stable under the force of a stronger gravity. A place where children of the Belt could grow up straight and healthy. Ceres, the center of learning. A dream from the past. What kind of alternative was it when there were these other children flying up in the sky, slim-boned and delicate, designed for microgravity, living in trees, with mothers, fathers, brothers, and sisters?

"Could we not learn to share?" he asked.

Buster said: *I wish we could.*

"And why can't we?"

Buster said: *Because Ceres is more than just a home to us now. Ceres is a means to an end.* This puzzled Cody. He tried to get more on this but the smell of creosote grew stronger. Buster was blocking. Buster changed the subject, went to the matter they were really here to discuss. *I've plucked whole from your mind Vesta City's counterproposal, have run models on just how long we could survive on Charon under the conditions and restrictions they demand, and have determined that we could survive on a subsistence level only, in a cold and hard place where there couldn't be many moments of joy. I'm afraid the answer is no. We will not leave. The negotiation is at an end. There can be no other answer from us. You and the others must leave. This is the only solution. You and the others must understand that Ceres is a dangerous place for you now. Ceres can never be what it once was. Ceres has been changed forever.*

As Cody watched the children disappear down the river on their pedal planes, as delicate as fairies, he knew that a renewal of the hostilities was all but inevitable now. He pictured the bombed-out buildings in Planck's Constant, hulking ruins sleeping in their own piles of rubble, and thought that there would never now be a cleanup or a reconstruction, that the classrooms of Newton would never again ring with the voices of children, and that once again the ruins would be simply places for soldiers to take cover in. He had come here with great plans. He had come here believing he was going to make a difference. The children on pedal planes finally disappeared into the misty light of the moons. He had never expected to inadvertently become the catalyst for a new war.

Axworthy stared pensively at his hands when Cody told him Buster's answer. He finally took a deep breath and ran his hand through his thick white hair.

"So he as good as told you that they have no weapons, nothing large or significant, just knives and this nano-putty, and their ability to hide really well. And then he refused our counteroffer, refused to give up Ceres even though I have enough firepower aboard the *Conrad Wilson* to blast the asteroid from the sky. You see what Jerry means when he says you can't negotiate with these people, even when they have a gun held to their heads?"

"Yes," said Cody.

"I don't believe it," said Axworthy. "How did Buster explain the surface silos?"

"He didn't."

"And what about the gravity-field projector?"

"We didn't talk about it."

"And what's this about Ceres being a means to an end? What does he mean by that?"

"I don't know," said Cody.

"I think he's lying," said Axworthy. "This is nothing but orphan double-talk."

"He can't lie; he can only omit. I would sense an out-and-out lie."

"And this place you saw, this Forest of Peace and Understanding, this City of Resolved Differences. You saw nothing that looked like military activity there?"

"No."

Axworthy rubbed his chin reflectively.

Cody thought about it. "Couldn't we send our children to Earth?" he asked. "Growing up in Earth's gravity would be just as beneficial to their long-term health."

Axworthy shook his head and smiled sadly. "That's a 320-million-kilometer journey round-trip under optimum conditions," he said. "Vesta would be bankrupt in six months. Trips to Earth are prohibitively expensive, you know that. I'm sure Vesta City's going to escalate the pressure somehow. Council has offered the Meek a more than generous chance. If they don't want to take it, then they're going to have to suffer the consequences."

"And what might those consequences be?" asked Cody.

"We'll have to wait and see."

Cody heard someone approaching from outside. He faintly sensed Azim, and a moment later Azim stood in the door. He had his hands clutched before him in an inadvertent gesture of prayer, and he looked uncomfortable, as if his intrusion were the grossest breach of etiquette he could imagine.

"Sir, I'm sorry to interrupt," he said, and bowed a few times, silently begging the commander's pardon.

"Go ahead, Azim."

Azim glanced at Cody, squeezing his lips together, then turned back to Axworthy and stroked his small pointed beard a few times in an effort to get his words in order.

"Sir, photo, satellite, and sonar reconnaissance indicate nuclear detonations at silos 2, 7, 9, and 13."

He gave Axworthy several quick nods, as if he felt he had to chase his words vigorously with these affirmative gestures, and rubbed his hands together like he was nervously waiting for the commander to believe him. Axworthy's face stiffened and he leaned forward. It looked for a moment as if Axworthy were indeed going to refute Azim's assertions. Yet Cody sensed that Azim was telling the truth, that he was dead sure of his facts.

"Detonations?" said Axworthy. Azim's shoulders sagged

a bit. "No launches? Just simple detonations? Detonations on-site?"

Cody could see why Axworthy was so puzzled. Why would the Meek stockpile nuclear weapons only to blow them up in their silos? Azim hoisted a nervous grin to his lips, a messenger hoping to keep himself from harm's way.

"Detonations on-site, sir," confirmed Azim.

"Were you able to obtain any triggering information?" Axworthy gazed at Azim with an expression of increasing mystification. "Were they intentional detonations or were they accidents?"

"Triggering data was unobtainable, sir."

Axworthy pondered all this, finally shook his head, then motioned toward the door.

"We might as well go have a look," said Axworthy.

Cody followed Axworthy and Azim to the control room. Claire Dubeau sat at her laptop analyzing the data as it came in. She looked as perplexed as Axworthy. Azim ran the footage from silo 7. First just the structure, in the dark, inactive. Then a blinding flash . . . and that was all they saw for a while. Azim flicked from camera-emplacement 1 to camera-emplacement 5, ten kilometers back, where the blinding flash at last resolved itself into not the traditional mushroom cloud such as might be expected in an oxygen atmosphere, but into a sphere of white light radiating off to the left, funneled through the silo's aperture. Cody noted the curious sideways thrust of the blast. And thinking of thrust, he quickly arrived at a hypothesis.

"Claire, could you access the GK navigational program?"

Axworthy joined them, interested in what he was doing. "What's going on?" he asked.

"The ejecta signature of the blast has given me a hunch," said Cody. "But in order to confirm it, Claire's going to need clearance to go into the *Conrad Wilson*'s current triangulation file."

"Why?"

"I want to check our orbital trajectory."

"For Ceres?"

"Yes."

Axworthy frowned. "But it's well known," he said.

"I think it just changed. I think the silos are thrusters."

Axworthy stared at him, taking this in, assimilating the ramifications, and how they connected to the four nuclear detonations. Then he walked over to the communications console and raised the *Conrad Wilson*.

"Valentini, I want you to give Claire Dubeau, GK 5, access to anything she needs on the CW. You will assist her with any communications or observations she needs, and connect her to any of the Belt's deep-space tracking installations." Axworthy nodded at Claire. "Go ahead."

Over the next fifteen minutes Claire sent and received messages from a variety of space-based observatories in the Belt and fed the data into the GK navigational program. When she was done, and the new figures for Ceres's orbital trajectory appeared on the screen, she looked at both Cody and Axworthy with wide concerned eyes. Cody peered over Claire's shoulder at the graphics inset, a diagram of the four inner planets, their positions, their paths, and a forty-day projection, Mars and Venus losing ground to Earth, Mercury cycling halfway around the sun ahead of Earth on its quick 88-day orbit. Ceres's new orbit, in green overlay, reminded Cody of the cellophane, Buster's orbital trajectories, Lulu's dream-projection of the moss-hung amphitheater, Buster's odd singing.

Claire said, "Ceres has decreased speed to 160,000 kilometers per hour." She double-checked the figures to make sure she was right. "She's in orbital decay, sinking sunward. You can see on this forty-day projection that in five and a half weeks Ceres will pass within a hundred thousand kilometers of Earth." She looked at Axworthy. "I guess Cody's right. The silos are really thrusters. And it looks like we're headed for Earth."

*   *   *

"They want us on standby," Axworthy said to Cody. "They're in emergency session right now and they should have an answer for us soon."

"Did they give you any indication of the way things might go?" asked Cody.

Axworthy shook his head. "No. But you have to remember, well over half the members fought in the Civil Action here thirty years ago. They see the Meek's orbital maneuvering as a deliberate escalation. They see it as a belligerent rejection of their generous offer to subsidize the Meek's exodus to Charon."

Cody sighed, disheartened by the way the whole thing was getting out of hand.

"Why would they threaten Earth?" he asked.

"Because they have the capability. Because this is what Buster meant when he said Ceres was a means to an end."

"Buster himself told me they have no offensive weapons. They live in a culture of peace and cooperation now."

"Buster's a liar. I don't think they're going to Earth for a holiday, do you? Fourteen of those silos are still armed."

"What do you think Council will do?"

Axworthy took a slow meditative sip of his coffee. "I think they'll give him another chance."

"You do?" Cody felt suddenly hopeful.

"They'll look into possible firing sequences for the remaining silos, try to devise a sequence that will lift Ceres back to its traditional orbit, then ask Buster to initiate that firing sequence. If the Meek are able to do this, Council will probably offer them another chance at Charon. The Council members aren't unreasonable. They'll exhaust all diplomatic measures before they resort to something firmer."

"Should I talk to Buster?"

"No. I'm going to send Lulu."

"Lulu?"

"Why keep her detained?" asked Axworthy. "I think we've gotten everything we can get out of her, and she can deliver to Buster whatever decision the Council finally makes. I just hope Buster knows what he's doing. I hope he realizes he doesn't stand a chance. He still has the opportunity to make amends. But he's going to have to address this orbital decay, I'm sure of it. That will be Council's first demand. If he doesn't, I imagine we'll be asked to storm the silos. We can rig our own firing systems to the silos. We're devising special suits up in the *Conrad Wilson* right now that will protect us against the ricin and this demolecularizer. I'm sure we can find a way to make the silos lift Ceres back into its proper place. But there'll be a lot less bloodshed if Buster does it for us."

"The Council won't order another bioextermination, will it?" said Cody. "There are 620,000 people here."

"The Council will do whatever it takes to get Ceres back. And if that means using the *Conrad Wilson* strategically, well, then . . . I'll have to follow orders. And since the asteroid is in orbital decay they'll have to make their decision soon. The *Conrad Wilson* can stay only so long before she'll have to pull away."

"How long?" asked Cody.

"About thirty hours. Council's asked all nonessential personnel to be evacuated to the *Conrad Wilson* within the next twelve. Like I told you before, I'm going to need eighteen of my own men. I'd like to conscript two of yours, over and above the crew you're going to need to keep here. Claire, because she's an ace programmer and we might need her. And Dr. Rudnick, because . . . well, with the death of Dr. Minks . . ."

"I understand," said Cody.

CHAPTER 16

Cody should have been sleeping right now. But he couldn't. He kept thinking of the children flying over the river. Lulu stared at him with growing apprehension. He knew she could feel all his misgivings. He was concerned about the Council's final ultimatum—whatever that ultimatum might turn out to be—the one that Lulu would deliver to Buster once Vesta City made up its mind. Would the Meek be able to restore the asteroid's orbit now if that's what the Council should ask? And would they finally concede if they were offered a second chance to go to Charon? Would Council even offer them a second chance? Or would it simply go ahead and order another bioextermination? Seven hours since he had spoken to Axworthy, and not a word from Council yet.

Crew slept around them in the bunkroom. Eight hours of sleep, then one more shift working on the emergency shelter, then the landers would come for the nonessential personnel. Axworthy wanted at least a skeleton crew working on the emergency shelter, patching whatever nano-putty holes remained in case his recruits should need the shelter as their first fallback.

Cody glanced out the doorway into the control room. Azim sat at the tracking console. Axworthy stood behind him looking down at the screen. Something wrong again? Buster chipping away at life support? Undermining the automated defense? Surprising Axworthy yet again? Azim kept switching modes, muttering commands into the voice-activated interface. Bruder stared at Cody from a chair just outside the door, kept patting the grip of his sidearm in a taunting fashion. Cody turned away from him.

Lulu reached up and put her hand on his cheek. She looked into his eyes and he felt her great loneliness. *I can't hear anybody, Cody.* He stroked her albino-white hair with his hand. She said: *This is what it must have been like for Buster at the beginning.*

He said: *They've killed all the marrow in Newton.*

She said: *I can hardly hear you.*

He nodded. She lifted some lichen from a bowl, chewed it for a while, then pulled him near. They kissed. Only this time it wasn't a kiss of communication. He felt her desire. It enveloped him like a warm cloud. He hadn't slept with a woman since Christine had died. He was a widower, and, yes, that made a difference; he had Christine's memory to think about. Only now, kissing Lulu like this, the habit of his self-imposed celibacy seemed to melt away. Lulu's desire infected him like a good dream come true. His desire, through the medium of the marrow, stoked her, and the two of them worked in tandem to ignite the whole thing, like fire feeding fire. An empathic sexuality, where desire was doubled because he couldn't help feeling his partner's passion. He placed his hand on her small perfect breast, amazed, astonished, and frightened that this strange blue woman should at last open the floodgates. She reached down and stroked his thigh. He heard Bruder shift. He turned around.

Bruder.

Watching them.

He had just about had enough of Bruder.

Bruder sat there grinning at them in a mean way, stroked the grip of his sidearm once more, then formed his hand into the shape of a gun. He pretended to shoot, all the while keeping the mean grin on his face. This was more than Cody could stand.

He got up, walked over to Bruder, grabbed him by the front of his uniform, and shook him.

"Do you have something to say?" demanded Cody.

Bruder's face turned red. "No . . . no, I . . ."

Still clutching the front of Bruder's uniform, Cody yanked the man to his feet and shoved him against the wall. "If I so much as find you looking at Lulu again, or threatening her in any way, I'm going to turn your face into mush."

"I just . . ." He could tell Bruder wanted to respond with force, but knew Bruder wouldn't dare in the face of possible reprimand from Axworthy.

Cody let him go. He didn't like confrontations, but he saw Bruder was the kind of man who understood things best through confrontations. Sensed Bruder's surprise, his anger, his frustration at not being able to respond. Cody stared at him hard.

"I'll be watching you, son," he said.

Cody found both Axworthy and Azim looking at him. Axworthy was obviously annoyed, but otherwise didn't say anything.

"Cody, come here and have a look at this," said Axworthy.

Cody walked over, trying to calm himself, letting the harsh energy of his anger drain away, and looked at Azim's screen.

The microgen tracking screen, only an hour ago registering every single Meek, now had only a few specks of green left—and those few were blinking off one by one.

"When you delivered our counterproposal to Buster, did he mention our tracking microgen?" asked Axworthy. "Could you sense it in his thoughts at all?"

"No."

They watched six more green dots go out. "Because the tracking microgen is one of our key defenses," said Axworthy. "Without it the antipersonnel emplacements are useless. Somehow they've found a cure for our tracking microgen. I don't see how that's possible since it takes its blueprint from a virus."

Superscience, thought Cody. He respected more than ever the resourcefulness of the Meek.

More green dots blinked off.

Finally the screen was clear. No tracking microgens left at all. Axworthy shook his head.

"They can overwhelm us any time they like now," he said. Axworthy looked ashen, truly shaken by the turn of events. "We won't be able to target them as effectively. About the most we can do now is draw a tighter perimeter, send out more scouting robots, and try to hang on until reinforcements arrive." He looked at Cody, gave him a tired grin. "They were always smart, Cody. That's what I remember about them. They were always practical and inventive. You think you have them, but then they turn around and do something that puts you on the defensive. They're formidable. They're resilient. Too bad they don't have more common sense."

Cody worked on airlock 6 of the emergency shelter the next day. Deirdre held a strip of dura-seal into the groove while Cody screwed it into place. Through the doorway and into the main auditorium and mess hall Cody saw the *Conrad Wilson*'s oxygen pod, a pressurized sphere, the old piece of equipment Axworthy had promised. Cody wasn't even sure they made them anymore. When he thought of oxygen pods he thought of the nineties. They were from a bygone era, lifeboats to be used in the unlikely event of a prolonged pressure wall breach. Prolonged pressure wall breaches didn't happen these days, not since the introduction of his own insta-seal.

It looked like an antique diving bell, such as they used on Earth and Europa for undersea exploration, had round porthole-like windows, an oval pressure door made of riveted steel, with an antenna and a small satellite dish on top. He liked old equipment. He liked to see how workmen from other decades, other centuries, put things together.

"That just about does it for this side," said Deirdre. "Do you want to test it?"

He looked at Deirdre, and saw a shy grin come to her face.

"Sure," he said. "Thanks for staying on, Deirdre. You're one of the best."

She shrugged, looked away. But then her eyes narrowed and her face grew solemn. "It doesn't look good for the Meek, does it?"

He paused. "No," he said. "It doesn't."

They gazed into each other's eyes, groping for a better understanding. He wasn't sure what passed between them as they stood facing each other but it was as if Deirdre had been rendered afresh to him; there was a new depth to her green eyes that spoke of silent struggles, an easier bearing in the way she carried herself, as if whatever existed between them had made her stronger. He exhaled, relieved, surprised and glad to feel a new fondness for her. He turned to the street.

"The marrow is coming back," he said. He pointed to a patch in the crevice by the curb. Talking just because he liked talking to her. Enjoying her company.

"It grows fast," she said.

He could sense it. Friends. Nothing more. No love, or at least only the love friends feel for each other. He put his hand on her shoulder and gave it a comradely shake. No romance. No sex. Crewmates. Working together. He liked that.

Deirdre had a passing thought of Lulu, and Cody sensed it. Her expression changed yet again; her eyes grew searching, her lips pursed inquisitively, and she looked as if she were on the verge of a breakthrough of some sort. He felt the residual recoding of the Meek still within her, and impressions passed between them—feelings, thoughts, images. An image of Lulu. Of Lulu accepting some marrow from Deirdre. Of two women, from different worlds and cultures, from different genetic brews, making peace with each other.

"You can sense that?" asked Deirdre.

"I can," he said.

"We've talked," said Deirdre. "We've kissed."

Cody nodded. "I'm glad," he said.

"She really loves you," she said.

Cody knew this but was still a little overwhelmed, still had mixed feelings about it all. Because of Christine. He had nothing to say to Deirdre, but he was grateful for her interest and concern. He lifted the Thermos and poured coffee for her. She took it with a grin.

"Thanks," she said.

"You look cold."

"I'm fine," she said.

They got back to work.

They were just setting up the equipment to check the seal on the airlock when Cody's legs grew weak. The Meek. He could sense them. He felt as if he were standing in a strong current again, like that first time, and that it was about to wash him away. He looked at Deirdre and he felt as if he were seeing her from the wrong end of a telescope. She gazed at him in alarm and he could tell the recoding wasn't strong enough in her for her to sense what he was sensing.

"What?" she asked. "What's wrong?"

He closed his eyes, put his hand against the wall to steady himself. He felt Deirdre's hand on his shoulder. A thousand chaotic aromas filled his mind. They were coming. He could sense them all around, seething with the same objective. They were coming to free Lulu. Even before Axworthy had a chance to let her deliver the Council's decision.

"Cody?" said Deirdre.

He put his hands over his ears and looked up at her, thankful she was here. Seven of them streaked by. Then another three. Deirdre turned, alarmed. Another five loped by. Their thoughts clamored in his mind. Deirdre clutched Cody by the arm and guided him into the airlock recess. He felt the Meek, felt anger feeding anger. Several more ran by, all of them toward the VDF bunker. He felt old resentments feeding old resentments. He heard the bunker alarm sound. A whole pack of them ran by.

He moved out of the recess.

"Cody, please," said Deirdre.

He looked down the street. Odd to see such a crowd of them all in one place, at least a hundred or more, all blue, all armed with knives, all silent. No war cries, no protests, none of the expected din a normal human mob would make. It reminded him of the photograph in Ptolemy Square, when they'd come to kill civilians during the war. Their anger was like a tidal wave in his mind. They swarmed the bunker like an angry bunch of bees, pelted it with nano-putty. The bunker began to steam and hiss, melting like a block of butter on a hot day. Security officers came out and fired laser rifles into the crowd but killed only a few Meek before they themselves were attacked. A couple of Meek slit their throats, then stabbed them repeatedly. *It's always overkill with them.* Cody saw Buster. And as if Buster sensed his presence, the old warrior turned his way. He looked down Rhenium Lane and narrowed his eyes, eyes that now looked as if they had black greasepaint around them. In fact, they all had black greasepaint around their eyes. Cody sensed from Buster that he wanted Lulu back, that before the battle was joined he had to get her into his own camp.

Buster turned away, shutting him out, then smoothed nano-putty over the side of the bunker and waited. Other Meek sabotaged supplies while Buster's nano-putty ate away the wall. He gave the wall a good kick and the putty-compromised piece collapsed inward. Then he threw a smoke grenade inside.

Out in the supply yard Cody heard a hiss. Some of the Meek wrecked the bunker's oxygen production unit, while others released oxygen from the extra tanks. Deirdre came and stood beside him. He sensed that she was afraid and put his arm around her to reassure her.

As the smoke from the grenade cleared, Buster and a half dozen others entered the bunker.

Cody saw Axworthy, Azim, Bruder, and some of the other security recruits stagger out of what was left of the bunker, coughing, their eyes wet with tears from the caustic smoke. The smoke didn't affect any of the Meek at all. Several of them ran away with supplies, foodstuffs, and oxygen tanks. Someone flicked on the floodlights but this time the Meek didn't run around blindly, weren't affected one way or the other—the new greasepaint around their eyes seemed to diminish the effect of bright lights. Buster came out of the bunker and surveyed the scene dispassionately, turning his head this way and that, taking it all in, looking as if he had stepped into an old memory. Lulu came out behind him, stumbling a bit for having been restrained so long, but now free, now out of shackles. She paused, searched the square, squinting against the bright lights. She picked him out down Rhenium Lane, stared at him with her big violet eyes. She didn't say anything. She didn't have to. He knew how she felt. He felt the exact same way. They didn't want to part. Buster grabbed her by the hand and yanked her off into the darkness of Isosceles Boulevard, as if he had the inalienable right to take her anywhere he pleased. She took one last glance backward. Cody didn't know whether she was going willingly or was being coerced. She seemed dazed. He took a few steps toward her, but, disoriented by all the emanations, he stumbled. Deirdre steadied him. When he looked down Isosceles Boulevard once again he saw that they were gone, all the Meek. The darkness had swallowed them up.

Cody and Axworthy sat on cable spools in the yard, sipping soup while they surveyed the aftermath.

"I'm having security recruits salvage what they can," said Axworthy. Cody watched three recruits drag cots, lockers, and undamaged equipment into the emergency shelter across the street. "The bunker is ruined. According to Azim our computer systems are intact, as is our communications apparatus. But half the equipment and supplies have been either destroyed or stolen. Fusion cells remain operational, but the portable oxygen production unit for the bunker is finished, beyond repair. All the pressure suit oxygen tanks have either been emptied or stolen. Two security recruits are dead."

"Vesta City's not going to like it," said Cody.

That Buster's attack on the bunker would darken Council's view of the whole situation and garner support for a full-scale bioextermination against the Meek was a foregone conclusion. Never mind the extenuating circumstances. He felt helpless.

Axworthy shook his head. "No," he said, "they're not." He looked up at the emergency shelter. "How long before the emergency shelter's ready?" he asked.

"We're going to double-check the structure one last time," he said. "We've got all the nano-rotted spots cleaned out and stabilized, all the breaches sealed, and plates over the larger holes. The damaged airlocks have been repaired. You have Deirdre Malvern to thank for that. She did a lot of retooling. She's a wizard in the workshop." Cody gazed up at the emergency shelter speculatively. "We'll finish our double-check and then go out to Actinium to make sure the Meek didn't wreck anything in the control room, and to see if we can get a few more solar panels on-line. It should take us three hours total."

Axworthy nodded. "Good," he said. "When you've done your check I'm going to have the landers prepare for evacuation of nonessential personnel to the *Conrad Wilson*. Once the landers have taken the evacuees to the ship I'm going to have them bring back a three-week supply of tanked oxygen for the rest of us. If your new seals on the emergency shelter don't hold, and the Meek actually succeed in depressurizing this place, we'll need all the oxygen we can store. Frankly, I don't know how long Vesta City will want us to stay. The situation is deteriorating. Have you assembled your returning crew?"

"Yes," said Cody. "They're going to help with the double-check; then they'll be ready to go."

"I'll have Bruder round up my people. It's going to take the landers three hours to gear up for the launch anyway."

Three hours later Cody went out to the surface to watch the launch of the landers. Returning personnel were now on-board and the main thrusters glowed white in the darkness. The *Conrad Wilson*'s two landers, though big, were meant to lower and lift equipment in what was essentially an open-to-the-vacuum cage—a cage that protruded like a giant thorax from the midsection. The cabin in front had space for ten. Cody's own evacuees included Wit, Dina, Huy, Peter, and Anne-Marie. The landers' engines began to increase thrust, kicking dust and debris into the vacuum, polishing away the gray carbonaceous dirt until there was nothing but bedrock beneath. The landers lifted off. He was glad they were getting away. Higher and higher they rose, shimmering like giant fireflies. They veered east, toward Equilibrium, preparing to orbit Ceres twice before making rendezvous with the *Wilson*.

Cody went back inside. Ben, Deirdre, Jerry, and Claire still remained. He descended to the center of the city on the Charles Darwin Memorial Turbo Lift, powering the unit with a portable power pack, sinking the equivalent of 130 floors in a minute.

Once back in Laws of Motion Square he helped the others set up operations in the main auditorium of the emergency shelter. He was just stacking some crates of food off to one side when he felt the oddest sensation in his spine, as if his vertebrae were starting to squeeze up one against the other. The food crate he carried felt heavy and he set it down with a loud bang.

Axworthy looked at him. "What's going on?" he asked. Cody could see Axworthy was feeling it too.

Claire turned around and looked at him. An electronic stylus rolled off her desk onto the floor all by itself. Cody had the sensation that he was in a high-speed elevator, just like the Charles Darwin Memorial Turbo Lift, but going up instead of down. He looked up at the rafters. Dust fell in a sudden bizarre straight line. He heard a distant rumbling. And then he felt the drag on his limbs.

"It's happening again," he said, trying to stay calm. "Everybody should get on the floor. Lie down on your back. There's going to be another grav-core flux."

Everybody did as Cody told them. And none too soon. A moment later there was a huge increase in gee-force. Cody felt as if five people had jumped on top of him. He heard groans from the crew lying on the floor around him. From out in the city he heard another low rumbling sound then a horrible bang. The grav-core spasmed, leaned on them with the heavy weight of five gees. He felt as if he had 200 pounds pressing against his chest. He could hardly breathe. He looked at Axworthy. Axworthy's face sagged strangely to one side, pulled groundward by the gravity. The commander glanced up at the communications console.

"Do we still have contact with the landers?" he asked.

But Cody couldn't lift his head from the floor to check. He heard another bang from somewhere out in the city, followed by something that sounded like thunder, rumbling and prolonged. He felt vibrations through the floor. A skyscraper tumbling down? he wondered. The walls of the emergency shelter creaked, groaned, and the temporary lights flickered, went out, then came back on. He heard Lake Ockham whispering distantly from the end of Isosceles Boulevard as it was jostled by sudden tides. Even the air inside the emergency shelter seemed heavy. Through the crush of it all, while his bones felt as if they were going to break, Cody couldn't help wondering if this gravity flux was intentional, if it had been timed to coincide with the lander launches. He couldn't help thinking of Joe Calaminci. He couldn't believe that Buster would deliberately jeopardize the launches when the people in the landers were essentially following his demand to evacuate.

This grav-core fluctuation went on a lot longer than the last one. Cody clenched his teeth against it. Tears came to his eyes and he broke into a cold sweat, such was the crushing pain of the thing. Incoming hails from the *Conrad Wilson* crackled over the radio. Azim struggled to pull himself up to the console but his arms started to shake and he carefully lowered himself back to the floor. Cody heard no hails from the landers.

Finally, after nearly an hour, the painful gee-force relented. Cody felt buried under rubble. He began to breathe easier and was able to push himself into a sitting position. Azim again attempted to drag himself to the com-link, and this time was able to acknowledge the *Conrad Wilson*'s hail. Cody glanced at Axworthy, who was leaning against the side of the console. The man looked old, his features pulled downward by the gravity.

The gravity lightened further, following its previous rebound effect.

Claire struggled up from the floor and went to her own workstation.

"Azim, can you raise the landers?" asked Axworthy.

"Nothing so far," said Azim. "I'm accessing the flight data."

"What about the *Conrad Wilson*?" asked Axworthy. "Are they okay?"

"They've moved to a higher orbit."

"Claire, do you have any data from site 19?" asked Axworthy. Site 19 was where the large round object was, the suspected gravity-field projector.

But she hadn't checked it yet. Cody saw that she was checking municipal pressure walls instead.

"I'm afraid we show a drop in pressure," she said. "A hundred millibars so far. We've got a slow leak somewhere."

"The airlocks?" asked Axworthy.

"No," she said. "Somewhere in the seams. If current leakage remains the same, we'll have to go to alternate sources of oxygen in less than three hours."

Axworthy's eyes narrowed and he lifted his chin. "The

landers were going to bring back oxygen tanks," he said.
"Azim, have you got that flight data yet?"

Azim turned to his commander, his face slack. "I'm
afraid they both went down on the outskirts of Equilibrium.
Biofeedback monitors for all crew and passengers show
nothing."

Cody turned to Deirdre. The two stared at each other. The
gee-force was easing up more and more, but, if anything,
Cody felt heavier. Wit. Huy. Peter. Dina. Russ. Anne-Marie.
All gone. If the deaths of Joe Calaminci and Wolf Steiger
had been devastating, the passing of these six additional
crew members staggered Cody. He stopped breathing again,
his throat tight. Deirdre crawled over, put an arm on his
shoulder. He shook his head. His legs were splayed out in
front of him. The mess hall floor was covered with dust, and
there were footprints in the dust, and some of those footprints
belonged to Wit, Huy, Peter, Dina, Russ, and Anne-Marie.
And that was all that was left of them.

"Cody?" said Deirdre.

Cody looked at Azim. "There's nothing at all?" he asked.

"Nothing," said Azim.

"Then that means our only source of oxygen is the pod,"
said Axworthy. The gravity reached about one gee and
everybody else struggled to their feet. "I'm sorry, Cody, but
we're just going to have to shake this off as well as we can
for the time being. I'm sorry about the deaths of your crew.
And all those recruits of mine. But we're stuck here. We
have to shake ourselves out of this and get the Actinium
OPU supplying oxygen to the emergency shelter as fast as
possible or we're going to be in real trouble."

Cody gazed at the commander blankly. He remembered
Peter Wooster's words. *The math doesn't add up.* Were they
going to face the same bleak equation again?

"I've got data from site 19 now, Kevin," said Claire, her
voice shaky. Cody turned to Claire, took courage from her,
at the way she was forcing herself to concentrate on the task

at hand even though she had just lost all those friends. "The gravitational field generator was activated," she said.

"Is it still activated?" asked Axworthy.

"No."

"How long was it on for?" asked Cody

"Forty-three minutes, seventeen seconds." As Claire scrutinized further data, a knit came to her brow.

"What is it, Claire?" asked Axworthy.

"The projection of the thing's gravitational force seems to extend for nearly a full astronomical unit." She looked more perplexed than ever. "Why would they do something like that? What do they use this thing for? Did you ever get anything out of Buster on it, Cody? Or Lulu?"

"No."

"Keep at it, Claire," said Axworthy. "Analyze everything you can."

The gravity lightened further and Cody felt his shoulders lift.

"Sir, I've had a communication from the *Conrad Wilson*," said Azim. "Vesta City says they want everyone off the asteroid as soon as possible. The *Conrad Wilson* says they can refit the unmanned explorer to evacuate the rest of us, now that the landers have been destroyed."

"Has Council reached a decision about what they're going to do about the Meek?" asked Axworthy.

"Not yet, but they still want everyone off. They've just received word of the catastrophe and they think it would be the best course. Engineering came up with this plan to refit the unmanned explorer and Council wants them to go ahead with it."

"How many do they think the explorer can carry?" asked Axworthy.

"It's big," said Azim. "They said it can carry all of us."

"How long will it take to refit?" asked Axworthy.

"They said about seven hours."

Axworthy lifted his hand to his chin, did some figuring. Then he looked at Cody. "We might make it yet," he said.

He paused, shook his head. "It's going to be close with that many people in the oxygen pod. But we just might get out of this mess. Cody, we still have the three remaining oxygen tanks from your own crew?"

"Only two left now, and those are only a quarter full. Six hours in each of them."

Axworthy nodded. "Can you and Ben take those tanks out to Actinium and spend the next six hours working on the OPU? If you two can get the OPU out in Actinium up and running for even just a little while, that will increase our margin. It might buy Engineering Section the time they need to refit the unmanned explorer before all our air runs out."

Cody nodded, still feeling shocked by the deaths of his crew, but forcing himself to think of the problems they faced and of the possible solutions they might devise. "We can do that," he said. He looked away as his feet left the ground. He imagined wreckage out by Equilibrium. He imagined bodies. He quickly shook these images away, feeling as if they were the mental and emotional equivalent of quicksand. But now he saw in his mind the Meek children on the pedal planes flying down the wide river. How was Vesta City going to react to this? Was there now going to be a bio-extermination? Is that why they wanted to evacuate everybody?

Axworthy looked around, startled as his own feet left the ground.

"Did this happen the last time?" he asked.

Cody nodded. "It seems to rebound with a repulsion effect for a few minutes. A sort of reverse field all around the asteroid."

Axworthy nodded, simply accepting it, then looked more closely at Cody. "What's on your mind, Cody?" he asked. "You have that look in your eyes."

"How do you think Vesta City's going to react to this?"

Axworthy shook his head. "I've got ten recruits poisoned, two with slit throats, my doctor killed by a suspicious suit malfunction, and now another twenty-one killed in crashes. Ceres will rendezvous with Earth in five weeks armed to the teeth with nuclear weapons. You figure it out."

"Another communication from the *Conrad Wilson*," said Azim. "They're telling us that they've revised their fuel estimates and will now have to leave orbit in six hours and forty minutes, that if they follow Ceres sunward much longer than that they won't have enough fuel to get home. They've asked Engineering Section to work as fast as they can on the refit, to see if they can get it done in under seven hours. We've also had another communication from Council. They've advised us that the *Conrad Wilson* is the only vessel close enough to make a military response."

"Have they advised a military response?" asked Axworthy.

"Not yet," said Azim. "But they expect a decision soon."

"Does Earth have anything available?" asked Axworthy.

"Nothing in a cruiser class," said Azim. "Everything's deployed. They have the *Theodore Richards* in orbit around Venus—that's the closest. They have their usual array of orbital defenses, but most of those satellites have been programmed to deal with hostilities Earth-side. The only way Terran authorities can launch a strategic strike against Ceres is to do it directly from Earth, and that means they have to trade distance for lift. That's got Earth awfully nervous. They don't want Ceres to get anywhere near Earth before they start firing at it. They'd sooner not risk any of the collateral fallout."

Axworthy nodded. "So the *Conrad Wilson* is it, then," he said. "We're the ones who'll have to make the strategic strike if the Council votes that way." His brow settled. Axworthy's feet sank back to the floor as the gravity stabilized to .5 gees again. He put his hands on his hips and looked around at everybody. "We're the ones who will have to end this stalemate once and for all."

CHAPTER 17

Cody and Ben were out on the surface again standing next to one of the sabotaged optic cables that led to the microwave conversion tower.

"I think it will take us too long to repair this cable now," said Cody. "It might be faster if we try to find fresh solar panels and sweep them off."

Ben nodded. "You're probably right," he said. "What a way to spend the last six hours of your life, though. Sweeping."

Cody's shoulders were still sore from his previous stint of sweeping. "I know what you mean," he said.

"I'm sure glad I found a way to divert pressure to the main auditorium only," said Ben.

"I guess that means less panels to sweep," said Cody. "How many do you think we'll need for the auditorium?"

Ben paused, did some figuring. "At least six."

"If we push ourselves, I'm sure we can do it."

"I feel highly motivated right now," said Ben.

Cody found a working solar panel a half-kilometer away from the microwave conversion tower, climbed the rungs to the top, and started sweeping away the coating of micro-meteorites. Far in the distance, in the harsh glare of the sun, Cody saw Ben sweeping his own panel. Here he was again, his life depending on sweeping. He checked his oxygen gauge. Just over five hours left. He wondered if the Council had made their decision yet.

He felt Lulu's presence. But the feeling was distant, tenuous, and quickly faded. He stopped sweeping and looked around. He saw some marrow growing in a patch a few meters away, walked to it, picked it up, crushed it in his hand, ran it over his suit, then threw it up into the vacuum.

He said: *Lulu?*

The communication he felt from Lulu was faint. Maybe coming from close by, maybe coming from a great distance, a stirring of a breeze that was nearly too difficult to detect, oddly encoded, as if she'd been told by Buster to end any and all communication with him. He was about to call her once more when he was interrupted by Claire Dubeau. Her holo-image appeared in the upper right corner of his visor.

"I'm communicating on a private link," she said.

"Acknowledged," he said, initiating his own reciprocal private link. "How's the air?"

"We've got thirty minutes before we move into the pod." she said. "I've been looking at the data from site 19. The gravitational device?"

"Yes?"

"Kevin still has me hooked up to all the deep-space observatories," said Claire. "Remember how I told you the artificial gravitational field produced at site 19 extended a full AU, 93 million miles?"

"Yes?"

"It actually goes much further than that. From that point, it arches. The sun's trying to pull the gravitational field into an orbit, and that's why I missed this. But I've tracked it out a lot further now."

"Why would the field arch?"

"Because it has a gravitational center just like a planet, and other gravitational forces act against it. That means the sun is trying to pull it into an orbit, just like it would a planet. The field extends all the way to Highfield-Little." She paused, waiting for him to acknowledge Highfield-

Little, but the name, though familiar, at first drew a blank from Cody. "Highfield-Little," she repeated. "The rogue planet entering our solar system."

Cody searched his memory, and slowly, bits and pieces fell into place. He remembered news of Highfield-Little three or four years ago but nothing much since that time, just occasional updates from various news providers about its progress; how, like an overgrown comet, it was going to drift through the solar system, missing all the planets, and finally tumble into the sun, nothing more than a spectacular light show for amateur astronomers who had the proper sun filters for their telescopes.

"I've heard of it," he said.

"I've done some digging," said Claire. "Into old news articles. They have a great news file up on the *Conrad Wilson*. You want to hear a little about it?"

"Sure."

"Just let me get it up on the screen here . . . yes . . . here it is." He heard Claire take a deep breath. "It says here it was first spotted six years ago by a couple of amateur astronomers on Mars, comet-hunters Charles Highfield and Rebecca Little. They thought it was a comet at first because it exhibited all the signs and eccentricities of a cometlike orbit. But as they continued to observe, they realized it a had a mass thousands of times greater than an average comet. Other astronomers quickly confirmed their findings. They went on to discover spectrographic readings suggestive of a full-fledged atmosphere composed mainly of nitrogen and oxygen. Rogues are rare. There've been only sixteen recorded cases so far and they're all light-years away from Earth. This is the first one in recorded history that's ever been trapped by our sun's gravitational well."

"So why are the Meek aiming their device at it?" asked Cody.

"I'm not sure," said Claire. "Right now the rogue's coming down at an angle toward the orbital plane of Saturn. The gravitational field projector hits it dead-on. The farther the gravitational field travels the stronger it gets. I've checked all the orbital trajectories, and guess what? If Highfield-Little maintains its current trajectory, it's not going to fall into the sun after all. The Meek are maneuvering Highfield-Little with the projector at site 19. They've somehow harnessed the grav-core, hooked it up to the apparatus at site 19, and are using it to alter Highfield-Little's orbital path. Current calculations have it dipping below the sun's south pole, swinging up and around the sun's equator, then its north pole, then heading back out into space at a greatly increased speed. Its mass and trajectory suggest it will never return to the solar system, that it will keep going until it gets attracted by another star's gravitational well."

Cody began sweeping again, thinking this over. "Why are they trying to maneuver this thing if they're just going to toss it out of the solar system? And what exactly is it? I'm not sure I know what you mean by rogue planet."

"It's a planet that wanders through the galaxy free from the gravitational pull of any star. I've accessed some interesting articles on the CW's more scientific downloads. In the case of Highfield-Little, what we have is an Earth-sized planet ejected, by some force, gravitational or otherwise, from an embryonic solar solar system maybe two billion years ago, before its star's increasing heat had a chance to blow off the rogue's atmosphere. As it began its travels through the galaxy, with no sun to hold it in an orbit, it cooled, and its atmosphere condensed to such an extent that it formed a greenhouse effect strong enough to trap the heat produced by the radioactive decay in the planet's interior. Highfield-Little's warm. It has its own furnace. It might be dark because it has no sun, but it can support life, and in fact, it has life, according to the latest data, the kind of life that doesn't need light, what you find around volcanic vents at the bottom of the sea, or under Europa's ice pack."

"So why are the Meek towing it with their gravitational field device?"

"Because I think the Meek want to move there." Cody

stopped sweeping, caught off guard by the idea. Claire continued. "They could conceivably live there. Especially because they seem to subsist on marrow, which grows without light and in even the harshest conditions. They don't like the light. They could subsist there at first, but then diversify their diet through the use of an ever-expanding infrastructure of agricultural lighting. Like they've done in the Forest of Peace and Understanding. Highfield-Little has lots of internal energy. It wouldn't take much to turn that energy into light, and to power whatever other apparatus they might need for agriculture."

Cody paused. The idea was startling, daring, and he could now see what Buster meant when he said that Ceres was a means to an end. Highfield-Little was real estate for the taking, and Buster was using Ceres as a down payment.

"So Buster's really going to make a try for it?" he finally said.

"It certainly looks that way," said Claire. "But he's taking a risk."

"Why?"

"Because I've been looking at the data," said Claire. "Especially the temperature counts as Highfield-Little draws closer to the sun."

"Where were the first temperatures recorded?"

"Out beyond Neptune," said Claire.

"And what were they there?"

"They varied. That's because the planet's orbit runs on a perpendicular plane, is going to follow the sun's meridian as it approaches perihelion, not its equator, and is tilted on its axis at 33 degrees. Accordingly temperatures in the southern hemisphere ran around 17 degrees Celsius, while in the northern hemisphere they sank to just below the freezing point. You have that atmosphere keeping the heat in."

"An oxygen atmosphere?"

"An oxygen atmosphere."

"And 17 degrees even out beyond Neptune?"

"But getting warmer. Here's where the risk comes in. The

rogue's going to get hotter as it transits the sun. Maybe too hot for human survival. The heat will drastically affect Highfield-Little's weather, particularly because it has such a big ocean."

"It has an ocean?"

"One continent, one ocean, and one inland sea."

"And signs of life," said Cody, wanting to make sure he had heard her right.

"Signs of life," she said. "Flora. Molds and fungi, stuff that can grow in the dark. At least that's what certain trace gas readings indicate. The jury is still out on fauna."

"So what do you think Buster's going to do?" asked Cody. He checked his oxygen readout: 4 hours, 45 minutes left. "Land on the planet as it leaves the solar system?"

"No," said Claire. "As it transits the sun."

"When it's close to the sun?"

"Yes."

"He can't be serious," said Cody.

"I've run some computer models on it. It looks like they're maneuvering the orbits of Ceres and Highfield-Little for the express purpose of effecting a rendezvous. Here on Ceres, they have fourteen of their eighteen nuclear thrusters left. I've entered the locations of all thrusters on a computer, their relative output, asked the GK as well as the CW to come up with a firing sequence, given the known orbital trajectories of each body. Guess what? In order for Ceres to achieve rendezvous with Highfield-Little, she needs a total of eighteen thrusters, four of which have already been fired. My computer model indicates step one in the sequence is the simultaneous firing of thrusters 2, 7, 9, and 13, which they just did. Four thrusters altogether. They're not headed to Earth, Cody. They're going to rendezvous with the rogue."

When Cody tried to raise Axworthy, Azim told him the commander was currently in communication with the Engineering Section, that the Engineering Section had run into a snag repairing the landing carriage of the unmanned explorer. Cody swept quickly while he waited. But the harder he swept the more oxygen he used, and by the time the holo-image of Axworthy appeared in the upper right corner of his visor his current-rate-use indicator showed less than two and a half hours of oxygen left.

"What's going on with the unmanned explorer's landing gear?" he asked Axworthy.

"Three of the load-bearing mechanisms are locked, frozen into place. Engineering Section's working on replacements but it's going to put them behind."

"A lot?"

"They don't know."

The two men fell silent. Axworthy floated before him, transparent, in unreal electronic hues.

"Any word from Vesta City?" asked Cody.

"No."

"Did Claire show you her data?"

The holo-image of Axworthy frowned. "She did," he said. "I'm thinking it over."

"You haven't told Vesta City yet?"

Axworthy's frown deepened. "As much as I trust the actual observations she's made, I'm not sure I completely agree with her interpretation. I don't see how Buster can mount a full-scale exodus to the rogue. We've scanned Ceres dozens of times. For a full-scale exodus he'd need thousands of landers. Big ones. We've detected no evidence of any landers anywhere. We've done a complete computerized axial tomographic inspection of Ceres, we've analyzed it layer by layer, and while at first some of the data was misleading, shrouded in their so-called technology of invisibility, our technicians have been able to break through all that, and they haven't found any landers. So I don't think they're going to land. Especially if the rogue's going to heat up like a barbecue coal as it passes the sun."

"I think you should tell Vesta City that under the circumstances a strategic strike doesn't make sense. I firmly believe the Meek don't have designs on Earth."

"That might be so," said Axworthy, "but it doesn't change the basic equation. They're running off with our asteroid. True to type, I'm afraid. Vesta City's not going to let that happen. If the Meek reestablish the normal orbit, Vesta City will be willing to negotiate with them."

"But maybe they don't have the means to establish Ceres's traditional orbit anymore. They've used up four of their thrusters."

"No. They do. We've analyzed sites 1 through 18. If they're all indeed thrusters, Azim says all the Meek have to do is fire thrusters 4, 6, 10, and 17, in that order, and Ceres will climb back up to its usual orbit."

"But can't you at least tell Council what Claire thinks?"

"Cody, I'll send Council the facts. After that, they can make up their own minds."

By the time Cody and Ben finished cleaning off the extra solar panels, they both had 45 minutes of air left in their tanks. They descended to the control room of the Actinium Oxygen Production Utility.

With his air running out, and the prospect of death looming large in front of him, Cody found his thoughts drifting to Christine. He keyed up the panels and got them working. Luckily, the orphans had not wrecked any of the controls in here. One memory in particular kept coming back to him, from the trip he and Christine had taken to the James Cook Coral Reef Habitat. Ben sat down with Claire's laptop and interfaced with the antique software. Claire's software ran through a half-dozen conversions before the two established a compatible link. As the computers did their conversions, Cody's coral reef memory persisted. Cody was in the water floating above a colony of rose-colored coral. Through the gemlike water he saw Christine swimming toward him. She wasn't wearing a diver's mask. She preferred to dive without one. Her hair floated like a cloud around her head.

Ben got up from the laptop and rested his hand on the large antique breaker switch.

"Here goes," he said.

Cody felt far away from it all. He felt the nearness of death. He couldn't stop thinking of Christine. Christine swam up to him and smiled. Angelfish swam by behind her. She beckoned. She wanted to show him something . . .

Ben closed the breaker switch. The kilowatt bar graph indicator on the screen began to climb. Ben left the breaker switch and watched the bar graph intently.

"It's reached the fail-safe," said Ben.

Cody shook Christine from his mind. He didn't exactly panic while he watched the bar graph hover at the fail-safe point. He just felt overwhelmed by an acute sense of stasis, as if time stood still. Yet time ticked by second by second in his visor readouts. Twenty-five minutes of air left. He checked the atmospheric pressure in the control room. Less than a hundred millibars. Newton's air was all but depleted.

"It's not moving," said Ben. "What's wrong? If we don't get at least 30,000 kilowatts out of that thing—"

But Ben was interrupted by Axworthy. Cody saw Axworthy's holo-image in his visor. "Any luck with the OPU?" asked the commander.

"The bar graph's not climbing beyond the fail-safe," said Cody. "It's stuck at 20,000 kilowatts. It's almost like the fail-safe is holding it back. We can't engage the system until it climbs above the fail-safe mark."

The holo-image of Axworthy seemed to crumple. "Oh," he said. He looked positively gray. "Then that's too bad," he said. He looked like a man who had just been told he had an incurable tumor. "Because I just received more rotten news from the *Conrad Wilson*. They have to replace yet more load-bearing units on the unmanned explorer before they can safely land it down here. It's going to take them another two hours. By that time we'll all be dead, and the *Wilson* won't have the fuel to stay in orbit anyway. Our only chance is to get the OPU working again and, if Council doesn't order the *Wilson* to strike strategically, hope a rescue ship comes for us at a later date."

Cody thought of Deirdre, of Jerry and Claire, of all the security recruits in that small antiquated oxygen pod, their air slowly running out.

"We're down to our last 25 minutes here," he said. "It looks like this might be it, Kevin."

"Cody," said Ben, "Cody, it's going up now. It's reached 21,000."

"Did you hear that, Kevin?" asked Cody.

"I heard. Keep working at it." Axworthy's face looked a little more hopeful now.

"So there's still no word from Council?" asked Cody.

"They still haven't decided," said Axworthy. "They're voting right now. By the way, I've been looking at the municipal street plan. There's a Security Detachment Office just down the way from where you are, on the corner of Niobium and Morse. If it gets to be fifteen minutes, and you still haven't got the OPU working, I want you both to go down and check it. Like Lulu says, they kept emergency oxygen supplies in all these old places. I know most places must be fairly picked over by now, but you never know, you might find something. The way I see it, the Meek wouldn't go much for the oxygen tanks, since they don't breathe the way we do. They might take a few tanks for lab use occasionally, but other than that . . . it's worth a try. If things get too tight, and you can't make it, or if Council orders the *Wilson* to strike after all, you've always got your chloropathoxin. I'm glad we had the extra units on hand. It's a much nicer way to go. A lot of pleasant dreams. Better than dying in the vacuum. And definitely better than being fried by gamma radiation."

The bar graph continued to climb, reached 22,000 then 25,000 kilowatts. Monitors showed robots in the oxygen pit running diagnostic tests on themselves, gearing up for work. The transom-valve panel indicated flow led directly to the main auditorium. They now had fifteen minutes of air left in their tanks, but they stayed despite Axworthy's urging to the contrary. The bar graph reached 26,000 kilowatts. The micro-wave converter, using Claire's program, was targeting perfectly, sending current out to the oxygen mine, then sending a portion of it back to the utility. The bar graph was just reaching 30,000 kilowatts when something went wrong with Claire's targeting program.

"What happened?" asked Ben.

"I don't know," said Cody.

They checked the outside monitors, quickly zeroed in on the microwave monitor.

The microwave dish swung wildly in the direction of the open-pit oxygen mine, its waves generating energy hot enough to melt rock. Cody watched the monitor as the beam slammed into one of the massive earth-moving robots. The piece of machinery exploded into fragments.

"Turn it off, turn it off!" he cried.

Ben leaped up and broke the connection. The bar graph quickly sank to 20,000 kilowatts, sticking at the fail-safe for a few seconds, then dwindling away to nothing. The panels and monitors died, and the targeting program went off-line. Cody listened to his own heartbeat, his own breathing. Biofeedback monitors on his visor indicated a rise in both. It was dark. It was quiet. And they had failed.

"What are we going to do?" asked Ben.

Cody checked his meter. Eleven minutes left.

"Let's look for oxygen."

As they walked quickly—not running; running would just deplete their oxygen faster—down Morse Street to the Security Detachment Office, Cody was surprised to see how much the marrow had come back to this outlying area of Newton, making its encroachment quickly from the neighboring suburb of Planck's Constant. The buildings in this area of the city were war-torn, bricks and mortar blown away from the underlying girder supports, lying in piles everywhere, strewn all over the street. The scene of dreary wreckage popped into relief in his guidelight beam, small circular snapshots of the end of the world, snippets of a nightmare rendered in the wan glow: a few charred skeletons over there, an overturned hovercar black and gutted on the sidewalk, and, of all things, a frozen horse in a lane lying on its side, emaciated, mummified, the insignia of the CDF Mounted Riot Squad tattooed in blue and white on its chest. Everywhere else, impenetrable darkness, not even any glowmoss out here, like he was inside the stomach of a giant beast.

They found the Security Office badly damaged but still standing. Though the main entrance had been bolted shut, the front window was smashed, its bars ripped away, one still dangling from the steel window frame. They climbed through the window. Cody swung his guidelight around the duty clerk's area, saw a chair lying on its side, broken glass all over the floor, and a vandalized particle-beam battering ram leaning against the wall. A picture hung next to it, a face from the past, now no more than a historical figure, a photographic portrait of Comptroller Leo D. Oliver, his cheeks hanging like the jowls of a basset hound, his blue eyes hooded by drooping and suspicious lids. Ceres's leader from thirty years ago, the man who had ordered the evacuation, the official who had signed off on Isosceles Boulevard's decision to bioexterminate. Cody swung his guidelight away. A corridor led to the back. He looked at his oxygen meter. Three minutes left.

"Let's check back here," he said.

They hurried to the back area and found another corridor running at right angles. Marrow grew here and there. He looked up and down the corridor. Which door to try? He had two minutes of oxygen left, two minutes to live, two minutes to find the right door.

At the end of the hall he saw a door stenciled with the word STORES.

"Down here," he said.

They ran down the hall.

They had to break the door down. Cody ran against it

three times, launching himself shoulder-first, trying not to panic, struggling to forget how quickly the seconds of his life were dwindling away. The door finally gave and he stumbled into the storeroom. He checked his oxygen meter again—1:23. Some old uniforms hung on a rack. Discarded computer terminals had been stacked one on top of the other against the wall. What else? A pile of evidence collection bags. A stretcher. Three truncheons. Someone's framed certificate from the Academy. A pack of chewing gum. A music stand. A large metal cabinet, locked, stood against the other wall. That was the only reasonable place to look. He took out his laser drill. Fifty-nine seconds left. He cut around the lock while Ben sliced at the hinges. The metal turned orange, then white. He cut a circle right around the lock and it popped out. He opened the door and jumped back. Thirty-seven seconds left. A dead orphan, mummified and wizened, in shackles and handcuffs, lay in a fetal position on the floor of the cabinet. No oxygen tanks anywhere in sight.

He turned, looked at Ben, tried to keep his panic in check, but he couldn't help thinking of snow again, the powdery stuff that came in the evening at the Chillicothe Alpine Habitat, and how, in day's final light it would glisten with all the colors of a diamond, white, but also blue, violet, and gold, something great, something he was going to miss.

"This is the shits," said Ben, and activated his chloropathoxin unit.

A blue gas steamed up into Ben's helmet, obscuring his face. Cody reached for Ben but he knew it was pointless. So this was it, he thought. You think about death, it sometimes haunts you when you go to sleep at night, you know it's out there waiting for you, but you never know where or in what circumstances it will finally catch up with you. Warning pings sounded inside his helmet. Ben slumped to the floor. Cody knelt beside him. He began to gasp for breath a few seconds later. Not strenuously, at least not at first; there was still residual oxygen inside his suit, but it was quickly being replaced with carbon dioxide.

"Ben?"

Ben didn't respond. Through the yellow visor and the blue mist, Ben LeBlanc's face looked green. His mouth hung open and Cody could see his overbite. Cody struggled for breath but he felt like he had a plastic bag over his head. He thought his exposure to marrow might help him, but he hadn't kissed Lulu in a while and his stomach was now proving useless as a respiratory organ. He looked around the storeroom. So this was where he was going to die. Every breath he took was more torturous than the last. He gazed at the music stand, at first thinking it was an odd object to find in here but then remembering that the Security Department on Vesta had any number of marching bands. He felt suddenly faint. He glanced over at the mummified orphan in the cabinet, thought how cruel it had been to shackle him, to throw him in there, then just forget about him until he died. He felt the lack of oxygen right down to the base of his spine. He breathed faster. He hyperventilated. Felt his hands start to tingle from lack of oxygen. Felt his muscles seize up as he began to panic. He couldn't breathe. He got up and looked wildly around the room. So this was it . . . but it didn't mean he wasn't going to fight it.

He ran to the rack of hanging uniforms and pushed them out of the way. Instinct told him to fight, even though the *Conrad Wilson* might end up launching a strategic strike anyway. He needed oxygen and he needed it now. His knees felt wobbly. His visor warned him that the carbon dioxide in his suit was now reaching dangerous levels . . . he ran over to the stack of old computer terminals and pushed them out of the way . . . thinking he might find an old tank behind there . . . but what he found was a French horn . . . sitting on its bell . . . its brass body dented . . . one of its valve keys stuck in the down position as if the musical instrument were playing a silent but eternal note . . .

At last, he decided he didn't want to die this way.

He wanted dreams.

He wanted euphoria.

Above all, he wanted peace.

He activated his own chloropathoxin unit.

A blue mist rose before him. Like the blue of those gem-like seas in the James Cook Coral Reef Habitat. He breathed in deeply. He sank to his knees, thankful that he didn't feel the panic anymore. He fell to his back and looked up at the ceiling where a colony of marrow grew in neat little rows. He closed his eyes. And he dreamed. Dreamed of those distant days before the collapse in Residential Sector 5 . . . when he and Christine had been together . . . when they still had plans . . . and when anything seemed possible . . .

CHAPTER 18

In his chloropathoxin dream Cody was underwater. The artificial tropical sun sparkled on the surface of the water above him, giving its underside a mirrorlike appearance. Christine swam down to him, her hair floating around her in a dark brown mane, her eyes the color of jade, that smile of hers on her face.

He reached up, cupped her chin in his hand, and felt all the old pain come back. *I understand your pain, Cody,* she said. But could anybody ever understand his particular pain, how he had suffered with it for five years, missing her every day, still getting used to the fact that he was alone, that there was now a major demarcation in his life, a discontinuity, and that at times, as with Buster, he felt like an island unto himself? She reached down and pulled off his diving mask and the water seemed to darken, to lose all its blueness, grow shockingly cold. She leaned toward him. To kiss him. He was so happy to see her again after all these years. The chloropathoxin made her so real. *Our life together would have been a work of art,* he said.

When Christine kissed him the water instantly warmed up. But it was more than that. She came into focus yet receded at the same time. He started to come to his senses. Christine didn't have green eyes but violet eyes; and she didn't have brown hair anymore but white hair; and her skin had turned robin's-egg blue. He knew this wasn't Christine at all but Lulu, here to make him breathe with his stomach, to withstand the lower atmospheric pressure, to survive the killer cold, to reactivate all the marrow he had already ingested so his chromosome 3 could repair the toxic damage of the chloropathoxin.

For a long time his muscles didn't—or couldn't—cooperate, felt locked in a chloropathoxin-induced paralysis. He was so tired, so worn out, as if everything he had ever done in his life had finally caught up with him. He didn't think he would ever move again.

He lay there staring at the circular glow his guidelight cast on the ceiling of the storeroom. Sometimes Lulu came to kiss him; sometimes she disappeared from sight. He lost sense of time. His lungs weren't working. His chest was still. He felt unarticulated yet reassuring emanations from Lulu. She didn't have to say anything, didn't have to form her thoughts into words because he already knew, could comprehend that nugget of brightness, recognized the way she felt toward him and found strength in it.

He turned, saw Agatha kissing Ben, a desperate CPR kiss. He thought Ben was dead. But Ben finally coughed. A small cloud of blue gas escaped from his mouth.

Ben opened his eyes. He turned his head weakly to one side, dazed and disoriented. Cody tried to speak, to ask Ben if he were all right, but there was no air, nothing to force against his vocal cords, and no medium through which sound could travel. He gave up on his impotent attempt to form words.

He said: *Will he live?*

Lulu stipulated: *He will convalesce.*

Her cool wind cleared the fog from his mind, and all the pieces of his current reality fit themselves together. He sat up, dizzy with the effort, and pulled on his helmet. He checked his visor readings, patched into the biofeedback monitors of the survivors in the pod, and discovered that only four of them remained active: Axworthy, Claire, Deirdre, and Jerry. He accessed the pod life support, had trouble with the connection, had to try a few times, finally got through and saw that the four survivors had 22 minutes of oxygen left.

He said: *Do you know where there's any oxygen? Any extra tanks anywhere?*

She nodded, beckoned.

He followed her down the hall on unsteady legs to a door at the end. She pulled her knife from its scabbard, pried off the control unit, did something to the electronics inside, and the door slid open. Stairs led to a basement.

In the basement, they found fifteen oxygen tanks as well as a rack of different adapters, one of which fit his own suit.

Oxygen not to breathe—he was breathing with his stomach now—but to speak with, to force his vocal cords to move.

Axworthy's holo-image smiled weakly at Cody. "I thought you were dead. When we saw the glitch in the targeting program we thought you'd had it."

"What happened to everybody?" he said. "I've got only the four of you left."

Axworthy looked away. "My security recruits used their units so the rest of us could have more air." He looked up at Cody, his eyes steady. "They were brave men and women."

"We've got fifteen tanks of oxygen here. We can be there in 35 minutes. Can you hang on that long?"

"It means we're going to be running on empty." Axworthy's face settled. "Not that it's going to make any difference now. They've ordered the strike."

Cody's blood quickened. His throat tightened with apprehension. "What strike?" But he already knew the answer to his question.

"Had you contacted us ten minutes sooner . . . the Council's voted for bioextermination. The comptroller's signed off on it. I've sent the order to the *Conrad Wilson*. I've had them abandon the explorer refit. They weren't going to have it done in time, and they'll need the fuel from the explorer to make their maneuvers anyway. I've locked in the strike command. The ship's on automatic strategic deployment. The crew can't stop it. They're just along for the ride now. Only I can send the abort command."

"Then send the abort command," said Cody. "I'm coming with the oxygen. You can't kill them all, Kevin. Send the abort command."

Axworthy's face hardened. "It wasn't my decision, Cody. And don't think it was an easy decision for the Council to make either. You saw how long it took them. They considered two possible options: a full-scale invasion or another bioextermination. They felt a full-scale invasion would cost too many Vestan lives and might not be effective enough in stopping whatever plans the Meek had for Earth. Plus they wanted to minimize damage, and the blast from neutron bombardment is quite small compared to the firepower they'd need to launch a full-scale invasion. They believe that Ceres might be recoverable at some point in the future and they want to optimize that possibility."

"You've got to send the abort command, Kevin."

"I can't do that."

"Please," said Cody, growing even more alarmed.

Axworthy frowned. "I've erased the software. I'm a soldier, Cody. You think I'd actually leave the software intact? I know how orphans work. The minute we run out of oxygen, the minute we're dead, they'll be in the pod hacking the bioextermination order. Only they won't find it. There'll be nothing there to hack."

Cody stared at the holo-image of Axworthy, his mind racing to find a way out of what was quickly becoming a checkmate situation. But he felt as if he were groping in the dark, searching for a solution that simply wasn't there.

"You mean the *Conrad Wilson*'s going to attack Ceres whether we want it to or not?"

"That's about the size of it."

Lulu put her hand on his arm, as alarmed as Cody.

"I did it for our children, Cody," said Axworthy, looking

annoyed that he should have to explain this to Cody. "I want
them to grow up healthy in the one gee, like I did. I want
them to grow up free from the fear of orphans coming in the
night. And I want them to know that they live in a society
that's willing to stand up for what's right."

"But what about the Meek children?" said Cody. "Have
you thought about them?"

Axworthy sighed. "The order's been sent, Cody, and it
can't be canceled. The ship's maneuvering for the best
strategic spread, and should be ready to fire in less than four
hours."

He ran like fury down Isosceles Boulevard, an oxygen
tank under each arm. He loped past the big government
buildings on Isosceles Boulevard, their tall pillars lit by the
fitful glow of the new lights Axworthy had strung up. Lulu
ran beside him with two oxygen tanks of her own.

According to his visor the oxygen pod's air had run out
two minutes ago. He couldn't let Deirdre die. He couldn't let
Claire die. Agatha was still back in Actinium with Ben. He
couldn't let Jerry or Axworthy die. Most of all, he had to
find a way to stop the *Conrad Wilson*.

In the main auditorium of the emergency shelter, a red
light flashed on the outside of the oxygen pod—an indicator
light. No oxygen left. Cody put his oxygen tanks down, exhausted by the long run from Actinium, staggered forward,
gripped the pod for support, and looked through the porthole
window beside the door. He saw the survivors lying on the
floor, gasping, eyes half-closed, like fish washed up on a
shore. The corpses of the sacrificed recruits lay to one side.
The carbon dioxide meter on the wall inside showed levels
close to the saturation point. The survivors wore pressure
suits, had helmets ready. On their belts they wore
chloropathoxin units. All they had to do was snap on their
helmets, activate their units, and dream their way to eternity.

He cycled the airlock, stepped into the pressurization
chamber, dragged the oxygen tanks in after him, and beck-

oned Lulu. Lulu got in. He shut the outside lock, cycled the pressure again, smelled the stale carbon dioxide air, and opened the inside airlock. Claire looked up at him. He sucked back a chestful of the stagnant air and spoke.

"Claire," he said, "we've got to get your targeting program back on-line."

He had finally come up with a solution.

Meek converged around the pod, summoned by the biochemical telegraph poles of the marrow, Cody's own weak call amplified through Lulu, replicated in the microscopic particles of marrow that floated in the vacuum, jumping from colony to colony, all the way to the City of Resolved Differences, to the Forest of Peace and Understanding. They converged around the pod and they accepted him. Buster was there and Buster accepted him too. In siding with the Meek, Cody had crossed a line, he knew that, and he knew he had to act accordingly. He had four of the Meek guard Axworthy. He was going to save them if he could, and, as much as he had grown to respect Axworthy, he had to prevent the man's interference.

With that settled, Cody went back into the pod to see how Claire was making out.

She sat at her console going through the 15,000 lines of code in her targeting program. Cody leaned over and watched the screen. He recognized only some of the machine language she was using. She scanned line after line, thousands of electronic hieroglyphs, and every so often she would shake her head and her brow would pinch.

"Any luck?" he asked.

"I can't find it," she said. "I've been through it twice. I've opened all the crunched bits and I've had a good look through. I can't spot any corruption. And there's no sign of a virus either. You're sure it couldn't be in the hardware? The interface to the microwave converter? Look how old it is."

"Our monitor indicated bad code in your software."

"I'll keep working," she said.

*   *   *

Cody and Claire stood on the transmission tower platform double-checking the interface between her microwave converter targeting program and the rest of the equipment. In the 270 square kilometers of solar panels below them, swarms of Meek, all wrapped in the orange reflective pressure tape, swept the astral debris and dust off the photovoltaic cells. Cody sensed their single-minded determination. More important, he sensed their unity; even though they still had their clans, they came together like this for the common good, thousands upon thousands of them. The white glare of the sun beat down on them from directly overhead. The orange tape was as bright as flecks of fire against the dark solar panels.

"I've had to modify the targeting software with the introduction of a joystick option," said Claire. "I don't know what they're going to throw at us, but I anticipate a multiple launch with multiple warheads. Forward and backwards are up and down. Right and left are right and left. The subsidiary thumbstick brings you back and forth through the grid. This trackball here changes the angle of view."

"I checked the GK historical file on the subject," said Cody. "Thirty years ago they used seven launches with two neutron warheads apiece. They'll fire at least that much if not more. Thirty years ago they launched from an altitude of 2,500 kilometers."

"What about warhead deployment?" asked Claire.

"The warheads separated from their launch vehicles at the 1,000-kilometer mark."

She nodded. "So we should try to intercept the launch vehicles before the warheads deploy. If the warheads deploy you'll be looking at twice as many targets. How soon till they launch?"

"Between ten and twenty minutes from now. I can't be more precise than that."

Claire glanced at the bar graph. "This is a great idea, Cody. We're up to 500,000 kilowatts." She put her hand against the microwave converter. "That gives this thing a range of 750 kilometers. If they deploy the warheads at a thousand it still means you'll be faced with all those extra targets. Do you think we can get any more range than we already have?"

He gestured toward the thousands of Meek. "They're working hard," he said. "If we can get the plant up to a million kilowatts, that'll give the converter a range of 1,500 kilometers, and that's well above the warhead deployment zone. At least historically speaking. That'll cut down on the number of targets considerably."

"Those launch vehicles travel at 600 kilometers per minute," said Claire, not at all encouraged. "That won't give you much time."

"I'll have just under a minute to shoot down as many launch vehicles as I can. After that, I'll have to deal with the separate warheads."

"And just under two minutes to destroy whatever warheads get through." She shook her head. "I don't know, Cody. Those odds aren't great."

"It's what we've got to work with. Key in the provisional parameters, but be ready to change them if we have to." She followed his instructions. "Now let's see what it looks like on the graphics."

She nodded, punched up the graphics. "The holo-grid in green here is for reference," she said, "with the distances marked horizontally and vertically along the sides. The *Conrad Wilson* will be represented by a blue triangle, the launch vehicles by yellow triangles, and the warheads by red triangles. Your targeting is represented by this white arrow. Once you've got your arrow in any of your target grids the microwave beam will automatically home in. If you've got two or more targets within the same grid the beam will pick off the closest, then the next closest, and so on."

Cody nodded. "Is the targeting lock mandatory or can you move to another square if it seems more pressing?"

"Just hit Enter and the targeting will disengage until you

move it to whatever grid you think is necessary. If you decide you want to stay in the same grid after all, just hit Enter again and the targeting will reengage."

He nodded.

He tried it in test mode, getting the feel of the joystick, the thumbstick, and the trackball, watching the arrow move through the grid sideways, up, down, backward, forward, the little white arrow growing larger or smaller to enhance the effect of perspective, the scene panning left or right as he tried the trackball.

"I should do okay," he said.

"I'm concerned about the strength of the microwave beam," said Claire. "And I still haven't located the glitch in my targeting software."

"Those are the least of our worries," he said.

"What do you mean?" she asked.

"We're trying to stop a full-scale strategic neutron strike with a piece of hydroequipment that's 200 years old," he said. "Might as well try to saw through a brick with a feather duster."

The *Conrad Wilson* appeared as a blue triangle, swimming along the top of the green holo-grid like a shark along the surface of the sea. Thousands of Meek continued to sweep. Every panel cleared showed a corresponding rise in power. Each rise in power meant an increase in range for the old microwave converter. He now had 750,000 kilowatts. That gave him a range of 1,075 kilometers, an unspeakably narrow margin, just a hair's breadth above the warhead deployment zone.

He looked up, squinting against the sun, which now slanted toward the west, thinking he might see the *Conrad Wilson*, maybe as a moving star against millions of stationary ones, but the ship maneuvered for attack 2,500 kilometers away, too far for the naked eye.

On his screen, he saw three yellow triangles detach themselves from the *Conrad Wilson* and head west toward the

Angle Territories. Cody pushed the joystick in that direction, but the arrow wouldn't rise above the 1,100-kilometer-altitude mark. He followed the yellow triangles along this power-deficiency barrier toward the Angles, the little white arrow reminding him of a helium balloon bobbing along a ceiling, unable to go any higher because of lack of power. The farther west he went, the more his arrow sank, trading altitude for distance. The launch vehicles breached the war-head deployment zone and the three yellow triangles turned into six red ones.

With a quick thump of his heart, he realized that the red triangles had sunk below the 1,000-kilometer-altitude mark, that he was within range.

He swung his white arrow all the way to the left, placed it in the target grid of the three nearest red triangles, and watched the three red triangles disappear. He then brought it over to the next square, was able to get two of the red triangles, but the last of them strayed to the next grid before target acquisition. He saw a flash on the horizon. He looked at the screen, at the damage-assessment window.

He saw that the City of Fair Argument, a city of 100,000 souls in the Territory of the Angle of Incidence, had taken a direct hit.

A hundred thousand souls. And nothing he could do. He felt momentarily shaken, that he was fighting against un-beatable odds, and that in the end he would be responsible for the deaths of thousands of people, but he shook these thoughts away, controlled them, concentrated, bolstered his nerve, and found a new resolve to fight harder than ever.

The *Conrad Wilson* launched another three weapons. He checked the power readouts. He had 900,000 kilowatts on-line now, a range of 1,350 kilometers. He moved the white arrow forward and to the left, then lifted it into the appropriate square. He knocked out all three launch vehicles before they reached the deployment zone. The explosions, visible to the naked eye, looked like big blue donuts

1,200 kilometers straight up. His success gave him courage.

He contacted Deirdre, who was out in the field supervising hundreds of Meek in the laying of new optical cable to replace the old impact-compromised stuff.

"Can we get any more power?" he asked her. "I think they're going to attack east next, toward the Forest of Peace and Understanding."

"We're just about ready to go with the panels in northwest grid number 16," she said. "That should give you an extra 50,000 kilowatts."

Which meant an extra 75 kilometers; an advantage of seconds, but every second was precious.

Eight yellow triangles left the lethal underbelly of the *Conrad Wilson*. The launch vehicles traveled through a wide range of grid squares, spreading out from each other like the legs of a spider, deploying over an area of 62,500 square kilometers. His gridwork reference immediately panned back, showed the entire northern hemisphere of the football-shaped Ceres, allowed for targeting straight through the carbonaceous planetesimal by showing the asteroid in transparency.

He targeted. He had a 1,425-kilometer range now.

He wiped out four of the eight launch vehicles before they could deploy their warheads.

But the others . . .

The others got through. Reached the warhead zone.

The four remaining yellow triangles turned into eight red triangles.

Eight neutron warheads he had to destroy in under two minutes.

He swung his white arrow two squares over and vaporized two of them. Then down three squares to get another three. The remaining three triangles hurtled eastward. One toward Equilibrium, one toward the Forest of Peace and Understanding, one toward the City of Resolved Differences. He pressed the joystick forward, caught the two trailing warheads, watched them burst into bright blue donuts on the eastern horizon, was about to move his white arrow into the next square where the last remaining warhead was heading ever closer to the City of Resolved Differences when a message popped up to his screen: ERROR IN TARGETING LINK 6579. Claire's glitch, Claire's software problem, Claire's invisible trouble spot.

The huge microwave dish, towering above him like a giant white flower, swung suddenly to the left.

He hit Enter, hoping to disengage the automatic targeting.

On the top line of the gridwork the *Conrad Wilson* pulled away, disappeared from his screen, its mission over, had to retreat because of fuel concerns, even though its attack had been only partially successful. The error message blinked off for a second, then came back on. The microwave dish swung ninety degrees to the right. The beam slammed into the oxygen mine's carbon slag heaps. The last red triangle had its nose down, dipping the 500 remaining kilometers toward the City of Resolved Differences.

He saw a blinding flash in the direction of the City of Resolved Differences and thought for sure he had failed, that the warhead had struck the Meek's primary city; but then he saw another blinding flash to the south, another to the north, and finally one to the northwest. He felt some gee force, grabbed on to the rail to steady himself, watched the four detonations light up the surrounding terrain, saw the explosions form themselves into white spheres. Nuclear detonations, such as they looked when fired from the silos. The Meek had just made another trajectory change, and none too soon . . .

On the screen the asteroid broke free of Claire's computerized targeting gridwork, ducking away from the oncoming warhead.

The warhead came to within 100 kilometers of the City of Resolved Differences, remained on its trajectory, was still too high to be caught by the asteroid's gravity well, kept going straight, even as the asteroid acted like a head ducking out of the way of a bullet. The warhead passed the asteroid, now headed away from Ceres in the opposite direction from which it had come, on its own straight tangent. Cody exited the targeting program.

The microwave dish settled down and finally grew still.

PART 3

CARSWELL

CHAPTER 19

Buster said: *We have no wide-scale relief capability for this kind of attack. We are a peaceful people. We have trained ourselves to be meek. To be otherwise would be the end of us.*

Cody and Buster rode in a skimmer over the bleak surface of Ceres. Thousands of other skimmers rode like a swarm of insects around them. Lulu was somewhere out there in one of them with Deirdre. Agatha rode with Ben. Jerry and Claire rode with Rex and Boris, ranking members of Buster's clan. Annabel, another ranking member of Buster's clan, drove a heavily sedated Kevin Axworthy. Sedated because he had insisted on resisting, such as was his legitimate duty. They went with the Meek because there was nowhere else to go. To stay behind in Newton, to wait for a rescue when all ships would be out of range for the foreseeable future, and when they had been given up for dead anyway, would make their chance of survival tentative at best.

Cody felt the thoughts of the Meek—the thoughts of thousands of them, thoughts of gratitude, of acknowledgment. He also felt the deaths of a 100,000 souls in the City of Fair Argument.

Cody said: *And you're sure about Equilibrium? My gridwork showed all warheads down over that area. I don't know how one got through.*

Buster said: *The Village of Mutual Tolerance sustained a*

direct hit with a partially compromised warhead. The bec-querels are still high—lethal—and casualties there could run as high as 25,000, even despite our code-written protection against it. For three decades our culture has conscientiously vilified arms. We carry these knives more as talismans than weapons. When we learned of the Conrad Wilson*'s attack we had no idea how we were going to defend ourselves. We owe our lives to your ingenuity.*

They continued over the cratered terrain, skirting far to the south of the contaminated area.

Cody said: *You owe your lives to your second firing sequence. The* Conrad Wilson *continues to retreat?*

Buster said: *They're well out of range now. In 22 hours we'll be within the orbital plane of Mars, well on our way.*

Cody said: *And there's no possible way we can help the people in the Village of Mutual Tolerance or in the City of Fair Argument?*

Buster said: *In response to this emergency we have in production a pressure tape designed to shield against the intense radiation. We'll dispatch aid workers as fast as we can but I fear it won't be enough. The doses delivered by the* Conrad Wilson *are much too high, even for us, and we expect a great number of fatalities.*

Cody hated to think of all those people dying slowly. All those people suffering and no one well enough to help anybody—a microcosm of Armageddon. He racked his brain trying to think of something else he could do, remembering the collapse in Residential Sector 5—all that suffering, a universe of suffering, people trapped in horribly injured conditions for days under all that rubble. The suffering in the City of Fair Argument and in the Village of Mutual Tolerance would be different. All the buildings would still be standing, all the infrastructure would be in place, but everybody would be sick and dying from the radiation, hair falling out, open sores forming, teeth falling out, with weakness, disorientation, nausea . . . a nightmare.

Cody said: *We have to do something.*

Buster said: *We'll send out as many as we can. We'll save those who can be saved. But mostly we'll just bring comfort. In the meantime the Father asks for you. He wishes to meet the protector of our home, the rescuer of our future.*

As they flew over the treetops of the river valley habitat toward the City of Resolved Differences, Cody saw that only a few skimmers flew in formation with them now, that others were breaking away from the main group and disappearing beneath the canopy of the forest. He felt tired. The life-or-death challenges of the last eighteen hours had exhausted him. The air was warm on his face, scented with the light perfume of a thousand different rain-forest blooms. Now that he didn't have to think about what he was going to do next to save not only his own life but the lives of everyone around him, he felt shaky, traumatized by the whole ordeal; not like a hero at all but like someone who knew how to grit his teeth and bear his own fear, squeaking by on willpower alone. He had done his best. He had done what he could, and despite the grief he felt for the dead he would just have to accept the outcome.

He slumped in his seat. That was it. It was over. The *Conrad Wilson* wasn't coming back. Cody was on his way to the Martian orbital plane with no idea of what he was going to do, no plan for getting back to Vesta. He didn't even know if he wanted to go back to Vesta. Would Vesta City even let him come back?

The forest canopy ended and he saw fields below. The skimmer dipped, flew two meters above the ground. He saw cantaloupes, big ones the size of watermelons, glowing in the light of the five moons. He saw tomatoes. Corn. Wheat. Peppers. Lettuce. They flew into ranchland. He saw cattle, slim-boned and elongated, produced to thrive in weak gravity. Sheep. Bison. Stegosaurs. Ostriches. A half dozen ungulates he didn't have names for, hoofed creatures concocted with designer genetic code, one looking like a cross between a pig and an elephant, another like a mix between a zebra and an ox, still another like a hybrid of wildebeest, wild boar, and donkey.

Buster said: *We are farmers now, not warriors.*

The river curved from the north, wide and flat, a mile across, muddy-looking, dotted with several effluvial islands. They skimmed across the river and came to the City of Resolved Differences.

The polished stone, flecked with pyrite, sparkled in the moonlight. It was a city of perches, not roads. Buildings soared for fifty stories or more, none of them just straight towers, all of them fanciful, each a creation in itself, designed in concert with the others so that there existed a unity to the composition of the city as a whole. One was a double helix. Another was a pyramid. Still another was like a roll of pennies knocked edgewise, creating a series of circular terraces going all the way up. The building gave the illusion that it might topple into the square at any second.

It was to this building that Buster took Cody.

They settled lightly into the square. Air pressure was at least 700 millibars.

Cody said: *If you don't need air to breathe, why do you pressurize this place?*

Buster said: *Our industry and agriculture depend on it. And we like the feel and the smell of air. We are of human ancestry, after all.*

Cody removed his helmet and took a deep breath. Beds of marrow grew in raised ornamental gardens, interspersed with genetically developed night-bloomers. The others took off their helmets as well. He looked around at his crew: Jerry, Deirdre, Ben, Claire, and . . . and Kevin Axworthy, still partially sedated, now being helped from his skimmer and out of his helmet by Annabel. Axworthy looked up at the coin-roll building with bleary eyes, then turned to Cody and stared at him as if he didn't know who he was.

Lulu looked at Cody too. He tried to sense what she was thinking but she wouldn't let him in. She kept glancing at Buster as if she were afraid of him again. Cody felt disoriented. He wanted to be near her. He wanted to touch her. If he could only touch her he knew he would feel greatly restored. Deirdre walked over and slipped her arm through his. He didn't mind. She was as distraught by the last eighteen hours as he was. Her touch soothed him.

They entered the building. Inside it, for at least the first seven or eight floors, was an atrium with a vast botanical garden, even full-grown trees. At the atrium's zenith a perfect scale model of Saturn with all its rings and moons glowed with a much higher holographic resolution than anything they had on Vesta, washing the entire area with a soft butterscotch light, brighter than the light of the five moons. As they walked through this atrium, they came upon small gardens and glades, where Meek could be seen conferring quietly. Cody came to understand that this was a place of government. In some gardens the Meek sang at shimmering blue cellophane, such as Cody had seen during his drug-induced interrogation of Lulu. Small waterfalls cascaded down the walls at regular intervals, and birds flitted through the branches of the trees.

They finally came to a garden at the back, an arbor hung with a profusion of crimson hibiscus blooms. In the middle an old man reclined on a hammock. He wasn't like the other Meek Cody had seen. He looked a lot more like a regular human being, with his limbs the customary human length, his eyes and ears normal, no bulge above his stomach. His skin had only a vague hint of blue. He had to be at least ninety, looked frail, as if his bones would break under the slightest pressure.

Buster said: *This is the Father.*

So. Not a god, not a deity, not an article of faith, just a man, not even a Meek man, or an orphan. Just a normal human man, showing only minimal signs of a genetic rewrite. The Father shifted in his hammock, struggled to a sitting position, lifted a cane from a hook on the tree, and stood up. Cody couldn't help thinking that there was something familiar about the Father, recognized something in him that he had seen somewhere before. His features. A broad shovel-blade of a chin, intense blue eyes, a hawk's beak of a nose. Cody saw that Kevin was staring at the Father with wide, wondering eyes.

"Dad?" said Axworthy.

He took a few steps forward, no longer needing Annabel's help and peered at the Father, shaking his head tentatively. His mouth opened, as if he were about to say something, then closed again, his jaw clamping down, like he was bracing himself to withstand the onslaught of a tidal wave. The old man looked at Axworthy, his face showing not so much surprise as resignation. The resemblance between the two men startled Cody.

"It's me, Kevin," said the Father.

Had to allow time for a reunion like that, for Kevin to be with his father for the first time in thirty years. Cody met the Father, spoke to him for a few minutes—to the man who hadn't been murdered and mutilated by the orphans after all—then gracefully made his excuses and left.

Finally Cody had a chance to rest, to be alone with Lulu.

She came to him while he reclined on a bed of moss in a small grotto built into the side of the atrium wall. She brought a plate of fruit, and they ate. He felt the cool wind of her menthol signature waves caress his mind. She didn't form her feelings into verbal signals, articulated thoughts, just let them flow into Cody as they came. She wore pants. Only pants. He looked at her breasts. At her hips. Felt desire. Emanated desire. Felt his own desire reflected and magnified in Lulu, then felt Lulu's desire reflected, magnified, like embers glowing in a fire.

He pulled her near, feeling fully and truly alive for the first time since Christine had died. She lay down beside him. He put his arm around her. She rested her cheek against his shoulder. The roof of the grotto flickered with the light of several bioluminescent moths, multicolored like the moons, enough light to see by but not a harsh light, a soft and muted light, evocative, ambient, liquid.

She said: *I was once like you. A human. A girl. So was Agatha. Buster calls me Lulu, that's the name everybody calls me, but that's a name I was given by the orphans, that's just the name I go by now, the name they gave me when they came and took me away from my mother and father. Back when I was a girl, a human girl, my name was Catherine. Agatha's name was Elizabeth. She was four and I was eight when the orphans took us away.* Cody felt Lulu's sadness. *We never saw out parents again.* Her sadness deepened. *Buster saved us from our kidnappers, the orphans of the Chryse Planitia Clan. We lived with the Chryse Planitia Clan in the caves and tunnels around Equilibrium until I was well into my teens. Both my sister and I are older than we look. We were at first used as child slaves. Then we were used as soldiers. And finally we were used as concubines. That's when Buster came to rescue us. I lie with you now, yet how can I turn my back on Buster? How can I wish to stop being one of his wives?* Her sadness modulated into fear. *Yet I no longer wish to be his wife.*

He sensed a much larger story in her words, not only of conflict between the Ceresians and the orphans but of conflict between the different clans. Of how the two separate lines of Meek got started, one line from the original crèche orphans, which she called the orphan line, the other line from kidnapped human children, from converted prisoners, from human volunteers, which she called the human line, the line that wouldn't suffocate, only get sick if you took away their marrow. She opened herself. He stepped inside and walked around, explored her thoughts and feelings, dug deep, saw her through and through, learned whatever he could about the clans, her place in them, Buster's place in them. How each clan named itself after a Martian geographical feature. How the biggest clan, Buster's clan, was known as the Olympia Mons Clan. How Buster was the leader of all the clans. How for years she had fooled herself into thinking

that her gratitude—the eternal thankfulness she felt toward
Buster—was actually love, and how, once she had touched
Cody for the first time, once she understood his own journey
through love and gratitude, and had delved into the depths
of his grief for Christine, she had at last realized that gratitude and love were two different things, that the first was but
a minor part of the much greater and kaleidoscopic universe
of the second. Knew love at last, and in so knowing, had
found herself reinvented.

Love.

Desire.

With a blue woman.

Who had violet eyes.

Who now slipped her hand under the mulberry-colored
tunic they'd given him to wear. Whose hand was small and
delicate, feminine but sure. He felt her love, how she was
surprised by it, that it should turn out to be so different from
what she had expected, felt her desire, and in so feeling it,
quickly reciprocated, turned, kissed.

Not a kiss of blunt practical communication . . . but one
of a deeper intermingling.

They made love.

And he could tell it was different for Lulu, that she had
never felt this fevered level of desire before. The reason was
simple. The reason was so elemental even a child could understand it. Yet it was something Buster had never grasped.
Her desire was so heartfelt and passionate because she had
Cody's *undivided* attention. For the first time in her life, he
thought, she was the center of someone else's universe,
wasn't simply there for the purpose of performing the biological function of sex, to scratch an itch, to ease a frustration, or to soothe the anger of the day's slights, such as was
typical for Buster. She was there as Cody's sun. She was
there as his sea. And he gloried in her.

When it was over, when they had spent themselves not
once, not twice, but multiple times, she collapsed in his
arms, some pink showing through the blue of her cheeks. He

pulled her near, hugged her, felt Christine's blessing, knew that he had finally rebuilt that part of himself he had lost under the rubble of Residential Sector 5.

He talked to the Father—Artemis Axworthy—the next day.

They sat in the Father's garden under the artificial light of the holographic Saturn, the light brighter today, nearly as strong as "daylight" on Vesta, like late afternoon, dusk, with shadows collecting on the lavender flowers that bloomed through the grass on the lawn in front of them.

"They started calling me the Father about twenty years ago," said Artemis. "I was surprised at first." Artemis's snowy eyebrows arched as he smiled at the memory. "But I see no harm. I think of them as my children now. As for Kevin . . ." Artemis looked momentarily puzzled. "I don't know what I'm going to do about him. I'm sorry I had to do what I did. I was his father, and I abandoned him. I abandoned his brothers, and I abandoned his mother. I tried to explain it to him yesterday, but I don't think he understands. He always was a child with a limited imagination."

They sat on a bench. The bench was made of pine, a rarity in the Belt because land use had to be so restricted. Cody couldn't help pressing his hand against it.

"So he's all right now?" asked Cody.

The old man raised his eyebrows. "I wish I could say he is. I should have been more attentive to him as a boy. I failed to recognize just how much he looked up to me. I spent too much time at the university. My head was always full of my work. You go along, you're thinking your own thoughts, you're just fighting for the things you believe in, working for them like anybody else would, and you don't stop to think about how other people are looking at you, or how the things you do or say can have such a lasting effect on their lives. When your kids grow up, you realize you hardly know them. I'm sorry about Kevin. I really am. I neglected to see how I really . . . well, how I really meant a lot to him."

They listened to the sound of the nearby waterfall for a while. A few bright birds flew by and disappeared into the hanging vines.

"So where is he now?" asked Cody.

"He's resting. It's going to take him a while. He must hate me as much as he hates the orphans. I hope he can learn to like me again. And I hope he can learn to like the Meek. I don't think I'm going to survive until we get to Carswell. I'd like to get it patched up before we leave."

"Carswell?" said Cody.

"Highfield-Little," said Artemis. "The Meek call it Carswell. After Lenny."

"Does Kevin understand why you did what you did? Faking your own death and so forth?"

"I told him Chryse Planitia would have killed me for real if I hadn't had Olympia Mons do something about it," he said. "I was their number-one target, the adulterator of their blood, the man with the rewrite codes, the man who wanted to brainwash them into being model citizens. They didn't seem to understand I just wanted to help them. They were a tormented people. And some of that bad code—no matter what you find in Lenny's papers he really wanted all that bad code in them. Make them paranoid. Make them angry. Make them understand the value of the pack, how there's strength in numbers. Lenny wrote all that into his engineered chromosome 3 because he knew they would need ruthless survival instincts if they were going to live on the surface of Mars with a minimum of life support."

"So they wanted to kill you?" said Cody. "Chryse Planitia?"

The old man nodded sadly. "And I told Kevin that they wanted to kill him, and that they wanted to kill his mother and his two brothers, and that the only way I could protect them was to have Buster come in with a corpse, mutilate it beyond recognition, coerce the investigation, corrupt the pertinent death documents, infiltrate data banks, and fake some of my DNA so the inquest would be satisfied with the pulpy mess they found in my bedroom."

A few children walked by, curious, waved to them, and disappeared toward a Tuileries-style fountain full of carp. Cody thought of his own father, as much of an academic as Artemis Axworthy but not as open, a snob unable to accept his son because his son had turned into a man with a hammer. The estrangement between Artemis and Kevin had more to do with the exigencies of war. Cody and his father had more or less abandoned each other. Artemis, for reasons that were mortally pressing, had abandoned Kevin, nothing mutual about it. He just left behind a twenty-seven-year-old officer in the Ceresian Defense Force, grief-stricken for the next 30 years over a father who had never really died and whom he never really got to know.

"I had to do it," said the Father, his voice now plangent with regret. "We were making a society out of the orphans. Buster and I, and all the various ranking members from the various clans. I don't know whether I made the right decision. You reach a point in your life and you realize that despite your best intentions, all your best efforts, maybe you shouldn't have been a father and a husband after all. I spent no time with my family. I spent all my time with the clans. Buster and I worked together right from the start. Lenny came up from Mars." Artemis shook his head. "Buster was so resourceful," he said. "And really committed. He helped us all survive after the first bioextermination attack. He had shelters everywhere on the asteroid. No more than tunnels and caves, really, special ones lined with protective materials. He had supply and food caches. He believed in what I was trying to do for them." The Father shook his head one more time. "The sad fact of the matter is, Buster's more of a son to me than Kevin is."

CHAPTER 20

The Meek supplied Cody and the rest of his crew with a conference room, a place of soft chairs, hardwood tables, potted plants, and a view overlooking the square. It was a conventional room modeled after staunchly Vestan antecedents. Lamps lit the room—not holographic replications of heavenly bodies. To Cody it was like the many meeting rooms he had used in Vesta City when he had occupied the number-three spot in the Public Works Department. They were here to talk about their situation. Cody glanced at Axworthy. Axworthy sat there staring at the middle distance, not paying any attention, a man whose mantle of authority had melted away like ice on a spring pond, who was still shocked by meeting his father after all these years. Deirdre kept watching Cody. He sensed a continuing love, a selfless love that expected nothing. Ben, fully recovered from his brush with the chloropathoxin, was restless, oddly detached, and kept glancing at the door as if he expected someone to come in. Jerry was talking.

"Has Buster or the Father confirmed any of Claire's data?" he asked. "Are they using this gravitational field device to maneuver Highfield-Little away from its collision course with the sun?"

"Yes," said Cody. He turned to Claire. "And your calculations for the orbital trajectory are for the most part accurate, Claire. The only difference is that the Meek are now going to try to maneuver Carswell into a higher orbit as it transits the sun. To avoid the hot temperatures. But even in the higher orbit, the temperatures are going to be searing."

Jerry considered this, rubbed his chin, then peered over the rims of his glasses at Cody. "And the Meek are then going to leave the solar system for good?" he asked.

"Yes."

Jerry frowned. "Then where does that leave us?" he asked. "How are we going to get back to the Belt?" Jerry took a deep breath, sighed, looked at the potted ficus next to his chair. "I just want to go home, Cody. I've got my wife and children back on Juno to think about. I've got my practice. And I'm getting really homesick."

Cody didn't have an answer for the doctor. "I've made Buster aware of our concerns and he's looking into possible solutions to the problem," he said.

Claire spoke up. "What's going to happen to Ceres?" she asked. "Once they abandon it, what are they going to do with it? Just let it crash into the sun?"

Cody shook his head. "They can't do that, not with the tiny black hole in the middle of it. The sun would just feed the grav-core, with potentially disastrous consequences. But they have to get rid of Ceres somehow. In modifying the grav-core to tow Carswell, the Meek ran into some unexpected problems. To put it simply, the grav-core is eventually going to destroy Ceres, and the Meek have no way to stop it. Their original plan was to give Ceres back to the Vestans once they were through using it. But they can't do that now."

Kevin Axworthy lifted his eyes, seemed to show some interest. "Why?" he said. "What's happening with the grav-core?"

"Well, rather than lose energy over time, the way a minuscule black hole like this one should," said Cody, "it's actually gaining energy. The only way it can gain energy is through the addition of mass. And it's gained mass. A lot of mass. The particle physics involved are complex, but the way it's behaving is something they never expected. The mass isn't coming from Ceres. Or from anywhere in the solar system. When they view signature spectrographs of various elements through the black hole they get crazy readings. Cesium, for instance. Cesium has an atomic weight of 140.12. But the cesium in the black hole has an atomic weight of 138.2. They think the extra mass is coming *through* the black hole from a place where the atomic weight of cesium might actually be 138.2."

The unspoken implication of an alternate plane was clear.

Claire's eyes were wide, wondering. "So what does that mean in practical terms?" she asked.

"One of three things," said Cody. "All this extra mass will make the black hole so strong that the Meek will no longer be able to contain the grav-core at its current .5 gees and the asteroid will be ripped apart by intense gravitational tides. Second, the black hole's event horizon will balloon in one sudden jump and surround the asteroid, forming a wormhole, and cast the asteroid to another part of the universe, maybe millions of light-years away. Finally, the asteroid could conceivably be catapulted into a different time. No matter what happens, Ceres is dangerous. Once the Meek get through with it they're going to use a final firing sequence—and they've just completed an extra silo for this purpose—to send it to the center of the galaxy, where theory suggests energy emissions are too great for any kind of life to survive and where the asteroid can't harm anyone."

The Tycho Brahe Observatory stood on Mount Pendulum in the County of Angular Momentum. Two-and-a-half weeks had passed. They were well on their way toward Earth.

Cody was out here with Lulu and Deirdre. Deirdre didn't say much these days. She seemed intimidated by the whole situation, liked to stay near him whenever she could; not, he sensed, because she still hoped, simply because she felt safe with him. Lulu stood beside him.

He pressed his eye to the eye-piece of the 300-centimeter refractor, and in the distance he saw a small blue ball: Earth. The Moon, still too far away to take on the contours of a disk, hovered beside it, not a finger's breadth away, like a fragment of gold.

Lulu said: *Ben and Agatha love each other.*

Cody smiled, thought of Ben. Never any girlfriends in his life, but always yearning for one. Thirty-one years old, seemingly too old for a young woman like Agatha. But Agatha was older than she looked.

Cody said: *I'm glad.*

Lulu said: *And Deirdre . . . Deirdre wonders . . . can you feel what she feels for you?*

Cody said: *I feel.*

Lulu said: *She needs comfort.*

He still hadn't sorted out his feelings for Deirdre. He glanced across the observatory. Deirdre's usually amber hair had turned lighter, was now golden from her partial genetic rewrite. Her freckled face had just the barest trace of blue. She turned to him, surprised to find him staring at her, and grinned self-consciously. He grinned back, tried to reassure her, to give her . . . comfort. She looked troubled. He caught from her a faint emanation, realized she was thinking of home. She turned away, looked out the window down the side of Mount Pendulum, 2,000 meters into the dusty gray valley. Home. He thought of his own home. The condominium he now owned in downtown Vesta City. A place to sleep. Not a home at all.

He turned back to the refractor and keyed in a search command. The telescope swung eighteen degrees to the right, then sank toward the horizon. He put his eye back to the eyepiece.

He saw it. Carswell—big, round, 150,000 kilometers away, rising over the pocked terrain of Ceres, shining half full, with the terminator just beyond the meridian; a white planet, completely covered by cloud, as bright as Venus; a vision of wonder, a tenet of hope. He checked some of the

readouts. Temperature at the equator was now 22 degrees
Celsius. Thirty-eight degrees Celsius at the south pole. Four
degrees Celsius at the north pole. With the south pole sinking sun-first along a perpendicular orbit above the solar system's usual orbital plane, and the equator and north pole
angled away from the sun at 33 degrees, these various temperatures made sense.

But eventually the temperatures would get hotter.

Too hot.

The seas would churn and the winds would roar.

Home. He wondered how Buster planned to turn that roving and unpredictable planet into a place the Meek might
call home.

Buster, now consumed with the details of the exodus,
delegated Rex to take Cody, Deirdre, Jerry, Ben, and Kevin
Axworthy to the hangar.

To call it a hangar was to greatly understate its size and
complexity. Nestled beneath what the Meek called the
Crater of Good Fellowship, the hangar extended for 14 cubic
kilometers underground, with 280 levels that housed 9,800
landers, 260 supply ships, and 826 satellites—satellites that
would be put into orbit around Carswell for a number of purposes. All this, completely missed by the *Conrad Wilson*.
Cody was again amazed by how the Meek had been able to
hide it. They were currently standing in front of lander 4,731,
on level 140.

Rex, a boyish-looking Meek with a particularly engaging
smile, jumped to the wing of the lander and, using the silent
language of the Meek, told Cody a bit about the lander program. Cody in turn communicated this information to Deirdre,
Jerry, Ben, and Kevin Axworthy. His empathic link with the
Meek was still strong, built upon the foundation of his early
childhood psi talent; the others now had intermittent links
at best.

"He says the spacecraft is designed for maneuverability
in an oxygen-nitrogen atmosphere such as we'll encounter

on Carswell." said Cody. "Hence the wings. Each lander's 100 meters long. Construction materials are from a nearby class M metallic asteroid."

"I trust they studied structural designs for the aircraft of Earth," said Deirdre, resting her hand on the spacecraft's fuselage. "Because I can't help getting nervous about a space-based people, none of whom have ever visited a planet with a breathable atmosphere, trying to design an airplanelike spacecraft. I'd like to know what kind of tests they've run on these landers. Are they weather-rated? I'm the only one here who's ever been to Earth. Earth is meteorologically unstable. You can't control the rain or the wind. Some places had hurricanes and typhoons while I was there, with winds up to 250 kilometers per hour."

Cody turned to Rex, who immediately flashed him an answer. The others waited for his translation. None of it was getting through to them.

"He says they've been studying Carswell's meteorological systems for a long time. He says to a large extent the greenhouse-type atmosphere moderates wide temperature fluctuations. This means the weather is generally stable. For instance, winds in the western part of the main land-mass are gusting at about 15 kilometers right now. It's raining over the inland sea, with 10 centimeters expected. And they have two tropical storms in the ocean, with winds gusting up to 90 kilometers per hour. Relatively calm compared to things on Earth."

Deirdre stared at the lander, then motioned at the overhead sky-gate, where Carswell floated three-quarters full. "So where exactly are we going to land on Carswell?" she asked.

"The landers will parachute into the inland sea," said Cody. "Weather patterns won't be as severe there as in the ocean."

She nodded, but still seemed anxious, nervous. "And then what do we do? What's the plan?"

Cody gestured at the distended half-sphere of Carswell.

"We migrate north," he said. "We travel nearly to the north pole as Carswell approaches the sun." He glanced at Rex, making sure he had this right, then continued. "Carswell will transit the sun rapidly. As it swings round, we migrate south." He again looked up at the white planet, pondering it, speculating about it. "As it leaves the sun, we migrate north again. We always stay with the part of the axis that is shaded from the sun. We travel with winter. We trek with the winter solstice."

But it was more than just a trek for Cody. Back in their conference room, he gave them the rest of the news.

"They plan to modify one of the landers," he said. "They're going to rig it to a crude thermonuclear thruster, like the ones they have out in the silos. As Carswell makes its outward journey past the Belt, they'll send us back to Vesta in this modified lander. The thermonuclear thruster will put us in range. Then we use conventional thrusters to rendezvous with Bettina, and finally with Vesta."

They had questions, of course. Would it be safe? What kind of shielding were the Meek going to install to protect them from the thermonuclear thruster's radiation? How long would it take to travel the 90 million miles back to the solar system's orbital plane from the elevated trajectory of Carswell? How long would it take for the conventional thrusters to push them into a rendezvous with Bettina? Would they refuel on Bettina? And then how long would it take them to get to Vesta? What kind of supplies would they take? How good was the life support?

He answered their questions as best he could.

"What kind of gee-force are we looking at when the thermonuclear thruster goes off?" asked Axworthy finally.

"Over ten," said Cody.

"That will crush us," said Axworthy.

"The Meek are working on that."

Axworthy let it go. Cody sensed the man still had reservations about the Meek, couldn't come to grips with the fact that far from killing his father they had conspired to fake his death in order to save his whole family. Over and above that, Cody could tell that Kevin Axworthy just wanted to go home. In fact, he could sense that they all wanted to go home.

And here's where he differed from the rest of them.

He wasn't sure he wanted to go home.

As the meeting broke up, he looked out the window across the spires and towers of the City of Resolved Differences to the river valley and the forest. The forest looked as if it had a million blue stars—glow-moss everywhere. Why should he go back to Vesta? Christine was dead. Investigators in Vesta City would eventually uncover his part in the interception of the neutron warheads and launch vehicles. And going back to Vesta would be like going back to the past. There were too many ghosts there.

What about Mars, then? So he could be close to his parents. He shook his head to himself, put his palms on the windowsill, and looked into the square below, where the collecting pool caught and reflected the light from the five holographic moons. He was estranged from his parents. They would make him feel like a working-class man—a man with a hammer—exiled among academics. What point to Mars?

He turned around and saw Deirdre standing there.

Then there was Deirdre, he thought.

No matter how weak her empathic ability had become, he knew she still sensed his ambivalence. Home. What was the meaning of the word? It was more than just a place to live. It was an idea. A dream. A goal. She crossed the room and put her hand on his shoulder.

"You're not coming with us, are you?" she said.

He turned around. Far to the north he saw a wide bend in the river. He saw some boats out there. He saw an airplane. She was close to him now. He could feel her heat. He put his arm around her, drew her near—didn't know why, it just felt like the right thing to do. He had no answer for her. She smelled faintly of peaches, the soap the Meek had given her to use.

"You miss your family, don't you?" he said.

She pressed her cheek against his chest, nodded. He caught a faint image from her, her mother, a woman with much the same coloring, tawny red hair, and freckles, sitting at a potter's wheel, spinning a pot, a shelf filled with beautiful crockery behind her.

"But I'll miss you too," said Deirdre.

He was faced with a decision he couldn't seem to make. Building things, engineering things, making changes in blueprints, selecting appropriate materials—professional decisions were always easy. But this was different. Lulu's ambivalence and fear, her connection to Buster; Deirdre's inner candle of hope—these made his decision difficult. A life on Mars? A return to Vesta with Deirdre? Or what promised to be a bleak pioneer struggle on Carswell with Lulu? He didn't know. He leaned down and kissed Deirdre on the forehead. Her skin was smooth. Silken. Warm. He felt a deep regard for her. But his regard didn't make the meaning of home any clearer, and he still couldn't come to a decision.

CHAPTER 21

Cody found the Father in his hammock the next day singing weakly at a suspended sheet of blue cellophane. Complex mathematical equations appeared on the sheet as the Father sang, many of the symbols arcane but nonetheless recognizable to Cody, others completely original, relational and quantifying symbols that looked as if they had been invented by the Father for the purpose of describing the problems, solutions, and theorems of the Meek's superscience. Even more startling was the human head on the table, eyes wide open, a grin on its face, alive, patient, amiable. Cody took a deep breath, realizing for the hundredth time that he should learn to expect anything from the Meek.

The Father smiled feebly at Cody, beckoned, but did not get out of his hammock. He looked frail today, frailer than usual. The head continued to stare at Cody, a friendly-looking man, with dark skin, lots of African blood.

"This is Comptroller Denneth Oldspice," said the Father.

Cody, of course, had heard of Oldspice. Comptroller Oldspice was a man of great power on Earth, leader of the Federated States of Appalachia, the eastern half of what had once been the United States of America. The comptroller's head was a transmitted projection; Cody was again astonished by the resolution and naturalness of the Meek's holography.

"How do you do?" said Cody.

"Hello, Mr. Wisner," said the comptroller after a pause commensurate with the interplanetary communications time lag that now separated Ceres from Earth.

"Comptroller Oldspice wants reassurance, Cody," said the Father. "With our approach to Earth, Comptroller Oldspice has put his strategic forces on highest alert. I've told him he has nothing to fear, that we have no intention of attacking Earth, but he's not yet ruled out a strike against us. Some of his aides have advised him that you and your four crew members are being held against your will."

The head on the table swung round and faced the Father. Cody realized that, while before he might have been an inadvertent catalyst for war, he now had an opportunity to promote a new peace. He felt both relieved and excited by the prospect.

"See that garment on the chair?" the Father asked him.

The garment in question, a pullover shirt with short sleeves, was gossamer-thin, see-through, made of a fine silver material.

"Yes."

"Could you remove your tunic and put that on?" said the Father. "It's a body-wide biofeedback input. It will help the FSA decide whether you're telling them the truth or not. They want reassurance, Cody. They want you to tell them that you and your crew are here through circumstance, not against your will. They want you to tell them that Ceres won't attack Earth. Also, they're planning a manned mission to Carswell of a scientific and exploratory nature with eight crew expected. The mission is going to rendezvous with Carswell before Carswell transits the sun and will use Venus as an orbital slingshot to get back to Earth once its mission is over. They want your assurance that all eight crew will be left unharmed. They asked for you specifically because you're a neutral third party. They plan to broadcast whatever you say to the people of Earth, most of whom are nervous. The media have run that quote from Matthew 5:5, how the meek shall inherit the Earth. The comptroller wants you to tell him that this particular biblical prophecy isn't about to come true."

Cody pulled off his tunic and donned the biofeedback garment, filled with a restless determination. He wanted to do this. He wanted to tell the people of Earth that everything was going to be all right.

"Where shall I sit?" he asked.

"Right there's fine," said the comptroller.

Cody sat on a wrought-iron garden chair and stared up at the bright pink hibiscus blooms trailing over the edge of the atrium. He had never been to Earth. The cost of such a voyage, as Kevin Axworthy had pointed out, was prohibitive. He had met a few Earthlings on Mars once, when he and Christine had gone there to visit his parents, and what he remembered most about them was how they stumbled in the light gravity, bouncing about like they were in a swimming pool, exerting far more muscle power than they needed to. He was a seventh-generation Vestan. His great-great-great-great-grandfather, a man named Seine Smyth, had come to Vesta 200 years ago from New York City, developed a deep-space lubricating oil that wouldn't freeze or gel up in the extreme cold or evaporate in extreme heat, an oil that was now used everywhere, even as far away as the outposts on Pluto. He smiled as he thought of the old photograph he had of Seine at home. He had to somehow connect with his ancestral past, to recognize the Earth he carried inside him, to remember Seine Smyth as a way to increase his empathy toward the people of Earth so they would be better able to understand what he had to tell them.

He stared at the camera, saw a Meek technician give him the signal to start.

"Greetings," he said. "My name is Cody Wisner and I'm the Vestan Project Manager for the Ceresian Reconstruction." He gave them the history of the reconstruction effort, even sketched in some of the more well-known facts about the Ceresian Civil Action, wanted to make sure everybody on Earth had their frame of reference right. "My survey crew and I attained orbit around the asteroid nine weeks ago. We of course expected to find no one there. But as you all know by now, we discovered a population of 620,000 genetically altered human beings."

He then recounted the events leading up to the *Conrad Wilson*'s attempted bioextermination of this genetically altered population.

"I had to stop them," he said. He told them of the evening he had seen the five children fly down the river toward the City of Resolved Differences on pedal planes, how happy they were, how much fun they were having. "I couldn't let the *Conrad Wilson* destroy that." He told them how he had enlisted the aid of thousands of Meek to sweep the solar panels in Actinium and how he had used the microwave converter to down the incoming neutron warheads and launch vehicles. "Despite my efforts, the Meek lost a significant percentage of their population." He then told them, all those billions of people on Earth, how the beast, the black hole, was alive and prowling in the center of the asteroid.

"The Meek wanted to give Ceres back to the Belt," he said, "but because of the increasing mass in the grav-core they won't be able to do that now." He explained how Ceres would be shaken apart by gravitational tides or otherwise catapulted millions of parsecs away or millions of years into either the past or future. "The Meek have to leave Ceres before Ceres falls victim to the grav-core. They must go to Carswell."

He told the people of Earth that Carswell, better known as Highfield-Little, was more than a rogue planet—that it was also humankind's first starship, and that the Meek were going to be humankind's first star travelers.

"The Meek, through the years and centuries, will send back observations and information to Earth, Mars, and all the inhabited moons. They'll do their best to locate other habitable planets among the stars, and to map them out for future colonizers. These people are your brothers and sisters, modified to survive in harsher conditions, brothers and sisters who can, and will, make the journey, not only for themselves but for all humankind." He leaned forward. "And does this kind of opportunity warrant a strategic response? I don't think it does. Would it not be better to give the Meek your blessing? They mean you no harm. Their intent is clear. To leave Ceres and make a home on Highfield-Little. You shouldn't stand in their way. In fact, you should do everything you can to help them. All they wish is peace, and a place to live. And that's something I'm sure we all can understand."

Two-and-a-half weeks later, Cody watched Claire as she interpreted incoming data on the new computer the Meek had given her. His body hurt from the latest grav-flux, the window was covered with mud from the river's violent surge and spray, and three pictures had fallen off the walls of the conference room and lay in shards on the floor. The firing of thrusters 7, 9, and 13 hadn't been much fun, either.

"Was the firing sequence successful?" he asked Claire.

Claire studied the readouts one by one, written in the idiosyncratic telemetry language the Meek had devised for the shifting of planetary bodies.

"It was successful," she reported. "The slingshot maneuver has put us well ahead of Earth."

"How close are we to Earth?" asked Cody.

"Put it this way," said Claire. "Ceres is Earth's second moon right now."

"Can you plug into any military communications?" asked Cody. "Are they upping their alert status?"

Claire switched to another screen, decrypted some military communications traffic over the next five minutes, and finally turned to Cody. "They haven't increased their alert status, but they're monitoring our trajectory closely."

"So no attack?"

"No attack."

"And what about the grav-flux? Did the Meek succeed in braking Carswell? Slowing it down?"

Claire switched to yet another screen. "Yes, they have. In three or four hours Ceres will make rendezvous with Carswell. Ceres will orbit Carswell, giving it a moon for the first time in its two-billion-year history. We'll be ready to start the exodus."

"What about damage estimates from the grav-flux? It was a lot worse than all the others, wasn't it?"

"I was checking that before you came up," said Claire. "It caused major quakes all over the asteroid. Clan scouts reported wide-scale destruction in Newton, with the collapse of over half its skyscrapers, major damage in Equilibrium, and tunnel collapses just about everywhere else. She's not going to hold much longer, Cody. It looks like we'll be leaving just in time."

The time for the exodus finally came. Ceres floated above the skies of Carswell. The hangar had its massive sky-gate open. Cody stood with Ben on the third level down. Ben LeBlanc had missed the final few briefings—his romance with Agatha had consumed much of his time—and he now wanted Cody to sketch in the latest information for him.

"We saw the most recent radar pictures," Cody told him. "Of the inland sea. Their cartographers have dubbed it the Sea of Humility. It's round. Perfectly round. Six hundred kilometers in diameter. For the longest time they thought it was a crater. But these new pictures change that."

"What do you mean?"

"They think it's artificial," said Cody.

"Artificial?"

"That doesn't necessarily mean they think the planet's inhabited by intelligent life," said Cody.

Ben looked at the nearest lander, thoughtful. "Well . . . is there *any* life?"

"Oh, sure, plenty of life. The Meek always knew about the flora from the earliest probes. But now they know there's a lot of fauna too. The methane content in the atmosphere has suggested the presence of animal life. With the satellites up and running, they've detected evidence of migration patterns. These new pictures show broad swaths of chewed-up land typical of the kind of scarring herd animals leave when they migrate. As for intelligent life . . . well, no. No radio signals, no burning of fossil fuels, no evidence of artificially produced radioactive emissions, no roads, cities, towns, or villages, no agriculture, no economic activity whatsoever . . . nothing but this perfectly round sea in the middle of the main landmass. Which, by the way, they're calling Our Home."

Above them, the first squadron of landers hung motionless in the stasis field ready for the journey to Carswell.

"And they've entirely ruled out the possibility of an impact crater?" said Ben.

"Yes."

"Why?"

"Because the depth of the Sea of Humility is an even six hundred meters from coast to coast, with no variation. Six hundred meters deep, 600 kilometers wide, with a perfectly circular island six kilometers across, right in the middle."

"An island?" said Ben.

"Yes. Made entirely out of glass," said Cody. He shook his head. "It's dead. There's nobody there. They think it's a structure of some kind. They've detected two other similar structures on Our Home, one to the south of the Sea of Humility, and one to the north. They haven't really learned anything substantive about any of them yet."

A clarion sounded and the first wave of landers floated up through the sky-gate, glowing blue as they breached the invisible barrier.

Ben looked away. "You know . . . I was a little upset to see . . . whoever arranged the flight manifest . . . why they didn't put me on the same lander with Agatha. She and I . . . we're . . ."

"I know," said Cody.

Cody realized that Ben was planning to stay on Carswell

with Agatha, that he was taking the biggest step of his life. Ben's face looked suddenly suffused with suppressed anxiety. "I think she might be pregnant, Cody."

Cody raised his eyebrows, stared at his friend, not knowing what to think. "Should I . . ." He peered at the man more closely, sensed Ben's ambivalence. "Should I say congratulations?"

The color of Ben's face deepened. "I guess you . . . you could," he said. "I just never thought . . . we didn't plan it this way. It's just that . . ."

"I know."

"A child . . . that's a big thing . . . and the future's not that certain, is it?"

"No," said Cody, "it's not."

"But we love each other," he said. He nodded, more to himself than to Cody. "And that should get us through."

Cody couldn't help thinking of his own situation. "It should," he said.

"Then that's good," said Ben. It was as if Ben had to convince himself of the future, persuade himself that he would be a good husband and father.

"She's picked a winner, Ben," said Cody.

Ben looked at him, a desperate grin on his face, mollified by Cody's confidence.

"You think so?"

"Why not?"

Overhead, the next group of landers took its position in the stasis field.

"Because . . . because Agatha's so damn beautiful," said Ben, looking worried again. "Why would she go for someone like me?"

"Ben . . ." Cody put his hand on Ben's shoulder. "Ben . . . I know you might think otherwise . . ." Cody grinned. "But the measure of a man is not taken by the size of his overbite alone. Believe it or not, you have other qualities."

*   *   *

Cody sat in lander 2,484. Weightless. In free fall. Seats were arranged in a commercial format, two on each side of a center aisle, fifteen rows, sixty seats in all, with three crew up front in the cockpit. Outside his window he saw the great white curve of Carswell spread out below him. Cody, Ben, Claire, Deirdre, Jerry, and Kevin Axworthy now had status, for the purpose of the exodus, as members of the Olympia Mons Clan, Buster's clan. As Buster was leader of all the Meek, it was decided that the humans, including the Father, would travel with him.

Lulu was on a different lander. Buster, in his jealousy, had made sure of it. Deirdre was the only other non-Meek on Cody's lander.

The lander angled for entry. Friction would be intense, Rex had told him. The craft's heat shields, made from a biological base, would burn away, regrow, burn away, regrow, again and again, like so many layers of onion skin. Gravity on Carswell was .8 gees, close to Earth gravity, stronger than anything any of them—Meek or non-Meek—had ever had to live in. To that end, everyone was fitted with a special suit. Bubbles melded with the black fabric responded to signals from antigravity satellites and would make the gravity at least a little easier to bear until they got used to it.

The lander dipped lower, skimming the ionosphere, and Cody felt the first distant pull of Carswell. Deirdre clutched his hand. In the skintight bubble-wrap she was a startling, provocative sight. Her hand was cold. He felt numb, neither afraid nor unafraid, just wanting to get it over with.

Outside his window he saw the heat shields flaring, chunks of ash flitting past as the biological base burned away sheet by sheet. Their lander descended into the clouds, and the view outside turned white. The roar of the lander's entry was loud, seemed to drown out all his thoughts. His stomach felt as if it were going to sink right to his feet. The gravity grabbed him like a claw and pressed his whole body heavily into his seat. The lander shook. Wind turbulence? The spacecraft angled sharply down. After what seemed like forever in the white limbo of the planet-wide cloud cover, they finally burst through to the other side.

Rain immediately battered the spacecraft, a withering precipitation a hundred times heavier than the showers the Weather Bureau in Vesta City produced every 36 hours for street-cleaning and agricultural purposes. Below, Cody saw the flat gray surface of the Sea of Humility, still at least two kilometers down. The lander leveled off, flew straight, then began to climb, angling sharply upward. The seats automatically released their catches and rotated gently downward in their braces. As the lander climbed, Cody found himself facing the floor.

The engines cut, and the lander began to fall thrusters-first toward Carswell, in free fall for less than a second. Then Cody felt the parachutes deploy, imagined the seven of them popping from the nose cone like sudden exotic blooms. As the spacecraft sank gently through the pouring rain toward the Sea of Humility, Cody realized he hadn't been breathing for the last several moments.

CHAPTER 22

Even through the pressurized walls of the cabin the smell of the place made itself known seconds after splashdown—a thick briny smell, like a tropical fish aquarium that hadn't been cleaned out in a long time.

The lander now floated like a boat, rocking in the two-meter waves, propelled southward by three screws, one on each wing, and one at the back of the fuselage. Out the window Cody saw the inflatable pontoons, off-white against the green sea. It was hard to see anything at all through the heavy rain lashing the glass.

The pilot made an announcement—a general telepathic broadcast giving them the facts: *We have landed ten kilometers south of our target zone and are moving at ten knots through a heavy swell. We will now have to navigate around the island of glass in the middle of the sea.*

Cody conveyed this to Deirdre, who had picked up only half of it.

Over the next fifteen minutes the rain abated and the swell of the sea grew calmer. Some of the younger Meek were suffering from seasickness. Cody felt a half-dozen different emanations from the clan members around him: apprehension, hope, misgiving, excitement, regret, and relief. The mist and rain cleared further, and out the window he saw it, the island, a shore of green glass lifting above the waves, a gentle slope rising quickly to several spires, all of them cylindrical, made of the same green glass, like a gigantic collection of old radio tubes, most of them so tall they disappeared into the clouds.

The pilot said: *I'll maneuver closer. We should learn what we can about the construct.*

Construct. A good name for it. Because as they got closer Cody could see that it really wasn't a city, it was more of an installation. A construct. The emanations of the Meek around him told him they concurred with the word.

They closed to within two hundred meters. In the dim gray light of the day he was able to see right through the green glass to the internal workings of the towers. What he saw reminded him of an arterial or circulatory system, trunk routes leading to smaller subsidiary branch routes, these smaller branch routes breaking off into a final subset of routes like a meaty lacework of veins. So eerie. So deserted. With the wind howling and moaning in a thousand different tones through the thrusting green spires, like a bizarre and forbidding Emerald City of Oz, no openings in any of the spires, no windows or doors, nothing that looked like roadways or streets.

Gigantic as it was, the thing looked more like a mummified corpse than like a building. Cody half-thought he was witnessing not the archaeological evidence of a long-gone civilization but the remains of an actual creature, as inhuman a creature as anything he had ever seen, stupendously large, bereft of movement, abandoned and lonely, with only the waves splashing against its shores to keep it company.

The antigravitational satellites interfaced with everyone's bodysuits ten or fifteen minutes before the north shore of the Sea of Humility came into view. Cody's eyes widened as he felt the sensation of lightness come to his body.

"Do you feel that?" he asked Deirdre.

She nodded. "I feel it," she said.

The little bubbles melded with the black fabric of his suit lifted Cody's limbs and his body, and he was able to breathe easier and not hold himself so rigidly. He lifted his arm, testing it.

"That's better," he said.

Deirdre pointed out the window. "Look," she said.

Outside he saw the north shore of the Sea of Humility. Ten of the huge supply ships, joined end to end, curved out from the imperceptibly arcing shore, floating on the water, forming a harbor for the rallying landers of the Olympia Mons Clan, each ship a hundred meters high and three hundred meters long.

The pilot maneuvered around the end of the last supply ship, and the water grew calm. They were in the harbor. Several of the landers had now been refitted into barges to transport food, materials, and equipment ashore, and moved back and forth across the green water, leaving wakes of silver foam. People crowded the shore, all of them dressed in the black bubble suits, going about the business of unloading the transports, getting ready for the migration. Several Meek engineers erected a crane, the sparks from their welding irons starlike in the mist that clung to the shore. Two other cranes had already been set up and were in full operation. The first wave of landers had arrived three days ago and Cody saw that the Meek had made much progress since then.

"Did Buster tell you how many of us there'll be?" asked Deirdre.

"In the clan?"

"Yes."

"Rex did," said Cody. "Thirty thousand. That's down from 40,000. They lost 25 percent in the attack. The other clans had roughly the same losses."

They docked and one of the crew opened the hatch.

Cody stepped onto the gangplank and took a deep breath. Thick. Moist. Warm. He immediately started to sweat. The wind tossed his hair. Clouds covered the sky from horizon to horizon, yet it was bright out, brighter than any artificial sky he had ever seen in Vesta City. Brighter even than the sky of

Mars. Mostly white but fading to gray in places. Many of the Meek wore the special black greasepaint around their eyes to cut down on the sky's glare. A big sky. A sky that made him apprehensive. As a seventh-generation Vestan, he found it hard to get used to the idea of a sky or the notion that if he kept going straight up he would eventually reach space, that there was just this thin skin of atmosphere protecting him, with no bulwarks or pressure walls to keep the killer vacuum out. Also, he was a man whose chief professional goal had always been to design a better airlock, and the idea that he couldn't close the door on any of it took some getting used to.

He and Deirdre were processed, as everyone was, like immigrants to a new country, injected with the Meek's own version of a tracking microgen, given work assignments, then allowed an hour to get their bearings, to get used to moving in their bodysuits, to accept the reality that they were on Carswell now, a planet nearly as big as Earth, a marauding heavenly body from who-knew-where.

They walked through the joined supply ships one after another, through their huge warehouselike spaces, through stacks of stores and hardware so endless that the aisles disappeared to vanishing points. Forklifts roved with persistent and organized industry. They walked and walked, a full kilometer, aided by their gravity suits, until they reached the shore.

Beyond the embankment stretched a flat area about sixty meters wide. At the end of the flat area hills rose all around, covered with a sparse green, yellow, and brown vegetation, a vegetation unlike any he had ever seen—non-photosynthetic, spores, molds, fungi, but arranged in grasslike formations, in bushlike clumps, even some widely spaced varieties that looked like trees. The hills stretched from left to right as far as the eye could see. The flat expanse between the shore and the hills now acted as a staging area for the clan. The twenty-five other clans had landed somewhere along this same stretch of coast, so Cody had learned, over 1,000-kilometer front. Bales upon bales of marrow were being unloaded. Cody and Deirdre stopped to watch the operation.

"They have a ten-week stockpile of marrow," Cody told her.

"Are they going to be able to grow marrow here?" she asked.

"Yes," said Cody. "They've been sending probes for years, and these probes have tested the soil extensively. The marrow will grow well here. But while we make the migration, the Meek will have to take what they're going to eat along with them. There'll be no time for cultivation and no real point to establishing farms until they settle down."

It looked much like an army operation, blue people with albino hair and violet eyes, all dressed in the skintight black bodysuits, working hard to unload supplies—much like an army operation except that there were children. The organized drills of inventory and delivery took place in the chaos of children running around through the mist, playing games, mothers running after them, some children already up in the hills, others pitching stones and grass into the sea. Cody turned back to the harbor, looked at the nearest crane.

"I wonder what those are?" he asked.

"Oh," she said, "I think you missed that briefing. I think you were with the Father that day. Those are carryalls. A more rugged version of the skimmer. Each one has a huge cargo rack underneath. We'll be making the migration in those."

The crane swung a stack of seven carryalls over the embankment. Triangular in shape, just like the skimmers, but with a frame made of black tubes, a hardy carbon-based alloy.

"They take seven people," said Deirdre, "plus all the supplies those people will need for the migration. They've got wind bonnets. You can't see them in that stack. They'll put them on later."

He had to admire the Meek. They had it planned right

down to the last nut and bolt. Despite the anarchic nature of
their ghost code, they were great organizers and had developed, from their long years of surviving as a dispossessed
people, an intense practical streak.

They watched for a few minutes while the Meek unloaded yet more stacks of carryalls. But then Cody got the
oddest feeling. He took a deep breath. He smelled her scent,
that cool menthol aroma he had grown to love so much.
Lulu. Somewhere nearby. Somewhere in the crowd. Somewhere close in the mist on the shore of this alien sea.

He left Deirdre's side and walked toward the hills, where
the mist rolled down over tiny flowers, lichen, moss, and
sparse stalks of sporelike grass. Sunless plants. Lightless
plants. He crouched at the foot of the hill, put his hand
against them. Dug right down and touched alien soil. He
looked up and down the row of hills. The visibility was
maybe fifteen meters through the mist. The sound of the
waves grew distant. He stood up. Sensed Lulu coming from
the right. Her menthol scent had been unleashed in his mind
like a snow-laden breeze.

He glanced over his shoulder and saw Deirdre approaching him tentatively. A half smile came to her face. She knew
what was going on. She stopped and waited. Giving Cody
some distance. He could sense Deirdre accepting it. Lulu
was on the way.

But it wasn't only Lulu. Over Lulu's enticing menthol
wind he now sensed the heavier creosote aroma of Buster.

Lulu said: *You're here?*

He said: *At the foot of the hill.*

From Buster, unarticulated jealousy.

They appeared out of the gloom together, the two of them
walking easily in their antigrav suits, fully adjusted to the
satellite-assisted lift. This was not a time for verbalized
thought. Cody and Lulu communicated to each other
through pure feeling. He walked quickly toward her. Lulu
tried to do the same, but Buster grabbed her, a detonation of
rage, quickly suppressed, exploding in his mind. Cody

stopped. Lulu shook Buster away, and Buster grudgingly let
her go. She ran to Cody.

They embraced. They kissed. They were back together at
last. Cody felt only a distant sorrow for the jilted lovers
standing on either side of them. His love for Deirdre was
like a candle. But his love for Lulu was like the sun. And he
felt as if his life had started once again.

Later, as night fell over Our Home, Cody stood with
Lulu and Agatha on the shore of the Sea of Humility staring out at the water, hoping he would see the lights of one
more lander easing into the harbor. Ben's lander. No radio
contact. No radar contact. He went through the facts one
more time. Analysis of satellite reconnaissance showed
Ben's lander veering off course after entry. Analysis of the
lander's own navigational readouts showed the same sudden
change of course, 180 degrees toward the south. Then a sudden breakup of the sonar-generated image and a final quick
descent before all readouts disappeared.

And still he hoped. He couldn't help remembering Ben's
dream, of being out in a boat with the Meek in the pouring
rain. He stared out at the waves and couldn't help wondering if Ben's dream had been a marrow-induced dream of
premonition. Stared out at the sea until he sensed surprise,
even fear from the Meek standing nearby. *Look up,* he heard.
So he looked up.

He saw a cluster of blinking lights riding high in the updrafts coming in off the sea, all grouped together in an area
of less than a square meter, each individual light looking no
bigger than a Christmas tree light, each one white. The lights
were no more than a hundred meters up, circling round and
round. Silently. Cody counted them. Nine in all. Always
keeping in a group, like a swarm, circling in a wide radius,
each blinking randomly with the bioluminescent glow of
fireflies.

"Can you make out any detail?" he asked Lulu, knowing

that the Meek, even of the human line, could see well in the dark.

She peered more closely and finally shook her head. She said: *No. All I see are the nine blinking lights.*

Another grouping of lights came up from behind the far hill and began to fly around the first set, each set spinning around the other. Over the sound of the waves slapping against the embankment Cody heard a faint cry. Then another cluster of lights sprang up from behind the hills and joined the others. Two clusters swooped down out of the low-flying clouds. In the peripheral glow of the blinking lights Cody now thought he saw a much larger shadow, caught a glimpse of a membranous wing, heard a cry again, an animal cry. He watched the lights grow more erratic, spin and career. Five more clusters sprang up out of the hills and latched on to whatever it was the lights were attacking; because that's what he sensed now, an attack, the lights packing together. He could feel it reminding the Meek of their ghost code, the lights attacking that thing, whatever it was, with the membranous wing. The blinking of the various lights became more frenetic.

Then the whole huge cluster of blinking bioluminescent lights went into a steep dive and disappeared behind the hill.

Cody stared at the dark hills for a long time. Wondering.

Then he turned around and stared out at the Sea of Humility.

Wondering.

Wondering why Ben's lander had gone into a sudden steep dive.

Wondering if Agatha's child would ever see its father.

Wondering how Ben's dream had ended.

The remaining members of Cody's crew, having come in from the Sea of Humility on different landers, reconnected with Cody and Deirdre the next day. Cody gave Jerry and Claire a hug, even gave Kevin Axworthy a hug. Kevin seemed to have regained his old vigor and was now looking around the staging area with intense interest. Kevin gave Claire a hug, and Cody realized there was something going on between his computer systems specialist and the VDF commander.

"I'd sure like to know how they're going to pull this migration off," said Axworthy. "It's already about 35 degrees Celsius. I really don't understand the orbital mechanics of this weird world or how we can turn it to our advantage by traveling with winter. I missed too many of those damn briefings. Would someone mind telling me what's going on?"

Cody turned to Claire. "I think Claire understands it better than any of us," he said. "She's been looking at it ever since she first realized the Meek were aiming their gravitational device at Highfield-Little. Claire, would you mind explaining it to Kevin?"

"Sure, I don't mind." It was the first time Cody had ever seen a flirtatious look on Claire's face. "Carswell spins at a 33 degree angle on its axis," she told Axworthy. She knelt down and drew in the dirt—the sun, Mercury, and Venus, then Carswell's present position high above the solar system's orbital plane equidistant between the first two inner planets. "Right now the sun is shining directly on Carswell's south pole. I've been following all the developments on the remote laptop the Meek gave me. The Meek's weather satellites are presently recording temperatures in excess of 60 degrees Celsius down at the south pole. Temperatures like that can kill a human being under direct and constant exposure in less than an hour. As Carswell pulls even with the orbital plane—and that will take another standard solar week—this intense summer will move north, not as bad as it could be because of the sharp tilt of Carswell's axis. At this point we should be close to Carswell's arctic circle, up on the northern peninsula of Our Home. That'll be week one."

She now drew a secondary position for Carswell.

"Week two's going to be a lot harder. Though the tilt of the axis makes the equatorial summer and sunshine diffuse, we'll have to turn around and travel as quickly as we can through this diffuse equatorial summer. Call it equatorial spring if you like. As Carswell dips under the south pole of the sun, this summer will move quickly north. The sun will be at our backs, lower and lower on the northern horizon each day as we make our way into the equatorial fall and toward the south pole's winter. Don't get me wrong. Every day's going to be a scorcher. With the greenhouse atmosphere, temperatures are expected to soar to 50 degrees Celsius, and those temperatures are definitely expected in our travel area. Which means we'll be traveling only at night during that particular segment of the migration, staying inside our carryalls during the day, under cover if we can find it anywhere."

Claire now drew a third position for Carswell directly beneath the sun's south pole.

"Week three will be easier," she said. "We'll be camped on the southern tip of Our Home, tilted directly away from the sun. There won't be any day, only night. We won't see the sun for a week. It'll give the Meek a good taste of what's to come once Carswell leaves the solar system for good. When Carswell leaves the solar system it will of course be night all the time." She peered at Axworthy, who nodded, letting her know he was following her. "We'll spend some time on the southern tip. After a week of nights, we'll have two days of northern dawns. The sun will again show itself above the horizon. We'll be on the move again, quickly traversing another equatorial spring. Again, during this portion, we'll travel only at night. We'll migrate all the way from the southern tip of Our Home right to the islands north of the arctic peninsula, a distance of 6,000 kilometers. It should take us two weeks. In week seven Carswell will finally be on its way away from the sun, and things should start to cool down. Also in week seven, Ceres will commence its final firing sequence and head off toward the center of the galaxy. By that time, the Meek will be scouting Our Home for the most advantageous settlement sites. Marrow cultivation will begin." She grinned again, looked directly at Axworthy. "Life will begin."

Life will begin, thought Cody. Yet he couldn't help feeling at least some sorrow for this final abandonment of Ceres, a place with a 350-year history. A place where generation after generation of children had come to grow up straight and strong. He thought of Newton, the most wondrous city in the Belt, then thought of the City of Resolved Differences, an equally wondrous city. Ceres was a civilization unto itself. And now it was deserted, a place of corpses and sad memories and destruction. Now it was a place that was going to be pitched like a worthless piece of junk into the inferno at the center of the galaxy. And he knew he would grieve for it.

Buster had Boris, a Meek who was extremely adept at long-range empathic contact, try to detect the mental emanations of any possible survivors from lander 2,692, Ben's lander. Cody watched as Boris closed his eyes and leaned forward toward the sea. The wind tossed Boris's albinowhite hair. He seemed to be sniffing the air for contact. He stayed in that position for nearly an hour. But finally he opened his eyes and turned to Buster.

Boris said: *They're not out there. I can't sense them.*

Cody felt a sudden woeful emanation from Agatha at the loss of her mate. Lulu put her hand on Agatha's shoulder, trying to comfort her, to calm her.

Agatha said: *Please, Buster, we've got to stay.* She looked frantically at Lulu, then back at Buster. *We've got to stay until we find him.*

Buster shook his head. He said: *I'm sorry, but to wait even another day will put us at risk. The sun is getting hotter. We have to leave today if we're going to survive.*

Unexpectedly, Agatha came to Cody for comfort in her grief an hour later. He put his arm around her and sensed she came to him because he was human, fully human, like Ben, and also because he was Ben's friend. She came because he too felt a great grief over the loss of Ben, a man who had been a good friend for the last five years, someone he could always talk to, whom he could lean on when his sadness at the passing of Christine became too much. Death had stalked Ben from the beginning. First his stroke. Then the chloropathoxin. He had survived both of those. But he hadn't survived his dream of precognition.

Agatha said: *All I ever wanted to do was go back.* He searched through the many unarticulated layers of meaning in this statement. *All I ever wanted was to return to my home, the way it was before the orphans took me away and turned me into one of them.* He received from her a brief tormented image of a much younger Agatha back when she still thought of herself as Elizabeth, an Agatha naked and in shackles, violated and abused. *I feel safe with Ben. I feel safe with you. Now I'm going to be a mother, and I need that safety more than ever.* She looked out at the thousands of clan members as they climbed into their carryalls for the journey north. She said: *These are my people now. I should love them. But I can't trust them. Maybe I have a bit of my own ghost code. Besides Lulu, you and Ben are the only people I've trusted since the orphans first took me away.* Her eyes filled with tears. *Ben's the only one I've loved, the only one I ever wanted for a husband. And now I've lost him.*

CHAPTER 23

Agatha insisted she ride with Cody and Lulu. Cody shifted some equipment and made room for her on the seat next to his. Lulu took her place on the other side of Agatha, giving Buster a peevish look. The mist was growing heavier, and the humidity was as thick as butter. Cody suspected Buster rode in the same carryall with them just to keep an eye on them. Cody tried to sense what was going on in Buster's mind but the leader was blocking. Deirdre, Jerry, and Claire climbed in as well and secured their harnesses. Down the shore Cody saw Kevin Axworthy helping his father into a separate carryall. Buster engaged the particle pulse propulsion system and their air vehicle rose toward the overcast sky, away from the Sea of Humility, climbing the side of the hill.

A light rain beat against the clear acrylic weather bonnet. A navigation screen showed direction, topography, wind speed, location of other carryalls, and the projected migration route north.

Higher and higher they rose, until they reached the top of the hill. To the north stretched yet more hills, an endless succession of them, all covered with lichen, moss, and flowering plants. These hills rose to between 100 and 300 meters high. He tried to concentrate on the various land features as a way to keep his mind off the grief he felt coming from Agatha. In the gullies between the hills he saw small stands of asparagus-like trees, just like the ones in his first mind-to-mind communication with Buster, no branches, just a trunk shooting straight up to a heavily seeded top. He also saw the occasional brook and stream. He was particularly interested in the trees, though, thought he might be able to use them as a building material.

For the next long while the terrain stayed the same. Hills, hills, and yet more hills. Cody was awed by how big the place was. Outer space didn't seem as big as this. The perspectives stretched forever, thousands of times bigger than the perspectives of Vesta or Ceres, even bigger than the perspectives he had seen on Mars when he had visited there with Christine eight years ago. The sky, despite the constant cloud cover, seemed limitless.

By midday the temperature had reached 39 degrees Celsius. The atmosphere was so thick and muggy that they were all drenched in sweat. Some of the ground-clinging mist burned away, the clouds climbed to a higher ceiling, and Cody could see further.

To the west the hills climbed rank upon rank, higher and higher until they finally reached a mountain range. Many of these mountains had concave dips at their peaks— calderas—and were in fact volcanoes. Five of them billowed steam and ash, more evidence that Carswell had its own internal furnace for the long cold night ahead. All were bereft of any vegetation.

Large birds, black specks, circled in the updrafts along the leeward slopes of these volcanoes and mountains. Cody wasn't certain if he could call them birds, but they were definitely flight animals of some sort, twenty or thirty of them, circling upward, then dipping, again and again, in an endless cycle.

They continued north for the next two days. On the third day the chain of mountains branched east, and they were finally forced to find a pass.

The pass they found was barren, a hardened lava flow, gray, basaltic, with only a few tufts of grass growing here and there. Cody saw a large four-legged creature scamper over the rock, five smaller ones following it, all of them gray, hard to distinguish from the rock.

The clan camped near an active volcano that night. Cody stared at the bare slope . . . and realized he had seen this volcano before. The glow of the lava from within the caldera a kilometer away stretched fingers of murky light into the night. This was what he had plucked whole from Lulu's mind, from Buster's mind. An image of precognition. With people walking up near the caldera, geologists having a close-up look, taking readings, measurements, trying to determine what kind of furnace Carswell had and whether it would keep them warm enough during the harrowing journey into the deep cold beyond colonized space.

They got through this east-branching range of mountains the next day by following the pass around a large volcanic lake. The water absolutely still, reflected the dull, overcast sky, and a lone island rose in the middle. After that the terrain settled again, grew hilly, the hills 100 to 500 meters high, with brooks and streams in between and more of the asparagus-like trees.

At midday, when the heat was at its worst, they stopped at one of these stands of trees for a rest. Cody and Lulu walked to the nearest tree, leaving Agatha in the care of Claire and Jerry. They walked silently together, reacting to each other's reactions, overwhelmed by the huge land, glad to get away, to be alone with each other. The tree was smooth, olive-green, with a delicate tracery of purple veins in it. It smelled musky, like a damp basement. He looked at Lulu.

He said: *Is she getting better?*

He meant Agatha. He wanted to get Lulu's take on the situation.

Lulu said: *She's all gray inside. She's beyond the point of numbness. She doesn't think about her child. She doesn't think about the future or the past. She thinks only of Ben and how the Sea of Humility has taken him away from her.*

He nodded. *That's what I thought.*

He wished there was something he could do for Agatha, but he knew there wasn't. Knew from firsthand experience.

Lulu said: *Is the wood any good?*

He pushed at one of the trees, and it fell right over. *Does that answer your question?*

On the fourth day the clan discovered three more constructs, green glass tubular structures thrusting upward out of the surrounding land. Cody and Buster looked at each other. Cody couldn't help feeling a bit of Buster's ghost code, a deep and abiding mistrust of anything he didn't understand. The three constructs were about five kilometers apart, all in a row, each half the size of the one in the Sea of Humility.

The clan stopped briefly to inspect one of them. Cody ventured with Deirdre into its canyonlike thoroughfares. They didn't see much, found a lot of dirt and windblown sediment clogging the passageways between towers.

"I wonder how these were built?" asked Deirdre. "I don't see any seams or rivets, no connective strategy of any kind."

Cody had no answer. Moss, lichen, and flowers, all non-photosynthetic, grew in the windblown sediment, which in some places was five meters deep. He could only gaze in wonder.

On the fifth day the hills ended. They entered wider flatter country, much of it flooded. Agatha clung to him. The wide open spaces seemed to frighten her. Lulu stayed close, too.

The wind increased steadily through the course of the morning, and their carryall was often buffeted about in the turbulence.

The wind got so bad they finally had to land.

The 3,000-plus carryalls of the Olympia Mons Clan settled on a broad floodplain like a flock of strange birds. A wide river meandered eastward toward the Ocean of Forgiveness—the name Meek cartographers were giving the world-spanning ocean.

A gigantic storm approached from the west. The Ocean of Forgiveness was undergoing its first heat-related convulsions, unleashing this violent storm in a place that had known stable weather for thousands, if not millions, of years.

Claire consulted her laptop. "Satellite reconnaissance shows a total of 19 hurricanes, and it looks as if seven of them are going to make landfall," she told Cody. "Most are south of the equator. But there's one directly that way," she said, pointing west, "over the Ocean of Forgiveness, and even though we're 1,000 kilometers inland it's going to spawn a good number of storms and tornadoes in our area."

Not that he was an expert in natural weather patterns, having lived his whole life in controlled weather, but Cody nonetheless felt he had to offer some advice, sensed that the storm moving in from the west was going to get far worse before it petered out.

"I think we should move to higher ground," he told Buster, shouting over the wind. "We should try to get out of the open. It's starting to rain, and we're not too far from that river. There could be flooding. The navigational screen showed a few hills 10 kilometers east. It might not be much, but at least we won't be exposed like this."

Buster agreed.

Keeping low to the ground, the carryalls, now acting more like hover-cars, skimmed over the soggy surface of the floodplain.

Fifteen minutes later they spotted the hills, striking in their loneliness and covered with a surprising growth of trees the likes of which Cody had yet to see on the planet. The carryalls entered the hills through a multitude of passes, and the wind immediately died down.

They set up camp for the night, rigging canopies to the sides of their carryalls. Cody knelt on the ground and hammered a guide rope into place. The rain grew heavier, running in rivulets around his knee. The children ran around in the rain, thinking it was great fun. He had to smile, even though the sight of so much rain made him nervous.

The storm finally passed five hours later, and the rain diminished. Cody ventured from the protection of the canopy carrying a hatchet from his Public Works tool kit.

By this time it was the middle of the night. The clouds shone with a dull phosphorescence, giving him just enough light to see by. He walked to the nearest tree and examined it. It didn't look so much like a tree as it did a form of giant fungal growth. Like a toadstool or mushroom, something that could grow in the dark. The trunk measured a meter across and tapered slowly to a height of 30 meters, where it was crowned not by branches but by dozens of stamenlike growths—long, flexible tubes, each with a pod the size of a pineapple on top. The trunk didn't have any bark. Instead, it was covered with thousands of little warts. Wartwood was the name the Meek had given it.

He pressed his hand to the trunk. The trunk was hard.

He ventured farther into the forest, touching trees as he went. He lifted his hatchet and chopped a wedge out of a trunk. He lifted it. Light but surprisingly strong. No evidence of wood grain or sap. He sniffed it. Musky. A smell akin to a fresh-cut mushroom. He felt his mood lighten. He might have a decent building material here.

He slept next to Lulu that night. They made love. Not much privacy with five other people sleeping under the carryall canopy with them, certainly not the best time or place for it, especially because Deirdre and Buster were right there, but the urgency of their need for each other overcame their caution.

Buster sat in the corner of their small shelter staring at them, a blanket around his shoulders, his eyes big and mean, a heavy creosote blocker making his thoughts menacingly impenetrable.

*　　*　　*

The wind woke Cody a few hours later.

Over the whispering of the wind he heard a sound he at first didn't recognize. He sat up. Listened. Water. Like the sound the lake made at the William Wordsworth Lake Country Habitat on Vesta . . . small waves lapping against a shore.

He glanced around at the sleeping people under the canopy. Buster dozed, still in a sitting position. Cody caressed Lulu's cheek with the back of his hand, then pulled the blanket around her shoulders. He went outside.

The wind was up, the rain had stopped, and there was a break in the clouds, a huge rift through which he saw Ceres—the *moon* Ceres—three-quarters full, lighting up everything in the valley below. At the foot of the hill water covered the floodplain, which now formed an inland sea. The river was gone, its banks overflowed, no sign of it anywhere. Even at its shallowest the water had to be at least three meters deep. Had they been caught out on the floodplain earlier, thousands of them would have died in the deluge, and much of their food and equipment would have been washed away.

Ceres painted a gold band over the waves. He was going to miss Ceres. He wondered how the other 25 clans were doing, if any of them had lost their way, if any of their members had as yet met with death, or had narrowly escaped it, such as Olympia Mons had just done with this flood. He wondered where they all were on this vast continent the Meek cartographers called Our Home.

He turned around and headed back to the camp.

He was just about to duck under the canopy when a sudden blinking of lights in the woods caught his eye. His eyes narrowed and he peered more closely. Blinking lights, a cluster of nine in all, each about the size of a walnut, hovered three meters above the ground, flashing in a quick random pattern. They went out. There was nothing but darkness for a moment. He waited for the blinking to start again. He took a few steps toward the woods. The lights flashed once more, a little farther away, then went out again. He approached cautiously, remembering the attack of the other blinking lights, how they had downed the creature with membranous wings.

He rounded the south perimeter of the camp and found a path that led into the woods between some steep hills. The lights continued to blink, this time up in the trees. He was close enough now to see that they weren't simply disembodied lights; they were attached to a much larger life-form. He saw, briefly, the life-form's outline in the peripheral glow of its lights. It was fairylike, much more so than the Meek, with arms and legs and a head, and huge transparent wings. The thing stopped blinking and Cody lost sight of it in the dark. He heard a low buzz, like the sound hummingbirds made with their wings on the shores of the James Cook Coral Reef Habitat. He felt wind on his face—not a natural wind but the wind of . . . of wings, pulselike and quick, realized the thing had swooped from the trees and now hovered in the dark in front of him.

He took out his small guidelight and flashed it a few times.

He sensed, more than he saw, the thing move away. Had he scared it? Where was it now? He couldn't see it. Was it clinging to the side of that wartwood tree? Or was it over in those bushes? A stillness descended over the forest. It was as if the thing were trying to figure him out.

Then he heard the buzz again, exactly like the quick flutter of hummingbird wings, felt the wind on his face. The thing was once more right in front of him. He stood rigidly, not in fear, just ready for anything. The thing blinked at him, nine lights flashing brightly, their glow shining on its body. He saw it clearly this time.

It measured a meter from head to toe and had what astrobiologists called "standard configuration" facial features—two eyes, a nose, a mouth—like any of the animals on Earth, but it didn't look like an animal; it looked surprisingly human. Its body was in "standard configuration" as well, with two arms, two legs, head, and trunk, all in the usual places. Humanlike, yet alien-looking. The creature had nine light-wands on its head. Its eyes were big, round, sensitive. What made it so alien-looking was its body. It was entirely transparent, with even its various internal body structures see-through clear. Cody saw right through its head into its brain and out the back of its brain into the forest. Its transparent wings flapped at least 200 beats per minute. Cody saw right through its chest. Saw its lungs. Saw through its lungs and out its back. The thing was like a ghost. A fairy. Clear. Brilliantly transparent, like glass. The creature blinked furiously with its headwands as if it were trying to tell Cody something.

Cody was just about to respond with his guidelight when someone pushed him hard from behind. Cody fell to the ground and lost his grip on his guidelight. The creature darted away into the trees. Cody struggled to his knees and found Buster standing over him. Looking into Buster's eyes, he realized Buster had finally been defeated by his ghost code, that he was angry, jealous, and resentful. Buster pulled out his knife. He was a different man now, thought Cody, a man whose temper, at last released, had grown murderous. Buster held the knife high over his head, preparing to attack Cody. His eyes glowed like glacial ice, their usual violet replaced by a frosty green.

Cody waited. He sensed Buster struggling against the shadow codes of his warrior days.

Buster said: *You take my love; I take your life.*

Yet still Buster hesitated, held the knife poised, his arm now shaking as he wrestled with his violent impulses. Cody felt Buster's emanations like a wrecking ball inside his mind. The emanations of a Meek man, then the emanations of an orphan, the thoughts and feelings of the two sides of Buster, each warring with the other. Thinking of revenge but asking for forgiveness, overwhelmed by suspicion but begging for trust, gripped by envy but filled with admiration.

The knife came closer. Buster stopped it again. Cody waited on his knees, knowing he was defenseless.

He at last felt Buster starting to get control of himself. He felt the compassion, understanding, and tolerance of a Meek man coming back . . . felt Buster's immense willpower as he challenged his own former nature. Cody tried to help. He projected himself into Buster, so that Buster would understand him as a man in full . . . his whole life—childhood, adolescence, adulthood—so that Buster would understand he meant no harm. Christine, grief, his five years as a widower . . . and now . . . now Lulu . . . how he loved Lulu . . . how he cared for Lulu . . . how he would protect her . . . using Meek empathy the way it was meant to be used, to establish a trusting bond, to make Buster realize he was not an enemy but a friend, and that this was not the end of his life with Lulu but simply the beginning of a new phase in it.

Buster let the knife fall to his side.

He turned away.

Cody got to his feet and put his hand on Buster's shoulder.

He was surprised. He felt Lulu inside Buster, yes, of course, that's what this midnight encounter was all about, but he also felt something else, something dark and troubling, something that seemed to sear Cody's hand as he touched Buster. Something that went far beyond his upset over Lulu. Something that incidentally might have provoked his upset over Lulu but that ultimately had nothing to do with it. Something that only Buster and a few other ranking clan members knew about. A new situation that now threatened the whole enterprise. Cody could sense it, could feel the weight of Buster's anxiety, but could hardly tell what it was. Only that Carswell wasn't as benign as it looked.

Buster said: *I'm sorry.*

Cody stared at Buster—still so odd to watch a man who, after such emotional exertion, wasn't breathing, no huffing and puffing, no chest movement at all.

"There's nothing I can do, Buster," he said. "I can't help

the way I feel." He peered more closely at Buster. "What is it? I can sense your . . . apprehension . . . your misgiving. What's happened?"

Buster said: *I think all this . . .* He indicated the wart-wood forest, the encampment, the floodplain, the asteroid Ceres. *I think all this was . . . ill-advised.*

CHAPTER 24

Buster called a meeting of ranking clan members early the next day. He invited Cody to the meeting.

They gathered in a clearing among the wartwood trees. Holographic equipment had been set up.

Buster said: *This is what the Phaethontis Clan reports.*

A holographic image appeared in the middle of the clearing, a panoramic shot of the transparent creatures—what Buster called Filaments—descending on the encampment of the Phaethontis Clan, ripping open crates of marrow, devouring handfuls of the stuff, clan members shooing the Filaments away, hitting them with tent poles, canopy poles, whatever lay handy, doing anything they could to protect their marrow.

Buster said: *They eat it. They like it.*

Cody sensed that this was the dark and troubling thing he had been feeling from Buster last night. He watched the holograph. Members of Phaethontis finally chased the Filaments away, but not without first losing 10 percent of their marrow supply.

Buster said: *The Filaments eat anything. They're voracious. Phaethontis now posts guards to protect its marrow. We will do the same.*

A new hologram appeared of a small test farm run by the Aetheria Clan.

Buster said: *The Aetheria Clan have made exceedingly*

*good time. They've already set up camp on the northern
peninsula. This has given them time to test-farm. They've
planted this marrow. See how the Filaments swoop down
and eat the seedlings? They don't even give it a chance to
grow. We might be able to protect our existing supplies but
we may not be able to protect our farms. We've tried some
conventional poisons against the Filaments. They don't
work. The Filaments just eat them. If we don't develop a
workable strategy within the next few weeks, many of us who
need marrow to breathe, those of the orphan line, may not
survive.*

A final hologram appeared, this one from the Tithonius
Lacus Clan. The Tithonius Lacus Clan had traveled north,
up the west coast of Our Home. The view showed a rocky
steep coastline. Hundreds of thousands of Filaments clung
to the bluffs, shoulder to shoulder, their wings fluttering,
packed so tightly Cody couldn't see the side of the cliff,
some flying out over the Ocean of Forgiveness, others diving
into the water, surfacing with fish in their hands. Like the
gannet colonies of Earth, he thought. They ate the fish, tails
and all. Buster was right. They ate anything and everything.
They ate ravenously.

And there were just so many of them . . .

He went for a walk with Agatha five hours later, during
the noontime break. The hills had given way to mountains
again. These mountains were small, no more than 1,000 meters high, peaks gray and bare, no volcanoes anywhere.
Broad valleys stretched between the mountains. The clan
stopped in one of these valleys. Here in this valley the grass
was high, straw-colored.

Agatha was quiet, subdued. She and Cody came to a
gorge in the middle of the valley. At the bottom of the gorge
was a small river. The strawlike grass had been flattened
here, just above the gorge, pushed over by the wind, was
soft, pliant, a good place to sit.

They sat down. Cody put his arm around Agatha. Her albino-white hair blew over his arm.

He said: *There's nothing I can do.*

And left it at that because there were no words for a situation like this. He remembered his mother's awkward attempts to comfort him after the death of Christine, how she had tried her best to say the usual things, but her words always fell short.

He said: *I could tell you about time. How with the passage of time you might feel better. I could tell you how you should think of your child. I could tell you how you should stop hoping—I know you want to run off, go back to the Sea of Humility, try to find Ben somewhere along its shores. But I'm not going to tell you any of that. I know there's no point.*

He pulled her closer.

She said: *Do you think he's still alive?*

He said: *No.*

She turned, looked down at the river. Seven or eight Filaments flew by in formation, following the river downstream.

She said: *He was humble. That's what I liked about him.*

He said: *He was also afraid of mice.*

She turned, stared, her brow arching in puzzlement. She said: *He was?*

He said: *We were out in the Great Plains Growing Region of Vesta one year fixing grain elevators. He opened an access door and a mouse scampered out. You should have seem him jump. I've never laughed so hard.*

She stared even harder. A grin came to her face, and he felt her cool pine scent in his mind. She understood. Here was a moment for her. A brief reprieve from her grief. He knew it wasn't going to last. He knew the numbness would come back. He sensed her hard kernel of grief still there, like a chunk of ice ready to freeze her heart again. But at least now, with this tiny anecdote, she might sense that the thaw might someday come.

*   *   *

The clan reached the northern archipelago of Our Home the next day, a vast curving arm of volcanic islands thrusting well into the northern ocean above the arctic circle, a group of islands Meek cartographers called A Hundred Second Chances.

On the way they discovered a group of 75 Filaments who had been caught under a rock slide. Surviving Filaments pulled rocks away. Cody, who now steered the carryall, brought the air vehicle down, landing on a grassy patch some way from the Filaments. He and Buster got out and observed the Filaments.

"I think they must be intelligent," said Cody. Cody preferred speaking to Buster now rather than using emanations, felt he expressed himself more clearly with the spoken word.

Buster said: *How can they be intelligent? They live in the wild. They scavenge. They hunt the same way hyenas hunt. They're beasts. Nothing more.*

"Beasts wouldn't show the same concern for their fellow creatures," said Cody. "Look at the way the survivors are digging the rocks away. They understand life and death. They value life. They're looking for survivors. They're trying to rescue their fellow kind."

Which was exactly what the Filaments did. They pulled rocks aside. They dragged injured survivors out. They dragged their dead out. They lined up their dead side by side, showing a sense of geometry, symmetry, and design that could be construed only as the work of intelligent creatures. They blinked their headwands at each other like they were communicating with light. The more Cody watched them, the more he grew convinced they were intelligent.

Buster, having walked through Cody's mind, said: *You make assumptions, Cody. Symmetry and design aren't necessarily hallmarks of intelligence. Look at a wasp's nest and you'll see symmetry. Look at a spider's web and you'll see design.*

The uninjured Filaments buried the dead Filaments. They

piled dirt, sand, and rocks over them. Several flew away behind the mountain and came back with handfuls of white
mud, the discharge of some geyser nearby, and smoothed the
white mud over the dark mud. Two of them then picked up
sharp rocks and drew designs through the white mud. Right
into the dark mud, so that the designs stood out in sharp relief.

"They're using tools, Buster," said Cody. "Not only that,
they bury their dead."

Buster said: *Several creatures bury things.*

"How can you plan to poison them when you can plainly
see they're intelligent?" asked Cody.

Buster said: *Again, you make assumptions.*

"No," he said, "I don't."

But then the Filaments did something even Cody couldn't
explain. They began to pile dirt and rocks on top of the injured survivors. They buried them alive. It was all Cody
could do to stop from interfering. Several of the injured
crawled away, plaintive cries coming from their mouths, but
they were dragged back and buried just the same. Buried the
way a cat might bury its business in a litter box. The way a
sea turtle might bury its eggs. The way a dog might bury a
bone. Out of instinct? Or through intelligent intent? He simply couldn't tell.

The migration continued over the next several weeks.

After camping for a night on one of the islands of A Hundred Second Chances, the clan turned south and headed
back through the scorching equatorial spring. For Cody, one
day blended into the next, a constant and endless cycle of
travel, then camp, travel, then camp. When it rained, the rain
was as warm as bathwater. They were plagued by constant
storms, particularly near the end of the day. They had to
stake down the carryalls so they wouldn't blow away.

The manned mission from Earth arrived in the middle of
the third week. By this time the Olympia Mons Clan was
three days south of the equator, into cooler weather, and

1,000 kilometers away from where the Earth mission landed. The Earth mission crew met with members of the Mare Tyrrhenum Clan. Buster monitored all contact scrupulously. Cody followed the whole thing with interest, an unusual and noteworthy occurrence in the monotonous succession of days.

"How big's their spacecraft?" Jerry wanted to know. "Can they take any of us back to Earth with them?"

Buster delegated Cody to investigate this possibility. Unfortunately, it couldn't be done.

"Their planned slingshot maneuver around Venus has been calculated to specific crew and fuel weights," he told a disappointed Jerry. "And the spacecraft is too small anyway."

The eight Earthlings were allowed to take their samples, conduct their experiments, take their pictures. And then they went back to Earth with no idea about what was happening with the Filaments.

The Meek had to ration their marrow in the interest of making it last until they came up with a solution for the Filaments; there would be no point in farming marrow, until they solved the filament problem. Cody watched as Filaments were captured and tested against a vast array of poisons and pesticides, none of which worked. Cody offered Buster his thoughts on the subject.

"In a place where food is scarce and nutrients have to be found in even the most unlikely places, the Filaments have evolved to eat plants or grasses that might contain toxins— toxins they can easily digest with no ill effects," he said. "As omnivores, they're equipped to deal with these poisons. All the plants and grasses on Carswell have mushroomlike qualities, can grow in the dark. We've learned that many of them contain a variety of poisons. The Filaments eat them all."

Buster reluctantly abandoned the poison and pesticide approach. He concentrated Meek efforts on developing an effective biological or viral weapon against the Filaments.

Buster, much to Cody's alarm, didn't at first see the irony of this plan. Cody pointed it out as bluntly as he could.

"What you're proposing is a bioextermination," he said.

Buster said: *We're still looking at other alternatives. The virus under development will be used only as a last resort.*

Once they reached the southern tip of Our Home, and had set up camp on the shores of the Bay of Redemption, five Filaments—Scar, Ears, Hunchback, Tumble, and Bigfoot (names bestowed for the attributes they described)— attached themselves to Olympia Mons the way stray cats or stray dogs might. The Filaments down at this end of the continent didn't seem as shy as the ones further north, Cody observed. They exhibited a greater degree of curiosity and fearlessness, as if perhaps there had never been any real predators down at this end of Our Home. Cody spent many hours watching them, sitting on a hillside above the sea, enjoying the ocean breeze on his face, remembering the ocean breezes from the James Cook Coral Reef Habitat. Scar, Ears, Hunchback, Tumble, and Bigfoot seemed to be a set group, and in fact, the Filaments down here seemed to travel around in such groups. Cody repeatedly observed their instinct to attach to a larger group, which at least partly explained why their five mascot Filaments attached themselves to the Meek. As it turned out, this was convenient because the Meek wanted to test some nonlethal methods for deterring the Filaments.

Buster said: *The five make good test subjects, a stable control group our scientists can identify from day to day and chart in a coherent fashion, without the anomalies unknown subjects might introduce.*

Olympia Mons established several experimental plots of marrow for the purposes of testing a wide variety of more flamboyant strategies. Cody went out into the field and helped break the soil. He wanted to work. He was getting restless, not having anything to do. Because the marrow grew so quickly—in less than 32 hours—they were able to grow enough of it to pilot a number of different options.

Cody observed everything. As the first seedlings poked through the ground the five mascot Filaments flew in from the surrounding hills and attacked the crop like a flock of marauding crows. They were quickly joined by swarms of others.

Olympia Mons tried sound, blasting music of all types through huge speakers mounted on big silver tripods, a variety of noises, dogs barking, lions roaring, but the Filaments simply looked up at the speakers, then went back to devouring the marrow. Cody stood by the side of the field leaning on his hoe, amused but at the same time apprehensive about the ineffectiveness of the strategy. He watched the bewildered scientists chart the dismal results on palmtop computers. Some technicians wheeled in an array of bright lights. Lulu came up beside him and slipped her hand onto his arm. Olympia Mons tried the light, but other than a bit of squinting, the Filaments seemed unaffected.

"They're impervious little guys, aren't they?" said Cody.

The next strategy was more drastic. Meek soldiers came in with particle beam rifles and shot the Filaments. (They spared Scar, Ears, Hunchback, Tumble, and Bigfoot.) The scatter-shot wiped out a dozen Filaments at a time. But it didn't matter. They were quickly replaced by others.

"Did they have to do that?" asked Cody. "I don't think it achieved anything, other than a lot of unnecessary carnage."

Next, they let Meek children shoo the Filaments away. Scar and the gang moved off no more than a few meters then settled back down, the way pigeons in a busy city square might.

They had a meeting about everything later that night.

Artemis Axworthy, growing frailer with each passing day, suggested the only humane way to solve the Meek's dilemma without resorting to the wide-scale deployment of a viral weapon against the Filaments was to rewrite the Meek's code so they wouldn't have to depend on marrow for their oxygen supply.

"But to rewrite Meek genetic code so you can breathe

without marrow . . . that would take at least a year," he said. "And we just don't have the time, do we?"

He shook his head as if he blamed himself for not having foreseen the unforeseeable.

Cody had a thought. "Can't we have the Meek of the human line go without marrow altogether?" he said. "Wouldn't that extend our marrow supply a little further and give us more time to find a better solution than killing all the Filaments? The human-line Meek might get sick, they might have withdrawal symptoms, but at least they won't die the way those of the orphan line will."

The Father shook his head skeptically. "We've already thought of that, Cody," he said. "Buster and I talked that over several days ago when we first realized we had a problem. Unfortunately fully three quarters of the Meek are orphan-descended. Even if the human line goes without, we can't make the marrow last forever. We have to grow more. And in order to do that we have to solve the Filament problem in the next couple of weeks."

Buster offered an update on the latest interpretation of orbital photographs: *After reexamining the trans-cloud satellite photographs, clan specialists have concluded that the so-called migratory scars detected on Carswell's surface earlier are in fact scars left behind by the extensive feeding forays of the Filaments.*

Cody shook his head as he came to his own depressing conclusion about the Filaments. These delicate transparent creatures who looked nearly human, who buried their dead, who spoke to each other in a language of light, and who daily showed a growing curiosity about the Meek, behaved more like locust, born to raze, scourging the countryside, stuffing their faces with a callous disregard for everything else.

Yet over the next few days, as he continued to observe them, he saw that they treated one particular species of native flora—known as the milkberry among the Meek—with unusual diffidence and respect. He watched as Scar crouched in a patch of milkberry bushes and delicately turned the small yellow leaves aside to look for the wild berries. There were hundreds Scar could have chosen but he seemed to be looking for the *right* berries. He finally picked out two. On occasion, Cody had seen him pick out three. Cody's eyes widened as he realized this was an unvarying pattern. The Filaments would pick two, sometimes three, never one, never more than three. Scar broke the berries open so the milky fluid ran over his thumb and fingers. Then he popped them into his mouth and flew away.

Cody couldn't figure it out. He watched Scar grow smaller and smaller and finally disappear. The Filaments never gorged on the milkberry like they did on everything else. He recalled the tests the Meek had run on the milkberry: highly alkaline, nonpoisonous, and loaded with complex carbohydrates. Cody got up off his haunches, walked into the milkberry patch, picked one, and tasted it. Sweet but tart. Nothing unusual about it at all. He wondered if it had pharmaceutical properties. Yet the Meek tests had detected nothing medicinal.

He looked around at the berry patch. So why did the Filaments treat the milkberry with such diffidence? Did it have a special significance to them? And if so, was it a cultural significance? A religious significance? A significance that confirmed their intelligence?

Lulu said: *She wants you.* Despite the perpetual night at the south pole, the weather was warm, balmy, and the air smelled sweet with the white-and-orange blossoms of a ground-clinging vine the Meek called Alms for the Poor. *She needs you. She loves you. Comfort her.*

The Bay of Redemption whispered beyond the wartwood-choked bluffs. Scar, Bigfoot, Tumble, Hunchback, and Ears played among the stamenlike branches, pulling them back and whacking each other with them, an activity that caused them no end of amusement.

Cody said: *And what of Buster? He needs you. He loves you. He wants you.*

She looked away, gasped suddenly for breath, her long-unused lungs from the days when she had still called herself Catherine spasming into life as she went into another withdrawal episode from marrow rationing. She coughed several times but finally caught her breath. Her hair had taken on a decidedly darker tint, reverting to the chocolate shades of her girlhood.

She said: *We give of ourselves. It's the way of the Meek.* Her emanations were weak, compromised by lack of marrow. *I've forgotten that. But now I remind myself. They need us and we should go to them.*

Cody lay next to Deirdre that night. He felt her fear and uncertainty. They lay away from the rest of the group under the open sky, their groundsheet emanating warmth, bio-therms stitched into the fabric. He held her.

"I think of you as my friend now," said Deirdre. "How long have we known each other?"

"Ten years," said Cody.

"I'm sorry Christine died," she said.

"I'm finally accepting it," said Cody.

She looked up at him questioningly. "Does sex get in the way of friendship?"

He knew he had to make a decision. He turned on his side, propped himself up on his elbow, and looked at her. She was pretty in an earnest serious way. Fair skin with freckles, green eyes. He pressed his palm flat against her stomach. She watched, waiting to see what he would do. She reached up, stroked his beard.

"You're going to go with them, aren't you?" she said.

He wasn't going to lie to her. "I love Lulu," he said.

She nodded, accepting this. "And I love you," she said.

"People can't help the way they feel," he said.

He leaned down and kissed her. Giving comfort, the Meek way. Her lips felt soft, sensual. He pulled away and saw that her eyes were almost closed, her breath coming in short warm gasps. They made love. He gave comfort and he received comfort. Sex as an expression of friendship, one of the oddest and perhaps most satisfying feelings he had ever had, free of all the usual freight.

When they were done Deirdre had a soft grin on her face.

"Whatever you do," she said, "I know you do it for the right reasons."

He nodded. "Thank you," he said.

Her eyes narrowed and she pointed past his shoulder. "Look," she said.

He turned around. Scar, Bigfoot, Tumble, Ears, and Hunchback hovered above them, ten meters up. The Filaments held hands, formed a circle. They turned clockwise, moved in a marked rhythm. Their headwands flashed in unison. Their shoulders jerked back and forth synchronously. Tumble moved to the middle of the circle and spun counterclockwise, his headwands flashing in the exact same pattern, only twice as fast, his shoulders jerking to the same rhythm, only twice as fast. Twelve other Filaments flew up from the surrounding grass garlanded with Alms for the Poor. These twelve formed a circle around Scar, Hunchback, Ears, and Bigfoot. In the middle, Tumble spun double-time counterclockwise, the other four turned normal speed clockwise, the twelve new ones spun counter-clockwise half-time. The twelve blinked the same pattern at half-speed, jerked their shoulders at half-speed.

"They're dancing?" asked Deirdre.

Cody stared at them. "I think so," he said. "The numerical relationships . . . the rhythms . . . the patterns . . . they're complex."

He grew more convinced than ever that these creatures were intelligent.

Tumble left the group and flew toward them. The others dispersed and disappeared into the night. Tumble came in for a landing, and as usual, he tumbled. He got to his feet, flapped his wings a few times, flinging bits of grass from them, brushed himself off, and approached Cody and

Deirdre with a bowlegged gait. Deirdre, still a little nervous about the small see-through creatures, moved closer to Cody. Tumble came right up and looked at them with his big round eyes. His headwands blinked, lighting up his face. He peered closely at Deirdre's breasts. He poked the left one.

"Hey!" said Deirdre.

Tumble rooted among the nonphotosynthetic grass and weeds and picked an Alms for the Poor. He sniffed the white-and-orange blossom a few times—Cody could see his little lungs expanding inside his chest—then offered it to Deirdre. Deirdre reached out and took the flower.

"Thank you," she said.

The two humans and the Filament stared at each other for a few moments more. Then Tumble flew away, his flashing headwands growing fainter as he headed toward the point.

The next day the sun rose for an hour above the northern horizon, brightening the cloud cover to a uniform gray; a brief taste of dawn after a week of nights, an intimation of the raging summer that would swoop down from the north.

Cody and Lulu went for a walk along the beach during this brief dawn. The sand under his feet was soft and warm (the planet seemed to radiate warmth), and the green and foamy surf rolled onto the beach in a musical rhythm. A grass-covered slope rose to the left, the grass bending in the wind coming off the bay. Shells the likes of which he had never seen before littered the beach, shaped like the triangular poppy seed turnovers his mother used to buy from the bakery down the street.

Lulu said: *You were with her?*

He sensed no reproach. Rather, she was glad he had given Deirdre comfort. He motioned at the deserted beach.

"I was," he said. He spoke to her, trusted his voice more than his emanations, could better control tone and inflection, felt more at home with his voice. "Tumble gave her a flower last night."

Lulu said: *He did?*

"I can't help wondering about it. I mentioned it to Buster. He frowned, wouldn't respond. But I think it's another indication, don't you?"

Lulu stared off over the waves. *Buster's had some of the scientists run intelligence tests on Bigfoot and Ears. Nothing. Their brain waves exhibit not the slightest trace of advanced cognition. But then there was a lot in the tests the scientists had never seen before.* She grinned. *I think giving a flower to a pretty woman like Deirdre is sign of intelligence, don't you?*

He grinned back. He had to agree with her. He lifted a stone and threw it into the ocean. "You've developed a taste for solitude," he said.

She said: *Now that our marrow rations are small the old codes fade. The instinct to pack weakens. Our empathic communications grow faint. I was solitary as a child, before the Chryse Planitia changed me. I like quiet.* She smiled as the wind from the bay buffeted her face. *Isn't that a wonderful smell? I've never smelled anything so fresh.*

He gazed out at the bay. Far beyond the east point the bay opened onto the Ocean of Forgiveness.

"Solitude has a lot to offer," he said.

They walked another half kilometer then climbed the slope. In the grass, patches of pink lichen grew in small conical pods, adding color to the otherwise drab brown, green, and yellow ground cover.

They had just about reached the top when they startled a pair of Filaments lying in the grass.

One them, the male, leaped up and approached Cody and Lulu, headwands flashing crazily in the gray dawn. Cody looked at the female. Birth water soaked the ground. Three newborns, two of them twitching their wings, trying to stand, huddled close to their mother. The third just lay there, shivering, deformed, born with badly crippled legs. The male picked up a lump of dirt and threw it at Cody. The intent was no doubt protective. The dirt bounced harmlessly off Cody's knee.

Cody took out his guidelight and flashed it a few times at the male. The male stared at the light. The female sat up weakly and gathered the two healthy newborns close to her. The deformed one she just left. The male looked over his shoulder, flashed something at the female. The female responded with a short flash of her own. Cody was sure they were communicating. They looked so small. They looked so helpless. They didn't look like the enemy at all. The male faced Cody again. He looked frightened, his little lungs pumping, getting ready to fight. Cody wanted to reassure him.

He stooped. Made himself smaller.

He searched the grass and quickly found a milkberry bush. He pushed the small leaves aside and revealed a dozen purplish-white berries. He did not pick them. The Filament craned, looked at the milkberries, flashed its headwands a few times, then turned away, walked back to its mate.

The male glanced over his shoulder and contemplated Cody and Lulu a second time. Then it dragged the deformed newborn a few meters away, where only a few stalks of spore-grass grew, and pushed sand over it, burying it alive. Cody was reminded of the burials at the rock slide. Now he understood. They buried the nonviable. The fatally injured. The dying. It was cruel. But in a world where food was so scarce, necessary.

The deformed newborn didn't struggle, simply allowed itself to be buried.

When the mound was complete the male Filament walked over to the same milkberry bush Cody had showed him, picked two of the small berries, broke them open, and mixed the juice with sand. The juice instantly whitened the sand, and the male spread the whitened sand over the mound. He plucked a stalk of grass and etched delicate lines into his child's burial mound.

Inside a large geodesic dome 18 Filaments struggled to stay upright. Cody stared through the clear acrylic. Jerry stood beside him watching. So did Buster, a number of ranking members of the clan, and several Meek scientists.

"It's not exactly a gentle virus," said Jerry. "But so many of the viruses they tried simply didn't work. This one directly targets the synovial fluid around their joints."

Cody saw that the knee joints, elbow joints, and ankle joints of the suffering Filaments were no longer transparent, no longer brilliantly see-through, but milky, translucent.

"So the virus essentially cripples them," said Cody.

Jerry's eyes narrowed, and an expression of regret came to his face. "That's about the size of it," he said.

"And we all know what the Filaments do to their cripples," said Cody.

CHAPTER 25

Cody and Buster huddled in the carryall, the temperature-control unit working hard to keep the interior temperature livable, the bonnet sealed in place against the intense 60-degree-Celsius temperatures outside. They were resting during the day in preparation for the evening's travel.

Buster said: *The mean temperature of Carswell has risen considerably. Because of these higher temperatures we have to broaden bodily tolerances and will need to increase our marrow rations in order to withstand the heat. Even you six humans will have to eat marrow to toughen your bodies. You won't be able to survive otherwise. This is going to deplete our marrow supply drastically and add yet more pressure to stop the Filaments. If we can't come up with an alternate solution for stopping them before we reach the Martian orbital plane, we'll have no choice. We'll have to go ahead with the virus.*

"But you can't kill them all," said Cody. "They're intelligent."

Buster said: *This dance you saw Tumble and the others do . . . several creatures exhibit ritualized behavior.*

"But what about the numerical intricacies of the dance?" asked Cody. "What about the way Tumble gave Deirdre that flower at the end of it?" Cody looked away, wiped the sweat from his brow, then turned back to Buster. "Let's add it up. First we have the headwands. In a world that's ultimately dark most of the time, doesn't it make sense that these creatures should communicate to each other with light signals?"

Buster said: *We can't be certain the blinking represents a language.*

"You were down at the brook with me last night," said Cody. "You saw Ears and Hunchback talking to each other. Ears blinked at Hunchback and pointed up into the branches of that tree. Hunchback looked up into the tree, then blinked something back at Ears. Then they both pointed at the tree. They finally flew toward the tree and disappeared into the branches. They were communicating to each other. Not just warning calls. Not just a food alert. Not even anything like the more complicated signals dolphins and chimpanzees send to each other. They were communicating in an abstract way. Think of it. They both have nine headwands. They blink them in combination, in sequence, dimly or brightly, at different speeds, extend the actual wands in different directions, curve them, bend them, cross them . . . you have the endless permutations needed for a complicated, varied language, one that might have more shades of meaning than English."

Buster said: *Just because it might look that way doesn't mean it is that way. And I've had them tested on sensitive instruments for intelligence. Nothing.*

"No," said Cody flatly. "Not nothing. You found a lot you didn't understand."

Not anything that indicates intelligence.

But Cody was relentless.

"What about the way they bury their dead? Just the other day we saw another burial. They didn't have any white mud so they chewed up milkberries and mixed it with the mud they had. The mud turned white, and they spread it over the burial mound. Two scribes made markings on the mound. If you look closely at the markings, you'll see a patterned relationship between them, a stylistic symmetry in the script."

Buster said: *I'm not convinced intelligence informs those markings.*

Cody sighed in exasperation.

"Okay," he said. "What about the way they treat the milk-berry?"

Buster lifted his head and gazed at Cody with wide violet eyes. It was as if for some reason the question had special significance to Buster.

What about it? he asked.

"Why do they treat the milkberry with such reverence? Why do they choose berries so carefully? Yesterday, Bigfoot took nearly two hours to find the ones she wanted. There were hundreds all over the place. Why did she finally choose the ones she chose? And they never take more than three at a time. Always two or three, never anything different. Don't you think that indicates numerical awareness? Just like the numerical awareness in their dancing?"

Buster grew pensive. He looked around at the occupants of the carryall, all of whom were asleep except for Agatha, who suffered through a bout of morning sickness.

Buster asked: *What do you want me to do?* Cody felt the emanations of Buster's moral anxiety. *Scar approached me when we were camped out on the Bay of Redemption. He came to me with three milkberries. He gave them to me. But first he offered me a choice. He held up two fingers. And then he held up three. It took me a few moments to figure it out. I held up two of my own fingers. He gave me two of the berries. We communicated.* Buster looked away, the torn expression on his face showing he did indeed grant the Filaments at least some intelligence. *So this is what I'm faced with. A decision that will have disastrous consequences either way. A decision that makes me act the way my enemies have acted, a situation that makes me order a bioextermination I have no wish to order. Even if they weren't intelligent, even if they were just wild creatures, I'd still be faced with the same dilemma, because I don't want to kill anything. It goes against what I've struggled diligently to become. But I have to. I have no choice.*

Cody shook his head. The irony struck home again. Just

as Vesta City had planned to exterminate the Meek, so now the Meek planned to exterminate the Filaments. The Meek were survivors. He knew they would have to go ahead and do it if they had to.

Buster said: *Do I destroy an intelligent race for the sake of saving my own? Or do I sacrifice my own race for the sake of saving the Filaments? My Meek code tells me to sacrifice myself, but my ghost code won't stand for it. I've been in contact with the other clans. So far 6,342 pesticides and poisons have been tried. None of them have worked. Many other strategies have been tested as well. The Ophir Chasm Clan built an indoor marrow farm, a protective structure of rocks, and hardened it with heat. They planted marrow inside. The structure was a meter thick, as tough as steel, with one small door. The Filaments came with tools, primitive hand axes made from a nickel-copper alloy, and hacked the structure to pieces, thousands of them, all cooperating systematically. They reduced the structure to rubble in a matter of hours and ate all the marrow.* Buster shook his head. *So you see, our options are clearly running out.*

Cody watched Kevin Axworthy and Boris carry Artemis Axworthy down to the lake—one of the many unnamed lakes in this vast continent—in a special chair, one with poles attached for easy lifting. The lake nestled in the bottom of a valley, as still as a mirror. The sides of the valley were golden with tall grass—grass that wasn't really grass but more a long-stemmed lichen, something that found its nourishment in the planet's internal heat and mulchy soil.

Axworthy and Boris eased the Father into the lake. Artemis Axworthy continued to sit in his chair. The water came up to the Father's waist. The Father weakly splashed his arms and chest. Axworthy looked on, the attentive son.

Claire approached Cody from behind, stood beside him, gazed at the tranquil wilderness lake. She watched Axworthy with a great deal of fondness. A hot breeze ruffled her short dark hair.

"How are they getting on?" Cody asked.

Claire paused before she answered. "He really loves his father," she said. "Artemis isn't well." She turned to Cody. "There's not much Jerry can do for him. He's 91."

The two of them watched. Axworthy, his father, and Boris seemed so small against the backdrop of the lake.

"And you and Kevin?" asked Cody.

She nodded. "Me and Kevin," she agreed.

"Is he coming to . . . to terms . . ." He motioned at the children playing in the water further down. "Has he come to accept all this?"

She thought about it. "Kevin knows how to compartmentalize," she said, offering Cody a compromise. "He knows that this is right, and he doesn't let all the other stuff get in the way. It's why I . . . he and I . . . he's a good man in a lot of ways. You just have to learn how to recognize it."

Cody nodded. "I know," he said. He watched Kevin Axworthy sponge his father with a wet towel; the old man was too weak to do it himself. "He's a good man."

Some of the Meek didn't survive the heat on the return trip north. Chief among the casualties were the old and the young; 9,000 deaths altogether, 100 in Olympia Mons, one of which was Artemis Axworthy.

They buried the Father a few evenings later, after the sun had set. News of his death was communicated through conventional nontelepathic means to the other clans; without a global distribution of marrow, long-distance empathic communication was impossible. Several emissaries arrived from the other clans to attend the funeral. The overcast sky was green with distant storms, and heat lightning flashed constantly on the horizon. Cody and Jerry helped two Meek dig a hole two meters deep in the hard-baked dirt. As Cody and Jerry laid the old man in his grave Cody sensed the thoughts of not any one Meek in particular but a joint communal eulogy, everybody in Olympia Mons saying good-bye to the great man, an outpouring of devotion, respect, and grief that fed upon itself until the whole hot plain seemed to vibrate with it.

When it was over, the crowd dispersed to make ready for the evening leg of the migration north. Cody took one last look at the grave.

Tumble, Scar, Hunchback, Ears, and Bigfoot—the five Filaments who were following the clan north—piled dirt on top of the Father's grave. Cody saw that Kevin Axworthy's eyes were narrowed under his impressive brow. The Filaments broke open some milkberries and whitened the mud. Tumble and Scar acted as scribes, drawing designs all over the burial mound with tiny sharp stones. Axworthy, always in control of his emotions, suddenly lost his rein. His eyes filled with tears.

"I'm really going to miss him," he said, wiping his tears on the sleeve of his antigrav suit. "But I guess I'm used to missing him."

Olympia Mons discovered five more green glass constructs on the way north. The five were all in sight of each other, rising out of the rolling hills, tubelike structures up to a kilometer tall. Cody gazed at them from 500 meters up in the carryall. Lonely and desolate, all of them catching the wind, making it moan. Many of these towers were so dirty Cody couldn't see through the glass to the arterial networks inside.

The sight renewed the question everyone had been asking right from the start: Who had built these constructs?

"It certainly wasn't the Filaments," Cody said to Lulu. "They're hardly beyond the hunter-gatherer stage."

The Builders, everyone agreed, had to be far more advanced than that. But where had they gone? Where had they come from? Had they originated on Carswell? Or had they come from somewhere else?

The clan settled near one of the constructs for the evening, and Cody, Lulu, and Agatha, in an attempt to find a cooling breeze, and to get a better look at the nearest construct, walked to the top of a hill. Agatha stared straight ahead, not watching where she was going, still grieving for Ben. Cody and Lulu walked a little apart from her, letting her be by herself for a change.

The accident happened a few minutes after they had reached the top of the hill.

One second Agatha was walking along normally, the next second the ground swallowed her up, collapsing beneath her feet like thin ice.

Cody and Lulu rushed over. A patch of grass, dirt, and clay had caved in. A sinkhole, by the look of it, thought Cody. He knelt on the edge of the hole and peered into the darkness. Lulu knelt beside him and sent emanations but got nothing in return.

Lulu said: *She's unconscious. She's hurt. Do you have your guidelight?*

Cody unlatched his guidelight from his belt and shone it down the hole. He felt further nonverbalized emanations from Lulu, concern for the baby, questions about whether the baby had been injured in the fall. Finally his flashlight beam found Agatha.

She lay on a flat surface below, a surface far too flat to be anything but a floor, a small pool of blood by her head. A dank, sweet aroma wafted up from the hidden chamber.

Cody ran to get a rope ladder while Lulu stayed at the hole, trying to wake Agatha. He came back with Buster, Jerry, Rex, and a half-dozen others. They came with a litter. Jerry had his med-kit. Cody threw the rope ladder down the hole and descended. Buster and Rex climbed down after him. Jerry had to struggle with the ladder but he finally made it down too.

They stood in a large vaulted chamber with stone benches built into the walls. At first glance this was all they could see. They didn't investigate further because they had much more pressing business with Agatha.

"Agatha?" Jerry called. "Agatha, can you hear me?"

No response. He took a neck brace from his kit and secured her neck. Then with Cody's help he carefully rolled her onto the litter, and they could see how bad her injury was. The left side of her forehead had an extensive laceration at the hairline.

"It's serious," said the doctor. "Maybe a fractured skull. We'd better get her back to camp."

They strapped Agatha onto the litter and hoisted her out of the chamber with a rope. Back in camp, Jerry and two other clan physicians took over Agatha's care. Cody and some other members of the clan went back to investigate the underground chamber.

They found engraved into the wall what looked like a design plan for one of the green glass constructs. With this evidence they concluded the underground chamber, too, was something the Builders had left behind, and quickly dubbed the site Builders' Mound.

They scrubbed an opposite wall. Under the dirt they found what Cody at first thought was an abstract mosaic made of ceramic tile: hues in the primary colors of red, blue, and yellow; geometric arrangements of squares, oblongs, and rectangles—parallelograms. The primary colors used in the wall mosaic were bright, fluorescent.

Cody theorized, "If the Builders used bright colors like these, in a world where the lack of light would always cause the colors to look gray . . ." And he explained how colors like these would need the reflection of light to gain their proper brilliance. ". . . then we can only assume that the Builders didn't come from Carswell, that they brought their culture of color and light from a place that had sunshine. We can't expect the use of color to arise on a place with no light. Knowing colors like red, blue, and yellow means the Builders *had* to come from somewhere else. A planet with a star. Not a rogue like Carswell."

But it was more than that. The red, blue, and yellow parallelograms, their various sizes, and their sequence led Cody to think that, yes, this might be an abstract mosaic of artistic design, but it also might be a written language. Was this alien cubist mosaic really so different from the alphabet? Visual patterns of any sort could always represent meaning. He wondered if the mosaic described the accompanying design of the green-glass construct.

Out of the three primary colors had great works, like the green-glass constructs, arisen?

Cody and Lulu watched Agatha sit on the edge of her cot staring at nothing, looking as if she didn't know where she was. Cody could sense Lulu thinking about the future of Agatha's unborn child.

"The temperatures are a lot cooler now," said Cody. "That's given Buster the opportunity to really ration the marrow. He tells me about half the human line have stopped eating it altogether, that they're trying to wean themselves off it. So Agatha's not alone."

Lulu stared at her sister apprehensively. "I wish she wouldn't be so stubborn about it," she said. She had been practicing speech, and at least she didn't sound like a deaf-mute now. Her words were rough and mispronounced—she hadn't spoken since she had been a girl—but she still spoke. "Buster said she can have as much marrow as she wants. Her whole system is depleted. She's never going to code for repair if she doesn't start eating it again. But what can we do? She refuses. She's rejecting the Meek. She doesn't want to be one anymore. She blames them for everything."

"We can't do anything," said Cody.

"How's she going to get better? Look at her. We're talking about her, and she doesn't even realize we're in the tent with her. Yet when you offer her marrow she fights you, opts to eat the traditional staples instead. Have you listened to her thoughts recently? They're all jumbled. They're not making any sense."

"I have."

They sat together in silence for a while. Out the canopy flap Cody saw the northern part of the Ocean of Forgiveness, deep blue, flecked with whitecaps, some Filaments hovering in the breeze. It was getting dark out already. The sun was far to the south. The clan had traveled the final leg of the journey north. They were on one of the islands of A Hundred Second Chances.

Jerry came into their carryall.

"How is she?" he asked.

"She's just sitting here," said Lulu. "She hasn't said a word all morning. She doesn't even realize she's having the baby."

Jerry took out a small flashlight and shone it into Agatha's eyes. "Agatha?" he said. Agatha didn't respond. "Agatha, can you hear me?" He shook his head, checked her heart and lungs with his stethoscope, then pressed the cold disk against her pregnant abdomen. "Everything checks out down here," he said. "And I've examined the ultrasound again. The baby's fine. As for Agatha, she's out of danger. I'm going to downgrade her condition from critical to stable. But I don't think she's ever going to fully recover. Even if we started her on the marrow. I'm not sure she's going to be able to be a mother to her own child."

When Jerry left, Cody and Lulu looked at each other. They communicated in the silent language of the Meek again.

Lulu said: *I'll look after her child when it's born.*

Cody said: *I'll help you.*

He had finally made up his mind. He was going to stay with Lulu. Going to stay on Carswell, leave the solar system behind forever. Not go in the rigged lander with the others back to Vesta. What else could he do? He had to be a father to Ben's child.

Cody and Jerry sat by Buster's bedside. Buster was suffering from congestive heart failure, what Jerry called forward failure, with the blood backing up into the pulmonary veins and capillaries of his stomach. Marrow was so scarce now and rationed so strictly that many orphan-line Meek had hypoxia and hypoxemia. Their stomachs mimicked symptoms of pulmonary embolism and chronic lung disease. Such was the case with Buster. The Meek leader was constantly fatigued, and his heart rushed in a ventricular gallop. His level of consciousness fluctuated, and even though he was offered more than his fair share of marrow, he refused it, accepting only the same ration everybody else got.

"Why is his heart failing when so many others aren't having that problem?" Cody asked Jerry.

Jerry raised his eyebrows. "He's old, Cody. Remember? Original Man. This kind of thing is bound to hit him harder than the young ones."

Buster, like an old man in the clutches of senility, grew excited when Cody brought up the subject of the Filaments.

Buster said: *How are we going to stop them from razing our crops, Cody? They're thieves.* His waves were weak from lack of marrow. Cody reminded Buster that the orphans were also thieves, but this seemed to make no impression. *Not only will they take our marrow, they'll take our grain, our orchard fruit, our cattle and sheep, our garden vegetables, everything we grow and raise. I've got to deploy the virus. I can't wait any longer. Unless we come up with a solution in the next twelve hours, I'm going to have to go ahead with it. We've got to stop these hoodlums.*

Cody asked, "Could we not just wait a little longer?"

Buster shook his head. *The migration's over, Cody. Ceres has been sent to the middle of the galaxy. The clans are choosing their settlement sites. It's time to start the business of farming.*

He knew Buster was right. Time was running out. The Meek had to plant their marrow and plant it fast. Cody told Jerry what Buster had just said. Jerry shrugged, not knowing how to respond.

Cody said, "Just a few more days, Buster."

Buster said: *I'm afraid I can't, Cody. The equation is simple. Either we plant now or we die. We're out past Mars. I'm sorry but I'm going to have to go ahead. Tomorrow morning I release the virus.*

Cody sat alone on a hill for several hours after that struggling to come up with a solution. The weather was remarkably calm and the clouds thin, so thin that he could actually see the setting sun, which appeared as a small murky white ball through the mist, reminding him a bit of the sun as seen from Mars. In the distance he saw some of the Meek burying casualties of the marrow famine, tiny black figures in the vast rolling landscape, performers of an age-old task. As the sun kissed the tops of the farthest hills he saw two dozen Filaments flock down from the wartwood forest and fly to the burial site.

That got him thinking.

Fly.

The Filaments landed at the fresh burial site, looked for milkberries, made the mounds white with the juice, and had burial scribes etch scrawls.

Then they flew away.

Flew.

That's when Cody finally came up with a solution.

CHAPTER 26

Buster licked his fingers and touched them to Cody's lips to strengthen his ever-weakening emanations.

Buster said: *What makes you think they're going to help us now? How are you going to negotiate with them when they think you're a turncoat?*

Cody was distressed by how sick the Meek man looked. Buster wheezed badly now. His lungs, having never taken breath, spasmed as his blood fought to get as much oxygen as it could.

"I'm not going to be the one to negotiate," he said. "Kevin Axworthy is."

Buster frowned. *He still views us with suspicion. He still thinks we took his father away from him.*

Cody shook his head. "I've convinced him that my solution will work. I know the infrastructure and support system on Vesta, and I've had Claire go over the orbital trajectories of Carswell, Vesta, and the seven proposed farms. Council would have a standard solar week to move the old ice and equipment transports into orbit around Carswell. I've had Annabel go over current marrow inventory. If everyone in the human line stops eating it, and we treat the withdrawal casualties as they come, we can extend the supply for another nine days. We'll have a two-day margin. It'll be close but I think we can make it."

Buster shook his head weakly. He said: *But Kevin Ax-*

worthy is a VDF commander. We killed many such men thirty years ago. How can you expect him to help us?

"It's because he's a VDF commander that I want him to speak for you," said Cody. "His word will carry weight with Council. No matter what old grudges he might have, he's a reasonable man at heart, he understands the situation clearly, and he wants to do what he can to save the Meek and the Filaments. Give us this one last chance, Buster. Spare the Filaments from extinction."

An hour later, Kevin Axworthy donned a biofeedback garment—a truth gown, as the Meek called it—such as Cody had worn for his broadcast to Earth, and prepared to talk to Council. Technicians of the clan established a com-link to Vesta City.

Axworthy began by telling Council about the loss of Benjamin LeBlanc and expressed his sincere regret to the family. He said nothing of Ben's child; he didn't want to complicate matters. Cody, sitting off to the side, gave Axworthy an encouraging nod.

"The rest of us are fine," said Axworthy. "The Meek have designed a return vehicle for us. Launch is five days away and we're expected to make rendezvous with Bettina in three weeks. Meanwhile the Meek suffer. Meanwhile the Meek die."

He then went on to talk about Carswell.

"It is perhaps a mark of the Meek's technological prowess that they discovered Highfield-Little a full 25 years before we did. They instantly recognized it as an opportunity. They knew that we would someday come back to Ceres. Once they found Highfield-Little, they began making sincere efforts to vacate Ceres so they could give it back to us. The first thing they did was change Highfield-Little's orbit so it wouldn't fall into the sun. Using the grav-core, they successfully moved the planet into a higher orbit."

Kevin then explained the unforeseen consequences of modifying the grav-core, how it acquired matter from who-knew-where, how its event horizon had slowly gotten bigger

and bigger, and how the Meek had finally had to jettison
Ceres to the center of the galaxy for the safety of everybody
in the solar system.

"Can we forgive them for that? I think we can. In alter-
ing Highfield-Little's collision course with the sun they
saved a race of intelligent beings, the Filaments."

At this point clan technicians transmitted some visuals
while Kevin continued with a voice-over. The visuals
showed the Filaments: Scar carefully picking some milkberries; a group of Filaments performing one of their nighttime dances; two of them having a conversation with their
headwands; a burial, with scribes turning the mud white and
etching dark scrawls on the grave; finally, a flock of 500 descending on a colony of marrow, devouring it in seconds,
then flying off, leaving the ground bare behind them. Kevin
recounted their problems with the Filaments.

"The pesticide approach seemed the most reasonable, at
least in the beginning," he said. "But unfortunately it didn't
work. Their unusual metabolism makes them immune to
every poison we've tried. We've tried light. Sound. Indoor
gardening. Even beating them off with sticks. Nothing
works. Now the Meek are faced with the deployment of a
virus that would wipe out in a single stroke every Filament
on the face of the planet. And they don't want to do that. It
goes against everything they've strived to become." He
turned to Cody, then turned back to the com-link. "We are in-
debted to Cody Wisner for coming up with a better solution."

He explained how the Filaments, though intelligent, lived
in a primitive, nomadic, hunter-gatherer society, with no
means of leaving their planet, and, because of the nearly
perpetual cloud cover, probably no concept of outer space.

"Why not use the space transports as vast floating
farms?" asked Kevin Axworthy. "If we grow the marrow in
space the Filaments will have no way of getting at it. I know
you won't have much sympathy for the Meek, but you were
going to give those space transports to them anyway for the
purposes of shipping them to Charon. Why don't you now

offer them as farms? The Meek can't use their own transports because they were designed as one-time entry vehicles. We've already sent you the refit specifications. Some
trays and some dirt—any damn dirt will do. You've got the
marrow I sent back with the *Conrad Wilson*. The stuff grows
like wildfire. You can get the crop started. By the time it
reaches us in seven days there should be enough to stop all
this suffering. The Meek can then ferry the crop down to the
surface in their landers. As long as it's properly crated the
Filaments won't be able to get at it."

Here clan technicians showed Bigfoot, Ears, and Tumble
trying to break open a special polymer-based crate, a recent
innovation designed to deal with the current storage emergency. The Filaments banged away with their crude metal
hand axes; the three couldn't even make so much as a dent in
the crate. The visuals shifted to a storage shed made out of the
same material. Axworthy explained how eventually huge indoor farms would be built from the same polymer.

"So you see, indoor farms will work, now that the Meek
have devised a Filament-resistant material. But it's going to
take time," he said. "The Meek are going to need those
seven transports to supply them with marrow for at least the
next three years." Kevin leaned forward and his eyes narrowed. "I know there are many hard-liners in Council," he
said. "I know some of you are going to argue against the ex-
pense of sending these seven transports."

Axworthy took a sip of water and cleared his throat.

"Let me put it this way," he said. "Through lax and possibly dangerous legislation on Mars several decades ago, the
Meek, in their first iteration as orphans, came into being. We
made them. We are their parents. We should shoulder our responsibility for them as their parents. We shouldn't abandon
them. They're different from us but they're still of the human
family. I won't say they're blameless. They're not. Most of
you in Council fought in the Civil Action on Ceres thirty years
ago, and there were atrocities committed there that will live in
your memories forever. But now the Meek find themselves

with a chance for redemption. If you offer the seven space transports as farms you'll not only be saving the Filaments, you'll be aiding the first group of human star travelers. You'll be the first to receive the observations and discoveries that such a momentous voyage is bound to produce. You'll be the first to know what is truly out there. And that, my friends, is something you simply can't put a price on."

Kevin leaned back in his chair. Cody was impressed by his performance; Kevin was giving them a moment to think about all this. Then his eyes narrowed further, with the shrewdness of a veteran poker player.

"I know that this won't be enough for some of you," he said. "Those transports are expensive. You've already lost Ceres. Why throw good money after bad? I'll tell you why. Right from the start we were all astonished by the Meek's technological ability. They subverted our surveillance satellites. They subverted all the sensory equipment aboard the *Conrad Wilson*. They hid a population of 600,000-plus for twenty-five years. They survived the first bioextermination. Now we learn they can move planets around and turn asteroids into spaceships. The list goes on and on. The Meek are willing to share their technology in return for those seven space transports. It won't be good money after bad. It will be the investment opportunity of a lifetime."

Axworthy glanced at some notes on his E-pad.

"I've been authorized by the highest-ranking members of Olympia Mons and the other clans to grant Vesta and the Belt complete control over any of the technology the Meek send you, a technology you'll be able to sell to Earth and Mars and the colonized moons. This technology translates into economic power, into the ability for Vesta and the other asteroids to revitalize themselves, and into the resources needed to come up with an effective solution to the juvenile-gravity problem. In aiding the Meek, you'll be aiding yourselves. And because the Meek will be traveling to the stars you'll not only be aiding yourselves but all humankind. I don't think you're going to get a better deal anywhere."

*   *   *

Buster died two hours later. The clan buried him, as they had buried the Father, out in the soil of the new world, and the Filaments came to whiten and inscribe his grave. Lulu cried. The clan had lost their leader. The Meek had lost their visionary.

Rex assumed leadership of Olympia Mons and, provisionally, of all the Meek. The first thing he did was make Cody a ranking clan member.

Rex said: *I want you as an adviser. You are the one who saved us from a second bioextermination. You are the one who brokered this life-or-death deal with the Vestans for the seven space transports. You're the man who convinced us that the Filaments are indeed intelligent. You're a man who cares, not only about the Meek, but about everyone.*

Three hours later word came of the Council vote. Cody conveyed the news to other humans. "They're going to send the space transports," he said, "pending the first transmission of technological data from the Meek. Rex assures me this will be immediately forthcoming. The deal is as good as done."

The next day Cody received a holo-transmission from his parents on Mars.

"We saw your broadcast to Earth," his father said, "and heard how you defended Ceres against the *Conrad Wilson*." His father didn't look too pleased about this. "Now we understand that Highfield-Little is outward-bound toward Pluto and points beyond." His father paused, his bushy eyebrows rising interrogatively. "You're not going to go with these people, are you, Cody?" he asked.

Much to his surprise, Cody could see that his father was alarmed at the thought of losing his son forever. Cody was also surprised to see how much older his father looked, with most of his hair gone, the flesh under his neck sagging, his eyes unsure and red-rimmed.

Cody smiled but his eyes were misty. "I'll be coming home in the return vehicle," he lied.

He couldn't bring himself to tell his father the truth. He

didn't know whether he was being kinder or crueler. He just felt that after so many good-byes in the last while he couldn't bring himself to deal with yet another.

His mother stood beside his father. She looked a lot thinner, more worn than he remembered her. He could tell by the look in her eyes that she knew he was never coming back. She gave him a slight nod, then turned away and walked out of the holo-image.

He signed off quickly and went outside, where he found Deirdre waiting for him.

"How'd it go?" she asked.

He looked away. Evening had come and the sky was filled with the twinkling of Filaments. "How many ways can you say good-bye without actually saying it?" he asked.

Maybe it was something in his voice, or the way he couldn't look at her, but she put her hand on his arm. He no longer wore his antigravitational suit; he wanted to get used to the gravity as quickly as he could, build up his muscles and coordination. He looked at her. Her eyes were serene but sad.

"Can you say good-bye to me?" she asked.

He took a deep breath and his lips tightened. He straightened up, squared his shoulders, gazed at the forest of wartwood covering the hills two kilometers to the north.

"Explain it to my parents, will you?" he said. "I didn't have the heart to tell them."

Three days later, Axworthy, Deirdre, Jerry, and Claire immersed themselves in pools of dim purple jelly, strapped oxygen masks to their faces, had technicians drug them intravenously with sedatives and muscle relaxants, and prepared to launch themselves back to the solar system's orbital plane on top of a multimegaton hydrogen bomb. The jelly and the drugs would help ease the terrific gee-force of liftoff.

Cody visited Deirdre in the command module one last time.

"They're going to need someone at Public Works to replace me," he said. "You should apply. A lot of the pressure walls in Vesta City have to be rebuilt. They're getting old. You know more about structural tolerances than anyone I know."

She reclined naked in her human-size acrylic birdbath full of gee-buffering jelly. Only her face floated above the surface.

"Do we have to talk about work?"

He stared at her. Truth be told, he really had no words for this. He was never going to see her again and he was going to have to learn to live with that. He leaned over and kissed her on the forehead. She smiled. A gentle smile.

"It's okay," she said. "You can go now."

She put her oxygen mask on, closed her eyes, and forced her head back into the jelly. The lid came down, the sedatives took hold, and she floated out of Cody's life for good.

Cody and Rex stood at the foot of Builders' Mound as sixteen carryalls arrived with the first load of space-grown marrow from the Sea of Humility landing site.

Rex said: *The farms are in full operation. I have lander pilots working around the clock to ferry the crop to the surface. We've got it all packed in the new polymer. That's why you don't see too many Filaments around right now, just those ones up on the Mound. They can't smell it through the polymer.*

At the foot of the Mound large tents had been erected as temporary shelters. Meek of the orphan line, feeble and skinny, many breathing with their lungs for the first time, lined up to get fresh rations of marrow. Cody tried to sense their thoughts but his talent was growing weaker; he hadn't eaten any marrow for a while, and Lulu, like others of the human line, had decided to go without as well, hadn't kissed him with marrow, hadn't primed his talent with her lips. Their kisses were just kisses now. He saw Lulu now across the square walking with Agatha in the perpetual twilight of a world that was speeding away from the sun. He turned his attention back to the Meek lining up for marrow. If he sensed anything from these Meek, it was patience. They weren't going to fight over the food the way they might have

fought over the best ice deposits in Valles Marineris fifty
years ago. The Meek had come of age.

He watched Meek children eat the new marrow. Immediately they grew less fidgety, less whiny; some even began to
play. Human-line Meek in the square watched. After wean-
ing themselves off the marrow the human-line Meek were
gaining the flesh tones of normal human skin. Their eyes
were shrinking to normal human size and turning green,
brown, or blue. Their limbs were returning to normal human
length according to the varying degrees of either Lenny Carswell's rewrite or of Artemis Axworthy's rewrite. Human-
line children ran around the square laughing, playing,
shouting, screaming. Children of the orphan line conveyed
their mirth telepathically, silently, and Cody was happy to
hear noisy children again.

He turned to Rex. "You realize that what you have here
now is really two peoples," he said.

Rex gazed around the square with his large violet eyes.
He said: *We have lived as 26 clans. Surely we can live as two
peoples.*

Lulu came up to them and stood beside Rex. Cody could
see that the difference between the two was now marked.
Lulu was indeed reverting. Her hair had darkened to the
color of coffee, her face was getting broader, her eyes
changing into human eyes, and her ears losing some of their
fairylike pointiness.

But . . .

But, like the Father, she retained a faint blue tint to her
skin. He smiled at her. Always lovely, she was lovelier still
with green eyes, full lips, and a more womanish, less girlish
cast to her face.

As they left the square and walked toward their tent, Lulu
said, "Should I go back to calling myself Catherine?" She
pulled a blanket around her shoulders; her tolerance to heat
and cold had diminished. "That's my human name."

"Catherine?" said Agatha, out of the blue, startling both

of them. They looked at her, then cautiously resumed their conversation.

"It's up to you," said Cody. "I like Catherine. I also like Lulu."

Down in the valley he saw Filaments squabbling over some apparently edible lichen, their headwands flashing contentiously.

"I met you when I was Lulu," she said. She took his hand. "I think of myself as Lulu now. I've lived most of my life as Lulu." Agatha began to wander away and Lulu pulled her back. "I feel like Lulu. I *am* Lulu."

They walked on in silence. Her menthol wind was faint now, just a presence, a sensation, something that warmed him from time to time. Lulu. That's the name he would use. This was the new language he spoke. He had once spoken the language of Christine. But not anymore. From now on, Lulu would be the language he spoke.

Six months later Cody and Lulu sat by Agatha's bedside in the new village infirmary. Agatha had given birth to her child the day before. She lay on her side, staring at nothing, a sheet pulled over her hip, the baby—a boy named Benjamin— suckling at her breast. She didn't seem to realize the baby was there. She had her arms tucked under her head, didn't hold the baby, didn't even acknowledge it. Benjamin didn't seem to care. He suckled fiercely without his mother's help.

Cody looked at Lulu's abdomen. Lulu was four months pregnant and starting to show. Down the corridor he heard the sound of hammers and saws. He wore a hard hat, work boots, and a tool belt. He had to get back to work soon. They were building the west wing of the infirmary now, and he was chief architect. Chief carpenter. Chief sawyer. Chief builder. The infirmary was made of sturdy wartwood planks. Wartwood cured straight. Far straighter than wood. It didn't split—there wasn't any grain. In fact, its unique cellulose *gripped* the nail once the nail was driven home. It was the consummate building material. And it grew fast. He gave Lulu a kiss.

"I should get back," he said. "Did the doctor say he was going to discharge Agatha today?"

"Yes," said Lulu. "Physically, she's fine."

Just then, Agatha seemed to realize she had a baby at her breast. She looked at Benjamin, gripped him with both hands, and pushed him away. He fell off the edge of the bed. Lulu jerked forward and caught him before he hit the floor. Agatha flung the sheet aside, and, with a complete disregard for modesty, got up, leaving the bloodied pad exposed on her bed, walked past them, kept going even when Cody tried to stop her, shook Cody's hand away, and left the maternity ward.

"Let her go," said Lulu. "She wants her chair." Cody had built a chair for Agatha, and she had grown extremely attached to it. "It's the only place where she feels safe."

So they let her go. Cody went out to the nursing station and spoke to the nurse.

"Could you have someone follow her?" he asked. "Just to make sure she gets home okay?"

The nurse nodded, speaking to Cody in the difficult way the orphan-line Meek spoke to the human line now. "She is our sister," said the nurse, the words badly formed, ugly. "We will look after her."

Cody returned to the small maternity ward to find Lulu rocking Benjamin in her arms, smiling sweetly at the baby. Benjamin had some infant acne and cradle cap but he was still the most beautiful baby Cody had ever seen.

"I guess he's going to have to depend on us now," he said.

Lulu's smile dimmed but didn't disappear. "I just hope he understands when he's older," she said.

CHAPTER 27

When Catherine was eight and Benjamin was nine, and Builders' Mound had grown from village, to town, to city, and everyone realized that Carswell wasn't going to get much colder than 5 degrees Celsius, Cody heard a strange sound outside his window. Like the sound of a thousand sheets flapping on a clothesline. And suddenly, miraculously, alarmingly, there was light in the sky.

He and Lulu hurried to the window. Thick beams of white light arched right up into the clouds, coming from the five constructs near Builders' Mound, connecting them with bows of brilliant luminosity. The beams lit the surrounding countryside uniformly, brightening the dark recesses of the various valleys and ravines, bringing color to what had been a world of twilight grays. The river in the valley showed up a spectacular blue-green, the nonphotosynthetic grasses on the distant hills shone a flaxen gold, and even the constructs themselves glittered like fresh-cut emeralds. Cody felt revitalized by the light. He was surprised by it, bewildered by it, had a dozen questions about it, but also derived some answers from it; about who the Builders were, how they were physiologically equipped, and why they had decided to light this world. This, it seemed to him, as he stood there with Lulu's hand in his, proved that there must be at least one commonality between humans and the Builders: They liked and needed light; their optical structures, as evidenced by the primary-color mosaics, were equipped to interpret light; and they had worked hard to supply this dark planet with light.

"That settles it," Cody said to Lulu. The children came to stand next to their parents, peering up at the bright sky in wonder. "The Builders didn't originate on Carswell." Agatha sat in her chair, oblivious to everything. "They came from somewhere else. A place with a sun. Why else would they build an apparatus like this? They built a civilization here. They left these lights . . . but then they . . . disappeared."

That's what Cody found so unsettling about the whole thing. That the Builders were gone. Were they extinct? Had they died out? And if they had, was the cause of their extinction to be found here on Carswell? As a family man he didn't like to think about it. He wanted Carswell to go on forever. He wanted his children to have children. The Builders were the ghosts of this place, a reminder, at least to Cody's mind, that extinction could happen to anybody.

He put on his jacket and walked over to the Civic Center. Meek had come out onto the street from their homes—no more tree-dwelling for the Meek, they lived in sturdy wood-frame homes built from wartwood, homes that could take some weather. They were looking up at the beams of light in hushed awe. Far off in the distance above the western hills rain slanted down from the clouds, catching the light, breaking it into the colors of the spectrum, creating a rainbow. Cody stopped short and stared. He had never seen a rainbow before. They had never made any rainbows on Vesta. Color. One of the things that made life worth living, he thought. And now the Builders had given it back to them.

At the Civic Center he talked to Rex, who had become one of his closest friends over the past nine years and who spoke fairly fluently now.

"We don't know where the power is coming from," he said. "We've been monitoring the constructs ever since they began producing this light an hour ago. You can see it here on this screen. Nothing suggests anything remotely related to the kind of energy we might use to power the constructs, no electromagnetic waves, no radioactive decay, fission, or fusion, nothing that suggests a conversion of heat into light, no subsurface sources of energy detected. We've scanned the light and there's nothing harmful in it, no gamma radiation, a bit of minor ultraviolet, but that's it, nothing the orphan-line Meek can't survive, nothing the human line can't deal with."

"Have you received communications from any of the other settlements?" asked Cody.

"We've received communications from all over. The light extends all the way to A Hundred Second Chances, down to the Bay of Redemption, and to both the east and west coasts of the Ocean of Forgiveness."

"Has it affected Filament activity at all?"

"There have been reports of increased aerial dancing," said Rex. "That's it."

"And have all constructs continent-wide been activated?"

"Yes."

Rex and Cody decided to have a closer look at the nearest construct, locally known as the Tower of the Helping Hand. They didn't use a carryall to get there, even though the distance was well over five kilometers; they walked because they wanted to see the colors in the fields, the small mushrooms—purple, turquoise, and yellow—growing up through the brown fungus grass, a profusion of color such as neither of them had seen since Carswell had left the brighter regions of the solar system years ago.

They passed a few indoor marrow farms, oval-shaped, rounded, made of the tough Filament-resistant polymer. The construct itself glowed like L. Frank Baum's legendary Emerald City. The technology behind the construct was daunting, God-like in its gargantuan proportions, and awe-inspiring in its capabilities.

"It makes me feel small," said Rex. "We think we have a sophisticated technology, but we're cavemen compared to the Builders. Look at the structural lines of these towers. They're architecturally impossible. They should fall over, but they don't. They go right up through the clouds. They're like out of a dream."

"Something's going on inside," said Cody.

The venous arterial network inside was indeed buzzing with activity, the delicate nerve endings twitching, the larger, aorta-like structures glowing with a faint pink luminescence. White light whirlpooled within the tubes, spinning upward, looking gelatinous and viscous, as if it were a solid, not an intangible.

"I wish there were some way we could get inside," said Cody.

But the green outer structures had proved impervious to everything, couldn't even be scratched. Cody and Rex climbed onto the base of the nearest tower. They felt a faint hum. For some reason Cody started smiling. So did Rex. Cody realized that the tower was making him feel happy in some way.

"Do you feel that?" he asked.

Rex frowned, but smiled in spite of his frown. "I feel it," he said. "I don't know what it is." He rubbed his hand against the tower. "But we're going to have to do some more testing, that's for sure, to find out what's causing it."

Which they did. They tested volunteers from all walks of life—old, young, teachers, doctors, farmers—and all professed to an overwhelming sense of well-being whenever the lights were on and they were near the constructs. Human line, orphan line, it didn't matter. The construct made people feel better, gave them a place to go for a cure-all.

The lights stayed on for thirteen hours. Then they went off. They stayed off thirteen hours, then came back on. For another thirteen hours. On and off in endless thirteen-hour cycles. No one knew why the lights started working when they did. But now that Carswell was way out past Pluto, well on its way to the Oort Cloud, the light was more than welcome.

*   *   *

Over the next several weeks, testing continued.

"We've detected no detrimental effects," Rex reported to Cody. "People picnic out there when the lights come on and they always come back feeling great. People who go there are moderately healthier and happier, and there have been zero side effects."

Cody shook his head. "I still find it unsettling," he said.

"What can we do about it?" asked Rex.

Cody shook his head. "Nothing," he said.

"It's perfectly benign," Rex assured Cody. "There's nothing to worry about."

Cody hoped it would stay that way: mild, benign, and innocuous. Feeling good because there was light was one thing; feeling good because of something you couldn't see, identify, or understand was quite another.

Life went on. A month passed. Another month passed. Some grain seed somehow got loose and spread quickly. Not an environmental catastrophe, but certainly an event that made the existing flora compete more fiercely for survival. Up through the fungus and spore-grass, wheat and barley could now be seen.

For the most part Cody was happy. When he felt sad, he didn't resort to a trip to the Tower of the Helping Hand, he just dealt with it himself. He continued to have concerns about the spalike qualities of the constructs, but gradually he got used to the idea, and sometimes he picnicked out there with his family. He always enjoyed himself, always came back feeling refreshed.

What bothered him most, and what he again found himself brooding about, was the disappearance of the Builders. What had happened to the Builders? He bundled up Catherine and Benjamin and walked with them to Wartwood Forest. The forest loomed before them, the trunks and stamenlike branches casting wild shadows all over the ground in the light coming from the constructs. Some Filaments flew by. If the Builders could disappear, if something on this world had made the Builders disappear, then what was stopping the same thing from happening to the Meek?

"Daddy, will the Builders ever come back?" asked Catherine, squinting up at the white bows of luminescence.

"Of course they won't, stupid," said Benjamin. "The Builders are gone. And besides, the Builders are great big hairy beasts. Who'd want them back?"

"Ben, is that any way to talk to your sister?" said Cody.

Ben, at the age of nine, had learned the joys of tormenting his little sister.

"Daddy, are they really big and hairy?" asked Catherine.

"No one knows what they look like, sweetheart."

"When I get older, I'm going to study the Builders," said Ben. "I'm going to run tests on the main construct on the Island of Charity in the Sea of Humility. I know I'll be able to make some breakthroughs. I have the primary-color mosaics on my computer already."

Ben, at the age of nine, had discovered the joys of computing.

"But they're really not big and hairy, are they, Daddy?" asked Catherine, growing more and more concerned about it.

Cody stopped, looked at the Tower of the Helping Hand rise into the thick misty atmosphere, a beacon of sorts, a testimony to a race who had had their time on this planet and now were gone. In a few years he would be 50. There would come a time when he too would pass. He felt, curiously, a poignant grief for the Builders. The truth was, no one knew anything about them, hadn't been able to interpret any of the available evidence into anything that gave even the dimmest picture of who they might be and of how they might have lived. All they knew for sure was that the Builders were gone.

Cody and his children entered the forest. Cody put his hand against the nearest wartwood. He'd grown to love the feel of the bumpy trunks. Yes, the Builders were gone. In his correspondence with Claire Dubeau (it now took more than six hours for their messages to travel back and forth) he had learned something interesting about rogue planets. Theoretically they could keep life going much longer than an ordinary planet, up to thirty billion years, because they didn't have to worry about a sun going supernova on them. So why, then, had the Builders disappeared?

And would they come back? His daughter raised a good question. Would they come back, now that Carswell wasn't going to crash into the sun? Were they out there somewhere among the stars keeping an eye on things? Had they been content to let Carswell crash into the sun? And if so, would they now recognize the Meek's legitimate claim to Carswell?

He took out his hatchet and hacked a sizable hunk out of the nearest tree. He would carve a cat for Catherine. And a pony for Benjamin. He wasn't going to worry about the Builders, how they had disappeared, or how the Meek might someday disappear as well. He was going to give his present life on Carswell his *undivided* attention. He would leave the wider concerns to others. He didn't want to end up with the same doubts Artemis Axworthy had had, didn't want to reach a point in his life where he realized that despite his best intentions, his best efforts, he shouldn't have been a husband and a father after all. He would worry about the Builders when and if they decided to return. He looked at his children then glanced back at the burgeoning city of Builders' Mound.

For now, he had more important things to think about.

Cody woke in the middle of the night. Sat up. Listened. The wind was blowing and he felt a lightness in the air, knew a rare high-pressure system was moving in. He pulled on his boots and stood up. He looked at the 26-hour clock. Daylight was precisely three hours and 42 minutes away. Lulu stirred beside him.

"Where are you going?" she asked.

"I'm going outside," he said. "I think the clouds have cleared."

She nodded. "I'll be out in a minute," she said. She, too, liked the sight of a clear sky. "I'll make some tea."

He went out into the yard and looked up at the sky. Sure enough, the nearly perpetual cloud cover had moved off, something that didn't happen more than five or six times a year, something he particularly liked to see at nighttime. Stars. In a sky as black as coal one star was bigger than the rest. The sun. Bigger, but even so, just another star now, a glimmer in the darkness, nine billion kilometers away. He checked the thermometer nailed to the side of the house. Six degrees Celsius, well above freezing; the volcanism, radioactive decay, and greenhouse gases were, as predicted, keeping the planet warm. Lulu came out the back door with two cups of tea. She handed one to Cody and looked up at the sky.

"Have you ever seen so many of them?" she asked.

"That big one over there is the sun," he said. "The one that's setting in the west."

She nodded. "So these over here in the east," she said, "the ones that are rising. Those are the ones we're heading toward?"

"Those are the ones we're heading toward," he confirmed. "The astronomers predict we won't be within probe range of any of them for at least another 500 years. Unless we make some miraculous strides in spacecraft propulsion. For you and me, and for generations to come, Carswell is it."

She looked at him demurely, slipped her arm around his back, and pulled herself near. "Is that so bad?" she asked.

He looked down at her, smiled. "No," he said. "Not at all."